FULL BODY CONTACT

FULL BODY CONTACT

Sexy, Sweaty Men of Sport

EDITED BY GREG HERREN

alyson books
los angeles | new york

© 2002 BY GREGORY HERREN. INDIVIDUAL AUTHORS RETAIN COPYRIGHT TO THEIR INDIVIDUAL ARTICLES UNLESS OTHERWISE STATED. ALL RIGHTS RESERVED.

MANUFACTURED IN THE UNITED STATES OF AMERICA.

THIS TRADE PAPERBACK ORIGINAL IS PUBLISHED BY ALYSON PUBLICATIONS,
P.O. BOX 4371, LOS ANGELES, CALIFORNIA 90078-4371.
DISTRIBUTION IN THE UNITED KINGDOM BY TURNAROUND PUBLISHER SERVICES LTD.,
UNIT 3, OLYMPIA TRADING ESTATE, COBURG ROAD, WOOD GREEN,
LONDON N22 6TZ ENGLAND.

FIRST EDITION: DECEMBER 2002

02 03 04 05 06 🅰 10 9 8 7 6 5 4 3 2 1

ISBN 1-55583-725-5

LIBRARY OF CONGRESS CATALOGING-IN-PUBLICATION DATA
 FULL BODY CONTACT : SEXY, SWEATY MEN OF SPORT / EDITED BY GREG HERREN.—1ST ED.
  ISBN 1-55583-725-5
  1. GAY MEN—FICTION. 2. GAY ATHLETES—FICTION. 3. EROTIC STORIES, AMERICAN.
 I. HERREN, GREG.
 PS648.H57 F85 2002
 813'.0108358'086642—DC21   2002028017

CREDITS
• STORIES BY AARON TRAVIS: "JOHNNY LAREDO" FIRST APPEARED IN *ALTERNATE*, DECEMBER 1980. "BACKSTAGE WITH THE BULLDOGS" FIRST APPEARED IN *MANSCAPE*, NOVEMBER 1986. © 1996 BY STEVEN SAYLOR. REPRINTED WITH PERMISSION OF THE AUTHOR.
• "WORKING IT OUT," © 1987 BY DAVID MAY, FIRST APPEARED, IN SOMEWHAT DIFFERENT FORM, AS "WORKING OUT" IN *HONCHO*, FEBRUARY 1987. ESSENTIALLY THE SAME VERSION OF "WORKING IT OUT" THAT APPEARS HERE WAS PUBLISHED IN *DRUMMER* #172, FEBRUARY 1994. REPRINTED WITH PERMISSION OF THE AUTHOR.

This is for two Pauls: one, my wonderful lover,
and the other, a dear friend who helped me
rediscover my joy in wrestling last year.
You guys both ROCK!
—Greg Herren

CONTENTS

ACKNOWLEDGMENTS

There are any number of people to thank for their cooperation and help in the compiling of this anthology. If I forget anyone, please forgive me.

Dan Cullinane was the first person to suggest to me that I should try writing erotica, about four years ago. After thinking about what he said, I sat down at my computer and pounded out my first erotic story, "The Wrestling Match," and I've never looked back. Thanks, Dan—I probably would never have thought about writing erotica were it not for you.

Jesse Grant and Austin Foxxe of *Men* magazine have both been tremendously supportive of my erotica writing endeavors and have always been a pleasure to work with.

Scott Brassart of Alyson has been a delight to work with every step of the way, with this book and others we have worked on together. It is always nice to find someone to work with who is funny and intelligent and who understands my occasional episodes of lunacy and doesn't hold them against me.

I would be more than remiss if I didn't mention my wrestling buddies, who over the years have provided me with a lot of fun matches as well as encouragement and support for all of my efforts. They haven't even minded being written about on occasion. So thanks to Scott, Kevin, Randy, Michael, Fernando, Doug, Al, Vic, Dave, and Tommy. You've enriched my life more than you'll ever know.

And of course, my beloved Paul, who makes getting out of bed every day a worthwhile endeavor.

—Greg Herren

Johnny Laredo
Aaron Travis

This is the true story of how I met Johnny Laredo. If his name sounds familiar, that's because Johnny was once a star, sort of. Not anymore. Johnny hasn't been on television for three or four years now, long enough for a lot of his old fans to have forgotten him. Oh, occasionally we'll run into somebody at the supermarket or on the street who recognizes him and asks for an autograph. But not often.

Which doesn't mean that Johnny doesn't get looked at just about every time we step out of the house. People look. People stare. I can't say I blame them. They can look all they want. But Johnny is mine.

And thereby hangs a tale.

This all happened a few years ago, right here in Fort Worth, Tex. It was the middle of the summer and hot as hell. I remember, because that was the summer that something called the Polynesian flu hit town. I was the first to get it, probably from some cracker coming in the clinic to have his bitch spayed.

That Saturday night when I first laid eyes on Johnny, I

was at home lying in bed, completely miserable, blowing my nose and flipping channels. There wasn't a damn thing on worth watching: an old Ronald Reagan movie, sitcom reruns, the local news, a werewolf flick on the Spanish station, and of course that goddamn 24-hour Christian network. Typical Saturday night TV in Cowtown.

I kept my finger on the button and watched the channels flip by.

"If you really loved me, Billy, you'd..."

"We're asking Mrs. White about the new, improved..."

"Win one for the gip..."

"Tornadoes are expected along the..."

"Flames of hell, consuming all the hummasexials, adultras, fawnicaytas!"

And then I flipped the channel one more time and saw something that made my fever-weak eyes snap wide open.

I hadn't seen professional wrestling on TV since I was a kid. Even then, I'd seen it only in glimpses, because in our house it wasn't allowed. My mother looked down on it; wrestling shows were for people who didn't know any better. And even as a kid I could see through the staged falls and rigged matches. Heroes and villains, cosmic Good and Evil shrunk down to a hard, lifeless core that the truck drivers and housewives could turn on to. When I was a kid the theme was still World War II, the Big One, being played out every Saturday night. The heavies were Nazi types in black leather with crazy German names, or pumpkin-shaped Sumo wrestlers. The heroes were hard-core American working types, big homely guys just a little past their prime, with broad shoulders and broader waistlines, heroes the ranchers and fry cooks in the crowd could identify with.

The heroes usually won, and the audience, self-styled

martyrs to a world of racial busing, welfare chiselers, militant fags, and women's libbers, could taste that sweet unstained victory of Good over Evil. Occasionally it was arranged for the villains to win, so the crowd could feel the rush of righteous indignation. Anyone with sense enough to get out of the rain could see through it. When I was older I got involved in high school wrestling, the real thing, and kept it up through college; my opinion of pro wrestling went from joke to bad joke.

But that feverish August night I discovered that TV wrestling had grown up, at least a little, and in a wonderful way.

There on the screen, talking and looking me straight in the eye, was one of the most gorgeous young men I had ever seen. Age: 22 maximum. Hair as black as ink, wavy and short. Bright blue eyes, smooth pale skin, red lips, square jaw. He looked like he had never shaved; his forehead and cheeks blushed warm pink.

He was practically naked, dressed in shiny blue trunks, high white socks and sneakers. He was lightly tanned, hairless, perfectly proportioned—an absolutely flawless physique. There wasn't a hint of coarseness; he didn't have a weightlifter's body, and certainly not a typical pro wrestler's. He was sculptured and lean, like a gymnast.

I put down the remote control and willed the TV camera to stay right where it was.

He stood with his hands on his hips, leaning down to a microphone held up by a short, pudgy announcer who was practically a midget. His lines were the standard claptrap ("Yeah, well, we'll just see how much of a man Killer Klaus Kurtz really is when I get him alone in the ring next week!"), but he didn't sound at all stupid. His voice was deep and soft.

JOHNNY LAREDO

My heart was melting. And draining molten into my cock, where it rehardened like cooling steel.

The camera panned away from the young wrestler to a close-up of the announcer, who was pointing his finger at the screen and barking like a used-car salesman. I growled at the TV. Then I heard the announcer: "And we'll be right back to see Johnny Laredo take on Big Donovan, right after these messages!"

I sat up in bed, fisting my erection slowly, while on the screen a skinny housewife in a cheap wig and a sleeveless blouse explained how a certain detergent got her husband's T-shirts really, really white.

Finally I was back in the coliseum, and the kid they called Johnny Laredo was jumping over the ropes into the ring. His opponent was a real monster: Big Donovan was a toothless, snarling, drooling bald giant with enough extra lard on his frame to heat a small city through the winter.

But Johnny, oh, Johnny. That face. That body. Talented too. He played to the camera with the natural instinct of a star, moved with the fluid grace of a young gymnast, showed off every perfect muscle as he danced around the ring. And when he fell, he fell hard, sprawling against the ropes and grunting while Big Donovan pounded away, making his pretty face into a mask of pain, wrenching in agony, suffering like a martyr for the screeching audience. Suffering for me at home with my greasy fist around my dick.

When he scrambled up, flexed his arms, and leaped, he was like moving sculpture. The camera caught him in a hundred shifting poses, each one more breathtaking than the last. Bent double with his ass reared up. Pinned on his back with his long, sleek legs in the air. Down on his knees with his arms twisted behind his back and his massive shoulders straining. Finally, straddling Big Donovan and holding him down, his torso gleaming with sweat, a blush of triumph on his angelic face.

It was over too soon. My final glimpse of him was his victory strut around the ring, his muscular arms held aloft and a beaming smile on his face while the crowd went crazy with excitement.

The housewives and truck drivers weren't the only ones excited. I had been slowly masturbating the whole time, my eyes glued to the screen. There was another commercial and I held off, thinking there might be more of Johnny. But when the show returned he was gone, and the next match was between a couple of female midgets. I switched it off.

My hard-on told me I was more recovered from the flu than I'd thought. I lay back in the darkness and made myself feel good, thinking about the amazing revelation of Johnny Laredo.

✪ ✪ ✪

From then on, I always had something to watch on TV before I went out on Saturday nights. And the more I watched, the more I started seeing how carefully choreographed Johnny's movements were. It wasn't just me and my dirty mind, I was sure. I wasn't just imagining it.

It was the poses: Johnny on his back with a look of agony on his face and his legs wrapped around his opponent, who huffed and puffed and bounced his gut against Johnny's rock-hard buns. Or Johnny on top, with the thug's head trapped between his iron thighs, while the announcer's gloated over Johnny's physique: "Isn't he an amazing young athlete, ladies and gentlemen? Just look at those muscles!"

JOHNNY LAREDO

What was all this but shifting images of man-to-man sex, sucking and fucking, with some sadistic violence and submission thrown in? How could even the dullest audience miss it? Or maybe they weren't missing it. Maybe they were taking it all at face value on the surface, but secretly, subconsciously feeding off the thrill of seeing Johnny nearly naked and posed for sex.

I had the hots for Johnny Laredo.

One Saturday night they announced a special offer of free 8-by-10 color glossy photos of Johnny to the first 50 people at the coliseum door. No way was I going to go down and fight the crowds. But I had to have one of those pictures.

How to get one? I wracked my brain for five minutes, then came up with one of those crazy ideas that you'd never believe could change your life. It almost seemed like a joke at the time. I wrote Johnny a fan letter. I made it special.

I found a ruled pad of paper and a number two pencil, then grabbed the pencil like an ice pick and scrawled out a letter:

Dear Johnny Laredo,

Hi my name is Tom. I am seven years old. I am your BIGGEST fan. Could I have a pitcher of you? I would like a pitcher of you IN ACTION. Thanks you a hole lot. My daddy heped me to rite this letter.

Yeah, I thought, a picture of you in action. Like down on your hands and knees naked, with your cute little ass in the air and your hard cock up against your belly. Or maybe on your knees with your mouth wide open.

FULL BODY CONTACT

But I was willing to settle for a simple shot of Johnny in his tight blue shorts.

I read the letter over and had a good laugh. I mailed it to Johnny Laredo in care of the coliseum and forgot all about it.

✪ ✪ ✪

The next Saturday afternoon I was busy with a friend in the bedroom when the doorbell rang downstairs.

The friend was Gary. Back then he was one of my steady tricks, a college freshman who still lived with his folks down the block. Blond, blue-eyed, slender, and hot as a pistol. One of those proud little whoreboys, the type who think about nothing but sex. Gary came out early. I met him when he was just out of high school and barely 18. He peeked through the screen door of my back porch one afternoon and asked if I wanted to subscribe to a magazine. I invited him into the kitchen and the next thing I knew he was cupping my crotch and asking if I'd like a blow job. The way he swallowed me in one gulp, I could tell he'd had a lot of experience.

I'd been seeing Gary at least one weekend afternoon a month. It was a trip, watching him fill out and mature into a young man. Watching his appetites grow. Feeding those appetites. I was the first to fuck his ass, and the first to spank it. After that he was always after me to get rougher and meaner with him; it's something a lot of guys seem to expect from me. Can I help it if I happen to have a 10-inch dick, shoulders as wide as a barn door, and a face so ugly it's cute?

That Saturday afternoon, upstairs in the bedroom, I had Gary stripped naked and kneeling with his back to the wall, right under the window that faces the street. I stood at the window with my hands pressed flat on the sill. The old man across the way was mowing his lawn. Kids on bicycles were doing wheelies in the street. I smelled the grass and felt the streaming sunlight on my naked chest while I gently rocked my hips and listened to the soft thump of Gary's head banging against the wall and the low, gurgling sound of Gary choking on my cock down his throat.

Every now and then Gary made a little whimper as he gagged. Maybe it was from the pleasure he was giving himself with both fists around his short, stubby cock. Maybe it was from the sting of the tit clamps I'd put on his pert little nipples, linked together by a chain I could reach down to tug on whenever I wanted to feel him swallow me extra deep.

Gary was working hard to get me off, loosening up his throat like a whore's cunt, but I was teasing him, giving him a hard ride, fucking his face with long, relentless thrusts. He kept choking and spewing saliva all over my balls and my thighs. Whenever he seemed to adjust I'd reach down and tug on his clamped nipples, listen to him whimper and fuck his throat a little harder.

Every now and then his long blond lashes would flicker open and he'd gaze up at me with glazed blue eyes. Then he'd shut them tight and suck harder, hollowing his cheeks, sliding his sweet red lips down to the thick root of my cock. His blond hair was dark with sweat, plastered across his forehead. His whole face was slick with spit.

I threw my head back and shut my eyes, savoring the sweet ecstasy of having 10 inches of sensitive meat buried down an eager-to-please teenage throat. I was close to coming, ready to pull out, when I heard the sound of a car pulling up and coming to a stop on the street just below. I looked down and saw a long purple limousine parked in front of my house. The windows were shaded, so I couldn't see any faces. I suddenly felt self-conscious, standing there on the verge of shooting a load all over Gary's twitching, cock-hungry face.

Then the limo doors started opening. I automatically stepped back from the window. Gary thought I was teasing him. My cock slipped out of his throat and popped from between his lips. He made a low whimper and fell forward onto his hands and knees to crawl after it. A second later the doorbell rang. I stepped back toward the window to see if I could get a glimpse of whoever was on my doorstep. My cock speared between Gary's wide-open lips and went all the way down his throat. He wasn't expecting it—he sprayed a throatful of mucus all over my crotch and sounded like he was drowning. Then I heard him gurgle contentedly and felt his throat muscles begin to ripple exquisitely up and down my shaft.

I couldn't see the front doorstep very well from the window. But I could see well enough to catch a glimpse of something that made me yank myself out of Gary's throat and start searching the room for something to wear. The doorbell rang again. I stepped into a pair of old, faded jeans and headed for the stairs. My hard-on kept popping the buttons open.

"Tom?" It was Gary behind me, sounding forlorn. "Tom, don't be long, huh?"

I turned around and grinned at him. He was hunkered down beneath the window, pulling his hard cock out from his crotch and letting it go so it kept slapping his hard belly. His lean, hairless body was slick with sweat, his chin was glossy with spit, his jaw was hanging slack. His face had the

JOHNNY LAREDO

glazed look of a cocksucker who's been gorging himself for hours and still hasn't had enough dick.

My dick throbbed and two buttons popped open on my 501s. "You come while I'm gone," I growled, "and I'll spank your ass." Gary moaned and looked like he might faint. He squeezed his aching red cock with one hand and reached up with the other to pull on his clamped nipples.

The doorbell rang again. I bounded down the stairs, through the hall, and across the living room. Just as the bell rang again I pulled the door wide open.

There were five of them in all, a little delegation gathered on my doorstep. Four of them were dressed in polyester double-knit suits and ties. The fifth was Johnny Laredo, wearing snakeskin boots, skintight jeans, a white felt cowboy hat, and a sky-blue T-shirt that hugged his big, meaty pecs like a second skin.

Johnny Laredo, in the flesh. Standing on my doorstep. My heart was pounding in my ears, and not just from rushing down the stairs. My cock was pounding in my jeans, and not just from Gary's interrupted blow job.

One of the men started talking, smiling the whole time. He was in his 50s and wore a bad hairpiece, had two solid gold teeth and a whiny East Texas bayou twang. "Howdy, suh, good aftahnoon. Is little Tommy heah? We got a big s'prise for the little feller."

"A surprise?" I said. I tried hard to look at the guy, but my eyes kept straying to the hard plates of muscles inside that sky-blue T-shirt. I could see Johnny's nipples through the thin cloth. While I watched, they seemed to crinkle and stiffen before my eyes. I glanced up at his face and could have sworn he blushed before he lowered his eyes. His face was almost too beautiful to look at.

The bossman gave me a big, glittery smile. "Wahl, now, suh, little Tommy-boy sent Johnny heah, the best goddamn wrassler in this state, pardon mah French, he sent Johnny a real sweet fan lettah, and we gonna s'prise him with a little sump'n."

"Uh, I'm afraid Tommy's not here right now," I said. "He's gone to his grandma's. Uh, with his mother."

The man frowned. "Ah see. Yes, ah see. Wahl, where's 'at? Cross town? We wanna give his s'prise to little Tommy in person." I caught him glancing suspiciously at my hands. There was no wedding band there, of course.

"Uh, out of town," I said. "Out of state, actually. Oklahoma. That's where my wife lives now. My ex-wife, that is. She came by and picked up little Tommy and they drove out of town this morning."

"Ah see. Yes, ah do believe I see." The man looked at me shrewdly. For the first time I noticed that one of the men had a camera on a strap around his neck. So that was it, a publicity gimmick, something for the papers: Wrestling Idol Johnny Laredo Answers Little Boy's Fan Letter In Person!

"Wahl, ah'll give you these things innyway, suh. You'll make sure little Tommy gits 'em, won't you?" The man winked and then elbowed one of the others, who handed me a wrapped package. It was the shape of a framed 8-by-10. There was an envelope taped to the wrapping.

"Hold it!" The photographer nosed in to catch the package changing hands.

"Don't be so trigger-happy, Darryl!" the bossman snapped. "Put 'at camera away. We won't be takin' inny pitchers today."

"But, Boss.."

"Hush up!" The man glared at him, then turned back to

JOHNNY LAREDO

me with a sickly sweet smile. "Wahl, we'll hafta be goin' now. You say hello to little Tommy for us." He turned and headed for the limo, waving for the others to follow.

"Hey, wait a minute," I said. "Don't I get to shake the hand of little Tommy's idol? I remember helping him write that fan letter. Why, I'm sort of a fan of Johnny Laredo myself."

They stopped in their tracks. Johnny glanced at the boss, then haltingly stepped toward me and put out his hand. The movement made his biceps swell up and fill the tight sleeve of his T-shirt.

I took his hand in mine. I looked at his face, so close I could have reached up and stroked his smooth cheek. He lowered his eyes, first down to my naked chest and then to the big bulge straining at the buttons of my jeans. He looked up and our eyes met for just an instant. There was something in his eyes that I couldn't quite make out.

"Come on, Johnny!"

He pulled his hand from mine and turned to go.

I watched them pile into the limo, then I closed the door and bounded up the stairway, clutching the package and the envelope. I ran to the bedroom window just in time to see the long purple doors slamming shut. One of the passenger windows rolled down and for just an instant I saw Johnny staring up at the window, looking me straight in the eye. Then the car wheeled around and sped off.

I felt something warm nudge against my crotch. It was Gary, masturbating with both hands and undoing the buttons of my fly one by one with his teeth, poking his tongue between the flaps to lick at my cock and balls. He undid the last button and it tumbled out, slapping him across the cheek. He tried to catch it with his mouth, but I stepped back. I reached down for the chain and pulled him hissing to his feet, then led him by his nipples to the bed. I reached into the dresser drawer for some lube and rubbers. Gary crawled onto the bed, purring and wriggling his ass.

Considerably later, after a long hot shower, Gary got dressed and went limping out the back door, with a grin on his face that wouldn't go away. I was grinning too, as I unwrapped the photo. The color was garish and the frame was cheap plastic, but it was Johnny. He was posed in a crouch, his shoulders hunched, his face set in a scowl. Even snarling he was beautiful. The inscription read: "To Tom Richardson, my BIGGEST fan, from Johnny Laredo."

The envelope contained two front-row tickets for next Saturday's match at the coliseum.

✪ ✪ ✪

Little Tommy couldn't make it, I'm afraid, and neither could his equally mythical mom, so Big Tom went by himself. I turned in the extra ticket at the box office and found my seat.

The arena was a madhouse. Kids ran up and down the aisles in rolled-up jeans, screaming and howling like animals. Women with cheap perms and bad makeup sat grimfaced, waiting for the kill. Men with big beer guts hanging over tight jeans burped and told dirty jokes.

I wasn't too out of place, in my freshly shined cowboy boots and my Western belt hand-tooled with acorns and leaves all around, with my name embossed on the back. I hadn't worn it since high school. Thirty-inch waist, and it still fit.

I looked up and down the front row. A gaggle of grade-schoolers were off to my left, along with an old woman doing her knitting; she was a regular I recognized from the Saturday-night broadcast. On my right there was a group of middle-age men in overalls, spitting tobacco juice on the floor and acting rowdy.

I looked over my shoulder and saw that the camera crew was stationed just a few rows behind us. Good, I thought, that meant the action would be played to my side of the ring. I squirmed in the hard wooden chair and waited for the lights to dim.

The evening got off to a slow start, for me at least. I couldn't get too excited about Big Donovan taking on Eric Samples, the Hillbilly Hooligan, or pseudo-Sumo wrestler Moso Hirohito rolling his 300 pounds of excess lard all over gone-to-seed bodybuilder Mickey-Mike Michaels— but the crowd warmed up right away. They were like wild animals, a seething mass of humanity plugged into a weird repressed sex and violence trip. They screamed, they hollered, they rose to their feet and shook their fists like football fans at the Superbowl. At one point the little old lady got so carried away she tried to crawl over the ropes and attack Moso Hirohito with a knitting needle. Some security guards escorted her, kicking and screaming, to the exit, with a ball of yarn trailing behind.

Then, finally, came the golden moment. The match we had all been waiting for: Johnny Laredo vs. Killer Klaus Kurtz.

Kurtz entered the arena first, to a raucous chorus of hissing and booing. I suppose at one time he must have had quite a body. His shoulders and arms were certainly massive, but generously marbled with fat; his gut was enormous. He was wearing a leather face mask and a leather harness and wore a German iron cross on a chain around his neck. He strutted around the ring, thumping his chest and bellowing insults in a ridiculously phony German accent.

Then Johnny came springing down the aisle from the dressing rooms. A wave of cheering replaced the catcalls. As he jumped over the ropes, I could almost feel the love that was pouring out from the audience, almost see it, as if it were a palpable thing like wind or light.

Unfortunately, the crowd was doomed to disappointment. Johnny didn't do well that night. I could tell early on that he was scheduled to lose, and he did. He played it magnificently, suffering beautifully and always getting back up to take more punishment from that brute Klaus Kurtz. I couldn't quite bring myself to join in with the screaming hysterics around me, but I can't deny that I felt the rush of sharing Johnny's struggle against evil and tasted the bitterness of his defeat.

The view from my seat was breathtaking. I was almost close enough to touch Johnny, and at times I could actually smell his sweat as he began to glisten and sparkle under the hot lights. I watched his body as he buckled, flexed, pounced and shuddered under the impact of Klaus's blows. They met, locked arms, broke apart, circled each other like wary beasts.

The images were like the most intense pornography, seen under glaring lights in 3-D. Johnny on his back, wrists pinned above his head, his long, lean legs spread open and wrapped around the Killer's waist; Johnny breaking free to roll forward and flip Kurtz onto his back with a thud, then scampering on top to trap Kurtz's face between his sweaty thighs; Klaus struggling free, getting to his feet and flinging Johnny against the ropes; Johnny, dazed, falling to his knees; Klaus, with a sneer of triumph, knocking Johnny

JOHNNY LAREDO

facedown to the floor; Johnny, trying to rise, thrusting his ass high into the air, wiggling his butt above unsteady, wobbly legs, flexing his taut buns inside his skimpy nylon trunks. Pointing his upraised ass straight back at me.

My palms itched. My mouth watered. My dick went stiff. And then—

Johnny looked back through his legs, his cheekbone pressed to the floor, his mouth crooked, like a young man in pain, or skewered on a cock. His eyes were barely open. His eyes were on me.

He saw the lust on my face. He knew what his pose was doing to me. Our eyes locked. He froze that way, his ass thrust toward me as he looked back at me, pleading with his eyes.

Suddenly Killer Klaus rammed him from the side and sent him tumbling. It wasn't planned that way. Johnny looked dazed and Klaus looked chagrined. They tried to get back into the rhythm of the fight, but their timing was shot. The match lost momentum, and when Johnny went down to defeat there was a certain spark missing. The crowd could tell, even if they couldn't tell why. Their boos at the end were a little forced and confused.

Johnny left the ring with downturned face and a towel over his slumping shoulders, looking more defeated than he should have. I watched him trudge to the dressing rooms. He turned at the door and scanned the front row until he caught my eye. He bit his lip and then disappeared.

I thought about leaving then, but it was easier to stay put and savor the weird high Johnny had given me. The next match started, but the wrestlers moved before me like ghosts. I barely heard the noise of the crowd, vague and distant like a roaring ocean.

FULL BODY CONTACT

Suddenly a little boy was standing in front of me.

"For you, mister." He thrust a folded piece of paper under my nose. As he ran off I caught the glint of a quarter clutched in his little fist.

I unfolded the note.

Meet me afterward? At the north exit. —J.L.

I looked over my shoulder. He was standing at the door to the dressing rooms wearing a blue silk robe, staring at me. I nodded, and he slipped out of sight.

★ ★ ★

During the last match I went to the parking lot and drove around to the back of the coliseum. Johnny was waiting for me on the steps, sitting with his hands in his pockets. I had expected to see him dressed the way he had been on my doorstep, in boots and jeans, but he was wearing sandals and cutoffs and a red T-shirt. His hair, still damp from his shower, looked jet-black.

We exchanged glances as he squeezed into the bucket seat. I drove slowly to the exit, glad to beat the rush.

"Hi," he said.

"Hi."

"Nice car. I like sports cars."

"Thanks. Anywhere in particular you want to go?"

"Well, there's a little bar off the expressway where some of the guys go after the show."

Just what I didn't need, I thought, a bunch of his wrestling pals hovering around us. "You want to go there?"

He thought about it. "No."

JOHNNY LAREDO

"OK," I said, "I know a place. Bert's. Kind of a funky establishment, in a little hotel downtown. Saturdays they've got a guy who plays acoustic guitar."

"Sounds great."

We didn't talk any more during the short drive to Bert's. I glanced at him every now and again, thinking how beautiful he looked under the glow of the shifting streetlamps.

Johnny ordered coffee and piece of coconut pie. I had a Lone Star. "You have a nice house," he finally said.

"Yeah, got a good deal on it."

"It's so big. You must make a lot of money. What do you do?"

"I'm a vet. As in veterinarian."

He smiled, showing off his perfect white teeth. "No kidding?"

"No kidding. I got a couple of assistants who take care of the pet work—dogs, cats, gerbils. I'm more interested in horses. One of these day I'm gonna find a place out of town and raise horses of my own."

"You like horses?"

"Yeah. I like to ride." Whether by accident or not, at that instant the calf of his bare leg made contact with mine under the table. I saw him blush, but he didn't pull it away.

"You really from Laredo?" I said.

He laughed. "Shit, no. Chicago."

"What are you doing in Texas?"

"College student. Premed; got a scholarship to SMU. Made the gymnastics team this semester."

"No kidding?"

He grinned, showing off the most perfect teeth ever to bite into a slice of coconut pie. "The wrestling's just something I fell into. Started back in Chicago, my first summer out of high school. Did a stint with Larry McMasters and the WPWC. He's the one who came up with the name Johnny Laredo. Came down here and I stuck with it; the hours fit and the pay's not bad."

"So what's your first name, really?"

"Oh, it's really Johnny. Just not Johnny Laredo. You live in that big house all alone," he said suddenly, "just you and little Tom?"

"Well, as long as we're being honest, all that stuff about my ex-wife and little Tommy was a bunch of crap. I'm the one who wrote the fan letter. Hell, it was kind of a joke, really. But I'm not sorry I did it."

"Neither am I," he said. His leg pressed against mine just a little harder.

Suddenly I didn't want to be in Bert's any longer. "My house?" I said.

Johnny nodded.

✪ ✪ ✪

We stepped into the living room. I tossed the keys onto the coffee table and switched on the lamp behind the sofa, coloring the room with a dim amber haze.

I walked to Johnny, looking him straight in the eye. I put my arms around him and felt him press his firm chest against mine. I kissed his neck, his ear, his lips. I eased my hands downward into the silky depression at the small of his back, then onto the hard rounded ledge of his buttocks. His body felt warm and firm inside his clothes.

"Johnny," I said, speaking quietly into his ear, "I want to see you naked."

He stepped back, out of my arms, and undressed until he

was the way I was used to seeing him, wearing nothing but his underwear and socks. His Jockeys were scooped low in front, made of sheer black nylon. I could see his hard-on inside, like a short, thick club.

"The back," I said, my mouth dry.

He turned around to show me his ass. The heartbeat in my cock was like a hammer as he bent to roll the skimpy shorts down to his ankles and step out of them. He stayed that way, bent over and clutching his ankles. He flexed the stretched muscles of his thighs, making his buttocks pull apart and spread wide open. Johnny was able to do things with his gymnast's body that I'd never seen before.

I wet my middle finger and pressed it against his hole. It quivered against my fingertip, then opened for me. Johnny gasped. I felt him clutching at my finger from inside, milking it with his ass. He opened and closed his taut cheeks, squeezing my hand and releasing it. I thought about what it would feel like to have my cock inside him, with him squeezing like that, and I suddenly felt dizzy, as if all the blood from my head had rushed into my cock.

Johnny pulled himself off my finger and folded gracefully onto the floor. He turned and faced me, kneeling. My middle finger was where he had left it, poking into mid-air. Johnny looked at it for an instant, then closed his eyes and took it into his mouth and began sucking on it. I sawed it in and out, fingerfucking his mouth, watching his eyelids flicker and his cheeks cave in.

I pulled my finger out of his mouth and traced the tip over his moist red lips, using my other hand to unbuttoned my jeans. My hard-on tumbled out and slapped the side of his face. Johnny blinked, staring at it cross-eyed. He split his mouth wide open.

FULL BODY CONTACT

I stepped back. Johnny followed on his hands and knees, his eyes almost shut, his mouth hanging open. Hungry for cock.

I made him crawl halfway across the room, backing up step by step. When I reached the stairs I stopped. Johnny looked up at me and made a whimper, as if to ask if he could finally have it. I nodded. I threw back my head and felt my cock swallowed up by his warm, moist throat.

He wasn't quite as good a cocksucker as Gary. But I guess I might have been a little disappointed if he had been. Besides, he could always learn. Gary had. All it took was being hungry enough.

I let him suck me to the point of coming, then gently pushed his face back. He hadn't touched himself the whole time. His cock, hard and dry, pressed up red and swollen against his belly.

"Let's go upstairs," I said.

I didn't tell him to crawl. He did it on his own, creeping on all fours up the stairway, his ass clenching and relaxing as he made his way. I followed behind him, with my cock sticking out of my pants like a compass needle aimed at his hole.

He crawled onto the bed and laid himself out spread-eagled, clutching the corners of the mattress with his hands and feet, lifting up his ass and spreading his thighs outward. I was in no hurry. I moved as if I were in a perfect dream, first lubing up my cock, hard as a steel rod, then slipping a condom over it, then lubing it some more.

I crawled into the space between his thighs, gazing down at the etched muscles of his back, and navigated my cock-head to the lips of his hole. He rose up a little and swallowed the head all by himself, letting out a little gasp of pain. I eased down into him, letting gravity force the whole thing into his bowels. Johnny twisted and squirmed and cried out, but he never stopped clutching the mattress. Once I was all the way in I pushed myself up on one hand and grabbed a handful of his black hair with the other, like a rein, and started riding.

Johnny was amazingly strong, lifting his whole body spread-eagled, rearing back to meet my thrusts, wrenching his hips back and forth on the bed, pulling against my hand in his hair. His back erupted in a river of sweat. He began panting and moaning, then making short, whimpering squeals, and then finally a long, ecstatic groan as I came inside him and felt his insides spasm from his own climax.

✪ ✪ ✪

"Johnny?"

It was a month later. Johnny and I were floating on the bed, spooned together, his back against my hairy chest, his ass cradled in my lap, my half-hard cock nestled up his butt.

Earlier we had watched the broadcast of his match with Junior Jackson. Johnny was worn out. He'd put on a good show. For me, he said. The wrestling show was long over, and the station had signed off. The screen had turned to blue snow. My arms were around him, my fingers absently stroking his nipples, all swollen and erect with a little hickey around each one. The blue glow of the television made Johnny's sleek flesh shine like silver.

"Johnny?"

"Yeah, Tom?"

"I want to ask you something, Johnny. It's kinda crazy."

"Yeah?"

I couldn't see his face, but I knew his eyes were open, staring into the darkness through droopy lids.

FULL BODY CONTACT

"Would you like to move in here with me?"

From the crinkle at the corner of his eye I could tell he was smiling. "Yes."

"You mean it? Right away?"

"Why do you think I always call it your big house, where you live all alone?" He cooed the words sleepily and snuggled his ass against my crotch. My dick began to stiffen again.

"It could be a good deal for you, Johnny. You're pre-med—I took a lot of those courses, went through all that grad school shit. I could help you out. And I make plenty of money. You could quit the wrestling if you wanted to."

"Tom, I'm convinced already." He breathed a long, slow sigh and squeezed his ass around my dick. I slid my hand over his hip and wrapped it around his stiff cock. The boy I lusted after on TV. Johnny Laredo the wrestler. I smiled. The look on his face was so peaceful, I knew in that very instant that it wasn't a passing thing, that something would come of it.

"Wanna fuck me again, Tom?" he whispered.

"All night, Johnny—all night long!"

JOHNNY LAREDO

Vanquishing the Captain
Lukas Scott

A thin mist of sweat and steam filled the changing room. Will stood at the door, his bulky rubgy player's physique still wrapped in the mud-caked shorts and shirt that he'd been wearing on the field. He steeled himself to enter the opposite team's sanctum, to ride out the barracking and abuse that only a loser could suffer. He was the captain, and as such he had a duty to his team and to his college. He was the only one who could do this—who *should* do this. Will was responsible for his team, and for their defeat.

It could have been the other way round. A few more conversions, a few more tries, a few more points and it would have been the rich kid Laurence coming into his dressing room. Will had wanted to beat the Sussex Horns so badly. He'd wanted his Epping Rams to be victorious, wanted to hold the prestigious Inter-College Trophy high above his head in front of the stadium crowd.

Instead here he was, awaiting a ritual humiliation that had been carried out for as long as any player could remember. As long as the trophy itself had been in existence. Of

FULL BODY CONTACT

course, only the players knew of the tradition. It could never be talked of outside the changing room. Only the lads themselves could understand its significance, its symbolic role in the completion of the competition.

Will could hear the banter between the victorious players inside their steaming chamber. They were laughing, joking, cheering. Rich, low voices from well-spoken and well-heeled college students, suppressed violence ordinarily clothed in button-down shirts and chinos but unleashed with rampant energy on the rugby pitch. Pretty boys who'd opted for rugby over boxing and would soon be in cricket whites for the summer. Their fathers were doctors, lawyers, professors, and ministers. Rugby was just a game to them.

Not to Will, the first of his East London family to attend college. It had only happened because of the sports scholarship. He'd worked his body into a mountain of masculinity, rippling thighs and wardrobe-wide shoulders. His body coursed with protein, dedicated to and tended for rugby playing. It was the only thing he'd ever done, the only thing he could think of doing. He *would* be a professional player, he would play in the great stadiums, he would be capped for his country.

It was one of the reasons losing the Trophy hurt him so much. It made him a loser, next to nothing. And now he would pay for it, in front of these rich bastard Sussex boys.

Will breathed deeply and tasted the sweat and blood hanging in the air, sharp masculine smells that assaulted his bruised nose. He went in.

The jeers started as soon as he entered their territory. Semiclad hulks sat on the benches pointing and laughing at the disgraced captain. They formed a double line leading Will on his procession of shame toward their captain,

VANQUISHING THE CAPTAIN

Laurence. He sat grinning at the end of the tunnel of flesh, sharing bawdy jokes with his counterparts, covered only by a small towel over his crotch. Will knew he was not allowed to look at the victorious player and kept his eyes averted. The insults from the winning team members continued until Will stood before Laurence.

Will muttered the time-honored ritualistic mantra: "I approach the Vanquishing Captain."

"The Vanquishing Captain orders you to kneel, Vanquished Captain." Laurence swigged an isotonic drink from a clear plastic bottle as he began to enjoy his role in this aftergame ceremony. Will belatedly dropped to his knees.

"The Vanquished Captain may kiss my feet." Laurence grinned, feeling the power of winning and the submission of his counterpart.

To a roar of derogatory jeers from the aisles, Will bent forward and lightly kissed first the top of Laurence's left foot, then his right. Will felt Laurence's steel-gray eyes staring down at him as he performed the ritual, aware of the very masculine size of the young man's feet and the rest of his body. He was well over 6 feet tall, well-built and well-toned. The light hairs that rose up his calves and his short, muscular thighs became an inverted downy triangle as they spread over his broad chest. Laurence's angular chin jutted out as he smiled arrogantly down at Will.

Half of the ritual was over. Will couldn't stop himself from looking up nervously at his conqueror. Laurence broadened his grin as he saw the trepidation in his opposite's dark eyes. He enjoyed the tension between them, playing it out for a long time.

Finally, in a low, guttural, yet articulate voice, Laurence delivered the command Will had feared.

"The Vanquished Captain may...kiss my arse."

The room fell silent, Laurence's teammates licking their lips in anticipation of this final humiliation of their rival. Will watched as Laurence removed his towel, spreading his thighs apart slightly, clasping his knees, and leaning back on the bench. He caught sight of Laurence's thick cock, nestling in a mound of dark hair, fleshy and ripe. Will felt himself being drawn toward the dark trail of hair leading to Laurence's backside, strangely hypnotized by the dark secret entrance that was being offered for him to kiss.

Again, but with greater force and an edge of impatience, Laurence repeated the command.

"The Vanquished Captain may kiss my arse."

There was no way out of this ritual humiliation, and Will closed his eyes as he moved his head forward between Laurence's thighs, making his way to the firm buttocks that spread before him. He felt the intense warmth that arose from Laurence's hot body, smelled the sweaty musk. Chin scraping the wet bench, his mouth made brief contact with Laurence's arse flesh, planting a recalcitrant kiss between the damp buttocks.

Laurence's teammates roared in fascinated derision while Laurence grinned even more arrogantly at this symbol of his ultimate victory. He dismissed Will by kicking him back against the floor, sending him sprawling on his back as the Essex Horns howled with laughter. Will found his feet, making his way back out of the changing room as quickly as he dared.

It was done, this stupid ritual, this ridiculous trial of masculinity. Yet even in his relief at the ordeal being over, Will could still see the soft curves of Laurence's cock and what he was sure was its twitching and thickening at his

VANQUISHING THE CAPTAIN

attention to the opposing captain's flesh. With surprise, Will realized that the memory of Laurence's arousal was arousing him as well.

He stopped, aware of a stirring in his shorts. He adjusted himself, feeling a lazy erection beginning to form, and willed it to stop. He remembered the sting of defeat, more than enough to terminate any budding tumescence. The memory felt like one of the kicks he'd received on the pitch—sharp, painful, and unwelcome.

Will returned in silence to his own team's changing room. They knew what the ritual demanded and couldn't face him as he joined them. They carried on showering and changing, quickly and quietly taking their leave without any of the usual aftermatch banter. Will waited until they had left before resignedly stripping off and hitting the shower.

Only under the deluge of warm water did Will start feeling anything other than shame and failure. He let the water beat down on him, washing away the dishonor. Switching the shower setting, he felt the water cool and then chill his skin, drops like cold hail against his bruised body. He soaped his battered form, feeling the tension in his muscles, slowly kneading them back into pliability. The smell of the soap was fresh and citric, reawakening his senses. His hands wandered over his body, one caressing his chest while the other massaged his genitals. The water provided a natural lubricant as Will stroked himself, lazily teasing his manhood into life. He wouldn't go further, he told himself, just a gentle stroke or two.

Will started as he realized that his showering pleasure was no longer solitary. There was only a sense of a presence at first, the knowledge that *someone* was lurking within the changing room. His hands froze where they were, one resting on the mat of dark chest hair above his right nipple, the other gently cradling his hairy testicles, wet and heavy. He stood still, the cold water splashing against his taut flesh.

Then Laurence was standing in front him, clad only in a pair of shorts, arms folded across his chest, staring at Will. After a moment, Laurence bowed his head slightly and coughed.

"I...the winner-loser thing...not my idea, you know," he stuttered.

"I play the game," Will said. "It's part of the game. I'd have expected the same of you."

"Yeah? Dunno if I'd have been able to do...that."

"No?" A tension was forming between them—a sexual tension. It felt as if their egos were crashing, masculine energies bristling against each other. "I'd have made sure you did."

"Then you should have won the game." Laurence threw the challenge right back at him, as quick and timely as any pass on the rugby pitch.

"It was a close thing."

"I guess you played OK. You're a player, all right."

"Oh, yeah, I'm a player." Almost unconsciously, Will moved his hand away from his genitals. Although Laurence continued to look him in the eye, Will knew he had been checking out his tackle.

Laurence shoved his right hand down the front of his shorts.

"The lads...they did you a disservice. The heckling and stuff. It was enough for you to do the ritual."

"You want to return the favor, Captain?" The challenge had escaped Will's lips before he was even aware of making it. If the other guys found out what he'd just suggested...but the way Laurence was staring was making him feel horny.

The grin that spread over Laurence's face showed that he wasn't shocked or surprised by Will's words. "Let's see the goods," he said.

Will smiled back and slowly began to turn around, modeling his sculpted butt for Laurence to admire. His white buttocks were well-toned, and he clenched them tightly as Laurence whistled his approval. "The Vanquishing Captain will put his lips on my crack," Will ordered him. He spread himself against the shower wall, leaning on it for support as he offered up his wet anus for kissing.

Laurence moved quickly forward and dropped to his knees. The cold water hit him as he bent to inspect Will's magnificent arse. His hair matted against his scalp, water dripping off his nose and chin, Laurence moved his head into position between Will's cheeks. His mouth made contact with Will's tensed flesh, and with loud smacking sounds he kissed Will's butt not once but over and over, his lips dragging over the wet cheeks. Will moaned in spite of himself and reached round behind him, grabbing Laurence's head and encouraging more intimate contact.

Lips became tongue as Laurence eagerly probed Will's arsehole. He pulled the cheeks apart and thrust his tongue toward Will's twitching sphincter. As he rimmed, Laurence began to rub himself through his wet shorts, his hardening erection showing through the material.

Will began to touch his own manhood, rubbing the thick pole in his right hand as he felt Laurence's tongue pleasing his butt hole. It felt good, this first experience of another man's tongue inside him, another man seeking to pleasure rather than defeat him. The tongue was warm and wet, and Laurence flicked it in and out, sometimes taut and firm, sometimes soft and relaxed. Will gasped, wondering if he could possibly have gone this much further when his lips were on Laurence. It was worth having lost the game to experience his rival's eagerness to match and outdo his own humiliation.

There were no more words between them, only the physical contact of man against man. The tribal divisions that had kept them apart on the pitch were gone; now they were united by a single-minded urgency. Gone was the pretense of antagonism that their sport demanded—their drive for intimacy and contact was nakedly obvious now.

Laurence tongued his way down to lick eagerly at Will's heavy balls, then took them in his mouth to suck on them. Will felt surprise at Laurence's sensitivity in sucking his testicles—could it be that this wasn't his first time ministering to another man?—and groaned as he felt the big lad's chin stubble brush against the underside of his ball sac.

He looked down as Laurence raised his eyes upward, holding Will's gaze before sinking his mouth over the pulsating purple cockhead. Will gasped as his cock entered the warm cavern of Laurence's mouth, his lips circling only the helmet. Will watched as Laurence rubbed his own cock through his shorts, entranced by the shape and size of the hard rod underneath. His own eyes closed in ecstasy, he pictured the unthinkable—his own mouth licking and tonguing his rival's meat. He grabbed Laurence's head, moving his mouth further down the engorged shaft, and sank his spear in right up to the balls. Laurence moaned in acquiescence, masturbating himself more frantically

The sight of the broad-shouldered rugby captain sucking his dick excited Will more than scoring a try, more than converting it, more than...more than winning the blasted

VANQUISHING THE CAPTAIN

game. Here was the victorious Captain deep-throating Will's excited cock, somehow knowing exactly where to place his tongue, when to quicken the pace of his cock-sucking and when to slow it down, bringing him to the brink of release several times.

It might have been Laurence and his Essex Horns who mastered the field, but now Will was master. He regretfully withdrew his hard-on from Laurence's attentive lips and rubbed his throbbing shaft over his face. The trail of sticky precome that marked its procession was all too soon washed away by the splatter of the shower. Will played with Laurence's willing mouth, occasionally slapping the hard meat against his face before entering and then withdrawing from the warm entrance. Laurence closed his eyes, moaning and rubbing his own cock faster and faster.

"I want you to come, Captain. I want you to shoot first, then wait for my hot juice to shoot over you," Will ordered him. "Bring yourself off for me."

Laurence opened his eyes and looked up at Will, then began to pull down his shorts.

"No," Will told him quickly. "Leave them on. I want you to come in your pants."

Laurence spread his legs, tossing off for Will's pleasure, his penis straining against the thin wet fabric of his rugby kit. His hand wandered over his own chest to pinch a hair-covered nipple, groaning at the intense pleasure it brought him. His breath quickened, and Will started pumping his own tool faster in front of Laurence's flushed face. Laurence began to whimper, then suckled on Will's cock tip as his body began to shake and his masturbatory strokes summoned his spunk to rise. Will watched in delight as Laurence's cock exploded underneath the shorts, issuing a sticky white goo that spread through the cotton fabric of his shorts.

While Laurence slumped against the corner of the shower, Will increased his own efforts, his climax approaching fast. He began swearing and grunting, more forcefully than he ever had in any scrum, his cock twitching in Laurence's face. A few furious strokes was all it took then and jets of hot white sperm were splattering Laurence's face and spraying the back wall of the shower. As the spurting subsided, Will allowed Laurence to lick the last few drops from his dick, rubbing the thick cream over his lips. Lawrence caught the final drop on his tongue, tasting it and moaning his appreciation of the forbidden delicacy.

The two men remained frozen in their positions as they recovered, both panting hard. It was Laurence who stirred first, raising himself to his feet. He turned off the shower, standing in front of Will in his wet and stained shorts. Without speaking, he grinned and began to make his way out of the changing room.

Will called him back gruffly. "Leave the shorts," he said, half demanding, half pleading. The Vanquishing Captain halted, stripped off his wet shorts, and threw them under-arm to Will, who demonstrated a perfect catch. Then he strode naked out of the room, leaving Will grasping his come-soaked trophy.

Just Another "Night With the Coach" Story

Clark Anthony

Hey, man—would you get up and take care of that? Just rewind the tape and get back over here. Let's do it again. We can definitely keep going, I just need a minute or two to recharge.

You're a nice guy, you know that? If you aren't a nice guy, my name ain't Danny DiMarco. Real sweet. Too bloody polite, but real sweet. I know you must think I'm crazy, but you're putting up with the tapes, man. Yeah, that's what I mean! You don't say it to my face, but I know you're thinking it...this guy is nuts! You think it, but you don't say it. You're a real sweet guy.

I mean, there's a story there. You must have noticed a running theme in these videos we been watching while we fuck. Older guy, younger guy, sports...c'mon, you know what I mean. One after the other, just another "night with the coach" story.

I mean, don't get me wrong, fantasy isn't weird or any-thing. Well, most guys' fantasies. There *was* this one guy I met on the Net. I got to his place, we talked, you know how it goes—figuring each other out, setting limits, whatever. He asked what ethnicity I was, and I told him, you know...Italian—purebred, straight-through Italian! And, man, this guy looked normal, but once he heard that he started spewing out *his* fantasies, begging me to pretend to be a Mob boss who's angry about a debt he owes or some shit. He wanted me to tie him up and beat him with his belt, threaten to kill his family. Man, I *was* tempted to beat his lousy ass. I mean, what the *fuck*! Fuckin' bastard has been watching too many episodes of the bloody *Sopranos*. The racist fuck. Besides, I'm Italian, man, and the Mafia is a bunch of low-down, dirt-scraping Sicilians.

Anyway, what was I saying? Oh, yeah, *most* guys' fantasies aren't fucked-up. I mean, there are a lot of guys out there who get it up for their coach. And the way I think about it, if you've had it happen to you, then it's not fucked-up.

Yeah, that's what I said. I told you there was a story behind why I like these videos so much, man! Yeah, yeah, it happened to me. I'm not ashamed of it or anything. What sport? Well, I mean, look at me. I'm what, 5-foot-2 when I'm standing really straight? And you've seen me with my shirt off down at the bar...hell, that's why you're here with me tonight, right? I'm fuckin' ripped, you know that's why you're here. Only one sport for a guy who's short and ripped. Up until a couple years ago, I was a gymnast.

See, there you go being sweet again, trying to hold it in, but it doesn't matter to me. Go ahead, man, you can laugh. I know, I know, it's not like most guys think gymnastics is a sport or anything—guys in tights instead of pads and helmets. Well, Danny DiMarco's ass had tights hugging it for a good 15 years, and from the way you look when I strip off my boxers, it's not like there's anything wrong with it after all those years.

My parents started me out in gymnastics when I was 4. Gymnastics may not look like a contact sport, but it is. Lemme tell you, if you get lessons with a private coach, that guy has his hands all *over* you from the time you're a little kid. Like I'm gonna do a handspring off a vault for the first time without some big, burly guy right there to put his hand on my little ass and stop me from falling? Yeah, right. So you grow up listening to everything this older guy says because he's like God, and if he's a good coach he keeps you from getting hurt out there. And if he lays a hand on your thigh a little too long or takes a couple looks at you when you're showering, who notices or cares?

That's not to say my coach had been scoping me out since I was a little kid. No kiddie porn here. When I started out with him, Coach Rick was just 22 and had finished a hitch in college gymnastics at some shithole like Southwest Georgia State. He was from my hometown and came back needing to get some young kids to coach to help pay the bills. Coach Rick was a damn good coach, and I was lucky to have him, but somewhere along the line he must have gotten some ideas about me.

By the time I got to high school I made every other gymnast in the state look like a little bitch. I was better as a sophomore than Rick was in college, and Division One gymnastics programs were taking a long look. I was the local golden boy. You're from around here, right? You probably saw my picture in the papers. They had some hot photos of me on the pommel horse. The photo where you could see my tights-covered ass made it to more girls' bedroom walls in this town than paint. More boys' walls too, for that matter.

FULL BODY CONTACT

All I had to do—*all* I fucking had to do—was place in the top two at the state gymnastics tourney my senior year and get to nationals. Didn't have to do jack shit at nationals, just win the state tourney and watch the scholarship offers roll in. Then I could get the hell out of this crappy town. I had kicked butt my junior year, but these top programs, they ain't looking at last year. They want results before they waste a scholarship on you. If I'm not as good at 18 as I was at 17, I'm not getting shit.

So I'm heading to the state tourney in Atlanta, and I'm fucking pumped. *Pumped!* I was rooming with Coach Rick at this big fancy hotel, all expenses paid. And, you know, man, I'm so pumped up the night before the tournament, I know I've got to calm down or I'm going to be a basketcase when it counts. So what the hell am I going to do in a hotel room but watch something on TV? I grabbed the remote from the night table and start surfing through, like, what, 80 channels? And wouldn't you know that there's *nothing* on.

Coach Rick is lounging there on one bed, no shirt or socks, just a pair of jeans. I'm laying on my stomach on the floor, wearing a tank top and a pair of those little gym shorts with the slit way up the side, like you see on college runners. I'm on my third flip through, stopping now and then out of desperation on that shitty entertainment cable channel—you know, the one with the show "Now That They Aren't Famous Anymore," tonight's special: "Pee-Wee Herman, His Rise and Fall!"—and I'm bored out of my skull. Rick sees that this whole channel surfing debacle ain't making me any calmer, and he gets up. "Hey, man," he says, "TV sucks. I brought a couple videos along with my stuff. You wanna watch?"

JUST ANOTHER STORY

Hell, yeah, I wanted to watch. Whatever he'd brought, it couldn't be worse than amateur home video of Paul Reubens in an adult movie theater. There was a VCR built into the TV, so Rick just stuffed the video in and sat on the bed again. I could see him a bit out of the corner of my eye, and I couldn't be sure but it looked like he had his eyes on me rather than the TV.

So this video starts, and the first thing I notice is that there aren't any credits, it just launches into the movie. There's this guy in a locker room, and he's taking off a football helmet. He looks pretty skinny and he's got this pretty-boy long blond hair all swept back and a little sweaty. Well, man, the helmet was just the beginning. He starts taking off all his clothes, real slow, and yeah, he's skinny, but kind of hot too. He has these blue eyes and this muscular ass, with a long, curving cock. Soon he's ready to hit the shower, and he steps under the nozzle and turns on the spray. The locker room gets all steamy and the mirrors fog up. The camera gets in really close on this kid in the shower, and pretty soon he starts to soap his cock. He's really into it, and then he ain't soaping it anymore, he's strokin' on it and jerking off.

Well, I may be a hick Italian kid from Georgia, but I've got a pretty good idea what sort of video *this* is gonna turn out to be. What surprises me though is when the kid starts jerking off, I look over at Rick, and he's staring at the screen. And man, wouldn't you know it, he's got this *raging* hard-on going.

I look back at the porno, and two guys have come into the locker room. One of 'em, this real All-American type kid, is cut like a rock, and you can tell just from the way he walks that's he gotta be the QB. He's carrying his helmet in his hands, and his face and neck and forearms are tanned like a farm boy. The other one is older but still looks like a youngish kind of guy. Real square-jawed, with a brush cut. He's carrying a clipboard, so I guess he's the coach. And right after they walk in, the blond stumbles out of the shower, still naked and with come all *over* his hands. And he gets real red in the face, but the coach and the QB don't look like they mind at all.

I'm not too surprised when I hear the bedsprings squeak a bit, turn my head, and find that Rick has stripped off his jeans and isn't wearing anything underneath. Rick's in his mid-30s, but he's still got all the muscle and definition from when he was a gymnast. He looks me straight in the eye. I know he wants me. And I'm cool with it. Hell, he's older than I am, but he's still a stud. "Take off the tank top," he says to me. So I pull it over my head. And just look at me, man. You ever seen a guy with guns like these for biceps? Look at these thighs. Fucking rocks. And I'm ready to just wrap 'em around Rick, but I turn back to the porno.

I'd completely lost track of what the guys were doing onscreen. When I turned back, the blond kid was on his knees, and the QB is standing over him. The QB has his shirt off and is standing there in pads. The coach gives an order: "Take off your uniform, Jimmy—Brett here is gonna give you a blow job." So Jimmy undoes the pads and yanks the sweat-soaked pants down his thighs and off. And Brett looks up at the coach, like he's hoping he isn't going to have to, but the coach says, "C'mon, suck him, or you're off the team." So Brett reaches behind and yanks down Jimmy's jock, and at that point I feel Rick kneeling beside me, and he starts to slide my gym shorts down my legs.

I just shift around so I can keep watching the porno. Jimmy has a monster dick, and Brett puts it to his lips and

JUST ANOTHER STORY

licks the shaft. And Rick takes my cock in one hand and slides it into his mouth until his face touches my abs. "Suck on it," says the coach, and Brett puts the head of Jimmy's dick into his mouth and starts to suck it real slow. It's my first time watching porn—well, gay porn, anyway—and the first time a guy has sucked me, and I can't hold back. Rick goes down on my cock for just a couple minutes and I'm coming down his throat. I flip my head back and gasp, still watching Jimmy thrust into Brett's mouth.

The coach is watching them go at it, and then he's taking off his clothes. Rick has gotten up and gone over to his bags. The coach gets naked real quick, and then he walks over behind Brett. He spits on his hands and rubs the spit up and down his cock. Brett's mouth is filled with Jimmy's dick. I feel Rick's calloused hands on my shoulders, and he shifts me around until I'm lying on my stomach. He takes my feet, one in each hand, and I let him spread my legs. The coach rubs some more spit on Brett's ass and centers himself behind him. I feel Rick's hands glide up my thighs, and then something wet and cold on my asshole. He centers himself behind me. The coach drives his hips forward and shoves his cock into Brett. Rick thrusts forward and down and enters me. Brett jerks with the force of his coach's cock, Jimmy's dick still sliding in and out of his mouth and down his throat. I relax my asshole, spread my legs wider, and push back on Rick's cock. I feel him expand inside me and thrust deeper. The coach's rhythm forces Brett forward onto Jimmy's dick. Rick holds my hips steady. He drives deeper, faster, harder. I'm impaled on his cock. I close my eyes, and Rick gasps. I feel him surging inside of me.

He comes explosively, and my insides are suddenly wet and warm. He gives a few more shuddering thrusts. I feel exhilarated. I don't care if anyone hears, I just throw my head back and yell like I'm gonna bust a gut.

I look back at the screen. Jimmy and the coach are walking toward the showers together, laughing and slapping each other on the back. Brett's head is bent, and he stays kneeling on the locker room floor. Man, I can't tell what the fuck he's thinking, but I'm jumpin' out of my skin. Rick pulls his cock from my ass, still trembling with the orgasm, and crawls to the VCR to turn it off. His cock is still dripping come. We cut the lights and get in bed, but there won't be much sleeping goin' on this night.

So of course I was totally fucked-up the next day. As my coach, Rick was right off to the side while I competed, all business, like nothing happened. But when he gave me a boost onto the rings, his hands on my calves reminded me of my legs being spread, him entering my ass. My arms shuddered and I could barely hold myself up on the rings. It was the beginning of the end. I couldn't concentrate. I fucked up the floor routine. I lost my grip on the uneven bars. I don't even wanna talk about the vault or the pommel horse. I finished ninth overall. Can't say I was surprised to be goin' to Northern Georgia A&M after that. Division fucking Three. So much for the Olympic team, right?

Rick? Yeah, man, Rick bailed out as soon as he knew I wasn't gonna be his ticket to coaching glory. All my knowing him got me was a partial scholarship to a shit school and a little fetish for coaches. I'm kinda at loose ends. Northern Georgia A&M doesn't really cut it for me. At least they got a gymnastics program, but I only do it now to keep in shape and keep the money flowing. That and it's the only thing I know how to do very well.

Hell, hasn't that tape rewound yet? Well, you don't

JUST ANOTHER STORY

wanna hear any more of this shit. Go on, press Play. Get over here and spread me. And, uh, man? I know you're only the football team's manager, but just for tonight could you *pretend* you're a coach?

The Playoffs
Mel Smith

Division Playoffs, Game One: Eastridge Community College versus Danville Junior College.

Players to watch: Cruz Santiago—catcher for the Eastridge Bulldogs. Nineteen years old. Born in Mexico, bilingual. Five-foot-9, 170 pounds, nothing but tight muscle and sinew. Deceptively strong. Practices in bare feet. When not playing baseball, he choreographs numbers for an all-girl hip-hop dance troupe. Majoring in music. An enigma to his teammates.

Rob Dunn—catcher for the Danville Blasters. Nineteen years old. Born in Danville. Six-foot-one, 220 pounds. Built like one of his daddy's stud bulls. When not playing baseball, he works on his family's cattle ranch. Dreams of playing professional ball. Majoring in physical education.

Bottom of the ninth. Eastridge is leading 2–1. Dunn is on second. The Danville second baseman is at bat. Two away. The batter drives an 0–2 pitch down the right field line. It's going to the wall. Dunn, a slow runner, is going to try for home. The throw from right field hits the cutoff man. Dunn has rounded third and is heading for home. The throw to Santiago is off target. Santiago is pulled off the plate. Dunn is charging hard. Santiago has the ball and is set, blocking home plate. The 220-pound Dunn is bearing down on the much smaller Santiago. They collide. Santiago's mask is ripped from his face. There's blood. Santiago hits the ground on his back. Dunn lands hard on top of him. Santiago is crushed. He couldn't possibly hold onto the ball after that kind of punishment. Wait. He's showing the umpire his glove. He has it! He held on! Eastridge wins!

After the game, Cruz is gathering his equipment, alone on the field. His teammates know to let him be. He likes to spend time by himself, going over the game in his mind.

His nose is broken from the collision and has been taped up. He is barefoot and still in his uniform.

Cruz sees Rob coming towards him. Cruz tenses, not in the mood for a confrontation with some redneck jock who's pissed because he got beaten by a skinny Mexican.

Cruz squats and concentrates on his equipment.

Rob stops in front of Cruz, towering over him. Cruz does not look up.

"Nice play. I can't believe you held onto it. I've never hit anyone so hard."

Rob's voice is flat, not sincere. Cruz shrugs.

"I asked around about you."

Cruz stiffens and stands up slowly.

"They say you're a dancer and you hang with a gang." Rob looks down at Cruz's bare feet. "And you practice barefoot."

Cruz stares at Rob and does not respond.

"Odd combination, seems to me."

Cruz shrugs again. "Predictability bores me." Cruz

looks down at his equipment, willing Rob to leave.

"You get off on the unexpected, huh?"

Cruz does not respond and starts to squat again.

Rob grabs the back of Cruz's neck, pulls him close, and kisses him on the mouth.

They stare at each other for several seconds, then Cruz squats. "I knew you were going to do that."

Rob shoves Cruz's shoulder and laughs. "Fucking liar."

Cruz stands again. "I knew you were a fairy the second I laid eyes on you."

Rob shoves him again and they both laugh. Their smiles slowly fade as they watch each other. Rob steps closer and slides his hand behind Cruz's neck again. They kiss some more. They take their time, each enjoying the feel of the other's body, the taste of the other's mouth.

The sun is warm. Neither one is concerned that they might be seen.

"I have my own place near here."

Rob smiles and pushes Cruz backward, toward the dugout. "Too predictable."

Cruz stops. He untucks his uniform shirt. With his eyes on Rob's, he slides his hands up inside his own shirt, stroking himself and pinching his nipples. Rob adjusts his own hardened crotch, anxious to see what's under Cruz's shirt.

Cruz pulls his shirt off. Rob licks his lips. Cruz's skin is smooth and very dark. His muscles are carved into his skin. His nipples are erect and a lighter, pinkish brown. They look like tiny targets marking his sculpted chest.

Rob runs his hand down Cruz's body. "Damn."

Rob's hand rests on the top of Cruz's pants. He looks at Cruz and Cruz smiles. Rob undoes the uniform pants and they drop to Cruz's bare feet. Rob steps closer and slides his hands along Cruz's chest, then around to his back. As Rob sinks to his knees, his hands run down Cruz's back to his bare ass. Rob grips the tight, round ass as he licks and chews on Cruz's jockstrap-covered cock.

Cruz strokes Rob's thick blond hair. He curls his fingers into some of it and pushes Rob's head against his crotch. Rob works his tongue under the strap and licks Cruz's balls.

Rob's hands run up Cruz's flat belly to his chest, fingering and lightly pinching the tiny nipples. His eyes are looking up at Cruz while he continues to slobber on his bulging jockstrap. Cruz smiles down at him.

Rob pulls Cruz's strap out with his teeth. He lets go with a snap and says, "Fuck me."

Cruz pulls Rob to his feet and they kiss some more. Cruz steps slowly back toward the dugout. Rob follows, still kissing him.

In the dugout, Rob pulls a condom from his jeans pocket and proudly holds it up.

Cruz laughs. "Boy Scout, right?"

"When I saw that you held on to that ball even after I crushed you, I knew I had to have your cock up my ass."

Cruz stops smiling. He pulls Rob to him by his waistband. He kisses Rob once, biting his lower lip before releasing him.

"Get naked, farm boy." Rob obeys. He pulls his jeans off, kneels on the floor of the dugout, and leans his elbows on the bench.

Cruz whistles softly at the sight of Rob's smooth pink ass. He expected a big, beefy ass, but Rob's is almost delicate: high tight mounds, flat and muscled on the sides.

"Hold up the rubber. By your right ear."

Rob opens the wrapper. He can hear Cruz getting out of

his jockstrap. Rob holds up the rubber as ordered.

Cruz's dripping cock slides against Rob's ear and pushes into the rubber. Rob moans as he tugs the rubber into place.

Cruz spits into his hands. He kneels behind Rob to moisten his asshole, then spits on his own latex-covered cock.

Rob feels Cruz's cock at his hole. "Hit me as hard as I hit you."

Cruz places his hands on Rob's shoulders and thrusts hard up into him. Rob's knees come off the ground and he yelps.

Cruz throws his body into every penetration. Rob tries to stroke his own cock but he can't hold on. His hands grip the back of the bench tightly, his knuckles turning white.

"Oh, fuck. Oh, fuck."

Cruz is merciless. When he feels himself getting too close, he takes a quick breather by changing Rob's position. He pulls him off the bench and makes Rob get on his hands and knees on the floor of the dugout. With one hand on Rob's shoulder and the other gripping his hip, he resumes his relentless pounding.

Rob is moaning, sounding almost delirious. His fingers try to dig into the concrete. He hangs his head down, gasping for breath. "Oh, God. I think I'm going to come."

Cruz releases Rob's hip and finds his balls. He squeezes their base, preventing any release.

"Oh, God. Oh, God."

Cruz pushes Rob's head down and he collapses forward, laying his head on his arms. Cruz then pulls Rob's hips up so that Rob has to stand on the balls of his feet. Cruz stands up and drives down into Rob's ass as hard as he can, over and over.

Rob can hold back no more and, with a howl, unloads thick strings of come all over the ground.

THE PLAYOFFS

Cruz pulls out of Rob's ass, rips off the condom, and comes on Rob's back. It runs down his spine and into Rob's hair.

Rob falls to the ground, his chest heaving, his body slick with sweat and come. "Oh, fuck. Oh, fuck."

Cruz lies on top of Rob's back. He kisses his neck and shoulders. "I guess we're even now, farm boy."

"Are you kidding?" pants Rob. "This was just game one."

Game Two:

Ninth inning. Danville is leading 4–3. Two outs. The speedy Santiago, who has not been thrown out a single time this season, is on first. The pitcher winds and throws. Santiago is running. He had a great jump. It's going to take a perfect throw to get him. What a rocket! Dunn comes up throwing. Santiago slides. He's out! Danville wins 4–3, sending these playoffs to game three.

Rob sits in the dugout, going over the game in his mind. And waiting for Cruz.

Cruz appears, wearing only jeans—shirtless and barefoot. He stands outside the dugout.

"Nice throw. No one throws me out. Ever."

Rob shrugs. "All streaks have to end sometime."

"I've been asking around about you. You're not a farm boy. You're a cowboy."

Rob stands. "Yeah. What about it?"

"You a good rider?"

A smile tugs at the corner of Rob's mouth. "I've broken my share of broncs."

Cruz unbuttons his jeans and pushes them down. He is not wearing a strap or underwear. "I've never been ridden before."

Rob moves to Cruz. He lays one hand on Cruz's cheek and the other on his shoulder. "You sure you're ready to be broken?"

Cruz starts undoing Rob's uniform pants. They kiss as Cruz pulls Rob's cock out of his jockstrap. Rob is not completely hard and he's already 8 inches and very thick.

Cruz raises his eyebrows. "Feels bigger today."

Rob laughs. "It's not too late to change your mind."

Cruz shakes his head. He holds their cocks together and strokes them both. "I want it, cowboy."

Rob gets a rubber from his pants before taking them all the way off, then he pulls Cruz into the dugout. He sits on the bench, his cock now close to 9 inches. It points straight up, leaking precome onto his crotch.

Cruz pulls Rob's shirt off. He straddles Rob's lap and licks his nipples, working their cocks together again while he sucks and nibbles.

Rob rolls the condom onto his cock. "Wish I had some lube."

Cruz smiles. "Feel my ass."

Rob slips his hand between Cruz's legs. He finds his hole and it is slick. Rob smiles. "Boy Scout, right?"

Cruz stands up on the bench, straddling Rob. He puts his hands on Rob's shoulders. Rob holds his cock steady, and Cruz lowers himself onto it.

"Oh, Jesus."

"Just relax. Take your time."

It takes a while, but the head of Rob's cock finally gets into Cruz's tight hole. Cruz takes a breather and they kiss.

When he's ready, Cruz lowers himself further, and his body suddenly opens itself and takes Rob in.

Cruz's eyes are huge. "Oh, God. God, it feels amazing."

THE PLAYOFFS

Rob kisses Cruz. The pressure and the heat on his cock take his breath away. They don't fuck for a while. They hold each other and kiss, making the feeling last.

When they do start to fuck, Rob lets Cruz do all the work. First Cruz rises up slowly and drops himself down, over and over. Then he rocks back and forth, kissing Rob while he does it. Finally Cruz returns to the up and down fuck until he knows Rob is close. He begs Rob to come inside of him. Cruz wants to feel the pulsing of Rob's cock while he comes.

Rob's head falls back and his hips thrust up. He holds Cruz down by the waist and pumps himself dry.

Rob puts his hand on the back of Cruz's neck and pulls him closer to kiss him, sucking his tongue violently while he strokes him to orgasm. Cruz coats Rob's stomach with thick, creamy gobs of come. Rob is still hard inside of him. Cruz spreads his come over Rob's chest, then he sucks his nipples clean.

"Tomorrow's the last game."

"Whoever wins is going to be celebrating with his teammates."

"And then my team heads home."

They stay together a while longer, then they dress in silence. They kiss once more before walking away from each other.

Game Three:

Three hours before game time. Santiago is at home, trying to get into his game day routine. He's having trouble concentrating. There's a knock on his door. He answers it and—it's Dunn! Dunn charges Santiago, just like in Game One. Dunn has Santiago in his arms and he's kissing him!

FULL BODY CONTACT

Well, it looks like we'll be going into extra innings on this one.

Cruz pulls away to catch his breath. "How'd you know where I live?"

"I asked around about you." He kisses Cruz again. "I had to see you once more."

Cruz starts pulling Rob toward the bedroom. "We don't have much time."

They strip and fall onto the bed, kissing. Rob licks down Cruz's throat. He sucks on his nipples and nibbles on the underside of his arm. He kisses his way down Cruz's stomach to his cock. He takes him into his mouth.

Cruz pulls Rob's hips toward him and soon they are on their sides, each with the other's cock deep in his throat, hands exploring the other's body.

Their sucking becomes desperate and passionate. They need to devour each other. They want to make it last. Rob gets all of Cruz's cock and his balls into his mouth. Cruz gets most of Rob's cock down his throat. Their jaws ache. Spit and phlegm oozes out of their mouths and down their necks.

It becomes too much and Cruz lets go. "Oh, God. I'm coming."

Rob releases him and they come on each other's face.

They stay 69'd, holding each other.

"I wish I wasn't going away to school. We could still see each other occasionally."

Cruz shakes his head. "Wouldn't matter. I'm going away too. I got a scholarship to San Diego State."

Rob springs up. "San Diego State? No fucking way. That's where I'm going."

Rob dives onto Cruz and they roll on the bed, kissing and laughing.

THE PLAYOFFS

"You know what this means, don't you? Only one of us can be the first-string catcher."

They eye each other as competitors, then Cruz jumps on top of Rob. "Fuck you for it!"

Sexual Sparring
Adam McCabe

Outer forearm block, step turn side kick, spin hook kick. I
tried to keep my mind on the blows that lashed out at me.
I wasn't as advanced as my sparring opponent. No one was.
Jim Durban was the 18- to 20-year-old champ for our state.
I was ranked 17th. I knew I was going to get my butt
kicked, but I wanted to try. That's how you get better. The
fact that he was gorgeous had nothing to do with my challenging him.

He swung his leg up in a crescent kick that hit my temple with a solid thud. I took a step back in shock. I'd worn
my headgear, knowing that this would be a rough match.
Jim wasn't one to pull his punches—or his kicks. I'd barely
seen that one coming. Two points for him. I brought my
right arm up in front of my chin, with my left guarding my
middle. Like it would do any good.

Jim smiled as he took another step toward me. He knew
that he had me beat easily, but he was still giving it his all.
He wasn't taking it easy on me, and I hadn't wanted him to.
I could see the sweat pouring down the sides of his face. He

hadn't worn any headgear; that's how confident he was that I wouldn't score a kick to his pretty face. His dark hair was damp with sweat. The drops got caught in the stubble on his cheeks and chin. I tried to concentrate on his quick hand movements, but the front of his gi had started to pull open, revealing a smooth white chest with only a few stray hairs. It was no surprise that they were flattened to his chest with perspiration. He never let up for a second. Even a match with me demanded his every ounce of concentration. I tried not to let my mind wander to what he'd be like in bed. I didn't want to think about what his lithe frame would feel like next to mine, not right now.

But the thoughts of Jim's body made me lose my concentration. Even though I knew I shouldn't, I took a step back toward the wall. That was all the incentive Durban needed. He spun and smacked the back of my head with a hook kick that threatened to knock my eyes clean out of their sockets. I stumbled forward, and he put out a hand to catch me. He threw one of those faster-than-lightening arms around my shoulder and spit his mouthpiece into his other hand.

"Sorry about that, man. Guess I don't know my own strength. You were putting up a good match." He walked with me around the dojo as I caught my breath. As soon as he figured I could make it on my own, he walked off toward the corner of the room. I took a few more steps and decided to sit down. I shucked the headgear and hand and foot protectors and threw them aside.

I pulled my legs up to my chest and watched as Jim took a long hard look at the heavy bag. He stripped off the top of his gi and threw it to the ground. I caught my breath as I saw his broad shoulders and the lean defined muscles of his back. His muscles started at the shoulders and ran V-like to a tiny waist obscured by the gi bottom. I tried to picture his muscular, round butt. He spun and kicked the bag, sending it hurling in the opposite direction—the same kick he'd used on me a few minutes before. He caught the bag as it thudded against his chest and held it tight for a second. I suddenly yearned to be the leather bag, tight in his embrace. He slowed the bag's motion and turned to look at me.

He had small but defined pecs. I could see the thick bushy hair protruding from his underarms. His nipples were perfectly flush with his chest, dark brown ovals that just cried out to be kissed. I felt the familiar rumblings in my crotch and was glad that I wore a cup, to hide my growing boner. Damn. I'd even jacked off twice that morning to keep from getting turned on during our match. Didn't look like losing two loads of jizz had done any good. I still wanted him in the worst possible way.

He placed a few more hook kicks on the bag, each one high on the leather. The room was silent except for the snap of his leg and the thud of flesh against leather. He kicked until I was tired just from watching, but he didn't seem to slow down or feel the strain. Each kick was well placed and up at head level. There didn't seem to be an end to his energy. I forced my brain away from wondering if he was like that in bed—enthusiastic and insatiable. I wondered how many loads he could fire off.

Finally he stopped, walked to his bag, and pulled out a towel. He patted himself down with it, then threw it to me. I wiped my damp hair, breathing in his musky scent, and felt my cock grow as I pressed the towel against my face. I stood up and took a few steps around the dojo. The wooziness had subsided. Jim walked over to where I stood, and smiled. He was still wearing his hand- and footpads, even

SEXUAL SPARRING

with his chest bared. Up close, I could see beads of sweat running down his chest and arms. I wanted to lap them up.

He jerked his head back to the sparring floor. I nodded and waited for him to put his gi top back on, but he made his way out to the center of the floor again. I followed him silently, watching the tight thick muscles of his back as he stretched one arm and then the other over his head. I couldn't see an ounce of fat on his upper body.

We turned to face each other, and he paused without bowing. "I'm gonna feel stupid if you don't take off your top too." He looked me over, grinning, but his eyes watched my every move like a predator, waiting for me to do something.

I looked at him again, trying to gauge his motives for wearing less. His face was expressionless. I untied the belt and threw the top of my gi against the wall. The dojo was cool, and the air felt good against my skin. My own chest was bigger than his frame. I had two solid slabs of pecs and a happy trail leading from them to my gi and below to my hard cock.

Jim paused a minute, and again a smile broke out across his face. Just the sight of that broad grin got me hornier than ever and I felt my dick straining against the cup; I'd have been fully hard if it weren't for the protector. Jim shook my hand to start the match, and the touch of his palm against mine shot electricity through my system. I wanted him that bad.

I threw my arms up in a sparring stance and waited for him to make his move. I stayed on the defensive when I was fighting Jim. I couldn't help it. I knew that I should attack, but every time I started to, he launched into a series of kicks that struck home in my ribs or against my head. It was all I could do just to block him.

FULL BODY CONTACT

The inevitable happened. A combination kick punch hit me in the head and left arm. I reeled back and landed flat on my ass. I wanted to crawl off the floor and find a place to hide. Jim didn't seem to mind. Why should he? He wasn't sitting on the ground. He probably knocked guys on their asses all the time. He spit his mouthpiece into his padded hand and gave me another smile.

He extended a hand to me, and I reached out for it. He grabbed my hand protector and yanked it off, leaving me with my ass back on the floor for a second time. I tugged off the other pad and shook my head again. He pulled off his pads as well and threw them to the side.

He offered me his hand for a second time, and again the electricity shot through me as we touched. Without thinking, I yanked him to the floor. I'd learned some ground fighting moves from my instructor and decided to put them to use. Most tae kwon do students are kickers. We might be more evenly matched at close range. On the mats, I had a chance of winning.

He caught himself and rolled a bit as he hit the ground. I had the weight advantage on him by about 10 pounds, so I used it to swing him around and climb on top of him. I shifted so that my ass was almost over his crotch.

The extra weight did the trick. At this range, his legs were useless to him. I pushed my palms against his shoulders and pinned him to the carpet. He didn't seem to put up much of a struggle. My body was pressed against his for almost our full length and I could feel the hard plastic of his cup through his cotton pants. As for mine, I thought I would burst free of my jock and cup at any second. I could barely take the heat of his body against mine.

I wasn't sure what to do now. I'd managed to pin him,

SEXUAL SPARRING

but I didn't want to let him go. Every nerve ending in my body was on fire as we lay there on the floor. I'd started to get up when I felt one of his legs swing behind me and wrap around my waist. I thought he was going to kick me till I realized his pant leg had pulled up and I could feel his leg against my back. The move was nothing from the world of tae kwon do, but from the world of gay sex I knew exactly what he wanted. Jim managed to slip a hand free, and I felt him press his palm against my chest. His fingers found a nipple and tweaked it hard. I let out a moan without thinking and I saw another flash of his smile. His arm went around my neck and pulled me in close. I felt an explosion of heat in my body as his lips found mine. His tongue slid between my lips and began its own combat with my tongue. He didn't let go of my neck—locking me in place, as if I had any intention of moving.

Our bodies ground against each other as we kissed. I could feel his cup rubbing against my leg. My dick had shoved my protector aside, and it leaked against the cotton of my jock and my gi. I pushed my crotch against his leg, ground it into his firm calf muscles. I knew he felt its hot demand. His hands still moved over my chest and nipples. He would tweak the soft skin around the tips, then flick them until they stood at attention—so different from his flat brown ovals.

His right hand followed the line of hair down my abs until he was at the waistband of my gi. I could feel his fingers fumbling with the tie belt, pulling it loose. My cock was at full attention, ignoring the cup and jock, which couldn't restrain my almost eight inches. I tried not to squirm as his finger ran under the drawstring waist and started to flick the head of my cock. I could feel it oozing precome at his touch.

FULL BODY CONTACT

The leg behind me tensed, and he pulled me closer until I thought we'd become one. I continued to grind against him, pressing his hand flat against my tight abs. His hand continued down into my pants, and I could feel the heat of his body as he grabbed the head of my cock in a stranglehold.

"Nice cock, man," he whispered as he started moving his fist up and down my shaft. The precome lubed up my dick and his hand slid easily over the length of my cock. I couldn't wait much longer for what I wanted. I grabbed his gi pants and tugged. They came down easily. I could feel his hairy legs now against my crotch. He wore a jock and cup, but his cock seemed ready to break free. His ass was exposed, and my hand assessed the muscled cheeks that had executed those punishing kicks.

He let out a low moan as I felt his ass. He tensed it so that it became two smooth orbs of muscle. My fingers slid to his ass crack and brushed the hairy hole. He contracted his cheeks again, inviting my finger inside of him. He took the finger without much problem, and I probed the puckered flesh around my index finger. He bucked his hips as I entered and nearly pushed me off of him.

Jim pulled at my drawstring and yanked my gi bottoms down around my knees. He had a firm grip on my cock and didn't seem to want to let go. He maneuvered the jock down past my balls, so that my hard dick was exposed. I could feel the cooler air against my cock, drying the sweat from our sparring. Jim continued to tug at it as I lay on top of him. I still had a finger inside of him, and he'd started to move his hips in a steady rhythm that pulled it deeper.

Before I could find out what he wanted next, he executed a quick roll from under me, flipped me over, and sat on my stomach. He'd been under me of his own choice. I hadn't

SEXUAL SPARRING

done anything to him that he hadn't allowed to happen. I felt a bit foolish suddenly, but those feelings were quickly supplanted by lust.

The silky hairs of his ass brushed against my abs. His jock still covered his dick, but it was damp around the waistband where he'd been dripping precome. That round circle of his man juice made my mouth water. I wanted to taste his cock through the cotton, play with it using just my tongue to make that spot grow until it covered the front of his jock. From what I could see, it was about seven and a half, only just shy of my own.

He straddled me, trapping my arms by my sides. I couldn't move, and yet I didn't think about defeat like I had 15 minutes ago. I didn't care if he had the advantage as long as he had me like this.

He slid back along my abs, teasing them with the soft fabric of his jock. I felt my dick stand straight up against him as he moved backward. He smiled sheepishly for a second and pulled a foil wafer from his jock. "I'd hoped something like this might happen," he said as he ripped open the package.

He grabbed my dick again and slid the rubber onto it. He didn't need to lube me up. I was spitting precome now, knowing what would happen next. I could feel the warm latex against my skin, even though I couldn't see him perform the action.

He leaned forward and hovered over my dick. I could see my cock tremble in anticipation of his tight hole. I wanted to have him, to be inside him. He sat on my cock slowly, inching it into him. I gasped a bit as I slid in, the shaft of my eight inches filling him up.

His face was beautiful as he took more of me. His brow

furrowed with concentration and pleasure. He had a smile that lit up his dimpled cheeks. I wanted to kiss him, but didn't want to disturb his moment. I could feel his balls against the base of my cock, and the downy hair around his asshole mingled with the thick tangle of my pubes. He shifted to free my arms, and began to use his thick muscled legs to move his ass slowly up and down on my cock.

I grabbed his cock, teasing the head and pulling just enough of it free to see the swollen head and the first inch of his veiny shaft. His rhythm on my cock grew faster as I traced the head of his with my forefinger. It trembled at my touch, eager to feel more.

His precome oozed between my fingers as I caressed his piss slit. I tried to take my mind off the fact that I was inside Durban. I'd beaten off so many times about him that I could blow just by acknowledging that it had become reality.

I pushed my hips off the ground to meet his thrusts, the move pushing me all the way inside of him. My pubes ground against his ass, and I could feel desire constricting my balls.

I played with his cock, using three fingers to stroke the shaft. Even without seeing them, I could feel that his balls were shaved. I took more and more of his cock in my fist as I jacked him. The combination of my cock inside of him and the firm strokes on his cock made his face go soft with yearning. He closed his eyes and swallowed hard as I kept up the pace. I matched the thrusts of my hips with the movement of my hand. He was definitely in my control. I loved seeing his firm body dance to my command. His mouth tightened and suddenly a load of come shot out of his cock. He moaned so loudly that I thought the whole town must have heard us. The streams shot out twice more, and then they tapered off to a small stream that leaked out of his reddened mushroom head. He breathed heavily, but didn't want to quit. We kept up the thrusts, him riding my cock like we were permanently joined. I was getting close. Feeling Jim's come all over my fist only made me fuck him harder. My balls tightened to prepare for the load I'd dreamed about so many times.

He must have known what was happening with me because he tightened his sphincter. The muscles gripped me and held me tight. The feeling was so intense that I couldn't hold back. I felt the jizz blowing out of me, pulsing through my cock in hot spurts. Four explosions, followed by countless smaller pulses. I whimpered and Jim eased off his death grip. He moved more gently on me now, coaxing the last few drops of come from my balls. I didn't know what had taken more out of me, 50 minutes of sparring or a single round of sex with the same opponent.

No Laughing Matter
Alex Hamilton

In high school, wrestling was my passion. There was nothing I liked better than rolling around on the mat with my aggressive teammates. The hot sweat of my buddies, the challenge to my struggling muscles, the power of pinning someone down in victory, the intense release of late-adolescent frustrations—all of these joys gave me a rush incomparable to any other physical experience. Even getting stoned couldn't compete with the feeling of having my legs and arms entwined with another boy's.

When I went away to college, one of my first priorities was to join the wrestling team. I had come to a small school in the Midwest, eager to get away from my family in New York. The men on my college team were much different from the guys I had wrestled with back home. Most of them were farm boys—tan, strong, and broad-shouldered from a lifetime of baling hay and carrying lumber in the sun. Though I had wrestled through all four years of high school, my build could not compete with theirs. I was a very good wrestler, but a city wrestler nonetheless.

That didn't seem to make too much difference to the coach. He accepted me for the team immediately. "You've got great skill, son," he said to me after tryouts. "You'll be a fine addition to our team."

Scott, the team captain, also gave me a hearty welcome. "We're glad to have you," he said with a Midwestern drawl, firmly shaking my hand. He was about 6-foot-2, with dusty blond hair and cheekbones sculpted by the gods. His body was incredible: massive chest and shoulders, slim waist, hard legs, and tight skin that clung to every muscle. He hardly ever had his shirt on. He had spent most of his life outdoors lifting heavy pieces of machinery and fixing the roofs of local barns with his father. Over the years his body had become as defined and statuesque as a Renaissance work of art.

The day after tryouts, my dorm phone rang. It was Scott.

"The next part of the tryout is tonight," he said. "We need you to be at the gym at 11."

"What do you mean?" I asked. "Haven't I already made the team?"

"Didn't anyone tell you?" he said. "There are two tryouts: the formal tryout and the informal tryout. You have to go through both to be on the team."

"Oh," I said. "Will Coach be there?"

"No," Scott answered. "This is strictly a team thing. Be there at 11 and we'll take care of everything then."

"That's kind of late," I said. "The gym closes at 10."

"I have the key," he answered and hung up.

I arrived at the gym at the appointed time. No one was there. I figured this must be some kind of initiation ritual. My new teammates would have their fun with me for the night, and then I'd be a real member.

FULL BODY CONTACT

A group of six wrestlers led by Scott arrived shortly after 11. I had only met a few of them at tryouts the previous day, so Scott did introductions while I shook everyone's hand. These were pretty big guys—not much taller than I was per se, but definitely more muscular. If their handshakes were any indication of their strength, they could probably crush rocks in their palms.

We all entered the gym. Scott locked the door behind us. As he led me through the corridors to the wrestling room, he explained the details of the "informal tryout."

"You see," he said, "Coach's tryout isn't enough for us. We need to make sure that our new teammates are going to have what it takes to win...to keep this team together. We don't want any surprises a few weeks into the season. So we have our own little tryout."

"I'm up for it," I said cheerily. Most of them were older and more experienced than I was, but I wasn't afraid. I knew I could hold my own against them.

"It's simple," Scott continued. "All you have to do is wrestle the team captain."

"You?" I said.

"Yup," he said grinning. "Me. We'll have three matches. You only have to win one of them."

"What if I lose all three?" I asked.

"Then you're off," he answered seriously.

We came to the wrestling room, where a large mat had already been rolled out on the floor. My six teammates surrounded the mat. Scott whipped off his shirt and walked to the center. He began removing his socks and shoes, and then his jeans.

"One more thing," he said. "You have to strip."

A few of the other teammates chuckled.

"Why is that?" I asked.

"So that nothing gets in the way," he answered. "Just you, me, and the mat."

"OK," I said.

I removed my socks, shoes, shirt, and jeans as Scott had done, and joined him on the mat.

"No-no-no," he said, shaking his head and pointing to my boxers. "You don't get to keep those."

"You mean you want me to strip *naked*?" I asked in horror.

"Of course," he said. "What did you think I meant?"

"I thought you meant down to my underwear, like you."

"No," he said. "I'm the team captain. I keep mine on."

I was somewhat embarrassed. I was going to have to wrestle around with this hunky guy on the mat in front of six other gorgeous teammates. I was afraid I might get hard. But what could I do? There was no turning back now. I peeled off my boxers and flung them to the side.

"Good," Scott said. "The rules are the same as they would be for any formal match. We'll go three times. If you don't pin me at least once, we'll have to say goodbye to you."

We began. Adrenaline rushed through me. I grabbed Scott's upper arms. My fingers pressed into his hard triceps. His muscles tensed beneath my hands and grew harder by the second. He flexed his biceps, forcing my palms away from him. His hands were on my shoulders, pushing me to the ground. A foot reached around my ankle. In a minute I was down.

We rolled around on the mat. I panted as I began to work up a sweat. Scott was on top of me now, his broad chest pressing down on my back with an almost superhuman strength. He reached down with one of his hands and grabbed my rib cage. I giggled.

FULL BODY CONTACT

"What's so funny?" he asked.

"Nothing," I answered.

He flung me over and forcefully pinned me to the ground. I managed to push him off but in a minute he had me flat on my back again. The heel of one of his hands pressed down on my right pec. His fingers jabbed into my armpit. I laughed again.

"What are you, ticklish?" he said.

"A little," I responded.

Then he crushed me with his full weight. I could feel his hot breath near my ear. The sweat of our necks mingled as I struggled to throw him off. One of the other team members counted three. I had lost the first round.

"Two more chances," Scott said, jumping up and stretching out his chest.

"OK," I said. I was already exhausted.

We started again. I laughed sporadically. Scott's hands kept exciting ticklish sensations on my stomach and ribs. I was used to competing in a wrestling uniform that offered at least some protection. In the nude, I was completely vulnerable. My naked skin was responding in strange ways to Scott's strong and agile fingers. I'd had no idea that I'd react so sensitively.

My ticklishness gave Scott the advantage. Every time I was about to gain a better position, I'd feel his fingers digging into my ribs and I'd have to let go of him. I was doing my best to disguise my weakness, but to no avail. I laughed as we wrestled, and Scott showed no mercy. We rolled all over the mat together, his legs wrapped around mine, his powerful arms pulling my own behind my back. His thighs held me immobile. His hands pressed my face to the mat. Though I posed a good challenge, I was no match for him.

NO LAUGHING MATTER

He twisted and turned me every which way until I had completely lost my breath. I panted and sweated as if I were a dying gladiator in battle. Eventually I gave out. In the end, I lost all three rounds.

I was really upset when it was all over. I figured he'd at least *let* me win one match. I mean, wasn't this supposed to be just some dumb initiation anyway? When we finished, I sat up with my elbows on my knees and let my chin drop down to my chest.

"Sorry," Scott said, wiping his sweaty hands on his boxer shorts. "That's the way it goes."

He walked away from the mat and gathered his teammates around him. When I lifted my head, they seemed to be whispering in some sort of huddled discussion. "What would I do without wrestling?" I though to myself. I felt like I was about to cry. Eager to leave the gym, I stood up and reached for my clothes.

"Hold it," Scott yelled from the other side of the room. "Don't put those on yet. We're going to give you another chance."

"I'm too beat," I said, breathing heavily. "I can't wrestle anymore."

"You don't have to," Scott replied. "In fact, you don't even have to move."

I really was about to cry and just wanted to get out of there. But if they were giving me another chance, I had to take it.

"What do I have to do?" I asked.

"Come back to the mat and lie down on your back."

That was easy enough. I stretched out flat on my back. I was still panting from my exertion.

Scott and the other wrestlers approached the mat. They

all took off their shirts as if they too were about to go head to head with one another.

Before I knew it, my hands were pulled above my head and secured to the mat by two wrestlers. They sat with full force on my wrists as my palms cupped their asses. My legs were likewise pinned down by two more wrestlers. I was flat on my back, spread-eagled with muscular wrestlers sitting on my wrists and ankles. I didn't know what was going on. I tried to squirm, but I could only manage to shift my hips a bit. I was completely helpless.

Scott and the two remaining wrestlers were standing above me. Scott walked around my body to the front and kneeled down between my spread legs. His knees pressed against the insides of my thighs. The other two wrestlers kneeled down next to my ribs on either side of me and sat back on their heels.

The sight of these beautiful men all hovering over me was almost too much to bear. I could feel my dick starting to get hard. I tried to think of silly things to get my mind off of what was going on...but I couldn't. Their brawny shoulders, defined pectorals, and sculpted arms kept seizing my attention. They all breathed down on me like bulls ready to charge. There was a hungry look in their eyes that frightened me a bit.

"Now," Scott said plainly, "we're going to give you another chance. All you have to do is sit still and do what I ask you to do. If you can manage to do that, we'll forget that you lost *all* three matches, and let you on the team."

"Uh...OK," I said, my voice quivering.

Scott placed his hands firmly down on my thighs, rendering even my hips immobile now.

"Here's the deal," he continued. "Our friend Jeff here

NO LAUGHING MATTER

has a stopwatch. Show him the stopwatch, Jeff."

Jeff was the wrestler who was kneeling beside my ribs on the right. He held a stopwatch up to my face. It was set to count down for one minute.

"Jeff is going to start that stopwatch," Scott said. "All you have to do is keep your mouth shut for one minute."

"Keep my mouth shut?" I asked in confusion.

"Yeah," Scott replied, "keep your mouth shut. That means completely shut. Your lips have to stay together. I'm going to be watching you very closely. If your lips part even slightly, you lose. Understand?"

I nodded my head. It sounded easy enough.

"Ready?" Scott said.

"Sure," I answered.

Jeff started the stopwatch. Scott nodded at Hank, the wrestler who was kneeling on the other side of me. One minute of keeping my mouth shut. What could be hard about that?

Then I felt it...an airy, tingling sensation in my left armpit. It felt like cat whiskers were brushing up against me, mingling delicately with my own hair. But that lightness lasted only a few seconds. I felt more pressure...not too much, but enough to make me realize that these were no cat whiskers. In an instant I knew what was going on. Hank was gently tickling my left armpit with one of his fingers.

"Forty-five seconds," Jeff said.

"Mouth tightly closed," Scott said, glaring down at me.

I giggled a bit, but kept my lips sealed. There was no way they were going to get me to break. Then Hank added a second finger to his tickling. I inhaled a big breath of air with my nose. Then I started to laugh.

"Don't open your mouth," Scott said.

FULL BODY CONTACT

"Thirty seconds," Jeff added.

Then Hank added a third finger to my pit...then a fourth, and finally his thumb. He began to slowly circle my pit with all five of his fingers, twirling them in and out of my armpit hair, repeatedly stroking the areas where my chest and back muscles met the pit cavity.

I couldn't take it. I burst out laughing. Hank stopped.

"Aw," Jeff said pathetically, "only 15 seconds to go."

"Now I told you not to open your mouth!" Scott yelled.

"I couldn't help it," I said. "It tickled."

"Oh," Scott said, "so you're ticklish?"

"A little," I answered.

"A little," he said smugly.

The other teammates laughed under their breaths.

"Well," Scott said, "that was a little unfair. You didn't know what we were going to do to you. I'm going to give you another chance."

"Really?" I said.

"Yes," he said. "Do you think you can make it?"

"Sure," I said. I was trying to play it cool, but inside I was terrified.

"OK," Scott said. "This time we're going to let Jeff do the work."

Jeff handed the stopwatch to Hank.

"Ready?" Scott asked, looking down at me.

I nodded.

Scott was still pressing down on my spread thighs. I was completely paralyzed.

"Don't forget," he said. "Mouth closed."

Hank started the stopwatch. I expected to feel Jeff's fingers in my right armpit, and I winced accordingly, but for the first few seconds, nothing happened. More time passed. I still

NO LAUGHING MATTER

didn't feel anything. "What's going on?" I thought to myself. Then it came out of nowhere. His hand was racing up and down the right side of my body. His fingers danced across my ribs like a swarm of insects, covering every inch of skin with fast, rippling movements. I howled with laughter.

"Wow," Hank said, stopping the clock. "He didn't even last half a minute on that one."

Jeff pulled his hand away as I tried to catch my breath. Scott was shaking his head as if disappointed.

"Looks like you're a little ticklish," he said. Then I saw him give both Hank and Jeff a knowing look and a nod.

Hank and Jeff began to tickle me again. There was no stopwatch this time. Their hands were just on me. One of Hank's hands was circling in my armpit, just as it had before, and one of Jeff's hands traveled up and down my other side, sometimes reaching up into the pit, sometimes not.

I began to laugh hysterically. What on earth were these guys doing to me? Were they getting some sick pleasure out of this? I couldn't believe what was going on. "This can't last long," I thought. "I'll die."

"I'm very disappointed," Scott said. "All you had to do was keep your mouth shut for one minute, and you couldn't even do that. Now I'm just going to let Jeff and Hank have a little fun with you...until you close your mouth."

He talked louder and louder as the volume of my laughter increased.

"Please stop!" I begged. "Tell them to stop! I can't take it! Please!"

"And your mouth is *still* open!" Scott shouted. "What am I going to do with you? Give it to him, guys. No limits."

He started to laugh himself. It was evident that he was enjoying my torture.

"Please!" I screamed. "Make them stop! OH GOD! PLEASE!"

"Oh, you want them to stop?" he said. "OK, I'll tell them to stop...just as soon as you stop laughing. If you stop laughing, my friend, I'll make them stop."

I was laughing uncontrollably. I had never realized how ticklish I was. It was absolute torture.

"FUCK!" I screamed.

I couldn't take it. Jeff and Hank were now tickling me with *both* of their hands. They had shifted positions somewhat and were kneeling on either side of me, directly over me. They didn't restrict themselves to the right or the left as they had before. Now their hands just ran freely over my entire torso—over my pecs, around my nipples, through my pits, up my arms, across and up and down my ribs. The tips of their fingers journeyed over my skin in a ferocious blur. They were light and nimble with their touch, and careful to cover every inch of my torso that was within their reach...all except for my abdomen. They never went anywhere near my stomach muscles. As I laughed in utter agony, I wondered why.

Then Scott said, "Boy, from the sound of things, he really likes this, don't you think? Let me help a little."

And then I thought I would die. Scott began moving his wonderful fingers in the air, and lowered them down to my stomach. He let out a frightening cackle as he tickled the muscles of my six-pack one by one, starting at the top and descending to my waist. Then he went below my waistline and tickled the extremely sensitive area just above where my pubic hair started. Often he would stop and tickle me in one spot for many seconds at a time. That killed me, but it didn't seem to bother Scott at all. The more I laughed, the

NO LAUGHING MATTER

more he seemed to get into it. I could not believe this was happening to me. Four big men held me down while three more mercilessly tickled me to the point of insanity. I thought I was going to pass out.

"Please!" I begged. "Oh my God...please STOP! STOP!"

"I told you," Scott said, continuing to twirl his fingers about my abdomen, "we'll stop as soon as you stop laughing."

They continued this—and I'm not exaggerating—for over an hour. Not one inch of my torso went untouched. They even held my head down by the hair and tickled my neck! At some points one of them would take a short break, leaving my body to the hands of the other two. At other points, all three of them would be tickling me with frenzied energy. Sometimes there were even six hands (60 fingers!) concentrating on one isolated spot of my torso. I didn't know what was worse—having their hands glide across every part of my torso or six hands tickling my stomach all at once.

At last the lunatics stopped tickling me. I was ready to pass out. I hadn't realized it, but my dick had been rock-hard almost the entire time.

"OK, my friend," Scott said to me. "We're going to give you one last chance."

"NO!" I yelled, heaving from exhaustion. "No more! Let me catch my breath! PLEASE! Let me catch my breath!"

"I'm sorry," Scott said, "but you don't have a choice about this one. This is your last chance and we're going to *make* you take it."

Oh fuck, I thought. I would surely die now. My friends would all read in the newspaper that I had been tickled to death by a bunch of psycho wrestlers.

FULL BODY CONTACT

"Here's the deal," Scott continued. "Jeff's going to start our little stopwatch…"

"No!" I begged. "No stopwatch!"

They all laughed at my useless pleading.

"Listen," Scott said. "Jeff is going to start our little stopwatch. You've got one minute to come. If you can come in a minute, you're on the team. If you can't, you're out of here. This is your last chance."

"Oh, fuck!" I yelled. "NO!"

But it was too late. Jeff had started the stopwatch. Hank was running his hands all over my upper body while Scott jerked me off with one hand and tickled my stomach with another. The sensations that surged through my body were mind-boggling. I felt like every nerve in me was being stimulated, from the tips of my fingers down to my toes. My torso felt on fire, and my groin area flooded with blood and burned with ecstatic pleasure. I screamed in both agony and sumptuous delight. Scott pumped my dick quick and hard, repeatedly running the sides of his thumb and index finger over the rim of my head.

"Kootchie-kootchie-koo," he said, moving his tickling hand back and forth between my ribs and my stomach. "Come on, old boy. You can do it. Let's see you come."

"Forty seconds," Jeff said.

It was all too much for me to take. I panted and gasped and laughed hysterically. Hank brushed over my pits, lightly tickled my ribs, and aroused my nipples with his expert fingertips. All the while, Scott's left hand twirled across the lower parts of my torso, as his right hand stroked my ever-hardening cock.

"Oh…*Oh…Whoa…Oh, fuck!…f-u-u-uck!!*"

I shot my load. I kid you not—I must have spurted six or

NO LAUGHING MATTER

seven times at full force. My jizz hit Hank's hands and coated my chest. It trickled down the sides of my pecs and puddled on the wrestling mat beneath me.

"Thirty seconds," Jeff said. "Not bad."

"Congratulations," Scott said. "You're on the team."

"Thanks," I said, barely able to manage the word.

"We'll see you at practice tomorrow," he said, gathering up his clothes and leading his group out the door.

My eyes were closed, and I lay there in a state of semi-consciousness. I had never felt so spent, so helpless. But I was in, and that was all that mattered. Then my muscles tensed with fear as I heard Scott say from afar:

"Wait until he sees what we have in store for him after our first match."

The Apple Falls, the Penny Drops

Kieron Devlin

Peter watches Boris slither up to him along the worn tiles—old Victorian schools are good for that at least. Boris slaps Peter on the back and slides his hand down under Peter's belt, under the Navy-blue regulation uniform. His fingers go into the back flap of Peter's pants, pressing the flesh of his upper backside. Red finger aureoles on white skin drive Boris wild and sweet. Peter wriggles away to stand with his back to the wall; boys like Boris just don't cut it anymore and he's bored. He removes Boris's intrusive hand.

"Get knotted." Peter carries on reading *Lady Chatterley's Lover.*

"Football practice in one hour. We have to. Renshaw gave permission, remember?"

"I know...keep your hair on."

Boris is a tad miffed by Peter's cold stance. He's arranged these coaching sessions especially so he can be alone with Peter, for whom he would dribble a mile. Peter glances back across the courtyard toward the medical office. There's this new older guy he hasn't told Boris about yet: silvery sideburns, dead cute, works school hours checking disease histories. The man's face peers out in Peter's direction. Then his eyes dart back to his tables and charts. Peter turns his back to Boris, hiding the smile. Yes, he can get this man. He doesn't want Boris to be a cling-on, not right now. It spoils the image of the loner isolated among more ape-like classmates, his more acute sensibility standing out. He puts distance, studies cool, looks down at his chewed nails, whistling. Boris and Peter have nice blue eyes, both—they could almost be cousins, people say. The older guy might get the wrong idea, might think he and Boris are hitched, no longer virgins, like Siamese. So truly gross.

Boys his own age are just no fun anymore—a pet theory of Peter's. Boris has become the pest, the tiresome lap dog it is necessary to slap down. The man in the medical office, on the other hand, reeks of tobacco and maturity. Nice, twice over. He's smart. He knows a thing or two about boys like Peter who know how to pick elder's brains, the bane of teachers' lives. There's going to be chemistry—and not the test tube kind. The med man's a dead ringer for D.H. Lawrence. Picture's right there in the book. Weedy, but refined. Limp, but agile, and driven by flesh-hunger. X-ray eyes, craving the comfort only a boy's ass can suggest. Peter waits for Boris to scram, but Boris lingers, jealously watches Peter's furtive glances. Peter doesn't care, gets closer to the window to take a look at his man, at the bulge in his pants. Hmmm, he has what it takes in the groin department.

Boris notices that too. "He looks half dead. If he fell into a grave, he'd be right at home."

"You can just tell—on the contrary, dear Boris—that he hasn't had it for months and he's consumed with boy-lust," says Peter. "It's like poetry. Music."

FULL BODY CONTACT

"He's a nerd, a wanker. Why do you like him?"

"I feel sorry for all loners. The insults—just like yours—they have to bear. Unjust."

"I'll bet all this week's lunch money you don't get him. Some other tart will."

"Done."

Peter licks the palm of his hand, slaps it in Boris's palm. They stroke hands, pull together. Peter breathes close on Boris's cheek, "Now go away. Leave me to it. You'll have your proof."

Boris laughs and bounces the football down toward the gym. He stops, bends over, slaps his behind for Peter to see. It used to work, to catch Peter's roving eye. But Peter ignores it in his very new mood these days. How tiresome young and pretty can be. Peter wants to get his teeth into some meatier experience. Boys just don't hack it anymore. Whatever was he thinking letting Boris cozy up to him so?

Peter faithfully hangs around the medical office each break time—looking lost, eager for a glance, for the man to know his allure firsthand. Peter plots how to get attention, how to stir things up: Fainting? Fits of unexplained nausea? Cartwheels? Split seams? Goose bumps on the inner thigh? Tapeworm? Will these work? Then he gets to fantasizing about freshly laundered bedsheets, clandestine dinner dates, fumblings at bus stops, the smell of leather in the back seats of cars, steamed-up windows, and the older guy in his arms, happily paying all the extraneous bills—a boy's necessary expenses. He dreams of landscapes stacked with all the naked bodies of the wrestlers and rugby players, the apes he's snubbed, discarded. A vision he wouldn't, couldn't, shouldn't ever tell his mother or she'll take him back to the shrink.

It has to be said, the older guy's a bit of jerk. He's so new it's embarrassing, doesn't know when a boy is hitting on him. He's the only one in the whole school wearing a dark blue suit, matching cuff links, and tie-pin—of all the nerve! In Peter's neighborhood, this dump of a school, this is gear for occasions. Peter wonders whether *he* might be that occasion. He begins to dress smart too, removes the Pop-star badges; scrubs the ink hearts from his knuckles, stitches up the "pot" burns in his best shirts; slicks back his fringe. Time to get classy. He wonders about underpants too, their color and texture, which areas are worn thin and which are not. It's the caress of the genitalia that does it. He just idolizes a threadbare undersection of a pair of briefs, enough to have dinner on them. The feel of it against his bare cheeks, brushing his nostrils. The essence of the wearer distilled in the smell.

From day one it was a gawking infatuation. Peter took one look at the med man settling in that office and couldn't believe his luck. The guy smiled back innocent, unsuspecting. Peter tore up to the window, panting. He puckered his lips and gelled a kiss against the glass window like a stuck slug. Peter heard his man fall off his chair in surprise and alarm, files in disarray as though he'd arrived at wild boy menagerie. Peter slid his lips down the window to disengage with dignity. He nodded at his onlooker, squeezed up his face and dropped his arm so it swung like a baboon; his eyes were filmy with ill-dimmed lust, like Boris in fact when he first clapped eyes on Peter at football practice. Peter left a grease stain, the dark purple coloring of fruit ice pops, a sugary trail all down the med office window. A love testament. It wasn't cleaned for a week, Peter was proud to note. The new man didn't know what from what. Perhaps he had heard of the crop of sick boys that year at school—the inex-

FULL BODY CONTACT

plicable diseases—and thought this was one of the symptoms. Peter dusted himself off—his territory marked—and strolled casually back to his biology class for rat dissection.

The med man is a picker-upper of crumbs, always bending over to fix his shoelaces to deny Peter the view. What a sauce pot. He gazes out above boys' heads in a superior fashion. *That* will change, thinks Peter. The med man preens his moustache too, and twiddles his tie, more than he should. He's maybe 30—completely ancient—though add another 20 years and Peter wouldn't care, he's going to bag his man. Peter's game of smiles hopes to divert more attention, inane one minute, geisha-like the next. First weeks, there was no reaction. The man is glued to the statistical charts, assumes the gestures of someone about to give dictation. If only Peter could be that secretary. Yes, sir. What did you say, sir? That's right, sir. One day. One day. He'd learn to type specially; top-speed shorthand; prepare tea and sympathy with killer timing; and, gradually—bingo!

Peter learns next day that the med man is also called Peter—destiny, paths colliding, simply meant to be. He is too shy to come out of his office without good reason. To rouse suspicion now would be fatal. He'll never satisfy Peter's longing with a deep-throat kiss in the schoolyard—there're scruples to consider. There's never any privacy there—boys butt into your business uninvited. Peter focuses hard: over-and-out, direct to the groin. A laser from his third eye, like Boris's demo in physics class last week. He held a magnifying glass aimed at the seat of another boy's pants. *It can start a fire*—Boris whispered—*or at least make a tart feel he wants to scratch his balls or backside, take his clothes off.* The boy in question rubbed his backside and squealed to the teacher, Mr. Broadcast. Boys could be little

THE APPLE FALLS

rats at times, always asking for punitive measures to be taken: spankings, chainings head-down over the toilet bowl—a favorite—humiliations, all the frills. But older men are not like this. They take things calmer. They are just...so reasonable.

Peter and Boris are on the field with all the other boys— the future lager drinkers. They bounce the ball from knee to head and back again. Boris is a good player, a real whiz— easily the best. No one, not even Peter, can get the ball from him in a tackle, no way. He has nifty tricks to monopolize the action. He's the number-one goal-scorer on the school team. Boris can do no wrong. Peter just plays defense, or not at all. Halfhearted. The lads, porkers and wimps alike, idolize Boris; they can't understand why he sniffs around Peter, who doesn't take the game seriously, who throws major nelly tantrums. Peter has other games in mind. While the other boys troop back to get changed, Peter works up a minor sweat kicking the ball across to Boris, who never lets him get it back. Boris can concentrate like a demon when his mind is off Peter's backside. He and the ball become one—a symbiosis that is quite mesmerizing to watch.

After the hour is up they go to the changing room, where the clamor and echoes have subsided. Boris and Peter are alone—that sudden rare privacy. They kick off their boots. Boris stands close to Peter and takes off his regulation shirt slowly so Peter can see his nipples. He flicks them like two pencil rubbers about to erase Peter's tongue. Peter sneers and takes his shirt off too. Boris pulls down his shorts and stands pink, white, and naked, gurgling, glowing, his dick raw like a freshly plucked chicken. He runs to the shower, behind the frosted glass, singing the number-one single of the day. Boris turns all the showerheads full

FULL BODY CONTACT

on, water gushing out hard on his spot-free back.

"Look at this," Boris holds up a pair of soggy under-pants one of the players has left behind, "one of the girls has dropped her knickers." He holds them over his dick like a cod-piece, whistles and wiggles his dick, checking to see if Peter is watching. Peter puts on the glum, give-over face and turns away. Boris gets like this in the shower. A cringe-factor for Peter. Boris striates the underpants into a long arm heavy weapon and slaps Peter—zing—right on his backside. Peter tries to dodge but is too late. A red mark appears on the back of his thigh. Boris moans, dumbstruck, holding onto his dick. It does his head in.

Peter grabs the underpants, "You won't be needing them. As you said in physics class, they get in the way." Peter locks them into a locker and runs naked back into the shower. Boris never wears underpants as they get in the way of masturbation. A hole in his pocket allowed him to do it undisturbed in class. Other boys tried to become orgasm addicts too, and thought it not bad—a boy's only solace outside of the tuck shop and football. Boris claimed he started the trend for do-it-yourself hand jobs.

Peter remembers the day in physics lab. Crouching behind the back table for experiments, he showed everyone his thingamy coming to a peak. Peter thought he was faking. But the boys were desperate to see. The teacher, Mr. Broadcast, a short man with glasses, was chalking the formula for Newton's law of motion on the board. "The apple falls, the penny drops," he droned, making it as dull as it gets just as Boris let rip a great fart. What had apples to do with anything anyway? It silenced the room and turned a hell of a lot of noses in Boris's direction. Boris pointed to a boy further up the lab table. "What a bloody great pong, sir! It's his."

THE APPLE FALLS

There was uproar, serious hilarity going on. Peter laughed too. Mr. Broadcast slammed his cane down across the desk. "What the hell is all this about!" He glared at Boris. "Explain yourself!'"

"Nothing, sir," said Boris, barefaced and tugging the slack on his pants. The class was locked in a tense hush. Mr. Broadcast waited.

"It wasn't a pong, sir. It was just a rather pungent aroma."

This would have been funny in any case, but Boris said it in Mr. Broadcast's very own warbling, affected voice—a goose swallowing pebbles, spot-on mimicry. Pandemonium. Laughs and giggles went into unstoppable reprises as the line was repeated and embellished. There was nothing Mr. Broadcast could do. Boris's remark chalked a new high in class lore. Mr. Broadcast fumed in a hopeless rage, a sinking defeat imploding on his face. The whooping didn't die down. Feet were stamping. His composure was lost. The remark would follow him for years. He knew it. Boris, the David to Goliath, the top lay, had scored again. Peter almost relented and let himself be Boris's little piece of stuff after that class. But boys are still boobies, lacking in experience, so he held off. The policy of teasing works just as well. Doesn't put Boris off. He'll do anything for Peter, except write poetry—poetry is scary.

Peter nips under the showers. "Yikes...the water's bloody freezing!" He backs out, shivering.

"Come on in, chicken," says Boris, splashing Peter with icy water. Peter steps in and splashes him back. Boris does a good Tarzan yell, holding his chest out, the muscles well under way to being splendiferous.

FULL BODY CONTACT

The water gets hot. "My nipples are hard," Boris says. "Feel!"

"Your tits are too big anyway." Boris turns to slap Peter hard on the backside. "Don't! I don't want your greasy paw marks anywhere on me. Renshaw might come in any minute."

"So? He won't say anything. He *likes* me...a lot. Got him round my finger."

"Yeah? Does he *do* it too? The dirty bastard. Does his wife know?"

"Fuck his wife too. Here. Give me the soap." Boris has a monkey grin on his face. Peter hands him the soap bar, hardened with dirt-soaked cracks like veins. "Watch!" Boris says. He bends over, lifts up his leg, rests it on the glass wall, and starts shoving the soap into his back hole slowly. Amazing, how it fits.

"What are you doing? You idiot! You'll shit bubbles for weeks. Give me that back."

"It goes all the way. Watch!"

"I'll bet," says Peter, turning his head away. "You're gross." Then he turns back to look. Boris doing stunts in the nude beats doing exam crams.

"Hang on. I've not finished. I'm going to fart a brick of bubbles. I've seen a guy who can play trumpet like this."

Peter watches. "You should be in a porn circus."

"Ohgodohgodawooooeee," Boris makes pleasure sound more basic than a Neanderthal. You can't say he sounds like he doesn't enjoy it. He squeezes out the bar of soap, washes it off, and hands it back to Peter. "Souvenir, my dear," he laughs.

Peter takes it anyhow.

"Oh, wait, I think I'm...com..." Boris gasps.

THE APPLE FALLS

"What's going on? You did the practice?" It's a harsher voice they recognize as that of Mr. Renshaw, P.E. master. Boris gags. He thrusts one of Peter's hands on his dick and covers his mouth. Renshaw's just walked into the changing room. He's heard the noise. He speaks across the frosted glass, the sound of water hitting the tiles. Peter can just about make out the pear-shaped outline of Renshaw's stomach, the result of too many late-night curries, and the bald head. Renshaw shifts uneasily. Boris is his finest player. It's not good to upset him as a rule. He doesn't know whether to look, what he might find. He decides not to.

"You boys just be good now, all right? Get back to class ASAP."

"Can't hear you very well, sir. We're just finishing," Boris shouts.

"How did the coaching young Peter go?"

"Fine, sir," says Peter.

"Can we get you out of defense, you think?"

"Maybe."

"He was gre-at, sir. Just great."

"Anything wrong with your voice there, Boris?"

"No, sir. Maybe a cold coming on."

"Don't stand about wet then. Get yourselves dry. Get a move on."

"Righty-ho."

Renshaw walks away scratching his bemused head, its one wisp of hair trailing from his crown over his collar. He'll never understand the murky business of boys.

Boris looks down, his mouth dropping open, as the gooey white stuff slushes into the soapy water. Peter holds on to his own dick like a shamed Adam—perhaps with a dash of Eve—evicted from Paradise.

FULL BODY CONTACT

"I can't believe you did that," Peter says. He's not going to come. He's saving himself for you-know-who. Boris doesn't notice. The noise drowning laughs.

Boris leans over to Peter, doe-eyed and passive. He lets the hot tap run down his back. "Ahhh. Feels good." He points to his shoulder, sore from a recent rough tackle. "Massage, please."

Peter massages Boris's shoulder. It's the least he can do. "That was the best yet. A record. Better than my girl-friend."

"You haven't got a girlfriend, Boris."

"I will have. Very soon. Know something?"

"What?"

"I love *yew.*"

Peter cringes. Why does Boris insist so? He looks at Boris—the prize—but the med man flashes through his mind. The elusive catch wins.

"Do you love me?"

"Dunno." A moment of agony on Boris's face. "I think I'm into someone else at the moment."

Boris's expression hardens. "Know something else?"

"What now?"

"That old guy's got a wife."

"How do you know? Are you kidding me? He's sup-posed to be single."

"They are made for each other. They are older than a couple of bats from hell. I've seen her."

Peter is not perturbed, not by the idea of age. Or of the female. The wife only makes it more intriguing. The two Peters are made for each other, it's clear.

"Here." Boris tries to kiss Peter on the lips. He's never done that before. Peter's mouth shuts tight. He steps out of

THE APPLE FALLS

the shower, silent. He wishes Boris wouldn't do this. Peter's not a goal to be scored, once netted to be mistreated. Boris must wait his turn. He puts the soap bar carefully in his jacket pocket.

The bell for class is about to ring. Peter, loitering, stares at the older Peter, who crosses his legs to hide a growing bulge. Peter relishes the impact he's having and clicks the score, finger in the air. It's time for history class, a dreary list of coups and beheadings. He gives a parting shout: "Want a fuck?" or was it "Good luck?" Who can tell through that window? He's no lip-reader. The man's head turns, alarmed. Peter gives a cheery wave. The man's head turns back, solemn. Peter loves this game—like pinball or Nintendo, it kills time; it kills being at school; it beats being in a scrum, picking bogeys, or instructing younger boys in the correct use of condoms. If he stays on track, he could reach the target by Wednesday lunchtime. And Boris will be squirming.

Peter doesn't do the lip-suction trick anymore. It was a mistake. Some subtlety is required, which, in a boy's school, takes less effort, it's true. Peter balances on the edge of the rock garden fountain, in full view of the med window, a tightrope cupid, imaginary bow in hand, about to topple from tiptoes. He fancies the med man might run out and catch him before he falls. He tries trailing his hand on the gravel till the stones make flesh bleed. Perhaps there is iodine, a bandage, a splint, words of reassurance in that office? But it doesn't happen. Peter fumbles absentmindedly across the buttons around his groin, absentmindedly opening one of them, slipping a finger in. The med man's riveted to Peter's other hand, slipping inside his regulation blue shirt, pushing up the vomit-brown tank top his mother

FULL BODY CONTACT

knitted to reveal the tiny curled mushroom on his belly. He watches the guy's eyes go there. Yes! He's got him. It's all about intention.

Class always gets in the way in this boys-only school from hell, designed to torment a young mind with lessons wasted, mostly. Never a moment away from boys who get crushes on you. Like Boris—dimwit, dipshit, but a football hero nonetheless.

✪ ✪ ✪

Next day, Peter is ready when the med man opens his window as though in need of air. He unbuttons his collar, loosens the tie, rolls up his sleeves, takes on that caged look. Peter catches his attention. He turns his head away quickly and crosses his legs. Peter runs to the bathroom, to catch the heat of the moment. The door is very near the med office door. Eyes meet, feet hover. Peter hints at the direction to go—no class was ever needed to learn this language without words. The med man dashes back to his office as if he's forgotten something. Peter shrugs. He's used to the sheer desolation of being a boy, that's what gives him strength. Who the hell else understands? There'll be time. Peter sees the notice board nearby, where the exam results are posted. His are the lowest in his year. Even at English he's hopeless. There'll be kickback for his abysmal academic performance, relentless advice about extra homework, which Peter would love to burn. None of the teachers has noticed his hanging around the med man. Peter and Boris agree, teachers are pretty dumb; they notice only unimportant things.

✪ ✪ ✪

THE APPLE FALLS

Late afternoon, and Peter decides it's way past time to attack. He hides behind a display unit in the corridor outside the med office. He should be in art class but he said he felt sick from drawing rotting cabbages and had to use the bathroom. He waits till the med man, the senior Peter, comes out of his office. He checks no one's there. Once the med man's in, Peter nips in behind him—the element of surprise. He's already unzipped at the urinal, taking a pee. Young Peter comes up to the stall at his side and looks down. The man hurries to zip up. Young Peter smiles demurely.

"Hello...ah...er.... You're the one who..."

"That's me. The very one."

The man's clearly tense, worried, his eyes don't stop darting back to the door.

"Hello. *Peter*."

"How do you know my name?"

"I know a lot about you. We've got so much in common."

"Oh."

"And how's your good lady wife?"

"She...she...doesn't know anything."

"That's cool."

The man moves toward the door. But young Peter has taken precautionary measures: An old mop and brush are cross-wedged against the door. It would be difficult for anyone to come in now. The janitor's lazy. His staff will not come for an hour or more. Peter's plan—always good to have one.

"Don't worry....it's what I want." Peter fondles his groin, flicks his eyes toward a stall. The man's eyes drag up and down the younger body in front of him. Young Peter kneels down. The man jerks back, looks at the door. Head level with the groin, Peter gets to work taking the dick right into his mouth and licking it softly. Then he bites down hard on the shaft and hears his victim gasp.

"No...no..."

The man recoils, but young Peter pulls him closer.

"Not here. Are you out of your mind?"

Peter releases him, pulls him to a cubicle.

"OK, here." Peter smiles.

There's a small pool of water on the floor, so Peter climbs up, his legs straddling each side of the seat. The man's eyes are straining. He keeps looking back, but it's too far gone now, he's lured in, his face a mixture of confusion and sheer release. Peter's working it, tearing at the shirt, the vest underneath, unbuttoning the pants. Young Peter wiggles and yelps. They go for it: touching, nibbling, kissing. It's what they both want, they can't deny. A frenzy growing. The man is tugging his dick out of his pants now—all the weeks of watching the young one, wondering where it would lead. It's a sure thing for Peter. He knows he drives the man crazy. This is where they go ALL the way.

Or stop.

Peter surveys his catch coolly, leans into his shoulder and sees the man's face in brilliant close-up. He sees criss-crossed lines, he sees the hairs; he sees capillaries that bulge blue over the surface like Roquefort or the strange surfaces of the outer planets. He thinks of cement drying with paw marks in it. He looks at the man's hands crawling over him like crustaceans on a food hunt, searching his nipples. How strange the man looks from this vantage point. The knuckles like rotten chestnuts. Veins under an extraordinary over-growth of hair. And freckles—and the pong. Sorry, "pun-

THE APPLE FALLS

gent aroma." Peter thinks, is this what turns him on really? Or just what he thinks turns him on. This is not the Lawrence who wrote *Chatterley*, this is like his joke of his deadbeat uncle who flashes from the bathroom window at women from the Church Hall across the street. The med man could lose his job, young Peter reflects, his marriage could be ruined. The power alone could make young Peter orgasm. But the feel of the med man's beard buried on his chest is a matchbox scraped across delicate nipples.

Something's very wrong. Peter pushes him away.

"No, don't stop. Don't stop now."

But Peter does stop, upset, but still pulling the strings. Those eyes are questioning him deeply, so much it's painful.

Peter buttons up. This isn't it. It just isn't IT. There's been a mistake. Too much for real. He thinks of Boris in the shower. Deprived of a climax, the man can't believe it has stalled so soon. A tangle new to him.

"It's impossible now," Peter says, cool as a mud bath.

"No. We can do it somewhere else." The med man moves forward to touch.

Peter pushes him gently, "—and you can't make me do it."

"What?"

"It's over, Pete."

"What are you talking about? Nothing ever began. You led me to this." The man's face is puce. He's on the brink of rage, or panic. Peter thinks mature men really ought to watch their hypertension. Could be dangerous. He's risked everything just for this letdown? He doesn't look pretty at this moment, Peter thinks. He looks—yes, that's it—old. Old is just not cute anymore. Old is dispensable. Old is just, well, OLD.

Peter pushes past the man, "Sorry, but you do have a wife. I don't. I'll never marry."

FULL BODY CONTACT

"But you have a boyfriend."

"Boris. Don't be funny. He's an oaf. A pickaninny."

Peter arranges his shirt buttons and studies his face in the mirror. He still looks ace. He has so many years ahead of him. He licks his finger and smoothes flat a stray hair on his eyebrow. He takes the bar of soap from his pocket. It's dried out now but he sniffs it calmly—*eau de Boris*—adds a little water and dabs the foam on his fringe like a mousse. Style is paramount at times like these. He flattens out the hair, giving it a dewdrop curl. It looks thick and glossy. The man watches, astonished, his hands extended. There's a moment when he could grab for the neck. But he's too scared. Young Peter gives him an admonishing look. He'd better not try. An afternoon strangulation would be very difficult to explain to the stuffy old headmaster. And very hard for the school to live down.

Conceding defeat, the old Peter reaches for the mop at the door. "Don't ever come near my office window again, you little trollop. You...Lolita."

This last is a great compliment to Peter, who's heard the name somewhere. "Only if I'm sick. Anyway, I've got to catch up my art—while there's *still life*. Ha!"

The man is not amused.

Peter adds, "That's a joke, you can laugh, you know." The man fumbles a lot, has trouble disentangling the mop from the brush from the door handle. Peter steps over to help, chivalrous enough to dewedge the door. "Anyway, *Peter*. You shouldn't be doing this at your age. You could get into trouble. You'd better make sure no one finds out."

That could be future tuck-shop money. Peter waltzes out right in front of him. What could he have been thinking all that time bothering with the med man? Besides, the older guy was just such an easy catch. No challenge. The experienced male so very overrated.

✪ ✪ ✪

It's 4 P.M. and Peter is talking to Boris. They're on the bus home as usual. The med man hasn't been seen. Rumor is he's got another job somewhere far away. Boris is chattering about girls, girls, girls. He's met one and she's a gas. She goes all the way. She lets him touch between her legs. Boris is looking better these days, Peter thinks. He's shaving his sideburns to a needle point. The freckles that Peter once pretended to pick off have faded into a subtle hue and his skin is tender soft. He wears out his pants easily. He's got hairs that ride his top lip like a ticklish centipede, sort of manly and streetwise. Peter listens to Boris, nodding at key moments so as not to lose him. Their hands touch when the bus jolts. Yesterday, the girl—Elise—agreed to watch while Boris sprayed shaving foam over his crotch and washed it off with fizzing cider. She laughed her head off at that.

"Remember I did that for you once? She has to be the right one if she didn't run away."

"Doubtless, she's the one for you then," says Peter.

"She let me do it. We've been doing it all week." Boris acts proud.

"That's great. Could be a record or something."

"Yeah, so we can have babies now."

"Babies? I love babies. They are so cute. They're so nice. And so young."

"Yeah," Boris goes on, missing Peter's irony. "We'll have boys though, not girls."

"Boris?"

"Yep."

"If you have a baby boy, will you promise me one thing?"

"Yeah, what's that?"

"Don't ever, ever call him Peter."

"Why not?"

"Just don't. I'm serious. I couldn't stand it, that's all. There are enough Peters in the world. I would change my name if I could."

"Crazy. OK, I won't," Boris grins. He's never thought of actually counting Peters till now.

Boris puts his hand on the seat where Peter sits. He worms his hand into Peter's back pocket till it feels that's where it always should be, warm and cozy touching Peter's soft behind. They make a good team, the two of them. Future football stars. Perhaps Siamese after all. They keep this position, talking and looking out of the window, until they get off the bus at their stop, at their tree-lined suburb. They walk down identical garden pathways to their front porch doors. Their mothers, longtime neighbors, have been peeking between the blinds, expecting their sons home anytime soon. Later on, after dinner, Boris may phone Peter, or Peter may phone Boris just to check if the other fancies kicking a ball around the lawn, see who can keep it in the air longest. Their eyes, everyone says, are the same blue— exactly—they could almost be cousins. Boris is ace with the ball, but Peter's got killer strategy.

THE APPLE FALLS

What Are You Going to Do?

Brian Lieske

"So," the gruff voice growls down at me, "what are you going to do?" He's a whole lot taller than me, a whole lot heavier than me, and I think he can crack coconuts between his thighs.

This is too damn much like work. I mean, he's hot and all, but why doesn't he just say what he wants instead of going through all this? "I'm guessing..." I try to move my hips, but they're wedged to the floor. "Unless you let me..." My arms are free, so I push at his chest, but the muscle slides over the rib cage. "Not a whole lot."

I feel the hard floor through the cold mat and wonder if the night is going to be a complete loss. First I get stood up, then the main playroom was almost deserted, and now I'm stuck under a big bully who isn't even wearing any leather. Except the boots, which I wouldn't mind licking.

He slaps my face, just hard enough to get my undivided attention. "Better try something, or this is going to hurt." He pauses for effect. "More."

OK, maybe not a total loss. I squirm and wiggle and roll

FULL BODY CONTACT

and buck against the weight of his body, feeling the crushing thighs tighten around my waist until I'm exhausted and gasping for breath. He's twice my size; I never had a chance.

He drops forward and pins my shoulders to the mat with his forearms, relaxing the grip of his legs. "Not bad for a first time."

"Thanks." I prefer rope, but the way he's got his body wrapped around, controlling me, feels good. And he's got pretty eyes.

I'm about to ask if he's done when he kisses my mouth and whispers, "But it still looks like you're going to have to suck me."

"Guess so." For form's sake, I try to sound a little disappointed.

✪ ✪ ✪

Monday at lunchtime, I'm still thinking about my big pal from the other night. When he grabbed me, I had been cruising the main playroom, trying to salvage some part of the evening and the party door price, hoping to get happily tied up and flogged after a top I'd been talking to online flaked on me. I'd been to that playspace a few times before, but I'd always stayed away from the little side room filled with guys who look like older, fatter versions of every jock who tormented me in high school.

For grins, I type "wrestling" into my favorite metasearch engine. 3,000,500 matches in .19 seconds. Great.

WWF; no. Undertaker; no. Chyna; definitely not.

Try "gay wrestling." That's better. Only half a million hits. Let's see. Freestyle, fantasy pro, NHB, gut punching... Ouch.

WHAT ARE YOU GOING TO DO?

Submission; that sounds more like it. Hell, one more mailing list won't kill me.

FROM: M4MRASSEL@YIPPIEGROUPS.COM
RE: Welcome

Welcome to M4MRASSEL, a discussion/meeting group for guys who like to wrestle. All styles and all orientations welcome, but be aware most members are gay and into freestyle, submission, and/or NHB. Use common sense when setting up a meeting, and be clear with each other about your style and stakes.

No spam, flames, or homophobes tolerated.

Feel free to introduce yourself and post a profile to the files section.

TO: M4MRASSEL@YIPPIEGROUPS.COM
RE: Dumb question...

Hi, I'm a total beginner. NHB?

"So, did you ever wrestle?" He's a lot smaller than my pal at the playspace but still bigger than me. Almost everyone is. A little older too; his tight dark curls have some white strewn around the temples. Very compact body. He has the kind of build you get from actually working with heavy stuff for a living, not gym lifting.

"Not since high school gym class," I answer, noticing the small reproduction of a Greek statue on the mantle. There's a training mat unrolled on the floor in front of the fireplace. I don't know exactly what I expected when he wrote back off list and said he loved coaching new guys—some kind of

FULL BODY CONTACT

locker room fantasy maybe—but this wasn't it. He's not even in one of those one-piece things college wrestlers wear, just shorts and a tee. It's a relief since I don't get the "gear" side of this scene and certainly don't own any.

Other than the mat and a few videos hand-labeled "NCAA Wrestling," there are none of the trappings around the place I'd expect from a fanatical fetishist. Besides the statue, there's not even any wrestling-oriented art. "At least not till I went to a play party with a wrestling room last week."

"Ah, the one up in town." He's relaxed, reclining on the sofa that's pushed all the way against the wall to accommodate the mat. "I meet a lot of guys who get back into this from there. I ought to go up sometime. How'd you do?"

I shrug. "I got my ass stomped. He was about 100 pounds heavier," I exaggerate, trying to scrape up a little justification for losing so badly.

"That's tough, but not insurmountable. Give me your arm."

I lean forward from my end of the couch, and he grabs just above my wrist.

"Pull," he says. I do. His grip is solid. We shift back and forth for a few seconds. "That's fine. You're pretty strong for a small guy. Obviously, you've got to use technique on someone who's that much bigger. Think you'll wrestle him again?"

I nod, not believing any technique can even things out that much. "If I get the chance. It's not my usual scene, but I had fun."

"You discuss any limits on moves or were you doing NHB?"

"What's that again?"

"No holds barred. Sometimes, if I'm fighting a smaller guy, I'll let him use chokes to even things out a little."

"I'd probably just piss him off if I tried something like

WHAT ARE YOU GOING TO DO?

that. Look, I'm not going to beat him. I just want to keep it interesting. I mean, how many times do you want to fight someone you can beat with one hand?"

"Fair enough. Want to give it a try?"

"Sure." I stand and follow him over to the mat.

He drops to all fours and says, "Let's start in referee's position. Throw-downs from standing are tougher and riskier. Easier to get hurt."

"Right." I kneel behind and to the side, dusting off the memory of the last time I did this, sometime in ninth grade. I settle into place, wrap my arm around his stomach, and put my left hand above his elbow.

"Closer. Don't leave space by the hips." I follow the instruction, feeling how solidly he's built. His gut is a little round on the surface and rock-solid underneath. He asks, "What are you going to do?"

I snort a laugh at the echo, then reply, "Try to take you down, I guess."

"Go ahead."

I reach across, grab his forearm and ankle and try to push him over. Before I know what's happening, I'm caught between his legs, getting crushed. He's not that much bigger than me, but I'm going nowhere. He squeezes progressively harder until I can't breathe.

"This is to submission; remember to tap out when you've had enough."

The sound that comes out of my throat is something like those cartoon panels that read "Aaaaaaarrrrrgggghhhhh!" This is a whole different kind of pain than I'm used to. I hear pounding in my ears. I realize it's my heartbeat. I finally manage to tap his back. Air rushes back in, but it's a moment before I can ask, "How the fuck did you do that?"

FULL BODY CONTACT

He grins back at me. "Trapping you or crushing you?"

Still trying to catch my breath, I reply, "Yes."

He laughs, "Come on. I'll slow it down."

Breathing heavier than I should be, I climb back up behind him.

It's a long, informative three hours. Sex never comes up once.

TO: M4MRASSEL@YIPPIEGROUPS.COM
RE: Endurance training

I thought I was in good shape till I hit the mat recently and couldn't breathe after five minutes. I've been doing swimming and weights for a few years. Any suggestions on improving endurance? Thanks.

When the next play night rolls around, I make a point of getting there early. Even though it's chilly, I wear a new pair of leather shorts instead of jeans and chaps. Keep my options open a little. I still head straight to the back, dodging past the wrestling room door.

After a half-hour, it looks like it's going to be one of those damn couple's nights. Everybody coming into the main room is entering in pairs. There's no one I'd trust to touch me—let alone top me—standing solo on the outskirts, cruising.

I head back up front. I hear my pal from last time's voice over by the mats. He's sitting on the sidelines shouting encouragement to a tall guy in rubber who's in the process of getting stomped by somebody not much bigger than me. "What are you going to do? Come on. Your arms are free. Grab him."

The tall guy tries to clutch at the other guy's hands. I'd learned that's always a mistake. The little guy has better position and is probably stronger than he looks. He forces

WHAT ARE YOU GOING TO DO?

the tall guy's arms into a lock and entwines his legs. Tall boy tries to squirm out without any luck then starts sounding like he's really hurting.

"Had enough?" the little guy asks.

"Say 'Uncle' if you have," my pal advises.

Tall boy isn't listening, or maybe he likes that kind of pain. The little guy ratchets the arms up more tightly, and the tall one finally calls, "Uncle!" There's an accent in the voice.

It's like hitting an off switch. The little guy relaxes and releases him, quickly climbing to his feet and offering an arm up. Tall boy looks suspicious for a moment, then takes the offered hand.

The little guy pulls him up, hugs him with a slap on the back, and says, "Good match." The tall guy nods and beats a retreat toward the back room.

My pal is chatting with the little guy when he spots me and calls me over. The hug is friendly then goes to strong and finally to really tight. He showered right before he came here. The crisp clean damp is still clinging to him. He stands up and lifts me onto the mat asking, "Game for another round?" The little guy sits down, grabs a bottle of water, and grins.

"Guess so," I reply. He pulls me to the floor and I forget everything my "coach" showed me, but I manage to keep my legs free.

He throws more of his weight on my chest and says, "Someone's been practicing."

I manage to grunt back, "Didn't want you to get bored."

He smiles at me and says, "Good boy," before he turns me on my stomach and locks my arms and legs.

✪ ✪ ✪

FULL BODY CONTACT

I visit Coach again the next week. "So you did better," he says, while we work on a speed drill.

"*Better* is a relative term." The endurance work I added to my gym routine is paying off; I can manage a conversation doing this.

"You got out from under him."

"Barely. I never got close to vertical, let alone control." This is going to hurt tomorrow.

"So, we'll work on that," he replies, coming at me. He takes me down and locks my arm against the mat over my head. "I don't care how strong he is, his elbow only bends one direction."

TO: M4MRASSEL@YIPPIEGROUPS.COM
RE: Training regimen

Obviously, I need to emphasize strength training more than I have. Any suggestions or links to sites with lifting sets geared for freestyle wrestling? Thanks.

The next play party, I'm in a headlock almost before I see my big pal. We're out in the social area near the fridge. He hasn't even taken off his shirt when he grabs me, so I bite down on his nipple through the fabric. I found out last time he gets off on tit play more than I do. The arm flexes around my neck, pulling my mouth tight against him. My nose gets covered too, but I don't care. He hasn't hurt me yet.

"Good job, boy," he says and tousles my hair with his free hand before loosening up, right when my lungs start burning.

"Thank you, sir," I reply, catching my breath. My cock's already hard.

"Am I tossing you around tonight?" he asks.

WHAT ARE YOU GOING TO DO?

"Guess so, sir."

"Good. Well, let's see who else is around." With that, he throws me over his shoulder and proceeds to carry me through the playspace like a sack of potatoes. Whenever he puts me down, I'm back in the headlock.

I don't walk from one room to another under my own power the rest of the night. My gut aches for two days after. I miss it awfully when it stops.

✪ ✪ ✪

It's Wednesday night, so I'm over at Coach's place. "What are you going to do?" he asks after an hour, while we grab some water. "You going to call him?"

"I don't know."

"You want to."

"Fuck, yeah. I love the way he works me over."

"Then why don't you?"

"Because he's still stomping me without breaking a sweat." I sigh. "And he didn't even notice the leg scissors hold."

"That's because you're still trying to outmuscle him," he chides softly. "You can't squeeze; you've got to lock your ankles and extend your legs."

"OK." I close the cap on the bottle and move out on the mat. "Let's put this together. If I'm going to his place, I am not going to just lie there and let him steamroll me. I'm putting up a decent fight and shocking the fuck out of him at least once."

"Think you can get away with joint locks?"

"That'd shock him all right. Think I can pull it off?"

"All technique, no strength. Not a problem."

FULL BODY CONTACT

I call my pal when I arrive home. His machine picks up. Shit. "Hi, sir. You gave me your number at the party last time, so I thought I'd call and see if you wanted to hook up sometime." I leave day and night numbers. "Thanks. Talk to you soon."

I hit the shower and beat off thinking about the way he felt under me the one time I managed to push him over last Saturday. When I shoot, the ache in my gut comes back to visit like an old friend for a few minutes.

TO: M4MRASSEL@YIPPIEGROUPS.COM
RE: Match wanted

Beginner, 5-foot-6, 125 lbs, wiry build. Dk brown/hazel. Tired of getting kicked around by giants, seeks freestyle or submission match with someone around my size. Stakes open for discussion, including for top (safe only!), but primarily looking to toss down with someone in my weight class for a change. Your pic gets mine.

Saturday night and Coach is busy, my big pal isn't returning my calls, and the only other local replies from the list are NHB fighters. That's for sure bruises I don't need, so I dust off my leather and head out.

I thought I had it worked out. I'm a bottom. Not a slave, not a boy, but I'm a damn good submissive bottom. Pretty much anything that doesn't do permanent damage is cool, and the right amount of pain just makes it better. All the same, my favorite bar seems less familiar and more quiet this week.

You'd think I'd be more enthused when a good-looking guy with three floggers on his belt picks me up, and I let him take me off and tie me to a St. Andrew's cross. But all of a sudden it feels like something's missing. They're nice toys, and he's really good at using them, but it's not satisfying. Even when we get to the sex. He's got a cock that fits my mouth perfectly, but it's only his cock, not him. He barely touches me. I get the feeling he's going through the motions because he thinks I expect it.

Plus, I just gave it up. He didn't earn it. I've been happily subbing for years. When the hell did that start bothering me?

The phone starts ringing when I walk in Wednesday night after practice with Coach. I figure it's a telemarketer, but I grab it anyway.

"Hey, boy."

"Oh, hi." When the fuck did his voice start making me hard? "Nice to hear from you, sir."

"Got your message. I was on a business trip last week. So, you're ready to come over to my place and wrestle?"

"I guess…"

"The stakes are higher, you realize."

"Oh?"

"When you lose here, I rape your ass."

Can't rape the willing, I think, but don't answer for a moment. "How's Friday night?"

TO: M4MRASSEL@YIPPIEGROUPS.COM
RE: Fighting up

How do you approach a match where you know you're outclassed, but you want to give your best? Thanks.

I don't get a damn thing done Friday afternoon at work.

I change clothes three times before I leave home and still manage to arrive at his place early. My palms are sweating. It's a nicely maintained suburban split-level in a quiet neighborhood with neatly manicured lawns and lots of curbside parking. I ring the doorbell.

"Hey, boy," he pulls me into a hug as he shuts the door. I melt against him and throw my arms around his barrel chest. "Ready to get tossed around?"

I'd sub out for him in a heartbeat, but he doesn't want that. Neither do I. "Ready to make you work, sir."

"Good." He throws me over his shoulder and carries me to the garage. We pass a foyer table with a statue like the one Coach has. I recognize it now as Hercules wrestling. Seems strangely apt, even though the demigod has his opponent upside down, gripping him around the waist, not in a fireman's carry.

"Take your boots off," he instructs when he puts me down. His motorcycle is parked by the door; most of the rest of the floor is covered with a regulation-size mat. From the setup, it's apparent it stays this way all the time.

I walk onto it and feel the foam distort under my feet. He puts his arm around my shoulder, and suddenly I'm on the floor.

We scuffle for a while. Periodically, he lets me up, and we shift to referee's position. I take him down once from the top starting stance. I don't think he expected that. He tosses our shirts over by my boots. I arch my back into the coarse hair covering his chest. He wraps his arm around my neck and holds tight, twisting my nipple with his other hand.

I'm catching my breath when he throws me onto my back and straddles my hips. "Not bad. So, here's the deal. You've got three minutes. If you don't get up, I get your ass." He puts

WHAT ARE YOU GOING TO DO?

his palms on my shoulders and presses down. "Better start."

I almost manage to pull off a reverse. I end up over on my stomach, but the effort costs me. He's letting all of his mass fall on me tonight instead of cutting me some slack like he has been at the party. Breathing heavy, I go into conserve mode to recover.

I catch a minty wisp of mouthwash on his breath when he whispers in my ear, "Two minutes. If you don't try, I'll beat you up too."

Much as I'd probably enjoy that, I twist and plant the heel of my hand on his chin, pushing his head back. It nearly gives me enough room to slip out from under the hold, but he pulls me back and lays on top of me. "Thirty seconds. What are you going to do?"

He humps my butt for emphasis.

I swing my arm around his neck and roll. If he hadn't had my legs locked, it might have worked, but I end up practically where I started. He compliments me. "Nice try. But time's up. Looks like your ass is mine."

"Looks like." I can't even manage to sound a little disappointed.

He opens his jeans there on the mat, and I go down on him. I know what he likes. He lets me have free rein for a while, then shoves me back down. He straddles my face and fucks my mouth, driving the back of my head into the foam. It's nothing new, and I wonder for a moment if he was serious about claiming my ass. I'm a damn good cocksucker, and he's earned my best. Pinned or not, I get aggressive and feel fresh sweat break out on his skin.

I smile when I hear a satisfied little growl come out of him just before he pulls out, hitches up his pants, throws me back into the fireman's carry, pulls off my jeans, carries me to the bedroom, ties me up, puts on a rubber, and domination fucks me in a variety of positions for the next several hours. When he's done, he sends me home with permission to jerk off.

I make it to the second stop sign under the yellow-orange glow of the halogen street lamp on his quiet suburban street before I engage the parking brake and do just that.

✪ ✪ ✪

It's Friday night. Coach and I worked out on Wednesday like usual, but I scheduled an extra cram session since tomorrow's a wrestling party night. "Take me through it." I flop on my back and gesture him over.

He straddles me and grabs my arms. "Like this?"

I nod.

"OK. Easiest way; bring your arms together over your head."

It's easier than I expected.

"Grab one of my wrists. Now pull straight up. Not off the mat, straight over your head."

I do, and his body lifts up off of me.

"There. Now keep the momentum going in that direction."

Three more tries and I finally get it more or less right. "You're not helping?" I ask.

He shakes his head. "Simple physics. Once you get the mass moving, it stays in motion. You've just got to direct it. Going for a rematch tomorrow?"

"Ask me again in an hour." I move back in to establish control. Once or twice, I do.

✪ ✪ ✪

WHAT ARE YOU GOING TO DO?

Saturday night and the wrestling group is smaller this time, with some new faces around as well. I turn down a match with a guy who's my size, wanting to stay fresh. Later in the evening, I'm about to see if he's still interested when my pal turns up. I put away his helmet and jacket for him before I go back to the mats.

He's really happy to see a huge, bushy bearded blond guy I haven't noticed around before. I hang back by the sidelines while they chat, then they move out on the mat. This'll be great; I've never gotten to wrestle him after he's had a real workout.

They're shoulder to shoulder, legs spread, arms around the back of their necks, vying for control. I think of Hercules and the Nemean Lion, then Jacob and the angel. Their breathing deepens and little involuntary grunts start springing out from both of them. The dance for dominance continues for what seems like several minutes, then the blond manages to throw his opponent down.

I actually have to stop myself from jumping up and trying to tackle him off. I've never seen anyone take my pal down from a standing start.

Control is fluid between them. There are near pins and reverses for I don't know how long until they finally declare the match a draw. Panting from the exertion, they hug and punch each other's chests. The thudding sound echoes in the small room. They kiss, and the blond heads off somewhere.

My pal's sweating and breathing hard. He sits down by the sideline while the next pair take the mat, and I look up at him from my knees with awe. He scratches my head and then rolls his shoulders with a deep sigh.

I spring up behind him and begin massaging the still-slick skin. He purrs, and I work harder. Eventually, we

FULL BODY CONTACT

move to one of the padded tables in the main room. I don't notice any of the other scenes going on around the space as I work every bit of tension out of him.

I'm practically creaming my jeans when I finally go down on him. The taste and smell turn me into an animal.

He shoots while I'm biting his nipple harder than I could possibly take. He shakes me by the scruff of the neck, says, "That's my good boy," and pulls me on top of him. We drift in the afterglow till the party ends.

I'm home before I realize I haven't come myself.

TO: M4MRASSEL@YIPPIEGROUPS.COM
RE: Decorating question

Has anyone found a decent desk-size copy of the Pankration statue available online (or anywhere else)? I've been looking for a few weeks, and the copies I've found are all either huge, outrageously expensive to ship from Greece, or have fig leaves added. The New Age bookstores have the statue of Hercules holding Antaeus off the ground, but I like the composition of the Pankration combatants better. I guess I sympathize with the guy on his knees in the armlock about to get punched. Thanks.

I wait a week before I call him. "Hello, sir."

"Hey, boy! Good to hear from you. Sorry I was too wiped to wrestle you last time."

"I didn't mind."

"Me either. What's up?"

"Free for a rematch anytime soon?"

✪ ✪ ✪

WHAT ARE YOU GOING TO DO?

Wednesday night; two more days to the rematch. "You're a maniac," Coach kids me.

"I'm tired of getting slammed into the mat." I pull harder.

"Turn your arm more so your bone is digging in on my muscle," he corrects.

I rotate my arm and yank back again. "Like this?" He's still trying to slip free, but I'm not letting him.

"Yeah! That's it." After one more try at breaking my grip, he taps out.

✪ ✪ ✪

Tonight starts off a lot like the last time. He carries me to the mat, and I let him throw me around the garage for a while before I ask, "So what do I have to do to get to fuck you?"

He snorts and says, "I think we've got a while before we have to worry about that."

"True," I reply. Then I reverse him and key-lock his arm. My weight is centered right under his rib cage, pressing his diaphragm, and my legs are scissored around his. He's not going anywhere. He tries, really tries, and I don't budge. It's taking everything I've got to keep him there, but I manage to get out, "What are you going to do?"

He laughs, warm and affectionate. I see stars when he does break free and slams me down, hard. My breath rushes out when I pull him on top of me into a long, deep kiss.

By the time he finally carries me off the mat I actually doubt I could move under my own power. I'm boneless when he pours me off his shoulder into bed and locks on the cuffs.

It's late. I'm blissed-out and drifting. Every touch registers as pleasure. He alternately fucks me and naps, spooned

FULL BODY CONTACT

against and in me the whole night. Eventually, I can't tell where my body ends and his starts. It makes me feel complete. We both climax noisily when the first light breaks through the window.

He strips off the condom, unlocks my wrists, and pulls me over on top of him. He's warm and soft and solid under me. We doze. I'm draped across him like a lion skin, or perhaps a lion cub, riding up and down gently as he breathes.

After we have breakfast and I'm heading home, aching a good ache all over, I realize I don't know if I'm ever going to beat him, but I do know I cannot fucking wait to try again.

WHAT ARE YOU GOING TO DO?

Working It Out
David May

I spend a lot of time at the gym because it turns me on. I like to watch men while they work out, see them flush red with the effort of reaching their peaks, their lips stretched open in a scream. It's like watching them come. But it's not just seeing guys pumping up their bodies and working up a good sweat. I also like the way I feel when I'm pumping iron, the way my body feels afterward. And the smell of the gym, that special combination of good, clean sweat and the plain soap gyms use because it's cheap. I even like the lousy disco they play to keep up the energy level.

Working out makes me two things: hungry and horny, not necessarily in that order. When I leave the gym my stomach's growling, my muscles are aching, and my cock's hard and begging for some attention. Sometimes it's so bad I've got to jerk off in the sauna before I leave, which is usually OK since a lot of guys need to get off after working out.

If it's a nice day, I walk home in my gym clothes. I get off on seeing other guys in their workout clothes, especially if they smell good and funky, so I go out looking for them dressed the same way. Sometimes I'll wear the same sweaty jock for days looking for the right muscled man to chew on it. Guys into jocks are like guys into leather—we dress the same way, get off on the same things, and can always spot each other on the street. The best place to get off with another body builder is the gym, though. It's what we talk about when we get together, and any chance we get to fuck in a gym we grab by the balls and go for. Because it doesn't happen very often, but when it does happen, it's hot.

✪ ✪ ✪

It was in the middle of a heat wave. It had gone on for over a week and most of the guys could hardly move at the end of the day, let alone get to the gym. But I stuck to my schedule because I'm a fanatic about it. I waited until the sun started going down and it had cooled off a little. There were only a couple guys there. I nodded to them and started my workout since I didn't have a lot of time to socialize before the gym closed. I wanted to concentrate on what I was doing. I could gab later.

I was resting on the incline bench between flies when I noticed him. The sweat was pouring down my face. My shirt and shorts were sticking to my skin. I licked the sweat off of my lips and started another set. He stood in front of the bench and watched me. I could hardly take my eyes off of him.

He was a big guy, 6-foot-2 to my 5-foot-10, and made entirely of muscle. His skin was taut and smooth, a deep golden tan and covered with a light blond down. His beard and hair were a sort of ash blond, and his eyes a deep blue. His T-shirt didn't begin to cover his massive chest. It was

WORKING IT OUT

just a rag, really, an old shirt he'd torn the sleeves and neckband off of. His shorts were almost as minimal, hiked up a little over his weight belt and exposing more than they covered. His substantial basket was at my eye level when I sat up on the bench. I saw movement in its damp confines and licked my lips again.

I nodded to him as I finished my set and looked around for my towel to wipe the bench off.

"How you doing?" he asked.

"OK."

I would've stood up but he was standing right in front of the incline bench. I tried to keep my cool.

"Looks like you're getting a good workout," he said.

"Working up a sweat."

"Looks good on you."

"Thanks. You're doing all right too."

I pointed to the patch of damp in his shorts, just above the crotch, where the rivers of perspiration running down his body had met.

"Yeah," he said, rubbing his hand over the beads of moisture glistening on his beautiful golden skin. "Yeah, working up a real sweat." He took a couple steps forward, bringing his crotch right into my face. I stared at the bulge moving under the shorts, and then glanced up at his face. "Maybe you'd like to lick it off for me."

My mouth was dry. I couldn't have said anything if I'd tried. He grabbed my head and rubbed my face into the sweet-salty rivers of his abdomen.

"Come on, baby, lick the sweat off."

I obeyed. There was too much of him to resist, even if I'd wanted to. He was bigger than me, taller by half a head, and unquestionably stronger. I buried my face in his body

FULL BODY CONTACT

and went to work. I took in the scent of his body. His sweat had that nice clean taste that healthy sweat has: no chemicals, tobacco, or booze stinking up his pores—just beautiful muscled meat.

He pulled the rag of a shirt off, and I moved my mouth from his navel to his massive tits. I'm always a sucker for a good set of pecs. I locked my mouth first on one nipple, than the other, alternating for some time. Even as I licked the sweat off, he perspired more in his excitement. His body was a mass of trembling muscles, his legs shaking like a newborn colt's.

Suddenly, as if he couldn't stand it anymore, he lifted me up from the bench and kissed me. Our lips met as we lapped at each other's tongue. Next thing I knew, he was carrying me in his arms—and I'm no lightweight—across the gym to a freestanding bench. He put me down and pulled at my clothes, tearing them off me. When I was down to just a jock and sweat socks, he pushed his face down in my crotch and lapped at the sweat around and under my jock. Then he was chewing on the strap itself. My already hard cock stood at attention. I eased his mouth to my cock and balls. Soon he was licking at them, sucking on my big hairy balls and cock though the jockstrap. I forgot that someone might hear us downstairs at the front desk and let myself groan out loud. It all felt too fucking good to keep to myself.

I grabbed his pecs, hard slabs of muscle covered with that soft gold fur of his, and held onto them as he pulled his body on top of mine. When his crotch was near enough for me to get my hands on it, I pulled at his shorts until they were down around his knees and I could see the monster cock swelling inside the ratty jockstrap he wore, the fat head protruding from over the elastic band. I held onto his

WORKING IT OUT

hips and pulled him toward me until he was almost lying on top of me, rubbing his raunchy jock in my face.

His cock swelled even larger as he was grinding his groin against me. I chewed on the smelly pouch that barely confined his cock and balls. I made love to the jockstrap, licked and chewed on it until it was dripping with my spit. Precome oozed from the dick head and over the waistband like it was drooling. I licked up the sweet ball juice to its source to tongue the head, then the piss slit. His body was thrashing on top of my face as he tried to get more of his thick cock into my mouth. I grabbed the torn pouch with both hands and tore it off of him, freeing his low-hanging balls and allowing me to pull the 10-incher from the waistband that held it close to his body. I opened my mouth and swallowed the whole thing, burying my nose deep into the man smell in the blond bush of pubic hair. I held on to the bench for support and pumped my throat around his meat until I could feel his head expand and start choking me.

He pulled his cock out of my mouth and stepped back. I looked up at him, at his huge cock sticking out into the air and glistening with my spit and phlegm. I could see the head pulsing, ready to explode, as he held it tight at the base to keep him from coming. For a moment we were both speechless. His face was twisted into a knot of pain from the effort of holding back his orgasm. I jumped up and grabbed his dick with both hands, stroking the length of it in my fists. He tried to pull away but I grabbed his balls, which must have been blue with pain, he was so close to coming. I jerked him off and pulled on his balls until he pulled my mouth down to his cock and forced it between my willing lips. It was already pulsating, expanding to what felt like twice its original size. There was a brief pause, a nanosecond that lasted a lifetime, followed by an explosion in my mouth. Cum poured out of him in long hot spurts. I swallowed several times before he finished, then sucked the piss slit dry, savoring the taste of his sweet, creamy come.

He stepped back. This time I let him go and looked up at from where I was kneeling with a satisfied smirk on my face.

"All right, fucker. Now it's your turn."

He kissed me long and hard, but before I was done kissing him he threw me on the floor. He was after my jock again, chewing on it, tearing it off of me with his teeth. His sweat ran onto my body, mingling with mine. He licked it all up, running his tongue across my hairy chest and abdomen, following the trail of fuzz to my crotch. He sucked on my nuts one at a time for while as he tugged on my hard nipples with his hands. Then he opened his mouth wide and sucked in both my balls. It felt so good I screamed. My body writhed out of control. Whenever he felt me slipping from his hold on my nipples, he gave a gentle pull with his teeth on my balls.

Finally I succumbed and my body stopped moving. It was like I'd come, but I hadn't yet. This was how he wanted me, exhausted from the workout he was giving me. He gently let go of my nuts and swallowed my fat dick in their place. He sucked it all the way down as one finger entered my sweaty, funky butt hole and gently caressed my prostate, keeping the head of my dick buried deep in his throat. I felt him use his throat on my meat the way I used my hand, squeezing and caressing it until I couldn't stand it. I pulled his face down into my crotch, pushing his nose into the dampness of my pubic hair, and let out a yell that filled the whole gym. I pumped what felt like a gallon of come down

WORKING IT OUT

his throat. He sucked me dry, all the while playing with my asshole. First one finger, then two. By the time I'd shot my load he'd managed to slip three fingers inside of me. Very slowly, he pulled out his fingers and rolled me over onto my stomach.

Next he was licking the sweat off my furry butt, following it to where it had formed a tiny stream down the crack between my cheeks. Before I knew it, his tongue was in my hole, lubricating it with his spit.

I felt as if all my juices had been sucked out of me with my come. There was no strength left in me to do anything but relax and breathe in deep as his tongue left my fuck hole and the battering ram he called his dick was put in its place.

I felt it push into my hole, stretching me open as he slowly shifted his weight on top of me. Getting fucked by a really big dick is like working out: It hurts so good. Then he was in me, all 10 motherfucking inches of him, pumping real slow and easy, letting me get used to the mass and girth of the monster rearranging my insides. He breathed heavily on top of me, the sweat rolling off of him and onto me. Our bodies stuck together with sweat whenever his pelvis ground into my buns, making sucking sounds when our flesh parted.

I took it all in, the sound of our fucking, the heady smell of man sex, the deep, urgent sensation of his fat 10 inches expanding inside of me. I was euphoric as it all ran over and through me. My cock was hard, squashed beneath me; the pounding of our bodies increased in tempo and fury. I was surprised again, this time at my own hard prick, and even more surprised when I felt myself on the verge of coming. He was pumping harder now, pushing his man meat into my hole with stronger, more determined thrusts.

"Hey, man. Don't come yet! I'm getting close again!"

If he slowed down or even heard me, I don't know. The pace of his fucking increased steadily.

Suddenly, he pulled me onto all fours, his dick still in me, and fucked me by moving my ass up and down his shaft. It felt too good in that position. The angle of his cock was just right as the huge head stroked my prostate again and again. I grabbed my own cock and pulled on it as the pounding reached its climax.

Then I came, shooting my load several feet in front of me. At the same instant, he pushed me back onto my stomach and with an animal yell, exploded inside of me. I felt his dick head swell as it exploded, felt the sperm splatter against the walls of my guts, forming a puddle on the gym floor as it leaked out of me.

We lay there for a while, our bodies locked together, until we heard someone cough. I lifted my head. I'd forgotten where I was, but now I remembered and was sure my gym membership was about to be canceled.

"Uh, excuse me, boss," said the trainer I'd seen earlier at the front desk. "Should I just close up like usual?"

"Yeah, I think so," said the man who'd just given me two outrageous loads of his come. "Just give us time to shower, OK?"

We pulled our bodies apart. I began looking around for the rags that had been my gym clothes an hour or so before and asked if he worked there.

"No. I just own the damn place. Like it?"

"Oh, yeah. I like it fine."

He grabbed me and pulled me closer and kissed me.

"Yeah? Well, you do one fucking fine workout."

WORKING IT OUT

Pinned
Hank Edwards

The mat was slick with sweat, and Paul's hand slid out from beneath him. Damn it! He felt his left shoulder hit the mat and then the crushing weight of his opponent as Jason Markham, an older, more powerful wrestler, maneuvered him into a pin. Jason's muscular arm wrapped around Paul's thigh and hauled his leg up into the air as his elbow rested directly on top of Paul's crotch. With his thick, broad chest, Jason easily pressed both of Paul's shoulders to the mat and held him there to the count of three.

"OK!" the coach called out. "Nice move, Markham. Good way to take advantage of his fall." The coach looked at Paul. "Tough break on the slip, Reed. But you're showing some good defensive moves. Keep it up. OK, next two!"

Paul removed his helmet and walked off the mat. Good defensive moves. Shit. That seemed to be all he could manage every time he took his position on the mat. He was smaller than the other members of the team, slimmer, not as thick in the shoulders and legs, but he was quick. He could wriggle out of almost any hold, given enough time and a dry mat. He just wasn't an offensive wrestler. His friends jokingly said he wore down his opponents because they had to chase him around the mat.

Sitting on the bench, Paul shook his head and grabbed a water bottle. Probably hadn't even been his sweat, either. Jason Markham was a sweaty beast of a wrestler with a tuft of dark hair between his hard, square pecs and big, broad shoulders. The guy more than likely broke a sweat just thinking about a wrestling move. He was also one of the most attractive members of the team. Paul had been resisting a growing infatuation for Jason for almost three months now, ever since the beginning of the semester. Raising the water bottle to his lips once more, Paul took a sloppy drink and raised his left hand to wipe his mouth. The palm of his hand was still wet from landing in the puddle of sweat during his match and he ran his tongue through the salty dampness. He closed his eyes and thought of how good it would taste to run his tongue through the dank, dark hair of Jason Markham's armpit. The image of his teammate lying sprawled out with his arms over his head and sweat beading up along his brow caused blood to rush into Paul's cock with surprising speed.

"Hey, Paulie," Jason Markham called from the other end of the bench. Paul turned his head and dropped his hands to dangle between his knees and disguise the rising lump of his erection. "You did a good job out there today." Jason wiped sweat from his forehead and mopped up his armpits with a white towel that he dropped on the bench beside him. "Good moves."

Paul nodded and raised his water bottle in salute. "Thanks." He turned to watch the match going on before him and tried not to think too much about Jason Markham.

Later that afternoon, Paul left the sports arena and

headed across campus, his hair still damp from the shower. He had almost bolted out of the locker room, trying to get away from the intoxicating smell of male sweat and the sight of all those glistening nude bodies standing beneath the showers. As he shouldered his way through the crowd of students between classes, Paul let his mind wander and soon found himself focusing on Jason Markham's thick, muscular body. The smell of Jason's sweat during their match was still fresh in his nostrils, and the feel of the man's strong, confident grip on Paul's limbs thrummed through his skin. Every touch Paul received from Jason jolted like a live wire fused straight into his groin.

During a break between his classes, Paul headed back to his room for some well-deserved time alone. His roommate, Russ, had classes all afternoon on Fridays. Paul locked the door behind him and fell heavily onto his bed. After staring up at the ceiling for a while, he reached down, unzipped his workout bag, and pulled out a small white towel. It was still damp, and he grinned as he held it up in his hands. He had left practice through the workout room and grabbed the towel Jason had been using to wipe himself down before the maintenance crew could come through and pick it up. And now he held it over his head.

Lowering the towel to his face, Paul took a deep breath and pulled the strong, musty scent of Jason's sweat into his body. His cock roared to life and rose up against the confines of his underwear. Paul closed his eyes and took another breath as he pressed the towel against his nose and mouth. He stretched his tongue out and ran the tip along the damp cotton, imagining it was the man himself he was tonguing.

With a trembling hand, Paul reached down and unbuttoned his jeans. He eased them down his legs and then hooked his fingers beneath the waistband of his severely bulging underwear and slid them off as well. His cock lay along the length of his belly, the cut and oozing head resting just below his navel. As he often did when he was alone and could revel in the sensation of masturbation, Paul assessed his cock. He lifted it from the small puddle of precome and turned it this way and that. Veins ran along the thick, pink shaft and up to the ridge of the wide, heart shaped head. The afternoon light coming in the window behind him caused the thick drop of viscous precome to glisten. Paul smeared the slick substance around the head with his thumb and sighed at the tingling sensation he felt spring up his nerve endings.

Another deep whiff of Jason's sweaty towel and the memory of watching the man mop his hairy, dripping armpits flashed into Paul's mind. His cock twitched in his hand and he groaned quietly. He remembered letting his eyes drop along the side of Jason's wrestling tunic, where it was darkened with sweat and plastered to his muscles. When they had left the workout room and headed for the showers, Paul had timed himself to fall in line behind Jason and let his eyes drop to the firm curves of his teammate's ass. Jason Markham had a firm bubble butt that begged to be eaten slow and deep.

Paul stroked himself and inhaled the stale musk of Jason's sweat. Releasing his grip on the towel, he let it rest over his nose and mouth so he could reach down and grab his big, softly furred balls with his left hand. His right hand was a blur of motion as he brought himself close to climax. His fingers squeezed tighter around the length of his 7-inch cock and brushed the ridge of skin where the shaft met the head as he closed his eyes and grabbed the towel with his teeth.

PINNED

A key in the lock brought him up into a sitting position and he hurriedly slipped beneath the sheets of his bed, stuffing the towel beneath his pillow and feigning sleep. His roommate, Russ, stomped into the room and tossed his backpack into a corner. Russ slammed drawers and tossed books around for several minutes, oblivious to his room-mate's presence as Paul felt his hard-on slowly subside. When he felt more in control, he sat up and glared at Russ's back.

"Marching band practice over yet?" Paul snapped and Russ jumped.

"Whoa," Russ said as he turned and blinked at him. "Sorry, Paul. I didn't see you lying there. Was I being kind of loud?"

"Nothing a shuttle launch wouldn't have been able to drown out." Paul lay back down. "Why are you here? I thought you had a class?"

"Canceled. Prof is sick." Russ sat on the edge of Paul's bed. "Let's go to that frat party tonight, what do you say?"

Paul rolled his eyes. "Frat party?"

"Come on," Russ said. "It'll be a blast. There'll be chicks drinking lots of beer."

Paul shook his head. "No, thanks. I've got a killer exam coming up on Monday and I really need to hit the books this weekend. Plus we have a tough match next week and I want to work out every night until then."

Russ shook his head and stood up. "All work and no play, Paulie."

"Yeah, yeah," Paul said and rolled over. He sighed as he thought about Jason Markham standing in the shower. The hot spray had reddened his shoulders and the back of his neck as the water sluiced down over his body and ran off the tip of his prick in a stream. Jason had a long, thick cock that looked half-erect each time Paul had glimpsed it in the locker room. Since the beginning of the semester he had been careful not to stare too long at the men around him. He did not want to be outed in the showers. He sighed and prayed for Russ to leave.

Evening came, and Paul still hadn't had a chance to finish getting himself off. Instead, he pulled on a sleeveless T-shirt, his jock, and a pair of baggy shorts, jogged around campus, and stopped in at the weight room designated specifically for the university's athletes. He worked his upper body for over an hour, sweat running along his torso in rivulets, and then entered the men's room to splash water on his face. Leaving the bathroom, Paul headed slowly down the hall to the exit. As he passed the wrestling workout room, Paul heard the squeak and scuff of someone practicing moves. He eased the door open and stepped inside.

Only two lights hanging over the main mat lit the room. A lone figure moved in the center of the circle drawn out on the mat. The muscles beneath the sweaty skin of his bare back bunched and released with each shift of his hips and arms. His hair was damp with sweat from his practice. It was, of course, Jason Markham.

Paul sucked in his breath at the sight of the man and released the door. It clicked shut and he felt himself blush when Jason stopped and turned around. The man had an irritated expression on his face until he saw who was standing in the shadows, then he smiled.

"Reed! Come on in." Jason waved him closer. "What are you doing here on a Friday night?"

Paul stepped onto the mats and shrugged. "Working out."

"Yeah? Let's see." Jason stepped up to him, the smell of his sweat enveloping Paul and making his head spin. With a strong grip, Jason felt the muscles in Paul's arms and then reached up beneath his shirt to feel his chest. All the while Jason kept his eyes locked on Paul's face.

"Are you a doctor now or something?" Paul asked nervously, but made no effort to move away from the suddenly intimate invasion of his personal space. His cock was fully erect and straining against the pocket of his jock.

"No," Jason said with a smirk. "Just wanted to see how far you'd let me go." He took a small step back and folded his arms over his glistening chest. "Care to practice some moves?"

Paul nodded. "OK. I could use the work."

"I'll say." Jason turned and walked back into the center of the mats. "Take off your shirt."

Paul stripped the T-shirt over his head, exposing his hairy chest and belly, then followed after Jason. They stood in the circle on the mats and crouched low, both ready and waiting. Paul nervously watched Jason's shoulders and hips for a sign of when he was going to attack. His dick was rock-hard and had begun to leak precome into the fabric of his jock. Paul worked to keep his eyes averted from the bulge in Jason's shorts and the patch of sweaty hair on his chest, focusing instead on the man's eyes.

Jason ducked low and lunged at him, wrapping his arms around Paul's thighs. The side of Jason's head pressed against the firm outline of his dick and Paul felt his feet lifted off the mat as he was pulled down onto his back. He landed with a deep exhalation and then Jason was climbing up along his body.

With a buck of his hips, Paul squirmed out from beneath

Jason's clutching hands and felt the waistband of his shorts grabbed as he darted away. His loose-fitting shorts peeled down his legs, leaving him lying across the mats in just his jock and shoes. His dick throbbed at the sensation of air on his bare ass and more precome drooled out of the slit. Paul crab-walked away from Jason and spun up to his feet, turning to find the man already up and heading for him.

"Wait! Let me get my shorts!" Paul cried.

"No stopping, Reed," Jason said. His eyes held a strange light as he feinted left and right. "We wrestle until one of us is pinned."

"This is stupid, Jason," Paul said nervously, trying desperately to hide his condition. "I'm not wrestling you in my jockstrap. What if someone comes in?"

Jason smiled. "I heard the door click shut behind you. It locks automatically. We can get out but no one without a key can get in."

"What about the janitor?" Paul dodged away from Jason's hands.

"He's already left for the night. I said goodbye to him myself." Jason lunged forward and tackled Paul with little effort, rolling him over onto his back and falling across him. Their bare, sweaty chests pressed together and Paul struggled to keep his erection from being discovered.

And then he felt the rigid outline of Jason's dick pressing up against the outside of his thigh. He turned a startled glance up at the man's face and found Jason staring down at him with lustful intensity.

"All right," Jason said as Paul stopped struggling. "How about this? I'll strip down to just my jockstrap so we're even. How's that?"

Jason got up and stood facing Paul as he let his shorts

drop to the mat. He stepped out of them and kicked them aside. A glance down at the pouch of Jason's jock revealed his long, thick boner outlined perfectly beneath the material.

"Ready?" Jason said. His voice was deep and throaty, tinged with lust.

"OK," Paul said and stood up. "You're pretty intense right now, you know? A lot more than at practice."

"This isn't practice," Jason replied. He jumped forward and locked his arms around Paul's neck.

Paul reached out and grabbed Jason by the neck and shoulders as well, each straining against the other. Paul could feel the damp sweat of Jason's palms where the man's hands gripped his shoulders. The sharp, fresh smell of Jason's sweat flooded over him and made him even more unsteady. His head was lowered and his left cheek pressed hard against Jason's, both of them grunting and huffing as they worked to offset the other.

As Paul's eyes skimmed down along the hair on Jason's chest and finally locked on Jason's wide, solid pole barely contained by the thin material of his jock, Paul felt a rush of confidence that took control of his body. His arms twisted like he had never been able to twist them before and his left leg pivoted beneath him with a fluidity he had never experienced. He pulled Jason's legs out from under him and pushed him down to the mat.

"What the—?" Jason said. He landed flat on his back and Paul turned his body to fall across him. Using his own shoulder, Paul held Jason's left shoulder down to the mat and then lifted the man's right arm up over his head and pinned it to the mat. Reaching down, Paul slid his right arm beneath Jason's thighs and pressed his forearm against the damp, firm outline of the man's dick.

FULL BODY CONTACT

Turning his head, Paul found himself looking straight down into Jason's sweat-drenched armpit. Beads of sweat had collected on the dark, tangled hair and the smell of him was thick. Paul took a deep, intoxicating breath and closed his eyes, relishing the feel of Jason's body beneath him and the essence of him in his nostrils.

Then Jason bucked his hips and tossed Paul off with startling ease. Before he could get to his feet, Paul felt the man's large, damp hands grab his hips and haul him closer across the sweat-smeared mat. Jason walked on his knees up along Paul's body and planted himself directly on top of Paul's painfully hard cock. Leaning forward, Jason pinned Paul's hands up over his head with one hand and reached down to playfully tweak Paul's nipple with the other.

"Hey!" Paul said.

"Good move there, Paulie," Jason said. "You got me down and almost pinned. Not bad...for you." He grinned at the irritation on Paul's face. "I think I know what could have caused that small break in your concentration."

Paul narrowed his eyes. "Oh, really? And what might that be?"

"This." Jason leaned forward and pressed his moist, ripe armpit over Paul's nose and mouth. "It was this, wasn't it? You get off on my sweat. I've known it since day one of practice." He ground his armpit against Paul's face. "Come on, Paulie. Open up and lick it clean. You know you're dying to."

Paul inhaled the sweet smell of Jason's pit and then opened his mouth wide and let his tongue hang out. He pressed his mouth against the wet, furry skin above him and began to suck the sweat into his throat.

"Oh, yeah," Jason moaned and pressed his hips down

over Paul's cock. Only a thin layer of cotton separated Paul's dick from the sweaty crack of Jason's ass. "Eat that pit out. Suck up all that sweat. Get it down your fuckin' throat. Yeah, lick it up."

Paul sucked and licked all along Jason's armpit and nearly cried out when the man lifted it away from his face. But a moment later the opposite pit replaced it and Paul began to slobber and suckle greedily once again.

When Paul had finished licking Jason's armpits, the man raised up and rode the hard bulge of Paul's cock as he twisted Paul's nipples. Paul groaned and pressed his dick up against Jason's sweaty perineum. His balls were practically exploding after his interrupted jerk-off session that afternoon, and his fantasy man bumping and grinding above him was getting him dangerously close to climax.

Jason leaned down and kissed Paul deeply. His tongue swept through Paul's mouth and battled with his tongue as his hands ran all over Paul's torso. Groaning up into Jason's mouth, Paul reached up and put a hand behind his head to pull him closer. He wanted to fill himself up with every inch of this man.

With a gasp, Jason pulled back and stared hungrily down at the man beneath him. He stood up and slid the wet and stained jockstrap off, tossing it in the direction of his jeans. Jason then reached down and ripped the jockstrap from Paul's body. He raised the wet pouch to his mouth and sucked precome from the material as he stared down into Paul's eyes.

Paul lay on his back and gazed with mute fascination at the man standing over him. Was this really happening? He reached out and massaged Jason's hard, hairy calves, then let his hands move down over the man's sweaty, hair-flecked feet.

FULL BODY CONTACT

Jason reached down and took hold of Paul's inflamed dick, looking it over as he slid his sweaty hand along its length. Paul moaned and closed his eyes, his hips automatically beginning to pump. With a few steps, Jason turned his back to Paul and then sat on his face. His damp and fragrant asshole planted itself directly over Paul's mouth, and Paul greedily set to work on it. The hot, wet pucker of Jason's sphincter gasped open at the touch of Paul's tongue and he drove it as deep into the man as he could.

"Oh, fuck!" Jason gasped. He held Paul's cock in a tight fist and stroked it roughly as he began to pump his hips over the man's face. "Yeah, get that fuckin' tongue up in me. Eat that asshole. Lick it clean." He rode Paul's mouth and tongue for a moment longer, then leaned forward and parted his lips to take Paul's throbbing cock down his throat. He swallowed the entire length of the dick in one gulp and Paul moaned up into the damp hollow of Jason's asshole. Jason held the rod in his mouth for a moment and increased his suction. Keeping his lips pressed firmly into the solid flesh of the shaft, he slowly dragged his mouth up along its length. At the ridge where the shaft met the head, Jason flicked his tongue through the slick of precome that had bubbled up from the slit and set to work sucking Paul with abandon.

Paul gasped at the ferocity of Jason's sucking, then urged the man's hips back and opened his mouth to swallow the thick, oozing cock jutting above him. Jason was bigger than Paul by about an inch, eight inches long and slightly thicker. The cut head of his cock was wide and blunt, and Paul wondered how it would feel forcing its way into the depths of his trembling hole.

They sucked each other for several minutes, both men

PINNED

leaving wet, glistening streaks of saliva along the lengths of the cock in his mouth. Jason worked his tongue over Paul's hairy balls and moved his hips to drop his own clean-shaven sack into Paul's mouth. Paul pulled and twisted the big, soft balls, sucking them deep into his mouth and then releasing them one by one.

With a quick move, Jason twisted around and knelt between Paul's legs. He smiled up at Paul, then raised the man's legs and pushed them higher until his hips were off the mat. Jason balanced Paul's lower back on the tops of his thighs and leaned down to begin rimming Paul's soft, puckered hole. He licked the length of the crack of Paul's ass, then popped the wrinkle of muscle open with his thumbs and drove his tongue deep inside. Paul groaned and gasped on the mat beneath him, his eyes closed and his mouth hanging open.

"Ready for a small visitor?" Jason asked. Paul nodded up at him and closed his eyes as the man slipped his thick index finger up inside the twitching hole. Jason finger-fucked Paul with one, two, and finally three fingers. He stopped every few strokes and let a thick glob of spit drop into Paul's open and inviting hole then used his fingers to work it deep inside him.

"Oh, goddamn it, Jason," Paul said. "I want your dick in me."

"Yeah?" Jason asked with a grin. "You think you can handle this big cock up that tight ass?"

"Oh, yeah," Paul said. "Get it in me. Fuck me."

Jason eased his fingers out of Paul's hole and repositioned himself. He spit into his palm and spread it along the pulsating length of his dick, then moved up and pressed the wide, glistening head against Paul's eagerly twitching sphincter.

With slow, steady pressure, Jason parted the lips of Paul's asshole with the head of his cock and drilled into him.

"Oh, fuck!" Paul cried out. His hands slapped the mats beneath him as Jason's cock kept pushing deeper and deeper into him. He didn't think it was ever going to stop!

Jason felt the hot, slippery muscle part before the battering ram of his thick-headed cock and closed his eyes. The rectal canal opened up before him and then closed back over the shaft of his cock with a velvet grip. He pressed further into Paul's widening hole and groaned low in his throat. The man's ass was like a long, hot fist. The muscles in his anal canal squeezed the entire range of Jason's dick as it tunneled further into him. He buried the full length of his cock up Paul's asshole and paused. Opening his eyes, Jason looked down along his own torso to the wiry hair of his bush where it was pressed up against Paul's perineum. Just a flash of the root of his cock was visible before it disappeared inside Paul's stretched sphincter.

"Oh, God," Paul said. "I can't believe you're inside of me."

"Completely," Jason said. He leaned down to kiss Paul, their tongues twisting together.

Paul felt the scratch of Jason's day-old beard along his chin and groaned. He pulled as much of Jason's tongue as he could get into his mouth and sucked on it as he had previously sucked the man's cock. Jason grunted at the sensation of having his tongue sucked, then pulled his hips back and rammed his cock home, driving completely into Paul with one thrust.

"Uh!" Paul moaned.

Jason pulled back and dove deep again, piercing Paul to the hilt. He raised up, his tongue pulling slowly from between Paul's lips, and took hold of the man's ankles.

Lifting Paul's legs a bit higher, Jason began to hammer at Paul's hole, fucking him with abandon.

"Oh, shit! Yeah, get that ass. Fuck me." Paul rode Jason's driving dick with his eyes closed and his fist wrapped around his own hard-on. Precome leaked from the slit and slicked the head and shaft with each pass of his hand. The angle and girth of Jason's prick was unlike anything he had ever taken up his ass and he was feeling sensations completely different from his previous anal experiences. Jason's cock was pressing firmly against his prostate with each thrust and shooting a blast of white-hot bliss straight to his brain. His balls pulled up and he felt the head of his cock begin to swell as he approached climax.

"Fuck me! Faster! Oh, God, get it in me. I'm coming!" Paul said and grunted as he shot a massive load of come up onto his throat and chest.

"Oh, yeah," Jason growled. Paul's asshole clenched down around his cock as the man blew his load, and Jason felt his own orgasm surging up from his balls. He pressed deep into Paul's willing hole, deeper than before, and closed his eyes as the come fired out of his cock and coated the inside of Paul's rectal tunnel.

"Oh, fuck," Jason hissed. "I'm shooting my fuckin' load. Shootin' it right up inside your tight ass."

"Yeah," Paul said as his orgasm faded and he squeezed the last drops of semen from his cock. "Fill me up with it."

Jason emptied his balls inside Paul and then fell in a sweaty, exhausted heap on top of him. They kissed for several minutes as Jason's dick slowly wilted in the confines of Paul's ass. Paul ran his tongue over the sweaty surfaces of Jason's face and then hissed as the man pulled carefully out of him. They kissed again before Jason helped him to stand up and handed Paul a jockstrap to wipe the come from his chest.

After cleaning himself up, Paul noticed that the jock he held belonged to Jason. He hesitated just a moment, then stuffed it into a pocket of his shorts before picking up his own torn jock.

"My jockstrap is missing," Jason said. He stood in the middle of the sweat-stained mat wearing just his socks as he looked all around. Paul smiled at the sight. Jason's dick was half-erect and hung down along his thigh. A drop of clear seminal fluid clung to the head of his cock. Paul walked over and stooped to run his tongue along the head and shaft. He swallowed the sweet semen and stood up to smile at the happily surprised look on Jason's face.

"That was really hot," Jason said. His voice was a dry croak and his cock twitched with interest. "My, uh, room-mate is gone for the weekend. Do you want to come over?"

Paul nodded. "Would we work on more wrestling moves?"

Jason grinned. "Oh, yeah. A lot more."

"Sounds good." Paul turned to walk off the mats.

"I just can't find my jockstrap," Jason said, still looking around.

Paul shrugged. "Forget it. Just pull on your shorts and shirt and let's get out of here. That's what I have to do since you tore off my jock."

Jason shrugged back. "I guess you're right. It's not like my name is in it or anything."

After Jason had pulled on his clothes, both men exited the building and crossed the well-lit campus in the direction of Jason's dorm. Every now and again one of them would lean over and bump into the other. As he walked beside Jason, Paul thought of the thick slab of meat hanging loose

PINNED

in the man's shorts and felt his dick begin to harden. If he was able to have as much private practice with Jason as he wanted, he was going to get damn good at wrestling.

Roughing the Redhead
Troy Storm

Usually, linemen murderously glare at one another, snarling behind our facemasks across a few feet of cleated turf at the opposing phalanx of human Mack trucks. Our massive bodies tensed, impatiently shifting our huge bulk like high-tuned muscle cars, we rev our engines while waiting for the snap of the ball to shift us into blitz gear. Then with howls to terrify the dead we gun forward to crash our bulky NCAA piles of hard plastic and foam rubber pads and straps and guards and girdle-protected frames headlong into one another.

But in today's game the hulk facing me was different. He was a big, bulky, overeager jock like the rest of us, but something in his excited green eyes communicated a thrill of the game, a sense of trying to do his job right, of making the play work, that indicated—I hesitate to use the word...I mean, I love my fellow tanks, but swift most of them are not—*intelligence.*

And therefore, he struck me as being sexy as hell.

All I had to do was peer deep into those green orbs

flashing over the high cheekbones and full lips—as much as I could see through his damn birdcage—and I wanted to know more: what kind of haircut Madsen, number 28, sported under his shiny helmet, what his real shoulders looked like stripped of their outsize pads, and what treasures lay snuggled and well-protected between his foam and nylon-secured slim swively hips.

His butt was to die for, that much I had been able to catch an eyeful of, but then most guys who play football have butts to die for—one of the reasons I got into the game. I've got a pretty nice ass myself.

And his thighs and calves were in fine shape too. With solid biceps and forearms and great six-pack abs. Down here in Florida we play in cropped outfits that give you a better shot at figuring out what the real man is like underneath the plastic and foam.

By the time the game was over, I had a pretty good idea what Madsen was like as a guy, and I knew he was a damn fine opposition player. He did his job—we slugged into each other, we took each other down—and his grins, nods, and slaps on the butt, even for the guys he was trying to smash, were friendly and encouraging. It's guys like Madsen who bring out the best in the rest of us. Both teams played a good hard game.

And I was good and hard, and more than encouraged to try and make a more intimate connection with Mr. Goody Two Shoes.

Both the home and visitor teams always showed up at the Rathskeller tavern right off campus. The furniture was basic and solid, in preparation for when, after a few beers, the teams invariably got into a hot furniture-throwing discussion of how their game had gone. Truth to tell, some of the players went to Raths hoping to tangle with some-body—anybody...even furniture—just to let off steam.

Me, I was always bushed. And at the same time jazzed by the amount of naked meat that had flashed before my eyes in the showers. And depressed by the knowledge that I was not going to get even the tiniest taste.

So I usually sat on the sidelines, nursing a brew, just looking.

I looked pretty hard when the other team came swag-gering into the place. They had won; they wanted to rub our noses—and whatever other parts of our sorry asses they could get a good grip on—into the sawdust-covered floor.

But not Madsen. I had to forcibly tell myself to close my sagging jaw. He was a front-page-of-the-sports-section win-ner. A damn fine-looking coppery redhead, square, ruddy-jawed hunk, with shoulders that looked like he might still be wearing pads and a set of pecs that not only stretched his oversize T-shirt to the limit but sprouted little peaks in the soft cotton to make my dry mouth flood with saliva.

Trim chinos encased his hips and showed his ass to per-fection. And the front of them looked like he might have neglected to remove his hard cup. My palms instantly started to sweat.

Pitchers of beer were guzzled, and within a few minutes the arguments began. Friendly and joshing at first, but you could tell the blood lust was rising. Madsen waded right into the middle and fought to keep the peace. I waded right after him and yanked him out of the path of a wild uppercut.

"Thanks, I appreciated that," he yelled as we stood on the sidelines watching the guys pound one another. He looked excited but discouraged, contemplating the making-war-not-love fighters. "I don't know why we can't funnel

ROUGHING THE REDHEAD

that energy into building a better team," he bellowed over the mayhem.

I shrugged. "You guys won. I guess some of your team-mates feel *funneled* enough. Now they just want to break heads." He looked even more conflicted. "You wanna go outside and discuss the deviant ways of the athletic college male ego?" I suggested.

He squinted at me in the dim tavern light.

"I know you. I remember you from the game. You were one of the good ones." He shook my hand heartily and flashed a grin that made my loose-fits suddenly seem constricted. "You fought honorably."

OK. So I figured I had hitched up with a raving philosophy major who was determined to change the world and who was trying to compute the fact that his very male muscles loved bashing into other very male muscles. Either that, or a religion major who just happened to be built like a Greek god and was determined to bring the message of peace and love to the lower orders despite his physical handicap.

Or. Perhaps there was part of him that he hadn't yet discovered, a part that might revel in the concept of making *warring love*—with me.

In the parking lot, halfway through yet another watered-down pitcher of brew, he contemplated my tentative suggestion. "You mean, since I obviously like being physical, but choose by playing football to protect myself *from* the physicality with all the padding and gear, *and* at the same time I also believe it's possible for all of us physical guys to get on like good buddies while doing our jobs of beating each other's heads in, there might be a connection somewhere?"

I couldn't have put it more obtusely myself, that was for

FULL BODY CONTACT

sure. Somehow I thought I had mentioned sex.

"I wonder if there's a way to find out?" He furrowed his broad, ruddy brow and scratched his scalp under the slightly long shaggy hair that reflected back copper-tinted highlights from the neon announcing the tacky Rathskeller establishment.

"Behind the gym, there's a little patch of grass that's pretty sheltered from prying eyes—unless, of course, it's being occupied by couples fucking their brains out. You and I could strip to our skivvies and try out some of our better moves from the game. And then you could see if that turns you on."

He blinked. He wasn't sure how our physical/philosophical discussion had ended up being about being turned on, but once his sloshed brain had gotten around the concept of our scuffling bare-assed in the grass, he thought it a brilliant plan and well put.

And off we staggered.

There was indeed a couple going at it in the surrounding shrubbery—the guy's pale buns glowing from the depths of the shadows as he pounded industriously up and down into his girlfriend underneath. We cheerily waved them on to go for the goal and to pay us no mind as we stripped for action: Madsen to his patterned Jockey skants and me to my FTL low-cuts.

At the sight of Madsen's trim, bared hips, side-lit by a lone and faraway campus light that brought out the impressive size and poundage of what my worthy opponent was packing in his straining bikinis, I dropped to my knees and slammed my face into his delectable basket of manly attributes.

Laughing at my drunken horseplay, he pulled me to my feet, and we crouched in the classic come-kill-me opposing

ROUGHING THE REDHEAD

stances of a football line and went at each other. We were both too soused to draw much blood. But not too numbed to thoroughly enjoy the physical contact of driving our near-naked powerful bodies into each other.

We started off very seriously, methodically blocking and tackling with Madsen grunting a running commentary about how a good player could knock the hell out of his opponent without resorting to the baser instincts of dirty cheap shots or roughing.

All I cared about was being able to get my hands on his powerful, muscular, sweaty flesh and hang on for all I was worth. Which, of course, soon degenerated into dirty cheap shots and we ended up rolling around on the ground grappling and groping and howling with laughter.

I managed to cram my hand into his sweat-soaked shorts and clutch his big semihard...and nearly pass out from the power that rushed up through my arm to bolt around in my chest and then shoot straight for my balls.

I licked his smooth bulging pecs and settled in to suck on a fat, juicy tit for the rest of eternity. Madsen threaded his fingers through my hair and stroked the side of my face. His other hand slipped down my backside and under the elastic of my shorts. When his fingers stroked my butt cheek and snaked into my crack, I almost came.

But Madsen's deep, soft, blurry voice shoved a whole fucking fist right up that possibility. "We can't do this, man. We're drunk as skunks. We probably wouldn't even remember it in the morning. That wouldn't be fair to...to what we think we want to do."

No problem, I mumbled. I'd just stay gripped to his dick and sucking on his tit until we both sobered up and then carry on from there. Made perfect sense to me.

He got glum. "We need some place to go and sleep it off,

but you've got roommates and my team's bus is taking off around midnight. I could miss the bus, but..."

The pair of rabbits in the bushes came over—the guy zipping up, the girl pulling down her sweater and straightening her skirt, two eager, wide-eyed freshmen obviously in the full flush of newly acquired freedom to act as their burgeoning hormones decreed. Madsen's lament had carried to them on the cool night air.

The young guy said, "There's a cheap motel not too far from here. No questions asked. Even for two guys. Hey, aren't you two...?"

The more discreet young lady he had been so vigorously boffing put a shushing finger to his lips. "Shhh, sweetie, it's the light. We all look like somebody else in this light. Right?"

A different light dawned in his dim recesses. "Oh, yeah. Right, babe. Cool."

Madsen modestly pried my mouth off his tit and rolled his hips over so that my hand in his shorts was crushed under his huge dick and balls. I lay on the ground, happy to be so agonizingly pinned.

"Then why aren't you two enjoying the comforts?" he asked. "Unless you have a particular fondness for being permanently grass-stained."

The guy shrugged and hugged his girlfriend close. "No bread. Blew it all on rubbers." She giggled modestly.

"What say we offer these nice young folk a freebie on us and get our boozy senior asses to some clean sheets?" he said to me, teasingly pinching my butt.

The kid gushed, "Ah, dudes, that would be awesome. We hadn't quite, uh, finished, had we, babe?" She grinned happily. "Awesome."

ROUGHING THE REDHEAD

Somehow I had expected the night air to clear our heads. But settled in our thin-walled cheap motel room, even with the sounds of our young companions already energetically going at it next door exhorting us to lay down and do likewise, Madsen was determined. We would sleep and then see how we felt.

We showered, and I pawed and clawed and grabbed and sucked as best I could, but he held me off from getting to the really good stuff. In bed, exhausted from the struggle and snuggled comfily into his muscular embrace, our hands possessively and protectively clutched around each other's rock-solid bones, I slept like a fucking log, my fucking log engaged in many blissful wet dreams.

And woke the next morning, realizing we were still pretty much in the same position, comfortably feeling each other up. The two humpers next door were already—or still—at it. *Jeez*.

"That guy must have a dick of iron," I muttered, realizing Madsen was awake. But the cold light of day and the clear head of reason made me wonder what new plan he would come up with to keep my hot bod from unleashing itself on him.

Oh, well, I thought, working my tongue over his pecs to the nearest tit, just being able to rub crotches would give me enough jack-off memories to get me through the rest of the semester.

"*You* seem to have a dick of solid steel," he noted pleasantly, his deep voice rumbling up through his nipple to tingle my suckling lips. "I'm fucking impressed."

"You wanna be impressed by what I can do with it?"

"I've been checking it out while you snored," he continued. "I think I could take it down. You ready to let me give it a try?"

FULL BODY CONTACT

I do not snore, I thought grumpily.

Suddenly, I was hovering over him, checking his face. I had heard right. He was grinning sexily. In an instant I was off the bed and tearing at my crumpled pants, digging for the Trojans. He snickered and waved an unwrapped one at me. I tried to grab it from him. "I want to do you first," I pleaded.

"No. I owe you," he stated definitively as he pushed me down on my back and worked the plastic down my throbbing meat. His touch almost set me off. His mouth certainly did.

His observation was correct. He swilled me down in one gulp. And the moment I felt his full lips stretching around my root and the head of my dick dug deep in Madsen's throat, I blew.

It was pretty cataclysmic. I had been hoarding up for so fucking long, held off for so long, tempted and teased so mercilessly, that when I finally uncorked I shot enough stuff to not only drain my balls but almost blow them out through the cannon firing down Madsen's gagging throat.

He was a pisser. He hacked and choked, fighting for breath, but he didn't pull off my gushing gagger. His throat muscles spasming around my fully-buried throbber only set me off more. I grabbed his head and slammed my hips hard into his face, driving every spewing drop deep into the containing condom, losing all track of time and space. My whole focus was fucking his handsome, guzzling face as I lurched up underneath him, my wracked body pulsing with powerful propulsive jolts.

He took it like the learning philosopher he was.

I finally hit empty.

I fell back, covered with sweat, gasping for breath, residual shivers coursing through my drained body. A

ROUGHING THE REDHEAD

final glop of mangoo pumped into the bulging plastic buried deep in Madsen's now-receptive, suckling gut.

My sorry ass slowly settled down to earth again. My pulse rate slowed to near normal. Madsen stayed glued to my shrunken meat, his face mashing my pubes, his glorious ass humped up high behind him. His hands were under my butt, massaging.

I must have been soft for about 10 seconds, maybe five, before I started to refill. His mouth caressed the spent meat and applied suction to draw fresh blood into the erectile caverns. Within minutes, I was bone hard in his gullet again.

He pulled his lips slowly up the full, throbbing length, until only the head of my dick was captured in his mouth. His thick lashes raised and he looked up at me and winked, then pushed his mouth back down, sucking in my straining rod completely again.

He repeated the slow, unnerving action, firing off every nerve ending in my dick, balls, and surrounding territory. Underneath my ass, his big hands slowly pried my buns wide as his fingers worked toward my butt hole. Up and down he slid his mouth, pumping my dick to even greater dimensions. My nuts felt as big as grapefruits and just as juicy; my buns, of steel.

I lay under him, legs wide, arms out, fists clawing the sheets. Madsen worked my middle like he had been sucking cock for years. He seemed to know exactly what to do with his mouth and tongue and lips to ignite my red-hot nerve endings into bonfires.

His fingers poked and probed my butt button, finally impudently pushing inside, then dipping deeper to ream it raw even as his mouth seared my dickmeat to charcoal.

FULL BODY CONTACT

I moaned plaintively and prayed the moment would never end. It got better...and *better.*

Finally, I blew another load, giggling and howling and snorting happily as I tried to plant my erupting seed somewhere deep underneath Madsen's belly button.

He pulled off me, grinning, stretching his jaw to loosen the tense muscles and massaging his neck. "Was it good for you too?" he smirked. I shoved myself upright and dove for his dick. He blocked me and we tumbled in a heap, ending with our faces in each other's crotch.

He pulled the packed rubber off my meat and knotted the plastic. Giving it a kiss, he tossed it onto the cheap bedside table and reached for two more protective circles. I snuffled around his huge hard member, sniffing up the tangy, savory scents, until my mouth found his tight, packed ball sac. As Madsen worked a fresh rubber over me and then rolled the plastic down himself, I washed his nubby sack of fruit clean with my worshipping tongue and nibbled teasingly at the raised ridge of flesh dividing his hard-working ovals.

The film of hair on his nuts and dusting his ass was a pale gold with coppery highlights glinting in the morning light. My mouth explored his butt, pressing into the muscular mountains; then my nose nudged into the dark canyon carved between. Acrid male smells spiced up through my nostrils, tempting me deeper and deeper into the tantalizing crack.

Madsen pulled my head out of his crotch. "I want you to fuck me," he said earnestly. "And blow me at the same time, if you can. I've always had kind of a thing about finding somebody who could do that."

I blinked. Flexibility is not one of the things linemen are noted for. But his dick looked big enough that maybe I

ROUGHING THE REDHEAD

could pull it off. We took a break and I did some stretching exercises while imagining my dick in his butt with his dick in my mouth, triggering pints of precome.

The thumping and groans were still coming from next door. Amazing. Madsen and I grinned at each other.

My hunk lay back and pulled his beefy legs up, spreading his muscular thighs wide. His asshole beamed at me. We had no lube, except the load of precome that had accumulated in his condom. I slid it off his dick and greased up my plastic-wrapped pole, rubbing the sweet muck up and down the throbbing length. I tried not to think about where the giant greasestick was about to go so I wouldn't blow another wad before I even got my dicknose near his butt.

Then I milked another fistful of his crystal goo out of the huge plum nose of his meat mallet and smeared it deep into his hole. He moaned as I fingered the tight anal ring wide and thrust my digits in deep. After sliding the rubber back on him, I hiked myself in between his legs and aimed my pile driver.

His bunghole tightened with every attempt to breach it. Fingers were one thing, but my boring bone was another. The big guy was breaking a sweat. I figured he needed diversion. I tickled his nuts, made dirty jokes about the freshman fuck team next door, scratched my way through his pubes and up over his abs to his tits, where I started doing a finger ring-around-the-titty dance, and soon he was snickering and chuckling while his ass relaxed and I eased in as slick as you please.

Once inside his virgin hole his O-ring snugged hungrily around the sucked-in head of my meat and proceeded to suck in more.

Madsen's big greens clinched and he threw his head back. "Ohyeahohyeahohfuckin'*yeah*!" Obviously this was

a stud who had longed to have his butt blown. I tried to ful-
fill his dreams. It took a little work, but soon my dank
sweat-soaked pubes were pounding against his sparse coppery bush. My nuts pummeled his fat perineum as his own
stuffed sack molded around the root of my bone.

The lineman's huge chest lifted and fell rapidly as I
pumped my dick in and out of his crammed colon. He
grunted viciously and slapped at the sheets with his big
hands as his teeth gritted together and sweat popped out on
his forehead, but never did he say no to my pile driving. My
throbbing meat pounded in and out of his fine ass. I
grabbed Madsen's pulsing dick with both hands and
stretched it toward my mouth.

Sure enough, by stretching my neck and going for the
gold I could slurp about half its massive length into my
mouth with enough room left over to whap it into shape
with my tongue. Pretty fucking neat. I sucked him as
viciously as I was fucking him.

Madsen chortled and moaned ecstatically, his fondest
fantasy now made blissfully real. "Ohmanohman fucking
awesome," he managed to breathlessly note. He grabbed
my tits and pinched and twisted mercilessly as I sucked and
fucked, my own hands working wicked rhythms on his butt
cheeks and balls. If my mouth hadn't been full I would have
agreed with his assessment even louder.

We both blew at the same time, nearly taking the creaky
bed down with us as we grunted and thrashed and shot our
loads. I almost blasted myself out of his ass, which drove
my head deeper onto his dick, devouring more of his meat,
which triggered his firing an even heavier load of hot milk,
driving me back into his ass, which set off another explosion in my nuts, which...

ROUGHING THE REDHEAD

Oh, *yeah*.

A couple of hours later, happily satiated, we hobbled next door to say goodbye to the still-humping couple. The kid answered our knock wide-eyed and buck-naked, his dripping, rigid hooked shaft looking like chopped meat inside its battered barrier. "Don't hurt yourself," Madsen admonished.

"Aw, no, man. When I start to raw up, she sucks me off until I'm good to start punching again. She's got a great set of chops. Right, babe?" he called back to his inamorata.

From the bed, she grinned modestly.

It worked for us too.

Two Sizes Too Tight
James Ridout

My name is Doug Reynolds. I play rugby with the Lion Hearts, for the city of Brewer in northern Wisconsin. We're a small town in the Midwest specializing in packing sausage for a big corporation. Most likely nobody outside of Brewer has heard of our town. Our passion is rugby. The whole town comes to see our matches. We play in an old minor-league baseball stadium, which houses 10,000 fans. We pack them in for every game. Rugby is the only thing happening in our working-class town.

I'm surprised to say that I still want to play rugby. So does Oseoli (pronounced "aussi-o-lee") McDouggle. Of course everyone calls him Asshole McDouggle. Don't parents think about what they name their kids? He tells everyone to call him "McDouggle." Sometimes they do. I call him Asshole....at least to myself. After everything that has happened, I still call him Asshole. I have to admit I'm obsessed with Asshole McDouggle. I hate him.

I'm going to tell you a story about me and Asshole McDouggle. I'll start somewhere in the middle instead of the beginning. Let's just say the events leading up to the middle of the story were that McDouggle and I hated each other. I can't say we're rivals. He's an asshole and he lets me know that I'm a wuss. We started out in grade school and worked our way to adulthood. After high school, McDouggle and I went to work in the factory packing meat. That's what everybody does in Brewer when they finish school. Guys my age live with their parents. I'm 21 and so is McDouggle. We seldom see each other at work since we're on different teams, and we certainly don't hang out with each other after work. The only time McDouggle and I get together is on the practice field and in the locker room. I'll start the story in the locker room.

Practice was over. The field was soggy as rain misted down on us the entire practice. When I think of Brewer, I think of weather like today. The skies are gloomy, spitting cool moisture into the air as it settles on the ground. Everything is always damp in Brewer. You might guess that the landscape is continuously green, and for the most part it is. However, for every square foot of green grass there is an equal amount of muddy ground cover. Ruby players love mud, because we stay covered in it for much of our lives. The field we practice on is soaked with mud, with little grass growing.

The guys and me were stripping off our practice uniforms to go into the showers and clean off the layers of mud caked to our bodies. It was impractical to be modest. We all had to shower before going home. Coach demanded it of us. We couldn't take public transit, which most of us used, unless we rinsed off, otherwise we would dirty the buses. Still, some were modest and rushed through their showers, got dressed, then hastily headed through the door. Others,

FULL BODY CONTACT

like Asshole McDouggle, pranced languidly through the rectangle-shaped locker room in full nudity as long as time allowed. If I looked like him, maybe I would do the same thing. I have to admit that he is fucking hot.

I'm sure the majority of the guys on the team are straight, but I know they admire McDouggle's body as he swaggers to the showers. How could they not? He has the most steel-perfect ass. It is hairless and smooth, without a single blemish. Each cheek is plump and has the juicy polished appearance of two nectarine halves. I know I'm young and lacking in experience, but I'm old enough to know that I want my face between those two mounds of pulpy flesh. I can feel my cock stiffening as I watch him brush past the guys across the long room to the showers. Who the hell does McDouggle think he is, parading around the locker room stark-naked and twitching his bottom from side to side like a woman? Yet his strut is manly just the same. I have to give McDouggle credit. Despite all his good looks and seductive movements, he is 100% man. He's all man on the rugby field and his ass looks to me like it could take a serious pounding. I can't figure it out. The more I hate McDouggle, the greater my need to fuck him. It makes my insides burn, as my hatred increases each day.

I guess you are wondering why my hatred for McDouggle runs so deep. You may wonder why I'm obsessed with him. Or why can't I just let him go? The answer is that McDouggle torments me. He deliberately pisses me off to no end. In grade school, he used to grab my lunch bag from me. He'd take what he wanted from my brown paper sack and then throw it back at me without putting the rest of the contents back inside. McDouggle was brawny even when we were kids. Now he has sculpted muscles on a butterscotch godlike body. He has wavy black hair with thick curls. He never mousses the curls to relax them. He's working-class and has no time for primping. I envy those curls. My hair is a straight mousy reddish-brown. My pubes are the same color, while McDouggle has those same shiny, black, tight curls nesting his dick and framing his asshole.

McDouggle seldom humiliated me in front of others when we were kids. I doubt he gave much thought to the mean things he did to me. For example, maybe he'd give me a hard shove to take my place in the milk line. Or he'd steal my algebra homework from my notebook. It was always quick and easy. I never fought back. McDouggle was strong and could easily kick my ass.

As we got older I became a brawny boy in my own right, but I never stood up to McDouggle. Nobody else stood up to McDouggle, but then I never really saw him bullying anyone else the way he did me. Was I his only target? Is his hostile behavior toward me our little secret?

By now you must be wondering what McDouggle looks like. He exemplifies your typical rugby player. He's from premium bull stock. He stands 6-foot-2 inches and weighs a solid 240 pounds. I'm not much smaller at 6-foot even and 230 pounds. His smooth legs have the polished appearance of caramel and look powerful when his muscles bulge as he sprints downfield with the ball. Mine are pale, with sleek and slender contours. It takes two or three men to bring him down. He's our most prolific scorer. He's not afraid of taking anyone on when he's storming down the ball field. His uniform shorts look at least two sizes too tight, since his butt is so heavily endowed. His jewels stretch the jockstrap fabric. As he sprints down the field, you can see the muscles in his ass expand and contract with each movement, straining the material of his shorts. He doesn't move fast...just powerfully. When he makes a score, he hot-dogs and runs around the field like a heavy gazelle. He finds the nearest person and jumps into his arms, straddling the guy's waist with his powerful interior thigh muscles straining around his hips. I dream about feeling that squeeze around my waist.

I don't think erotic thoughts when I'm on the field or in the locker room—except where McDouggle is concerned. My fantasy is to grab him on the playing field after he scores one of his goals, throw him belly first in the mud, and then with one hand, rip those tight shorts at the inseams, pull down my own shorts, and fuck him silly. Of course he hates it, but he doesn't resist. Not very realistic, eh? Or, when he's prancing around the locker room loosely carrying a towel in one hand as he heads for the shower, I imagine myself slamming him against one of the lockers and pushing my dick into him. Of course he curses me, but he lets me finish my business.

Does McDouggle have a big dick? I don't know. I haven't seen it hard. It seems to dangle OK. I'm more inter-ested in his ass. All the guys watch his ass. I love it when McDouggle saunters past some of the guys on his way to the shower and one of them snaps a towel at those glossy plump cheeks. He smiles back at the offender as the towel makes its cracking sound against his satin flesh, leaving a red welt. McDouggle never retaliates. He continues his casual saunter to the shower, sometimes taking two or three more snapping towels on that voluptuous, powerful ass. These scenes always make me hard. I have to sit for a few minutes by my locker with my legs crossed to wait for my erection to die down. Then I have to wait for McDouggle to finish his shower before I can tiptoe in for mine, staying just long enough to rinse the mud off. I keep to myself in the locker room. If one of the guys wants to hang out after practice I tell him to wait for me outside. I say I got my ass kicked today in practice and I'm moving real slow. There's a lot of truth to that. McDouggle makes sure I suffer in practice... at least I like to believe he does. He's hard on me. If he has a choice to run over one of three men to get to the goal, it's always me... at least it seems like it. He runs right over me. My ass is stuck in the mud, while he scores the goal.

McDouggle is full of cheap shots. Sometimes I manage to keep up with him in his charge to the goal. It's nothing for him to use a forearm or elbow across the side of my face. I'm bloodied after every practice. He's even kicked me in the nuts a few times. If I protest, he says, "Be a man, Wuss, and stop crying like a little girl." The most I can say is "Fuck you, McDouggle," which he of course ignores. I can't think of anything else to say. I just sit in my locker stall with my bruised nuts, waiting for him to finish showering, with my legs crossed. Even with sore nuts, I know I'll spring a hard-on in the shower if I'm near him.

One day everything came crashing down on me. It happened one Saturday afternoon in the middle of the season during an away game. My game was coming along pretty good and Coach wanted me to start handling the ball more often, so I was pretty excited. The guys were in the locker room changing for the game. Of course I stayed at the opposite end from McDouggle. I didn't want to be distracted by him. He would only do something to piss me off and then I wouldn't be any good for the game. But McDouggle wasn't going to let me off so easy.

FULL BODY CONTACT

"Fuck it!" McDouggle shouts, throwing his gym bag to the floor. "My mother didn't pack my jock or put my shorts in my bag." McDouggle stomps to the other end of the locker room, where I'm stripping down to suit up. He picks up my gym bag like he used to pick up my lunch bag and goes through it to find what he wants. He takes out my only pair of shorts and a jock. After getting what he wants, he throws the bag in my face and struts back to his locker. I'm pissed, so I can't speak. That's what happens to me when I get mad. I keep it all inside. Meanwhile, I'm turning red in the face and nobody says a thing to McDouggle. The prima donna can do anything he wants. All I can do is stare at McDouggle in clear contempt. I watch him slip on the elastic jock and then struggle into my shorts. My ass is not near as big as McDouggle's, so I wear more than two sizes smaller than he does. After a lengthy struggle, he pulls them over his hard buns. They're so tight, I know the shorts have to be racking his balls. He doesn't seem to notice. His mood instantly changes from foul to jubilant, and he prances out to the field.

"Here, Reynolds. I have an extra pair," a teammate says, tossing me a pair of shorts as I sit bare-ass on the locker-room bench. "Sorry, I don't have another jock."

I nod my thanks and hurry to finishing dressing. Everyone else has followed McDouggle out to the field. I pull on the shorts, and they are more than two sizes too big! I'm having trouble keeping them around my narrow little waist. Most rugby players are big-boned and fleshy like McDouggle. While I have a lot of muscle flesh, my waist is narrow and I broaden out at the chest and shoulders. As I stand, it seems like they will be OK. They have to be. This is going to be my big day. I'm going to see some action.

TWO SIZES TOO TIGHT

The match starts. My game has been going pretty quick these days, so my defense is good. The past few games I've gotten some good steals and have been feeding the ball to the other guys, McDouggle ending up with it on the offensive attack. This time, the opposing team is extra big and strong. Coach wants me to hold onto the ball longer if I get the opportunity, because I'm quicker than the big guys and I'll advance the ball. The strategy is working... well, almost.

When I get the ball, I see a clear path, but I don't get very far. It isn't the other team who's stopping me. No, it's Asshole McDouggle who's just as quick as me and wants the ball. In the first half, he strips the ball from me three times. As we come out for the second half, I'm determined to fight him for the ball...even if he is my teammate. I'm sick of McDouggle and I'm not going to take it anymore.

Then it happens. After a steal, McDouggle tries to wrestle the ball from me. Incensed, I slug him in the mouth. I can hear the crowd *ooh* and *aah* as I bloody his lip. He retaliates by kicking me in the balls, at the same time outmuscling the ball from me. So I tackle him. It isn't long before both teams are on top of us. Meanwhile, while we are piled up on each other, I can hear the ripping of McDouggle's shorts. The stretched seam that hugged the crack of his ass has split. At the same time, my shorts are falling down to my knees as guys scrambling for the ball tug at anything they can get their hands on.

In the middle of the pileup, I forget about rugby. The grunts surrounding me squelch the noise of the crowd. My dick is jammed inside the fold of McDouggle's ass! As I realize where it is, it springs to life. I can feel his ass twitching and wiggling against my dick as he struggles to hold on to the ball. It's more than I can take. I feel the hot lather of sweat between his ass cheeks. I know what to do. It's right there. I move my hand just enough to guide my hard dick to where it wants to be, in the inferno of Asshole McDouggle's butt. As I pierce him, I feel his asshole twitch. Then as McDouggle realizes what's happening, he starts to shake his ass in fury, trying to ward off his intruder. Since we're in the pileup, he has little recourse. I plunge in and start to really fuck him, in and out with hard long strokes. I don't think about the crowd or the other bodies around me. My mind is filled with the image of McDouggle's hot, tight asshole, which is sucking my dick inside him. A few more violent thrusts, and I come. As I come out of my trance, I see that everyone has extricated themselves from McDouggle and me. My teammates and the guys from the other team are circled around us, dumbstruck. The crowd is silent as they stare at me, ass-to-the-sky, engaged in McDouggle's butt. I do what any gentleman would do at such a moment. I pull out of McDouggle's ass and briefly rest on my haunches, contemplating what I have done. I feel the years of frustration released. I get to my feet and pull up my shorts. McDouggle lies facedown in the mud. The asshole looks like he's learned some humility. I tear my eyes away from him. I don't think I'll be playing any more ball today, so I head toward the locker room. Everybody stares at me as I enter the building. The enormity of what I have done hits me as I walk through those doors. What's going to happen to me? Will I ever get to play rugby again? I go to my locker and sit on the bench before it. I open it and grab a towel and start to wipe my face. Then I hear a sound. I turn to see who's coming. It's McDouggle, still wearing my now-tattered shorts. They're ripped and dangling on him. He's taken the liberty of removing his jersey.

TWO SIZES TOO TIGHT

He won't look at me as he heads toward his locker.

I can't take my eyes off him. His face has a defeated look I've never seen in all the years I've known him. He seems tamed. I watch his smoothed, muscled arms fumble through his locker. As I watch him, I once again feel the stirring in my loins. I must be crazy! What I did to this man on the field was close to rape—with 10,000 witnesses—and all I can think about is balling him again! I shift my gaze to the locker in front of me. I want a shower to clean the mud off, but McDouggle is already headed there. Fuck it! What do I have to lose now? So what if I get a hard-on in the shower from being so near him? I get my shower gear and march in there after McDouggle.

He is soaping up his torso as he warily watches me enter. I go straight to the showerhead next to him and let the stream fall on me. McDouggle continues to soap himself, and I feel the tightening in my balls. My dick is growing, but I don't care. What can he do to me now? Kick my ass? I've already gotten the best of him. I watch the soap suds roll from his body and wash down the drain. Then he moves closer to me, and I can feel the heat of his body cover me. He turns and braces himself against the wall of the shower. He turns his head the opposite way from me. At first, I'm not sure what he wants me to do. Then he spreads his legs apart and lets his ass protrude outward from the wall as his hands slide down the tiles to adjust his position. I'm breathing hard. He still has power over me even though I tried to take it from him out on the field. Like an obedient son, I go in behind him. I watch the muscles tense in his back as he braces against the shower wall. I spit into the palm of my hand and apply the slippery substance to the head of my cock. I'm not trying to be gentle.

FULL BODY CONTACT

I push the head of my penis into the tight curls between McDouggle's ass cheeks. I don't have to sear the right place very long. The head of my cock can fee. intense heat of want permeating from his asshole. My d. knows where it's supposed to go. Contacting the fiery coa. of his hot center, I push with a hard thrust, not caring if i hurt him, and McDouggle bucks backward. My dick is lodged in him. He lets out a gasp of pain but I ignore it and push again. My dick is three-quarters of the way in. I draw back slightly and jam it in a final time. Another cry of pain, as his ass meets the base of my dick. I start to pump him good, but not with the violence I used out on the field. I want to get off inside him. I couldn't care less what he's feeling. I want victory over him, but McDouggle seems to relax. He's no longer in pain. I'm so close to coming that his lack of misery doesn't quell my excitement. As I'm entering my final approach, I notice him jack his dick while I fuck him. I fuck him with all my might, as he moves his hand up and down on his dick as fast as it will go. I feel the tightening around my cock as he starts to come. I spend my load inside him. He stays braced to the shower wall and I feel the squeeze of his asshole surrounding my cock as he continues to come. I let myself slide out of him and return to my shower.

Catching his breath, McDouggle finishes his shower. We haven't said two words to each other. As we head back to our lockers, the guys start coming into the locker room. I guess the game picked up again after McDouggle and I left. Why not? What else could they do? The guys seem happy; I guess we won.

"McDouggle! Reynolds! In my office right now!" Coach barks. It's time to face the music. I trudge behind

McDouggle into the visitors' office. We sit in two chairs in front of Coach's desk. He hasn't bothered to close the blinds to the rest of the locker room.

Coach glares at us. "I don't know what the fuck happened out there with the two of you, but it had better never happen again. Do you understand?"

Coach looks at me. "You must be fucking crazy, Reynolds. What were you thinking?"

I shrug.

He turns to look at McDouggle. "You had it coming, Asshole. Don't think I don't know what goes on around here. I would can both your asses, but you two were the reasons we won today. I want both of you to leave what happened on the field today. No problems from your parents. Got it?" He barks.

"Yeah," McDouggle and I both mumble.

"Now shake hands," Coach orders, getting to his feet.

"Aaah, Coach," McDouggle complains.

"Do it!" Coach orders. McDouggle and I follow the old man to his feet. I cast a glance over to McDouggle, who stretches out his hand first. I place my hand in his and I'm jolted with a shock. *Damn! I came twice inside him and he still electrifies me.* McDouggle feels my reluctance to squeeze his hand. As he lets mine go he whispers, "Wuss."

"Fuck you, McDouggle," I mumble.

"That's enough, you two, now get the fuck out of my office." As we open the door to the rest of the locker room, Coach screams, "And no more fucking in front of the fans and God. Geez, you'd think the man forgot to give the two of you brains."

The guys all stare at us as we go to our respective lockers.

FULL BODY CONTACT

It would have been great if it could have been like Coach said and we'd left our differences on the field. McDouggle and I were slapped with a temporary suspension by the higher authorities. I can't imagine a life without rugby. I've been playing ever since I started coming up. McDouggle made a small protest, claiming that since he was the one who got fucked, he should be excused and be allowed to play. It's my guess that the higher-ups were all guys and they figured a guy that gets fucked is as much to blame as the fucker.

Someday maybe I'll move to another city. I could play rugby there without being remembered for fucking a guy on the playing field. I thought about going to some factory town in western Pennsylvania that maybe had a gay bar, so I could meet a cool guy and find a job in one of the plants. I don't need much to keep me happy. I'd like to have something like what my dad has with my mom. Maybe a nice boy to prepare my meals, do my laundry, and clean my house—who won't give me too hard a time if I cheat on him every once in a while. I could play rugby and maybe get together with the guys for cards every now and then. So what's stopping me from leaving? Of course it's Asshole McDouggle.

A couple of months pass. By this time, I'm only jerking off thinking about him every three days instead of two or three times a day. Still, my Friday nights are spent at home beating off and thinking about fucking McDouggle, while he and the other guys are out with the chicks.

TWO SIZES TOO TIGHT

One Tuesday afternoon after work, I'm sitting on a park bench outside the factory before making tracks toward home. I look up from my daze and there's McDouggle standing in front of me.

"Hey, Wuss, didn't you hear what I said?"

I look at him like I'm stupid.

"Yeah," he says, scratching his head. "What do you think about coming over and hanging for a shake?"

I nod and get up to follow him. I don't know what he wants with me, but I'm obsessed with him, so I follow. I keep my eyes glued to that ass of his on the walk to his house. I'm sporting a major boner. Of course we don't talk along the way. I just wait for instructions.

We get to his house and his mom is in the kitchen. "Hey, Ma," McDouggle says. "Wuss and I will be in the basement."

Mrs. McDouggle stops her busywork to scold him. "I don't think your father will appreciate you bringing him here, Oseoli."

McDouggle blows off the tight-lipped woman. "Yeah, whatever," he says, "He won't be here long."

I follow McDouggle down the basement steps. It's a living area with a sofa, chairs, television set, and a couple of recessed windows. McDouggle starts to strip off his clothes. I watch in amazement. "Don't just stand there, Wuss, take your fucking clothes off," he ordered.

I begin to get steamed at his audacity, but I comply. My dick is raging hard.

"You shower at work?" He asks. We get grimy in the factory so many of the guys clean up at work before going home.

"Yeah; you?"

FULL BODY CONTACT

McDouggle nods. "Come on, Wuss, I haven't got all day." I'm awestruck. I can't believe this is happening. I've dreamed of this, yet he pisses me off. "Fuck you, McDouggle" is all I say.

After I strip, McDouggle gets on the floor on his elbows and knees, ready to be mounted. I can't get a good look at his dick, because he's starting to stroke it.

"Are you going to squirt all over the carpet?" I ask. I'm standing to the rear of him.

McDouggle is astonished. "I don't give a shit. Why should you? Are you going to fuck me or are you going to stand there like a pussy?"

McDouggle is starting to get on my nerves, so I nestle up behind him on my knees, ready to make him pay. I'm afraid to touch my dick for fear I'll come all over his smooth ass before putting it in. I spit several times in the palm of my hand to get plenty of lubricant, then smear it on his hot hole and aim the head of my penis at his asshole. I start to apply some pressure to get it in. After a few moments, nothing. There isn't any give to it.

"Hurry up, Wuss! What's your problem?" McDouggle says, looking back at me.

I push harder in response, not caring if I hurt him. I push so hard my dick hurts. Still, the hole won't give. Then instinct takes over. I take a deep breath and take the dive. I start to make love to his asshole with my mouth. I hear him gasp in disbelief, as my first tongue flicker hits his magical button. I stick my tongue in as far as it will go. It tastes sweet and the scent of his musk sends shivers to my dick. Now I rise back up to put my dick inside his big ass. He's begging to be fucked, his buttonhole is pulsing, anxious for my dick. I don't have to push this time; it glides inside him.

TWO SIZES TOO TIGHT

McDouggle winces in pain and bites his forearm. I'm a big boy, so my dick has some length and girth to it. Right now it's straight as a police club. I spare him no mercy. I'm not going to be careful. I want to hurt him. He needs to pay for every fucking "Wuss" he's ever uttered. Yes, I'm fucking him. I'm fucking him long and hard with my big dick. I'm determined to make him a sore boy when we're finished. I slow the pace at times, because I don't want to come right away. I want my desire to die down some, so I can start the onslaught over again. My purpose is to cause him as much misery as possible. I look at his face. It has a look of pure agony on it, red and beaded with sweat. Why isn't he stopping me if he's so miserable? I slam his ass even harder. I see him grimace and close his eyes tight, struggling for breath. That's all it takes for me to come. A few short pumps and I spend my load inside him. I collapse on his back and happen to look at the floor. McDouggle has shot his load on his mother's blue carpet. I feel the rug burns on my knees; McDouggle must have some of the same. I have no energy to pull out of him at that moment, so I lie on his massive sweat-soaked back with my dick still inside him. I let my head rest between his shoulder blades. He lets himself collapse on the carpet, and there we lie together for a few moments, catching our breaths. It's the only intimate moment we've had. As much as I hate him, I don't want to let him go just yet.

"Come on, Wuss, you're heavy," McDouggle says, shaking me off. "Come on," he prods, "get the fuck off."

I comply. I get into a push-up position as my dick slides out of him. I roll over on my ass and sit with my legs crossed.

McDouggle gets up and starts pulling on his clothes.

"Well, I guess Ma will be starting supper soon. You'll be needing to get going."

I don't want to stay for dinner. I couldn't face Mrs. McDouggle. I know she had to have heard us fucking down here in the basement. I suppose she was grateful it was down here and not on the rugby field.

"Hurry up, Wuss!" McDouggle barks. "Sometimes I think your brains are in your ass."

"Fuck you, McDouggle," I reply. I get up and pull on my clothes.

✪ ✪ ✪

I still haven't made it out of this wretched town. My mind is stuck on Asshole McDouggle. Every few weeks, he'll come find me and we'll have a fuck session. Sometimes I get to suck his dick. If I seek him out, he brushes me aside, sometimes knocking me over. We fuck on his terms, which makes me seethe inside. Each time I fuck him, I'm determined to make him pay for his disrespect. I figure some day I'll give him the ultimate fuck and then he'll submit to me forever. Fat chance—McDouggle continues to play me like a harp.

TWO SIZES TOO TIGHT

Zoran's Big Meet
Duane Williams

As soon as the list was posted, I checked to see if Zoran had made the team. My name was on the list, of course. This was my third year as team captain, and my last before graduating from Lister. My goal was to make the varsity team at university and, eventually, the Olympics. Zoran's name was on the list, written just under mine. Zoran Vujnokovic. I went home after school and jacked off to the thought of wrestling Zoran in the nude.

Our first practice was the next day. I changed and was leaving the locker room when Zoran came barreling through the door, crashing into me head-on. "Sorry," he said. He was out of breath, and his black hair was hanging in his eyes. "Hey buddy, I'm late for the practice. Tell Mr. Sanger I'll be a few minutes."

During the practice, Zoran came up and apologized again. "Hey, don't worry about it," I said. I wasn't exactly upset about Zoran running into me. He looked even hotter than I'd expected in his singlet, which he packed full in the crotch. The other guys were checking him out too. It was

FULL BODY CONTACT

hard not to notice. "Congratulations on making the team," I said. "I'm team captain, so if you need any help with the training, let me know."

We trained every day after school through the fall. Because we were so closely matched, Zoran and I were always paired up during practice. Zoran couldn't beat me, and that burned his ass. He came close a few times, but his technique wasn't nearly as slick as mine. He had power, but I had flexibility and speed.

"Think you'll ever win?" I asked Zoran one day at practice. I had him in a killer gut wrench on the mat. The other guys were standing around watching, cheering me on. Zoran was hurting bad, I could tell, but he was showing no sign of giving up.

"Fuck. For sure," he said. He was grunting the words through his teeth. "You're a horse meat fucker." Zoran was from Yugoslavia. His English was good, but not always correct. Sometimes he said things that didn't make much sense.

"In your fucking dreams, loser!" I laughed and let Zoran go, giving him a shove off the mat.

"Fuck yourself," he said, getting up on his feet. The veins in his forehead were popping, either from my wicked hold or from his being totally pissed off.

"I guess somebody has to beat me someday."

"You're a fuckhead asshole," he said. He took off out of the gym and the door slammed behind him.

After the coach finished bawling me out for laughing at Zoran, I went into the locker room to apologize. My timing was perfect. Zoran was just getting out of the shower. I pretended to be squeezing a zit in the mirror, but I was watching him out of the corner of my eye. He had a dark, thick bush. His cock and balls looked heavy. I stopped looking

ZORAN'S BIG MEET

because I was getting hard in my singlet, which makes a woody very obvious. When he stepped out of the shower, I acted like I was surprised he was there.

"Hey, Zoran…how's it going?" He looked at me but didn't say anything.

"Sorry for calling you a loser, man. I was just joking around, you know."

He still didn't say anything as he toweled off. It was hard to keep my eyes off his cock. He was uncut, which was unusual in the showers at Lister. He dried off from the bottom up, starting with his big, muscular feet. He looked at me as he lifted his balls and dried between his legs. "What is the fuck with you? Are you jealous of me?" he said, looking at me with blue eyes. He threw the towel on the bench and stood there with his hands on his hips.

"Hey, I've got nothing to be jealous about," I said. "Let's not forget who's been captain for three years."

"Ah, fuck you!" he said, and blew me off with a flip of his hand. He grabbed the towel and walked away naked. His ass was as perfect as the rest of him.

Next practice, Mr. Sanger matched Zoran and me together, as always. Zoran looked pissed off as we stepped on the mat. Mr. Sanger blew the whistle, and I was quickest on the draw. I grabbed Zoran through the legs and dumped him on the mat, squeezing up his balls against my arm. I got a good grip around his waist, but Zoran was a strong mother. He kicked his legs up over his head and broke out. When he flipped back, his face landed in my crotch, which was on the swell.

"OK, guys," Mr. Sanger hollered. "Warmup's over. Five minutes on suplex, belly to belly."

"I'm ready now," Zoran said. He grabbed his singlet by

the straps and twisted it back into position, rearranging his bulge. Zoran didn't wear deodorant. His ripe pits were turning me on. Mr. Sanger blew the whistle and we grabbed each other by the shoulders.

"You want my dick in your face again?"

"It is so small to notice," he said. I threw him over, my best flapjack, and pinned his shoulders to the mat.

"You'll notice it when you're sucking on it."

✪ ✪ ✪

The final meet of the season was the provincial finals in Toronto. We had to stay overnight at a hotel, and Mr. Sanger put Zoran and me together in the same room. He was always trying to get us to like each other, or something. "Neither one of you will win if you're fighting each other off the mat," he said. "Great athletes learn from their competitors."

From the balcony of our hotel room, we could see the CN Tower and the Skydome. We arrived the night before the meet, but the coach said no, we couldn't go check out the prostitutes on Yonge Street. "You're 18. You probably wouldn't know what to do with one anyhow," Mr. Sanger said. "Unpack your bags and get some sleep. We didn't train all fall so you two could blow your wad on some pussy."

Zoran and I got unpacked and changed into sweats. Zoran wore his without gotchies, and the sight of his big cock bouncing around inside was making me horny. We stood on the balcony and looked out over the city. "Cool, eh? All the lights look so cool. Far fucking cry from Lister, that's for sure."

ZORAN'S BIG MEET

"Yeah…it is beautiful. Not like Sarajevo. The war destroyed my city," he said, leaning out over the railing. He was staring down at the street, not saying anything more.

"What war's that?" I asked after a while.

"The people look like bugs," he said, looking down at the street. I asked him again about the war, but he didn't want to talk about it, so we went inside the room to see if there was any alcohol in the bar fridge. It was empty, but I had some juice packs in my gym bag so we drank those instead. We discovered a porn channel on the TV, but neither one of us had the cash to pay for it. Just the idea of watching porn with Zoran was making me hard.

"Nervous about tomorrow?"

"Not too much," he said.

"Well, I guess you've already sized up the competition." We were each other's only real competition. Except for some guy from Sudbury, there was nobody in our weight division who was anywhere close to being a threat. "But I'm still planning to whip your ass," I said.

Zoran pretended to laugh hysterically. "A fat fucking chance," he said.

"Fuck you. You don't stand a chance," I said, twisting his arm in a wringer. He quickly broke the hold and pushed me on the bed. He jumped on me, and we wrestled around for a bit, fighting but not fighting.

"You want to suck my cock, buddy."

"You're the cocksucker," I answered. Zoran was on top of me, holding me down with the full weight of his body. "At least I have a dick." I could feel his cock pushing against my back.

Zoran was hard. "Yeah, you don't have a cock like me," he said. He was grinding his dick against my back. His pits

FULL BODY CONTACT

were hot and musky, and I took a deep breath. I tried to flip him back over so I was on top, but only ended up turning myself over. He was sitting on my chest now, holding my arms down. His cock was pitching an enormous tent in his sweats. Zoran leaned forward so his crotch was pushed up against my face. I turned my face to the side and pretended to fight him off.

"Get the hell off me," I said.

"You want my cock," he said. "I seen you many times looking down there."

"Whatever," I said, "Now get the fuck off, gay boy." Zoran reached into his sweats and pulled it out. It was the biggest cock I'd ever seen, muscled and leaking jizz as he slapped it around on my face.

"Maybe I'll let you win tomorrow," he said. "If you suck my cock."

My dick was about to explode. His crotch was musky like the rest of his body, but hotter and more intense. I turned my head and did it: I reached out with my tongue and took his cock. "Oh, yeah... Fuck, that is good," he said, pulling out of my mouth after a minute. He was getting close. He let my arms go and braced his hand against the headboard. With the other hand, he held his cock at the base and pumped my mouth slowly. He was groaning so loud that I thought the guys in the next room might hear. He gave my mouth one deep pump, then pulled out again, his whole body flexing as he sprayed a load on the sheets.

When Mr. Sanger came by to see if we were in our room and asleep, Zoran answered the door without his shirt on.

"You guys aren't fighting in here, I hope."

I was sitting on the floor in my sweats, stretching out

ZORAN'S BIG MEET

my quads. Zoran looked at me and rolled his eyes.

"Come on, guys, it's time to get some sleep," Mr. Sanger said. "Do I have to remind you that tomorrow's the biggest meet of the year?"

"It is mine for sure," Zoran said.

"I wouldn't be too sure about that," I said. "You haven't beat me once yet. Face it, man...you're a loser."

"You two are perfectly matched," Mr. Sanger said. "You both have swollen heads. Make sure one of you wins, OK? Now get to sleep. I'm not kidding." He left our room, and Zoran locked the door.

Zoran walked over to where I was sitting on the floor. "You're an asshole," he said. He pulled down his sweats and pushed my face in his crotch. "You haven't won nothing yet," he said.

FULL BODY CONTACT

The Pass
M. Christian

"What a beautiful day for a game, Howard. The sun is shin-ing, there's not a cloud in the sky. I'll tell you, this is the kind of weather the game was meant for."

The Rookie stepped from his car and into a freezing rain. The sky was dark, an inhospitable mixture of night and storm clouds. The rain went from a stern pattering on top of his head to a cold shower—a wall of needle-cold pin pricks—in his face, as a hard wind changed direction and then changed again.

Only a glowing front window pulled the house out of the pitch night. The curtains were drawn, but light still splashed and played against the pale muslin. Reflections showed the shimmering cement of the walk, the porch, and the hardwood of the front door. Stopping for a moment, the Rookie shook himself free of some of the icy water and knocked on the door.

"It is indeed a quite spectacular day for a game, John—a truly remarkable atmospheric display. I'll wager the teams are as eager as we are for them to get out there and really

show us the strength and elegance of this noble game."

The Pro was backlit: his broad-shouldered body nothing but a broad-shouldered silhouette. His black form shifted, and a big, pale hand emerged—open in welcome.

The Rookie smiled and accepted its grip and the firm pull that drew him inside to the warmth of the house.

"And what teams they are, Howard: two of the league's major players in a contest to decide who goes on to the division finals. Two titans of the gridiron locked in a competition to see who goes on and who gets left behind."

The place was homey without being too artistic. Testosterone furnishings: leather, steel, raw wood—but without drowning in it or boiling away comfort in machismo. It was a man's house, but not a belching, scratching, farting guy's house. Welcoming, but strong.

The Pro showed the Rookie where to toss his wet coat—a dark cave of a bedroom—and offered him a beer. The Rookie smiled warmly and took it.

"That's what makes this the spectacular game it is, John—this is what it's all about. Today we're in for a special match: a classic contest between an established titan of the gridiron and an up-and-coming, very promising all-star. Today promises to be a true battle royale over who will dominate the other and who will go on to possible greatness."

The couch was a great beast, a once-yellow, now-tan jungle cat that dominated the living room. In front of it was a cigarette-scarred coffee table, the dark freckles of old, cold drinks polka-dotting its veneer. In front of that was the tube—a gigantic, high-tech monster—the images of the game flooding out of it.

The Pro gestured toward the jungle cat, and the Rookie sat—the perfect cushions welcoming his buttocks in a familiar embrace of corduroy—moving only when the Pro sat down as well, the undulations of his ass's impact making the Rookie rise, then settle back into the sofa.

"Two competitors at their best, Howard. These pros are hot off a long line of spectacular games—what some are calling the best of the season—while the newcomers have been showing signs of becoming legends in their own right. Today we'll see if the Giants still have it in them or if the Young Turks will take away their crown."

Beers emptied, the Pro got up, vanished into the darkness of the kitchen, to return a few seconds later with two six-packs of frosty brew. Handing one to the Rookie, the Pro sat down again—even closer—and toasted him, can to can, ass almost to ass, and took a huge swallow.

Shyly smiling, the Rookie sipped, then—when he realized the Pro was still drinking, drinking, drinking—kept drinking. The Pro finished first, laughing and crushing the can in his huge hands. The Rookie finished shortly thereafter, also crushing his can, but more tenuously, more nervously.

"And there they are, John—and what a sight they are too: You can almost feel the tension, the opposing forces between these two powerful groups of men. Muscles aching for the battle of the gridiron, jaws clenched in determination, both of them just straining to get in there and compete for the roars of the crowd."

The Pro made a joke, his laughter at his own humor a deep quake. More in sympathetic vibration than real humor, the Rookie echoed—his own tones higher, more musical.

The sounds died slowly, leaving the two of them—just the two of them, on that big, big couch—until something flashed across the screen and their attention was pulled back to the action.

THE PASS

"I'm wondering what tricks the champions have up their sleeves today, Howard. They sure have a lot of them, scoring as often as they have, but they'll have to use some pretty good ones today to dance around these Turks. That's why they're on top, though—no one's meaner, tougher, or more determined than they are."

The screen hypnotized them for a few minutes, during which the Pro stretched, pushing his big, hairy legs out further. He wore too-tight running shorts, a too-tight T-shirt, and nothing else. No shoes. His feet were big, full of visible muscles and tendons, hinting at the bulges under his shirt and especially the one in his shorts.

"Just look at those magnificent men taking up their allotted positions, John. You can feel the tension, you can feel the excitement. These athletes are at the peak of their form, at the height of their physical prowess, waiting for that simple moment when the game will begin."

The Rookie shifted in the intimate embrace of the couch, momentarily uncomfortable. He wore a green turtleneck pushed up to his elbows and a pair of properly roughed-up jeans. Socks. Battered boots. Only his hands, his forearms, and his face were visible in the wash of lights from the set, but what did show was firm, coordinated, sculpted.

"—and there they go! The champ drops back, back, back, looking for an opening, any opening—"

Feigning a stiff shoulder, the Pro twisted, reached his arm around the Rookie's thin shoulders—and stopped, resting it on the back of the old sofa: close enough to be sensed, but not close enough to be felt...yet.

The Rookie took a moment to lunge for his almost-empty beer, rocking himself away from the Pro's heat, putting a few fingers of distance between them.

FULL BODY CONTACT

"—and it's no good! The champs are down! It looks like they might be losing their touch, Howard, to be knocked down that quick. We can only hope that they're just feeling the other guys out and it's not the sign that this is where it all goes wrong for them."

The Pro laughed at the screen, slapping the Rookie on the knee—but not hard, or for too long. His eyes scanned, sought the other man's, pulled them into his own, turned the stare into an earnest appreciation.

The Rookie laughed as well, but with fragile tones, and he shifted, but didn't pull away. His eyes met the Pro's, but then he blinked, blinked again—and then dismissively patted the Pro's hand, smiled, and turned back to the game flickering on the screen.

"I wholeheartedly agree with your assessment, John. It does indeed look like this could be the very game where the champs give up their title as kings of the field. You can see the pain and disappointment in their eyes. But it also pays to remind ourselves and our viewing audience that the game has only just begun, and many things never foreseen can change the outcome at a moment's notice."

With a sudden flash of a wry smile, the Pro slowly—then much more earnestly—began to fan his face. To add credence, he tugged on his collar, as if to let some of his building steam escape. Finally, dramatically much, much too hot, he reached down and pulled off his T-shirt—revealing a tightly formed, finely sculpted, hairless chest. His nipples seemed to change color like spastic streetlights from the TV's wash. His skin was thinly coated with sweat, making his body subtly gleam like something expensive, high-performance, and full of all kinds of optional extras from a halftime commercial.

THE PASS

Entranced, the Rookie could do nothing for a long minute but look at him. His eyes, much to the delight of the Pro, seemed to hum in their sockets, so fast were they going from ab to nipple, belly, shoulder, waist, and back again.

"What moves, Howard! Did you see that? Hell, how could you have missed it! Right out of that clumsy take-down to get within spitting distance of the end zone. Now that's a great game well-played!"

A quick swallow of beer went down the Rookie's throat wrong, and he explosively coughed, foam flecking his pants. Waving the Pro back down, he accepted a quick point to the bathroom and quickly stumbled toward the back of the house. A tap was turned. Water splashed. He returned, smiling, excused himself—and sat even further down the couch.

"Oh, no, John—it looks like the champs took a real firm knock on that last one. These newcomers to the major leagues might be inexperienced, but that does not diminish their ability to put the champs in serious trouble."

The game was well-played, and both the Pro and the Rookie cheered and slapped the couch, raising little clouds of dust, which miraculously didn't make the Rookie's nose even twitch. In the heat of a thundering play, they booth stood, their basso roars thundering in the room, and came together quickly in a very tight hug, slapping each other on the back.

There was a pause, maybe half a heartbeat, as they held each other. The Rookie looked nervous—and the Pro? The Pro just smiled.

"What's this, Howard? If I didn't know better I'd say that the champs are intentionally loosing yardage—but that can't be right. In all my years covering the game, I've never

seen anything like it. Either they're going to prove for us today what makes them great or we're seeing the last act of a once-great team."

Gallantly, the Pro gestured the Rookie back to his seat and then sat down next to him: not too close, but not that far away either. After a few moments, the game again drew their attentions in, and their cheers and laughter again filled the room.

As he laughed, and cheered, and roared, and clapped, the Pro also absently scratched his strong thigh, lifting his shorts just a bit to show the geometry of his muscles, the depth of his tight skin.

The Rookie, his head turned toward the game, still managed to carefully watch him out of the corner of his eye.

"I believe the young Turks don't know what to make of this new development, John. This could very well prove their ultimate undoing, their strength and speed falling to the inexperience of the champs."

The scratch turned into a rub. With palm flat, the Pro stroked the tight, hard muscles of his thigh, moving from the side to the top. As he rubbed—as if to alleviate a cramp—his arms and shoulders flexed and shifted, giving the Rookie a show of skin and muscle.

Back and forth he rubbed, working tight muscle against tight muscle, making his nearly naked body shine even more, filling the suddenly very small room with the sharp smell of man. Stopping, the Pro gave a sudden stretch, pulling his long body out all the way, turning his well-sculpted chest into a masterpiece of male anatomy.

The Rookie, no longer even feigning interest in the game on the screen, watched, slow blinks his only movement for a very long time.

THE PASS

"I'll tell you, Howard, this is what makes the game great. A few minutes ago I would have bet the farm on these young kids—but I'll give it to the champs: Their performance here has a real chance of proving why they are all-American."

Seeing the Rookie watching, the Pro laughed and playfully slapped him on the shoulder. Gesturing toward the kitchen and getting a slow, almost hypnotized nod in return, the Pro slowly, carefully got up, taking his time, as if he was using each corded muscle in his thighs and calves to accomplish it. After vanishing for a moment, he returned with two freshly opened beers, both topped with rising mounds of foam.

As if in courtesy for his guest, the Pro carefully put his lips to one can and slowly sucked down the foam, and then offered it to the Rookie—

—who looked at it, looked at the Pro, smiled, and took a big, hefty swallow.

At this, the Rookie roared again, and again slapped him on the shoulder. But this time his hand stayed there, gently massaging the Rookie as his laughter mixed with the younger man's.

"This is what truly makes this a magnificent game, John: the grace, the artistry. Surely this is not a sport but a performance of humanity's struggle against itself and overwhelming odds."

Sitting together now quite closely, they continued to watch and cheer the game. Somehow—some clever sleight of hand, wrist, and arm—the Pro managed to get his arm around the Rookie's shoulder. Somehow—some clever use of laughter, safety, and desire—the Pro managed to get his hand on the Rookie's thigh.

FULL BODY CONTACT

Watching, yelling, cheering—all the while the Pro's hand gently, ever so gently massaged the Rookie's thigh. But then, as if suddenly realizing he was under the water and air was in doubt, the Rookie shifted slightly away.

"Fumble! What a disappointing break for the champs, Howard—and they were so close to running rings around these newcomers. Still, the night's young and so are those other players—who knows how long they can keep ahead of the champs, or if the champs have even more tricks in store for them."

The room became fragile with tension, as if any move would shatter the air. The Rookie looked at the Pro, his young face a mixture of confusion, suspicion, lust, and, well, a lot of lust, but also suspicion and confusion. The Pro looked at the Rookie, his older face geologically sliding from eye-twinkling charisma to fuming excitement to simple joy.

Against that, the Rookie could only do one thing: smile.

"This could very well be the final conclusion for these tired old champions, John. This could very well be their last moment to turn a possibly humiliating defeat into a chance at regaining their status as masters of the game."

With an exaggerated leap, the Pro was on him, wrestling and tickling the Rookie till his voice shifted several octaves and his laughter became more like a scream.

Together, arms and legs alternatively locking then flailing, they tumbled off the sofa, landing heavily on the floor, their laughter never diminishing. Finally, the coffee table having been pushed aside—a beer can toppling and a slow, fizzing Rorschach spreading across its surface—they slowed, then stopped. Chests heaving like they'd just run the mile, they remained entwined: his leg over his arm, his arm over his leg.

THE PASS

Slowly, their breath returned. First the Pro's, then the Rookie's. For a moment the room was quiet, then the Pro shifted his body "just so" and gave the Rookie a good, hard, long, deep kiss.

"What an upset, Howard! Just look at the expression on their faces. Boy, I'll bet those young guys never saw that coming—took them completely by surprise: a wonderful lateral pass, end run. Just beautiful!"

The Rookie seemed, at points, to want to break the kiss, but his body, trapped by the other man or trapped by something deep within himself, didn't move. As they kissed, the Pro lifted his big hands and gently caressed the Rookie's forearms, shoulders, neck, and the sides of his head.

When the kiss finally ended, the Pro dropped his head down to the Rookie's shoulder and kissed the firm muscles through the younger man's green turtleneck, then started to chew, slowly working his strong jaws into the tense skin. The Rookie, arms playing over the older man's back, moaned deep and long.

"An absolutely magnificent moment in the history of the game, John. A turning point, if you will, where the age and experience of the champions may very well prove to be too much for the youth and passion of these up-and-coming players."

Then the Pro's hands were down around his waist, then the Pro had twin hands full of green turtleneck, and then the Rookie was naked from the waist up. The younger man tensed, anticipating the same firm force that had been applied through the shirt now on his bare skin, but the Pro surprised him, melted him, by starting with a slow parade of gentle kisses, building moment by moment, nibble by nibble, chew by chew, until the Rookie was in his tight embrace, his face lost in pleasure.

FULL BODY CONTACT

One of the Pro's hands, though, dropped down, toward his crotch.

"Look at that bastard go! He's at the 40, the 30, the 20—no one can stop him!"

Down between the Rookie's legs, the Pro's big, firm hand found the ridge of his very hard cock. Gripping it tightly, he started to work it through his jeans, rubbing its oh-so-stiffness with the firm material. Caught in the Pro's free arm, the Rookie moaned deep and low, his hands dancing all over the Pro's body, stopping here or there to grip hard or to suddenly caress gently.

Arching his back, the only sound the Rookie made when the Pro neatly reached his fly and methodically crawled it down was a low growl of earthy permission.

"I believe this could very well be the turning point in what up to now has been a case of the power of youth versus skill earned through years of diligent practice. Only time will tell—"

Skilled, the Pro only needed a few simple moves to separate the boy from the man's jeans. Naked, the Rookie was glowing with sweat, his cock bobbing almost with his pitter-pattering heartbeat, the tip glowing with a bead of sweet precome.

"Touchdown! My god, what a play—there was no stopping that damned steamroller. He wanted that goal and went after it like a heat-seeking missile. Defense didn't even have a chance. Wonderfully played, John—one of the best plays I've ever seen in my years in the booth. Just wonderful—"

Giving the Rookie a wicked glance, the Pro bent down and neatly swallowed the length of his cock. The Rookie almost screamed—not out of fright, but for his unearthly precision: no teeth, barely the tight ring of lips. For the

THE PASS

Rookie it was as if a wet, hot, firm tunnel had impaled itself on his cock. It was a performance worthy of applause—which he wasn't capable of—or awe, which the Rookie did express as a long, deep, primordial moan.

With his mouth, the Pro could count the Rookie's heartbeat, the cock in his mouth beating out a fast rhythm in synch with it. As he sucked—lips and tongue in perfect harmony and licked, painting the Rookie's cock with hot saliva, he also fondled, digging his big hands down to his balls, which he gently squeezed, firmly pulled, and even twisted.

"A remarkable upset in this contest of gridiron titans, John. The Turks may have had vigor and vitality in their challenge to this great throne of football, but the champions have proved that their skill as players of this noble game sets them far and above any other players."

Up and down, using his powerful mouth and strong yet soft lips, the Pro worked the Rookie's cock, with each stroke, each suck, tugging the come out of him. Down in the tangle of hair, his hand also pulled and twisted at his dark balls, even occasionally squeezing them together as if to see which out would break first.

The Rookie, back arched, hands pulling then pushing then pulling again at the Pro's back and hair, felt his whole body suddenly develop a heavy quake, one separate from the spasms that rocked back and forth through him. The quake grew in intensity until his whole body was moving with it, the quake of his coming.

"There's the gun! What a wonderfully played first half—the champs once again proving why they're masters of this game. The Turks are going to need a miracle if they hope to come back from being pounded into the ground like that."

The Pro swallowed and swallowed and swallowed some

more, but still come oozed out from around his lips, pattering down onto the Rookie's stomach, crawling down his thighs. Panting like a racehorse, the Rookie could do nothing but breathe, his body and will having been shot out of his cock, completely emptied.

He was so exhausted, so lofty from having been blasted high in the air by his shattering come, he didn't feel the Pro's hands gently rolling him over onto his belly.

"Yes, John, another truly magnificent example of the skills of these magnificent athletes at the peak of their form. Watching them perform today has been a true honor and, yes, even a privilege."

The Rookie felt the weight, the hands parting his cheeks, and the firm pressure of something—his blown mind literally not being able to connect at first what it could be—pressing against his asshole. When he did regain enough consciousness to understand, it was too late to do anything about it.

The Pro's cock pushed hard into the younger man's asshole—a steady, patient push that was rewarded by a sudden slide deep inside. Biting his lip, the Pro grunted three times, then slowly, carefully, began his strokes.

"There is just no stopping the champs today, Howard. They're not going to stop until they've given it to these younger players every way they can."

The Rookie grunted, the Pro fucked, one action immediately following the other, but it wasn't clear which caused which—the grunt that made the Pro smile and push harder, the pounding dick in his ass that make the Rookie grunt. On the living room floor they chased each other's tails, grunting and fucking, grunting and fucking, in an almost endless circle.

THE PASS

But with each spin, the distance between grunt and fuck grew shorter and shorter, and harder and harder, and louder and louder. Finally they met in the middle, a powerful, butt-slapping impact, a cock burrowing deep into the steaming hot recesses of a tight young asshole meeting a deep, guttural moan.

Strings cut, the Pro sagged, then collapsed onto a similarly panting, heaving Rookie.

"*I think we can all agree that this has been a battle of titans on the gridiron battlefield, a test of strong men with even stronger wills, and even though, John, there are some among us who would claim that the winning of the game is the only goal, I would have to disagree with them after seeing this contest of giants here today. This sport may be called football, but the contest is as eternal as the sun, and the only real loss in these contests of great men would be the day when the game stops being played.*"

Together they lay. Together they snored—the Rookie loud, the Pro soft. Smiles on both their faces.

FULL BODY CONTACT

Pinch Hitter
Dale Chase

Randy grew up in baseball and played all through high school and college; while he never made the big leagues, he made many a teammate along the way. Which left him with a lifelong love of the game—and its players.

He and I go to a lot of games. He's a San Francisco Giants fan, reads the daily stats, and has a crush on the catcher though he won't admit it. I don't mind because that hunk squatting behind the plate makes even me take note.

Randy watches games on TV and yelps and carries on when great plays are made but he also gets enthusiastic when things turn subtle, when the gracefulness of the game—"the dance," he calls it—begins. It's then that he gets hard. It's then that I get his pants off and suck his cock.

It's kind of an off-the-wall feeling to have a broadcaster calling a game while you're blowing your partner. The announcer's voice rises and falls, he gets excited over strikes and balls, and I chuckle when I hear this and happen to have one of Randy's fat nuts in my mouth.

He looks past me to the television as I push his legs apart

and get down between them. I'm playing with his cock, have it all stiff and wet, then slide down to his dark little pucker, push in a finger. He lets out a yell and I know it's because he likes getting something up there while watching his guys do their thing on the diamond.

So I get him squirming, get a couple fingers into him, and pretty soon he's got his hand on his dick, pulling frantically while some guy runs the bases. And when Randy comes I hear applause and he lets out a strained series of *yes*es which I know are a combined response to both kinds of action.

I don't care about the goddamn game, I just want to fuck him. The good part is this distracted mode of his is a turn-on. It makes me want to spear him again and again, to get my dick so far up him he'll choke. He knows this, of course, so he makes me work at it, keeping his eyes on the game as I get him over onto his stomach, get his ass up where I can get to it. And as I shove into his spongy chute, I know our little game makes the one he's watching even better.

The inning ends as I ram my cock into him. A beer commercial begins and Randy breaks his concentration, murmurs a "fuck me" as I get moving, rocking deep into him in a smooth, rhythmic stroke. His pucker gobbles my cock and while he's tuned to me instead of the game, he squeezes his muscle, sucking dick like he's starving. But then a new inning starts and he turns his head toward the TV, gone again.

I learned early on not to resent this intrusion but to use it. "Look at that ass," I'll say as the catcher squats behind home plate. "I can almost feel my dick up there," and I pound a little harder for emphasis. "Can't you just see him in the shower later on, huh? Big dick all soapy. You'd like to sit on it, wouldn't you, ride it until it shoots a load up

FULL BODY CONTACT

you. Big piece of meat screwing you like this." I grind his ass and hear applause. Randy hoots because his team has scored or something.

I ride him for most of an inning and he takes it like he'll never get enough. His own cock is hard but idle. Time later for that. For now he's getting pumped and when I'm ready to shoot I borrow the vernacular. "Grand slam," I say, or "Major league," or "Launching one." Things I've heard the broadcasters say. Randy likes it, and I pound him, unleashing a torrent because he has the sweetest ass that ever shed a uniform.

I try to come between innings because then he's mine for those few minutes. Then I pull out, toss the rubber, and kiss him; get him onto his back, legs spread, dick up. I'll handle him until the first batter steps in, and when play resumes, so does ours. I suck his cock into my mouth and lick and pull. He's off into his world, I'm off into mine.

His cock is big and thick, the best mouthful I've ever had. I think about all the mouths that have tasted it, all the asses who've received it, and wonder how many went on to the major leagues. He won't say who exactly but I always suspect we're watching somebody he knows quite well.

So the Giants get into the divisional playoffs and things get intense, Randy going on about how we can take the Cardinals. As I listen I think not about victory on the field but about really taking the Cards, a shower scene, all that bare ass and dick. So the playoffs become our thing, a last wild fling before the season ends and, spare me, football begins. Thank God Randy hates that game. If he didn't, we wouldn't be together.

It becomes a ritual, hurrying home from work to catch the 5 P.M. games. I insist Randy wear only a jockstrap. He

PINCH HITTER

obliges in his distracted way, as if this is standard uniform for watching a playoff game. Me, I'm naked.

Snacks, drinks, and supplies are set out. He does everything, rushing around all excited, telling me what a match it is. I listen, nod, but instead of anticipating the game, I picture the two teams in a jerk-off competition, rows of hard bodies and stiff dicks, cheers going up as come shoots down the line.

Randy is right about the teams being well matched. The game is awesome, home runs, wild-ass steals, diving plays, and a hit batsman that starts a melee. Who says baseball's not a contact sport? During all this I fuck Randy twice and blow him once. He's hard for about half the game, he's so into it, and when catcher-baby slams a three-run homer, Randy grabs his dick and holds on. I watch him watch his hero, then I lower my head to his lap, get him into my mouth and suck for all I'm worth. I know he's probably telling himself it's the catcher doing him, but I don't care. It's *my* tongue working while I get a finger up his well-used ass. Catcher-man won't do this, I want to say, but I know he gets the idea.

Divisional playoffs are best three out of five and I hope like hell they'll need all five. I root for our team, but when they lose the second game I'm secretly happy. Make it last.

Randy is frantic as that second game turns toward the opposition, and when his hero strikes out at a critical moment he is crushed. His limp dick lolls on his thigh and I take hold, offer a consoling squeeze. He murmurs his approval and when I get him into my mouth, he starts thrusting. I let him fuck my face and he yells as he unloads. He's pissed off; his climax is huge.

He's still out of breath when the Cards get up to bat and

start scoring big. I roll him over across my lap, work a finger into him as he watches the runs multiply. When the third baseman makes a costly error, Randy swears and I know what he needs. I suit up, get in behind him, and fuck him while the Cards turn the game into a rout. As runs stack up, Randy stops watching. He grabs his dick and starts jerking frantically while I pump his ass. Baseball is suddenly the lesser entertainment. As my come goes up Randy's chute, I think of it as a consolation fuck, soothing my poor baby the best way I know.

Tied one game each, there's a respite as the team travels from the visitor's park to its own. It's a day of respite for us as well. Randy works late, I visit friends, and when we reconnect late that night, it's only to fall into bed, to sleep. Like athletes, we save it for the game.

With the home field advantage for game three, the Giants roar back with an early lead, then waste it and end up trying to hold on. Extra innings means the game is almost four hours long. By the time we win, the room reeks of come, Randy's ass is pink, and his pucker's cherry red. When I pull out the final time, it gapes and the sight makes me want to go back in. I run my finger over it, prod enough to get a moan out of him, then a chuckle. We're both so very done, but I can't resist. I get my face down there, start to lick. I'm blissfully tired and wish I could fall asleep like this, down where I live. As it is, we turn off the TV, stagger to bed, and totally crash.

Next day Randy is totally psyched. Up two games to one, this could be it. The Giants could clinch the division. He gets home early, is sitting cross-legged in his jockstrap watching pregame, everything we need carefully laid out on the coffee table—food, drink, lube, condoms. "Pitching

PINCH HITTER

change," he tells me when I settle beside him, naked. "Really?" I ask. "Why?"

He explains how the scheduled pitcher's hamstring has seized up and as he goes on about the consequences, I slide a hand down to his crotch. He unfolds his legs, stretches out, but does not stop talking or looking at the TV. I feel his soft prick, balls full of come, and then the game begins and he sits up straight, leans forward. My hand stays put and as the first batter strikes out, I work a finger under the jockstrap, play around his cockhead, poke his piss slit. He's getting hard now and I know it's as much the game as me. I glance at the screen, think about shoving my cock up the catcher's ass, and next thing I know I've tossed the jockstrap and am sucking dick. Fuck baseball.

The unscheduled pitcher becomes a hero as he strikes out batter after batter. As the K's mount, Randy gets more and more excited. I spend half the game with his cock in my mouth. Every time he unloads another wad I come up for air, and just about then another batter bites the dust and Randy gets frantic again. So I go back down for yet another ballpark doggie.

I don't fuck him until the fourth inning, which is some kind of record, but when I do it's awesome. The taste of come lingers in my mouth and makes me anticipate what I'm gonna do. He shrieks as I suit up—another strikeout— and then I roll him over, shove my cock up him. He groans as he takes it and keeps on groaning in that pleasure-ache kind of way. He's so vocal I'm almost convinced it's about the sex but when the Giants get up to bat and his hero hits a grand slam, the moan is the same. Still I ride him, ride that edge, ready to let go a gusher. The timing turns out perfectly—commercial break and then the rise. An SUV

FULL BODY CONTACT

roars across the screen as I unleash my load and Randy bucks up into me, eager now, everything pure fuck. I pound him until I'm dry, then slump across him, but the game has returned and my soft dick slides out as the pitcher claims yet another victim.

Randy chatters during the game but doesn't need any reply. It's not conversation, it's observation, pure excitement. He sees all kinds of stuff I don't and rattles on and on. Most of the time, my mouth is full of dick, his words running past.

So it's a no-hitter into the ninth inning and Randy's so agitated I can't get my mouth on him. I move down between his legs and work a couple fingers into him and that's where I am when the Cards knock out a single. Randy lets out a cry, swears, never mind that our team can still win. I take advantage of the respite, push his legs back and get my face down to his pucker. He's eager now, squirms in readiness. I feed while he works his dick and seconds after we win the division he comes for about the sixth time. When I surface I find him yelping with glee, victory gobs all up his stomach. "We did it!" he cries.

"We sure as hell did."

Lying in bed later on, I start calculating. As Randy lightly snores, I savor what lies ahead: league championship—best four out of seven—then the World Series—again four of seven. That's a possible 14 games, the best of the best squared off against one another. I think about Randy and me and our own brand of squaring off. Play ball.

PINCH HITTER

The Punishment
Darrell Grizzle

I'm not sure who started the fight, or even what the fight was about. But I was mad as hell, and so was Brad, and in a flash we were locked together in a brawl, there in the locker room at the college gym, both of us naked and still wet from the showers. My fist slammed into his rock-hard abs as his uppercut nailed me in the chest. He thrust his huge arms around me in a bear hold and wrestled me to the ground, our 21-year-old bodies rippling with the muscles that had made us both stars at college powerlifting meets. He had me pinned on the dirty locker room floor and was delivering blow after blow to my ribs, almost knocking the wind out of me. But my rage—along with the fact that everyone else in the locker room was watching and cheering us on—made my adrenaline surge and I began to beat him brutally on the back and sides with both fists. Part of me was aware that with him on top of me, our cocks were grinding together. I could feel a surge of excitement in my balls, which infuriated me. *No, this can't happen here, I can't let my cock get hard!* Brad must have felt it too,

FULL BODY CONTACT

because he suddenly got even angrier. He stopped punching my torso and started trying to hit me in the face, but I had just enough room to maneuver my forearms up to deflect the blows. He then returned to battering the side of my torso, focusing blow after blow on just one spot, just below the ribs on my left side, with such speed and force that I almost passed out. I got in two or three forceful blows to the side of Brad's chest before Coach Green walked into the locker room and dragged us apart.

"OK! Show's over!" he yelled to the other guys in the locker room as Brad and I, breathing heavily from exhaustion, struggled to our feet. Coach Green looked at both of us angrily and said, "You two! My office! Now!"

Brad and I both headed for our lockers to grab a towel, some shorts, anything—we were both naked and covered in sweat, and now our cocks were halfway hard. "*Now!*" Coach repeated. He grabbed each of us by the arm and led us forcefully into his office, with all the other guys on the team watching and laughing.

Thankfully, the back door to his office led into the locker room, so we weren't dragged out into the hallway naked. He slammed the door behind him and looked at us like we had both lost our minds. Brad started to say something but Coach put up his hand. "I don't wanna hear it," he said, "from either of you. I oughta throw you both off the team!"

We both knew that wasn't going to happen, not with the regional powerlifting meet coming up in less than a week. I started to say something, to apologize, but Coach halted me with his hand again: "Shut up!" I thought he was going to start hitting me himself.

As he stood there fuming, I started to shiver a little. Coach's windowless office was air-conditioned. I looked over at Brad and saw that the cold air had made his nipples hard as diamonds. His cock, though, was still half-erect and seemed to be getting larger as he looked at me, the anger still blazing in his eyes. I realized with horror that my own dick was fully hard and pointing straight at Brad.

Coach Green noticed it too. His voice softened a little as he said, "It's pretty damn obvious what's going on here. But you two are too scared to do anything about it." We both started to object—*I ain't no homo!*—but Coach wouldn't let us. "Deny it all you want, but the body doesn't lie. And don't think I haven't noticed the way you two look at each other, the way you always spot each other on the bench-press so you can get a good look at each others' baskets."

That was true. It always just "happened" that Brad was my spotter. Having him spot me as I bench-pressed was the closest I had gotten to that massive bulge between his legs. And I loved the way he put his hands on both sides of my torso sometimes when I did squats—"to make sure we keep proper form," he said. Yeah, right. And I always returned the favor, thankful for the excuse to feel his muscles ripple as he lowered and lifted the weight. Many times I had longed to hold my hands there even longer, to wrap my hands around the front of his chest, to caress the nipples on his heaving chest.

"Listen," Coach said, "I've lived most of my life afraid of what others might think. I gave up a good shot at a body-building career when I was your age because my old man said it was all just vanity. If you two have feelings for each other," he said, looking at Brad's cock, which was now just as hard as mine, "and if you want to act on those feelings, then don't let your fear of what others might think get in the way."

FULL BODY CONTACT

He went around to his desk and started looking through some drawers as he continued talking. "I'm not gonna kick you off the team. But I do have to punish you, or at least make the rest of the team think I am. So here's your punishment: I'm going to leave now, and I'm going to lock you two in my office so you can work things out." He finally found what he was looking for: a box of condoms, which he tossed onto the desk. "The door dead-bolts, and I can lock it from the outside. There's no way out, and no way for anyone without a key to get in. I'll tell the rest of the team that you're having to alphabetize my files."

"Can't we get our clothes? It's fuckin' cold in here!" said Brad.

Coach shook his head. "No. And it's going to get even colder. I'm turning the AC down to 55. You'll have to figure out a way to keep each other warm." There was a gleam in his eye as he opened the door. "I'll be back in two hours," he said. We could hear the door lock from the outside.

Brad and I looked at each other. Our faces were both red with embarrassment at the way Coach Green had been talking so plainly about something we both were afraid to admit. I didn't know what to say. Brad looked down at the floor, his cock still pointing right at me. I turned away from him, tried to think of something—*anything*—else, but my cock remained hard and it was throbbing, almost painfully.

I looked at the red mark Brad's fist had made on my chest, right on the rounded mound of muscle of my left pec. The soft nipple and the hard muscle beneath it were bruised. So was my left side, where Brad had beaten me repeatedly with his fist. I put my hand on my side and breathed deeply. This was really going to be sore in the morning.

THE PUNISHMENT

"Hey," I heard Brad say behind me. "You OK?"

"Yeah," I said, still looking away. I didn't want to look him in the eye.

"Looks like we both beat the shit out of each other. Look at the number you did on my abs."

I turned around and saw where his washboard stomach was red. So were both sides of his torso. I couldn't help but laugh. "I wonder who would have won," I said.

"We might have both ended up in the hospital," he said, smiling. His eyes lit up as he smiled. *God, he's so beautiful,* I thought.

He kept looking at me, and I couldn't bring myself to look away. We had known each other for three years now, since our freshman year in college, but we had never had a real conversation before. The animal magnetism between us had been too strong, too frightening to both of us. Now, with both our cocks raging and nowhere to go for two hours, we had to do something about it or—

Or what? Explode? God, it felt like my cock was about to explode any second. I started to stammer something but didn't know what to say. I couldn't feel anything at all but desire for this magnificent young man. My cock was still throbbing, but now my nipples were too. My whole body was throbbing. I longed to reach out and touch him but I felt like I was paralyzed. I couldn't move.

"Here," he said, moving toward me. "I really messed up your chest, didn't I?" He put his hands on both sides of my torso and bent down just a little, just enough to put his lips on my left pec, gently kissing the bruise around my nipple. When his lips touched my chest I felt like a bolt of electricity coursed through my body. I put my arms around his shoulders, relishing the feel of our hard muscular bodies

FULL BODY CONTACT

together. He circled round my nipple with his tongue, licked the nipple, then softly bit into it and started sucking.

I never knew till that moment that my cock is directly linked to my nipples. The manic throbbing in my dick got even more frantic, and I swear my cock got even longer. I tossed back my head, trying to remember to breathe as my body felt waves of pleasure it had never experienced before.

He let go of my nipple, tugging it out a little with his teeth before releasing it. We looked each other in the eye for a split second before our lips joined together in a kiss.

We had both been waiting so long for this moment, and now we didn't want it to end. We kissed each other ravenously, our lips and tongues locked together with an overwhelming passion. Suddenly we were on the floor again, his powerful body on top of mine, our muscles rippling together, our stiff cocks grinding into each other. Our lips still hungrily tasting each other, I could feel his dick throbbing against mine. I was overwhelmed with sensations: his rock-hard muscles beneath my hands as they moved across his body; his powerful chest with its thick blond hair grinding into my tender nipples; his thick legs twisting against mine as we wrestled together on the floor; the weight of his balls as they pressed against mine....

At first I didn't realize Brad had pinned me again. His hands were clamped down on my forearms, holding them roughly against the floor as he raised his hips, then lowered his long hard dick between my legs, which were still clamped together. His cock plowed across my balls, all the way to the patch of hair behind them as he started thrusting, up and down, his dick playing my sweaty, throbbing balls like a bow across a violin. The tingling in my balls began to spread throughout my whole body as he fucked me between the legs. I was powerless. I couldn't move, and I didn't *want* to move, even as my balls grew numb from the force of the brutal beating they were taking from his cock.

Finally he let my arms go as he raised his dick out from between my legs and exploded with a jet of come all over my stomach and chest. His dick was still hard as he pressed it against mine, and I let loose with a gasp, covering his heaving chest with my come as he towered above me.

We were both still breathing heavily as he smiled that beautiful smile and said playfully: "I win."

"No," I said, forcefully pulling him down to the floor with me, our chests and ab muscles sticking together as we locked into a sweaty embrace. "We *both* win."

The following week we both took home trophies from the powerlifting meet. All I had to do before each lift was look over at Brad, and I could feel my testosterone levels surge as I lifted weights I'd never achieved before.

The Glorious Fourth
Simon Sheppard

Well, sir, Independence Day rolls around, the mines are shut down for the day, and damn near every man in Bodie is drunk as a hillbilly at a rooster fight, not to mention Father Kowalski. And the talk of the whole damn inebriated town is the arm-wrestling contest to be held that night at the Bella Union Gambling Hall.

Now, men have ridden in from miles around for July Fourth in Bodie, amongst them a great grizzly of a man, Josiah Britt by name, who rumor has it has killed more than one man barehanded by simply snapping the poor feller's spine. Well over 6½ feet tall, Britt has been strutting around shirtless all day, the sweat on the matted black hair of his chest and belly asparkle in the warm light of Helios. And unsurprisingly, Hiram, already in his cups, has been seen lurking around the big man, hands in his pockets stroking on a hard-on that's lasted for nigh on the whole afternoon.

"I figure I can beat any man around," says Britt, cocky as the king of spades. And in demonstration he holds up his right arm and makes a giant muscle, all impressive as fuck, though the smell from his sweat-soaked armpit damn near knocks the bunch of us flat.

"I would be most willing to wager," says pale, handsome Lars, the Standard Mine owner's son, "a substantial sum on your doing just that." Lars usually ain't much of a gambling man, but face-to-face with Britt he's got a twinkle in his eye, which gets a mite stronger as his gaze slides south of Britt's belt.

The Bella Union has dug a big barbecue pit out in front, where for a silver dollar a man can eat and drink until he's ready to puke, and many a man has been doing that very thing. The hot sun sets and big blasts of dynamite are set off in the hills above town, Bodie's own version of patriotic fireworks. The noise gets me to being a tad thoughtful, remembering back to the cave-in in the spring that took the life of Texas Joe. But the melancholy passes fast, it being unwise to dwell upon the Big Jump. For we miners all, each and every man of us, know that what puts grub on our table is risky as walking in quicksand over Hell, and what happened to Joe could have happened to me, and no hallelujah to that.

I'm painting my tonsils with another drink when Sy Tolliver, the proprietor of the joint, steps to the front door and announces, in a booming voice to be heard above the sound of drunken arguments, "Gentlemen, the arm-wrassling contest is about to commence."

Over in the alley between the Bella Union and Van Dine's Barber Shop, Hiram looks up from where he's been sucking on the swelled-up penis of Big Owen, the town blacksmith, and when he sees Josiah Britt heading into the Bella Union, without a word he gets up off his knees and follows him, leaving Big Owen standing there leaning up against the wall, his long, wet prong now unattended to. I,

FULL BODY CONTACT

unwilling to let a pretty thing like that go to waste, walk on over and slide Owen's prodigious foreskin back and forth, frigging him faster and faster until Owen's knees sort of buckle and, with a low-pitched moan, he spends his jism in big, wild spurts. Some of his spunk lands, to my dismay, on my dungarees, which, on account of it being a holiday, are my best pair, and recently laundered at the Wo Fat Laundry to boot. I rub some of the muck off with the palm of my hand, and Owen grasps my wrist and, pulling my hand to his mouth, licks his own seed down; when he lets me pull my hand away, his bushy beard is smeared with it.

The Bella Union is packed to the rafters with odoriferous, drunken men. Sy Tolliver is standing before a chalkboard on which he's written the names of the contestants, all 16 of them. The combatants themselves are in the center of the room, seated two to a table, mostly stripped down to their waists, it being one hell of a hot night. And while Josiah Britt's barrel chest is maybe the most impressive of the lot, many another fellow has a muscular, well-formed body that holds the promise of a hard-fought contest ahead.

All the men are present; that is, excepting Big Owen, who I reckon is still recovering from the pump-draining I've just provided him. "Gentlemen," says Tolliver, "we shall get started now. And it looks as though there's already a forfeit on the part of..." and he looks at the chalkboard, back at the men, back at the board, and calls out Big Owen's name.

"Not so fast!" comes a shout from the doorway. It's Owen, his swagger a trifle undone by the fact he's plumb forgotten to button up his pants.

"Owen," says Tolliver, "it's about fucking time, and that's a fact. You're over there, across from Duncan McCutcheon," and Big Owen goes and sits.

THE GLORIOUS FOURTH

There's a judge standing at each table, for as the prize for the competition is $100 in gold, a certain amount of attempted dishonesty is only to be expected in a hellhole like Bodie.

Tolliver is explaining the rules when another voice is heard.

"Is it too late to join on in?"

We all look around to see who spoke. It's a stranger in town. He's as blond as our friend Lars, but whereas Lars is willowy and handsome, this fellow is quite the opposite: thickly built, with the neck of a mastiff and real big shoulders and chest. He's got the beginnings of a double chin, though he's only maybe 20 years old, and his blue eyes have a slightly crazy, determined glare. There is, truth to tell, something about him that draws my excited notice and makes my britches stir.

"Well, sir, it is indeed too late. These other men have signed up days ago for this competition," says Tolliver with a glare.

The big blond looks like he's disappointed enough to smash Sy Tolliver's head in.

"C'mon, Sy," I hear myself saying. "Allow the feller to enter the tournament." A few others say similar as well.

"All right," says Tolliver, "if none of you object, he's in, but as there's now an odd number of men, you—" and he looks straight at me "—can be this man's first match. What's your name, newcomer?"

"Will Shively," says the blond man, stripping off his shirt and heading in my direction. The approach of such a prepossessing man makes, quite naturally, my prong as stiff as a pine tree.

"Only one thing," says Tolliver, "we are short one judge

FULL BODY CONTACT

now, on account of there's an additional match-up." At
which Lars speaks up and volunteers to judge our match,
and though it's widely known that Lars and I are well-
acquainted (and indeed many a man knows that Hiram and
I have tied Lars up and plowed him on a schedule near regular as Wells Fargo's) such is the Norwegian's reputation
for rectitude that not one man objects.

Shively and I head over to the one empty table amidst
the throng of spectators, and as we do additional wagers
are being made by the miners, most all of them, I reckon,
backing the big blond.

At the touch of Will Shively's strong, calloused hand, I'm
near overcome by desire, and I know then damn-well certain that I shan't be winning the arm-wrestling crown. Still,
it was at my initiative that the new man was included in the
contest, and so I am well-resolved to do my utmost, or at
least nearly so.

Lars is standing beside our table, ready to adjudicate our
struggle. My muscles tense up, getting nearly as hard as my
member. And then Tolliver speaks out, all stentorian,
"Gentlemen, the first round of the Bodie Independence Day
Arm Wrestling Championships is about to commence." A
half-drunken hush sets over the room. "On your mark...get
set...wrassle!"

Well, this Will Shively isn't as strong as he looks. No sir,
he's *twice* as strong, and it takes every ounce of my will
power not to just let him have his powerful way and have
done with it. As the crowd cheers their favorites on, Shively
applies his considerable leverage against me. I look into his
eyes and they, steely blue, gaze implacably back. Then I
make my fatal error, that of allowing my eyes to trail downward. The sight of Will Shively's broad chest, nipples erect

THE GLORIOUS FOURTH

in a thicket of blond fur, sinews straining, sweat coursing down his bare flesh...Jesus Lord, it's quite disconcerting. For one fraction of a second, all I want is to be overpowered by this handsome man, and in that split second he senses my weakness and slams my arm to the rough tabletop.

"Winner over here," calls out Lars, even-voiced as can be, and that settles that. Only it's with some hesitation that Shively loosens his now-painful grasp on my hand, and the lingering of his strong touch upon me makes my defeat seem of no import whatsoever.

Whatever chagrin I might feel vanishes when I look around me and see that most all the other matches are likewise concluded. Big Owen has beaten McCutcheon, Britt has won his match-up, and only two of the contests are still ongoing. Scrappy Juan Hernandez is grunting with agony, his eyes a-pop with the strain of battling Bill Logue, and Easy Averill and liquored-up Penn Cobb are also still in battle, locked in a sweaty stand-off. But inch by inch, Hernandez pushes Logue's arm to the wood, and then Cobb defeats Averill, and it's the end of round one.

Hiram has come over and he says to me "Good try," but he's looking at Shively while he says it, and when he claps his hand on the victor's muscled shoulder I wonder if there's ever a time when Hiram isn't hankering to drop his drawers.

The late addition of Shively to the contest has left an odd number of men to be divvied up for the next round, nine to be exact, but Sy Tolliver's quandry is solved when the inebriated Cobb leans over and hurls his guts onto the floor. It might not be official grounds for disqualification, but Cobb mutters something and makes for the door as one of Tolliver's barbacks sluices the reeking mess away and then pours a pile of sawdust onto the wet floor.

FULL BODY CONTACT

"In Penn Cobb's honor," calls out Tolliver with a grin, "the next round of neck oil is on the house!" And every man cheers loudly.

The second round sees Britt pinning Frank O'Rourke in less than a minute flat. Hernandez wins his match-up, too, as does Big Owen, and Will Shively damn near busts poor Abel Asch's arm.

Meanwhile, Lars, no longer needed to referee, comes up to me and asks, "Who do you make for the winner?"

"I would have said Britt till this Shively showed up," I reply, "but now I ain't so sure."

"Me neither," says my bosom friend Lars, "and it has me a bit worried, for I've laid a considerable wager on the fortunes of Josiah Britt."

"Lars!" say I, surprised. "I never knew you to be a gambling man!"

"That's usually the case," says he, "but oh, hell, it's the Fourth of July."

The four remaining contestants, Britt against Hernandez and Big Owen paired up with Shively, make ready for their battles.

There's much to be said for the matching up of man against man, testing muscles and mettles one against the other, and not the least of them is the smell that arises from the brutes. As I stand near the two tables that hold the remaining combatants, each and all of them stripped to the waist now and covered with the sheen of sweat, I can discern the animal reek that rises from their bodies, and if my interest had ever flagged this odor serves as a tonic.

At Tolliver's say-so the matches begin.

As Britt bears down on Hernandez, it's clear the two are mismatched. Though the Mexican's arm bulges with muscle, Britt's bicep is twice as big, and from the first the advantage is his.

"Sweet Jesus fuck Mary fuck Mother of God!" curses Hernandez, and then lapses into something Spanish that is no doubt at least as obscene. Hernandez does his best to arrest his arm on its downward path, but it's plum obvious that Josiah Britt has got the upper hand. Britt bares his teeth as he gets Hernandez's hand just inches from the table, and though Hernandez stalls it there for a bit the effort takes a terrible toll, and with one final loud "Fuck!" the Mexican lets his hand touch wood.

Meanwhile, Lars is touching wood, as well, after a fashion, for his hand is now down the front of my pants, and if anyone anywhere in Bodie might ever have objections, the drunken night of Independence Day is nowhere near the time. The delicate fingers of the mining engineer, well-schooled in the moves that please me and Hiram, is working my prong into a lather, wherefore my crotch is damn near sopping wet.

Meantime, Owen and Britt have been struggling mightily. Hand to calloused hand, their hairy forearms bulging with tension, they seem evenly matched, first one gaining advantage then the other. But then Britt gets a real funny look on his face and steadily forces the blacksmith's hand further and further down till Owen's arm is pinned, and a cheer goes up from the onlooking crowd.

I look over in the corner, and there's Juan Hernandez, salving his defeat; he's opened his fly and is stroking on his big brown dick, pulling the long foreskin back and forth over his swelling penis-head. And danged if Penn Cobb doesn't weave back into the Bella Union and head over to Juan. They stand there glaring at each other for one long minute, and I figure they're maybe going to fight. But then Cobb reaches out for the Mexican's organ and starts to frig it. Hernandez relaxes and grins and leans against the wall, and Penn Cobb drops to his knees and with alacrity takes the other fellow's stiff penis into his mouth.

It's down to the final contest now, and Will Shively and Josiah Britt, their naked torsos streaked with sweat, are seated across from each other, ready to tangle it up. Wagered money's been changing hands throughout, and it's fair to say a quite sizable amount of cash is riding on the result.

"And now, ladies and gentlemen..." Tolliver looks around and starts again. "And now commences, gentlemen, the final round of the Bella Union's first Independence Day Arm Wrestling Championship. Will Shively here will test his mettle against Josiah Britt, and may the best man win. On your marks, get set..."

Just then the bar room air is rent by a piercing "Yahoo!" from Juan Hernandez, who's loudly shooting his seed down Penn Cobb's throat. And though Tolliver has yet to officially start the match, Britt jumps the gun and is straining away, forcing Shively's arm, inch by laborious inch, down toward defeat.

Tolliver tries to sputter out his instructions, but the match has started without his say-so, and he realizes it's too late to do any different. Meanwhile, big blond Will Shively is refusing to let his opponent gain more ground, and their linked arms are stalled midair in an even-matched show of strength.

"Jesus," says my bosom pal Cal Callahan, who's slipped into the Bella Union without me noticing, "I hope to holy hell that this new fellow doesn't win, for at Lars's urging

I've laid a sizable sum on Josiah Britt's victory."

Now this concerns me, for Lars comes from money and can always be bailed out of a jam by his wealthy father, but Cal has worked hard for his poke of gold and doesn't have any to spare. Meanwhile, Shively is gaining the upper hand, having muscled his opponent's arm partway down to the table's surface, and Shively's handsome face is all screwed up from the strain. Just watching the struggle has made my penis good and hard, and I'm not the only one, it seems, for here and there throughout the Bella Union are half-dressed miners pawing at one another. Indeed, tipsy Penn Cobb, having drunk deep of Hernandez's sperm, is now sprawled face down across one of the tables, trousers around his ankles, his fundament spread wide, his hungry hole exposed and up for grabs. Noticing this, Easy Averill lumbers over, his short, fat prong poking out of his fly, and dang if he doesn't spit on Cobb's butt and commence to plugging him right there in the midst of the tumult.

"Fuck! The newcomer's winning, and there goes the two months' wages I gave to Lars to bet!" Cal is sounding frantic now.

Indeed, Will Shively's concentration is nothing short of amazing, his blue eyes drilling into Britt, and it would seem that nothing short of a major distraction could divert him from certain victory.

At which point I get an idea.

Now it's true that the judge of this contest is the sheriff, but I've done him a favor or two in my time, and he's liquored up to boot, so I figure he won't stop me. I elbow my way through the crowd, over to the table where the two men are locked in combat. Then I drop to my knees and scoot under the table, positioning myself between Shively's massive, sturdy legs. I unbutton the fly of his pants and reach inside, pulling out his soft root. Opening wide, I take the thing into my mouth, inhaling the high smell of his crotch, tonguing his foreskin, and hoping like hell I can distract Shively sufficient for him to flinch.

Within a matter of moments, the prick has gone from soft to stiff, and I'm sucking away with thorough enthusiasm. I was afraid that Shively would try to kick me away, but he kind of grabs me between his muddy boots instead. So I take him all the way down my throat, till I'm almost gagging as Shively shoves himself into my hungry mouth. Though the shouts of the crowd have gone from a tumult to a full-on ruckus, above it I hear Cal Callahan bellow to me: "That's the ticket! SHIVELY'S GIVING WAY!"

So I suckle on the meaty piece some more, then slide myself back a bit and use a hand to stroke at it, squeezing Shively's copious precome from his big piss-slit. I quickly swallow him down again, wrapping my arms around his tree-trunk legs, and suck so hard I feel his calves tense up and start to quiver. My throat milks his cockhead most vigorously, at which point Will Shively can take it no longer. His whole body goes rigid, which bangs my head up against the table, and he shivers and shouts as he pumps load after load of sweet cream onto my tonsils. Which is when I hear the loud thwack of one man's arm pinning the other's—the sound of Shively's defeat I'm certain—and I feel a flush of pride at having helped my buddy Cal out of a jam and that's for sure.

It's not till I've gulped down the very last of Shively's jism that I perceive the roar of the crowd, which is full-out deafening now, a huge human cry of horny, jubilant men. I back off the now-deflating penis and, out of sheer

THE GLORIOUS FOURTH

politeness, stuff it back into Will Shively's pants.

I slide from beneath the table and rise to my feet. And it's then that I see what's happened, for the two men are still sitting there stock-still, a stunned kind of look on Josiah Britt's bearded face. His arm has been pinned to the table by his competitor, and beneath Will Shively's control it remains. It's just the opposite, fuck it all, of what I labored so mightily to achieve.

"Tarnation!" I say to Cal Callahan. "I'm sure dreadful sorry! What in blazes happened?"

"It was a nice try you gave it," says Cal mournfully, "and Britt nearly did have Will Shively pinned. But at the moment he spent his spunk, Shively of a sudden gets all rigid, his arm having a mind of its own, and he just plain pushes Britt's hand straight down to the tabletop."

By this time Britt and Shively have relaxed their death-grips and stood up from their table, and, as all the onlookers—winners and losers both—cheer, they wrap each other in a big manly hug, bare torso to naked, sweaty chest. Then Shively reaches down to Josiah's crotch, and he roars out, "Why the fuck should I be the one who's havin' all the fun?" And he unbuttons Britt's fly and adroitly pulls out the victor's swelling cock.

Which is when Lars comes up to us and says to Cal, "Well, I have a confession. I'm afraid that I just thoroughly forgot to wager that money you gave me. Comes to that, I suppose it all ended up for the best, as you otherwise would have lost it. And if you fellows would come to my hotel room tonight"—and here he smiles that most pretty grin of his—"I'll be most happy to return it to you then."

I have no way of knowing whether Lars is telling the actual fact. For though the handsome young man values the

FULL BODY CONTACT

truth, he values friendship more. And, if it comes to that, he knows full well that he shan't receive more diligent attention than what Cal and I have given his naked, tied-up body all those nights at his room at the Grand Central Hotel.

Well, now, watching the arm-wrestling matches has gotten me all lathered up, and sucking Shively's erection got me even more so, and when I look over and see that Averill has finished drilling Penn Cobb's butt, but that half-conscious Cobb is still slung over the table, his hairy ass spread, his shiny hole inviting the next visitor, I mosey over before anyone can get there first, pull out my bone, and slide it up inside Penn Cobb's wide-open hole.

As I'm pumping away, and a bunch of the boys have commenced singing "The Whorehouse Bells Were Ringing," I feel a hand on my shoulder.

"Thanks," says Cal, "for tryin' to help me out."

"Shit," I say, not missing a stroke into Cobb, "ain't that what friends are for, buddy?"

And he leans over and kisses me gentle on the cheek. "See you a bit later at the Grand Central," he says, and goes off to get another whiskey.

And I for my part pump ever harder, slipping damn near out of Cobb, then pounding my way back in, all to his groaning delight. Meantime a bellow rises above the crowd, and when I look over there's Josiah Britt, hands behind his head, sweat pouring from his furry pits, his big hard dick pumping out gob after gob of thick sperm upon Will Shively's grinning face. And after a minute or two more, I myself can hold no longer, and shoot off my sperm like big-city fireworks, all over the slick walls of Penn Cobb's guts, a most truly befitting end to one hot Independence Day in Helldorado, and God bless America.

THE GLORIOUS FOURTH

Inside the Slaughterdome
L. M. Ross

INTRODUCTION

In 2033, Testosteronic tensions reached an explosive boiling point on the Big Blue Ball, known as Earth. Gays, liberals, progressive livers and thinkers alike were given two options: Either remain repressed citizens of a turbulent planet or forge a Brave New World on the Moon's frontier. Many chose the latter. It proved a massive macho-filled exodus. Once Moon-bound, the immigrants' gravity problem was solved by a complex system of mass magnification. Pure oxygen was supplied by microchips installed into nose rings. Life was good: the sports, spectacular; the sex and the sexing, sensational.

Each year since that Great Gay Flight, Moon's best and bravest homosexual inhabitants and the Earth's best heterosexual players went beef-to-brawn and cock-to-cock in Greco Slaughterball Games. Gay men on the Moon were a gruff and burly breed, and they took these athletic

FULL BODY CONTACT

competitions very seriously. Part vicious laser hockey, part blood-sport Greco wrestling, the Games were a manly badge of honor where one winner took all, including the asshole of the defeated, as roaring crowds cheered. For hard-core enthusiasts, the Slaughter Games were the best voyeuristic displays of brute strength, cock-and-ball free-for-alls of the new millennium.

By 2069, instead of the lavender astro-plains of the Moon, the blue planet's Australia was chosen from a lottery to showcase the events. Earth's beefiest barbarians were weeded away during the preliminary trials. From the best of the best, a titanic tribe of warriors were brought together in teams of six. The teams were then pitted head-to-head against Moon's most superior athletic specimens in a clashing, bashing, and eventual ass-fucking, take-no-prisoners finale. Make no mistake—these games were not for sissies. Greco slaughterball was the sport of Masochistic Champions.

My name is Chan Zeron. My lover, Blade Andros, was Captain of Team Moon. His mission: to defeat Earth's undisputed big-dicked universal legend and reigning champion of the Greco Games, Luc Dane. Blade always hated how "The Great Dane" lorded over the title. Blade wanted nothing more than to beat Luc Dane's straight, cocky ass, and then fuck it long and hard before the howling masses.

THE PREPARATION

From the clank of iron and rising funk of the Andromeda Gym, Blade Andros was beginning to feel that burn: the monumental ache and burn of muscles, tendons and sinews he never knew existed. His body was frighteningly overdeveloped. As his trainer, I admired his dedication as much as the jut in his aluminum-plated jock. But all this sweat and sinew was starting to boil my booster rocket, and I had to let him know. "Blade. C'mon, give it a rest, man! We both know you're the fuckin' best Moon has to offer! Besides, my dick's screaming for attention here," I teased, holding my raging bone.

"Look, if you're not gonna take the Games seriously, I'm fuckin' firing you as my trainer!" he huffed. Tough guy. Tough talk. But I knew his weakness. Blade was determined to keep his edge by refusing to fuck. But I was bound and determined to change his dedicated mind, and coast his big regimented dick out of dry dock. As I bent, licking the beads of sweat from his large man-tits, he released a stubborn sigh. Blade's iron-hard abs heaved as that 500-pound weight quivered in his grip. His attitude was hard as his fucking body. With the Games a week away and no time for sex play, he barked, "C'mon! Stop it and spot me, damn it! Get it over my head, or go put on a fuckin Gortex toga, you bitch! I need you supporting me. If not, then stop wasting my goddamn time!"

I knew Blade was struggling with his lust, so I let his verbal lashing slide. Still, it's rough to turn a blind eye to my package. I'm no slouch in the muscle department either; and my Afro-Asian roots render me "exotic" here on the Moon. I stand 5-foot-11, 220 pounds of crunched, carved, carnal manhood, with a dick-bulge chiseled for sin. But then, every man on the Moon is practically an Adonis. Maybe that's why lunar flights have reached an all-time high in recent years.

"Hey! I see you've been working that muscle out without my help, buddy. Been using that hydro-powered pump I got for your birthday, huh?" he asked, eyes like green lights shooting over me.

"Nope. Must be all those fist gymnastics I've been giving it since you started competing," I said.

Staring at my rocket, he said, "Hell! This is the 21st century, Chan! No one uses their hands! Why didn't you just get a good grip on the Orgasmatron if you wanted to get off without me? Been using your fist, huh? You fuckin' primitive! Well, a little fist-action would be all right, I guess," he grinned.

Man! I knew something hot was about to happen when his Gortex jockstrap rolled past his hard, awesomely cut thighs and fell to his superior calves. He whispered, "Come on. Let's grab a steam."

To see Blade Andros in the buff is to witness a stunning piece of human sculpture brought to life. He lay like some aroused god on the table inside the hot solar room, and I began to massage his flesh. I touched his warm, tanned skin and kneaded his rippling torso. That chest alone was endowed with enough muscle to open its own gym. His tremendous biceps coursed thick with bulk and veins. His massively ripped pecs draped so low they were nearly rectangular. Yes, Blade was one beautiful piece of iron man. I traced down eight-iron abs and stroked his huge iron cock. A long, thick, and veiny bull-cock, it shot out from my fist like a bronzed comet of steel and flesh.

Pulling the base made his large, smooth balls wag as the columns of his quads jutted. Ah! What a cock! Its planetary crown was juicing. Some powerlifters' bulk diminished the size of their dicks. But Blade's got the biggest thing I've ever seen growing between a man's thighs that wasn't alien in form! That 11 inches of extra-thick fuckmeat adorned his already mighty package like an exclamation point. And there it stood, high, hard, and so fuckin' statuesque I just

INSIDE THE SLAUGHTERDOME

had to suck it, and get the Moon beast to eject, correctly.

"You been aching to get fucked for a long time, huh?" Blade taunted, smacking the globes of my naked ass. "All right. On your belly!" he demanded. I obeyed gladly. As Blade lay atop my quaking flesh, I felt the hot, wet smear of his early jizz as he humped me in smooth, rippling waves. Kissing my burning neck, he pulled my legs apart and thrust his cock in between. I waited for the slice of his pole to give me what I'd been missing. But he didn't dick me. Damn him! Yet even with no anal insertion, my cheeks trembled against his thick battering ram.

"Tighten your legs around it!" he instructed. "C'mon! Squeeze the fuckin' come from my balls!" I tightened my legs viselike around him.

"Ahh! Yes! That's it! Make me feel it!" he roared. My thighs are long and leanly muscled now, thanks in large part to training alongside Blade. But then, his massive body and huge cock pounded beneath my ass while I gripped tight to the hot thick meat surging near my chute. *Mmm. Awww!* I bucked my restless flesh into a bed of Moon steam. I was so freaking turned-on I could barely breathe. When Blade left that crevice I'd created for him, I thought he'd weakened, given in to the fever. Our pricks stood vertical, as hard cocks on the Moon tended to do. Yes. I really thought he'd weakened. But, no. He still refused to fuck!

"No, no, Chan! Not until the Games are over!" he insisted, positioning himself before me, letting his raging prick bob at my sweating face. I grabbed it by its root, and he smacked my hand away. Horny as I was, I wanted to kick his big bronzed competitive ass, and *make him* fuck me!

Sensing my anger, and eyeing my niner, he fell like a capsized spacecraft beside me, and we contorted into a blazing 69. Blade's tongue roamed along my throbbing tube, sucking down my meat like ancient astronauts used to suck Tang. With his wide cock knob leaking inches from my blowhole, he lobbed the fuck pole between my lips, and we both commenced to buck and suck, buck and suck.

The engorged slab pistoned hurriedly back and forth, choking me in the sweetest way possible. Oh! I lunged and slammed my prick down his muscular throat with the wildest frenzy. I hated those games, and Blade knew why. If he emerged a Level One winner, according to the rules some other earthling would have to suck that same hot, throbbing dick crowding my lips! Gay or hyper-straight, whoever sucked it was bound to fall in lust with Blade's cock. Soon, the liquid friction of his lashing tongue became too much to bear.

Blade cunningly kicked off his space crugers and slyly removed my specially approved gravity boots, and we floated to the ceiling of the gym. Oh! There we were, floating and sucking, tumbling and licking dick, both of us spinning out of control! Soon, we blasted in duel versions of the Milky Way all over each other's sweating, cock-gobbling faces.

And then, to kill the moment, Blade asked the fated question that instantly made me go limp....

"So, you think Luc Dane will like the taste of my come? I plan to make that fucker swallow it!" I floated away from him, pissed, jealous, my crystallized load trailing me in mid-air.

One week later: After a three-hour flight to Earth, we docked in Miami, took another flight across the continent, and a half-hour later we were in "Outback." An airbus zipped us to a chrome and iron castle in the sky, where thousands awaited admission to the 2069 Slaughterball Competitions.

INSIDE THE SLAUGHTERDOME

Announcer: "Citizens of the Earth, masochists of all ages…welcome to the Slaughterdome! Players, rev up your turbo-powered blades, zoom to the arena's center, and let the games begin!"

Inside the Slaughterdome, a 200,000-strong crowd cheered, and the bloodthirsty roar was deafening! The scope of that fantastic arena housed the thundering throngs in iron spirals leading up to the 100-story ceiling. Team Earth, lead by Luc Dane, jet-propelled into the stadium in one speedy hydraulic thrust. The players wore red, white, and blue aluminum helmets and aerodynamic unitards. Plates of armor coated their knees, forearms, and chests. And there was Luc—a big, toothless, vicious wad of strange beef, if there ever was one: 6-foot-6, 300 pounds of head, neck, chest, thighs, and attitude. All that bulk was made more menacing by Dane's mechanical left hand. The original was lost in a freak swoosh of the laser puck, two years before. His other five teammates were a posse of snarls and threat.

Then Team Moon propelled into view, only with far less fanfare—we were, after all, visitors on a hostile planet. Of course, our costumes ROCKED! Lavender and midnight-blue, with clusters of stars along the codpieces and streaking comets flashed across the asses; our helmets jutted forth like deadly boners over the faceguards. And my man Blade never looked more magnificent.

Announcer: "Good citizens, please direct your attention to the rules posted on the scoreboard. Now, as you know, there are few holds barred, short of killing your opponent. However, to compete, each of tonight's competitors must be amply equipped with the following: 1) Eye of the Cobra (a fearless determination), 2) Beef of the Bull (muscles of iron), and 3) Saber of Death (at least an 8-inch cock—all the

FULL BODY CONTACT

better to humiliate and brutally force-fuck the tight ass of the loser).

Players, retreat to your home stations for round one, level one of Slaughterball! Now, of course, the ball is actually a laser puck, controlled by the players via their sticks. The object is to lead the puck across the steel-enforced field and into your team's respective goal. I understand Team Moon has a killer offense. But we'll see. Aggression is the key here. Team Earth, lead by Captain Luc Dane, is favored to take this round. But let's see how the game shapes up."

The period began with a center face-off spot. Because Team Moon was the visitor, we were given possession.

The puck moved at a breakneck pace from teammate to teammate, heading toward Team Moon's goal. That small blue glowing beam represented our destiny as it zipped from stick to stick. Once in the sure control of Blade's stick, we all saw visions of glory. But they were quickly dashed. Luc Dane body-checked Blade and drew a takeover as the wild multitudes clamored for our blood.

Announcer: "Good citizens, the force of velocity on this field is simply incredible. There's Dane, flying full-speed ahead. Oh! He's nailed Andros with a merciless wallop! And so it goes, in this theater of physical savagery! Look at him control that laser puck! Yes! He's sending it directly to the goal. Yes! Score! Oh, Moon's goalie, Rad Cumson, looks like a complete incompetent!"

Things went on in that way. Puck possession, then checks, body checks, and goal points. By the end of third period, Earth was up 5–1. It seemed *all* we had going for us, as the biased announcer was quick to point out, was that we "looked good" in our uniforms. In the interim, a personal grudge match simmered and waged between Blade

INSIDE THE SLAUGHTERDOME

and Luc. They racked up numerous calls for holding, charging, tripping, high-sticking, and slashing. That last call sent both teams and alternates rushing the floor with fists blazing! Didn't matter. We'd lost level one of Slaughterball.

Announcer: "And to the losers go the spoils. In this case, the spoiled, sweaty cock of Team Earth's ultimate player. Looks like this game's become a feast for the eyes and the groin alike. As is tradition, the captain of the winning team may choose the form of humiliation he'd like to inflict upon the challenging captain. Luc?"

"Well. Let's see. Since Team Moon looks so damned cute in their little outfits—I'm sure you all agree—I'd personally like to see how cute Moon Captain Blade Andros will look with my big thick cock in his mouth. Get over here, Andros, and whip this fucker out for me!" a surly Luc demanded.

"Suck that dick! Suck the dick. Suck that fucking dick!" the restless crowd chanted.

Blade wearily stepped to the hub of the packed arena, where Luc's cock cast a massive shadow.

"Suck that dick! Suck that dick! Suck it! Suck it! Suck that dick!" the entire arena screamed.

There stood beefy, bombastic Luc Dane, removing his helmet as a mess of sweaty blond curls matted his huge skull. "On your knees, faggot!" Groups of 100-foot video monitors recorded every hard, veiny trail of that blood-engorged prick as the fucker grew thicker on Blade's tongue. Shit! Luc Dane must've hit Earth's penis lottery. The man's dick was so damned ginormous, it was freakish!

Announcer: "Don't know about you fellow cocksuckers out there, but Luc Dane looks like a throatful! Never tried dick myself, but that thing seems a tad too much to suck! Check those muscles flexing in Luc's ass as he whips that cannon forth. Oh! Poor Blade! Aww, the humanity!"

The crowd leaned forth, oohing and ahhing as Blade bitterly allowed the slimy head then the shaft inside his mouth. I prayed he wouldn't gag or choke on that schlong, and lose those critical style points! But no. Blade was handling Luc's spit-slicked hard-on, a little *too* well.

Announcer: "Yes. Blade Andros is swallowing his defeat. But Moon dudes lack no experience in this area. Whoa! What's this? Oh, my! Luc is ramming those lips, power-fucking Andros's steely jaw. Yes! That cockhead is threatening to bust right through Blade's cheek! Well, no one's ever called Luc Dane a gentle champ. Jeez! Luc sure is woolly around the penile area. Someone grab a razor!"

"Like 'em hairy, huh? Bury your fuckin' nose in it, Blade baby! Inhale all that funk and sweat!" Luc taunted. "Get it all down! Yeah, take that dick, you Moon-licking fag!"

The buzzer sounded. Though Luc Dane didn't come, those five raunchy cock-sucking minutes had seemed like an eternity to me. Blade rose from his knees, turned, and spat on the arena floor, while the charged crowd booed. He walked back over to the team, and I gave him a swig of mouthwash.

"That motherfucker needs a bath! Tasted like something damned! But don't worry, fellas. We'll kick his ass in Level 2 and 3!" Blade assured us.

Level 2. Speed Skating Competition: the objective, to massacre your rivals, produce as much bodily injury as humanly possible, and still remain on your blades. For two arduous hours of no-holds-barred rough-and-tumble, bodies skidded, teeth flew, and neither team escaped unscathed. But thanks to the never-say-die power-thighs of Apollo Davis, and a strong show of adrenaline from Fearless Flash

INSIDE THE SLAUGHTERDOME

Williams, we managed to squeak out a tie then scored the final point by Blade head-butting two Earth players out-of-bounds and, thus, out of the competition. Yes! Team Moon did indeed have balls!

Announcer: "Will someone please, PLEASE wipe the field clear of blood, guts, and testosterone? Good citizens, we promised you a show, and by God, we're delivering here tonight! Now for the finals, Level 3. It's winner takes all in Greco Wrestling 3000!"

Wrestling was clearly our strongest event, plus we sported killer unitards. The asses were cut out, showcasing the best sets of taut male rump the Moon had to offer! Rad Cumson, all butch, blond, and bulging, used a cross-ankle pickup on his opponent and drove him down. When the whistle blew, that Earthling's unitard stretched with more meat shank than before that match had begun. Such closet cases!

Cock-strong Apollo was up next. Every black sinew rippled as he grunted, gripping his rival's thigh and pushing back with all his might. All eyes were glued to his glorious buttocks driving forth. Yes! Apollo easily defeated his adversary, pinning him within the first 30 seconds.

You could feel it. The hordes were turning. Of course we had the gay contingency—but little by little the bicurious and straights who wavered on the fence were starting to root for Team Moon.

Announcer: "And now for the Blood Match we've all been awaiting. Let's have a rousing ovation for Universal Champion Luc Dane! Yes. Soak it in, Luc. You deserve it. And now, the challenger, Team Moon's captain, Blade Andros. Come on, let's hear it for the lunar queen, er, uh, I mean, the man who would be king! All right, you warriors—time to lock and load!"

FULL BODY CONTACT

They came to grips, standing in a tie-up, both sets of arms wrapped tightly about the other's thick neck, their eyes fixed in brutal determination. Finally, Luc's ham thigh stretched and his foot tried to disable Blade's firm hold on gravity. But Blade wasn't going anywhere. They were locked in mortal combat. Every muscle of their mammoth torsos labored against the will and unwavering power of their opponent. Luc peered at the crowd, grinned wickedly, and bit Blade's neck. The ref didn't call it. Damn! You could almost feel the sting when Luc hauled off and whacked Blade with his mechanical hand! "AWW!" All hell broke loose! They were a symphony of raging never-say-die struggle. All grace was abandoned to walloping groin kicks, vicious bites, gouges! A near fall granted Blade three points. Yes! A reversal gave Luc two. Boo!

The vying of two ferocious titans became a fantastic war of brawn, brains, and balls. At times, as their super-buffed bodies stressed and squirmed against each other, you'd swear they were engaged in some violent act of gladiator fucking. Watching them, a man could bust a nut from the driving exhilaration of tendons tightening; humps of hammering flesh pounding flesh. As Blade lay twisting on his back, he used some inner force to pump hard and throw burly Luc to the mat.

Then Blade bounded up and drove headlong into Dane, and with the swell of his chest, managed to pin one shoulder. But the hard, humpy sight of Blade's tight, hairless bronzed ass must've weakened Luc. He lay there, huffing, puffing, every part of him clearly exhausted except his dick. That earthbound slab of cock was throbbing, bobbing up his panting belly.

Seeing the specter of that bone, Blade slammed hard and

INSIDE THE SLAUGHTERDOME

rode against it, using his weight to pin both of Luc Dane's robust shoulders soundly and without question to the mat! Blade lay on top of him a good 10 seconds as the crowd hushed. Finally the whistle was blown. And Blade leapt up, both arms raised. Hell, yes! Victory clearly belonged to Team Moon! We roared!

Announcer: "Good citizens, we have an UPSET! Yes. History has been made tonight. Luc Dane has gone down in defeat to THE NEW UNIVERSAL SLAUGHTERBALL CHAMPION, BLADE ANDROS! Behold your new god. Every square inch of him forms a fucking muscle! Check those cheeks of stone and jaws of square granite. Let's go to the stats: 23-inch biceps, a powerful 52-inch chest, thighs 27 inches. And that ass—two globes glued together by space-age polymers to form one perfect sphere. Is he real or synthetic? Only those closest to him know for sure. Doesn't matter, tonight. He and Team Moon go to the Hall of Champions. Congratulations, Blade! And yes, the whole lavender team. I guess the better man has indeed won...."

Steel thighs thundered with each step and stride Blade took about the floor of the arena.

"Go on, guys! Go join him. It's a victory for all of us," I told the other players.

"Naw. Let him savor it right now. Blade was the hungriest of us all," Apollo insisted.

His chest swelled with pride and his Herculean shoulders seemed to fill that giant arena as the crowd went wild. Blade gazed back at me. He looked hot and absolutely wet-your-jock triumphant. Jade-green eyes were silently fucking me with one piercing glare. The thrill of the game, the lust at emerging winners had swollen his dick thicker, longer. Standing victorious, he shoved Dane to the mat. Then, crouching over his sweaty face, Blade dick-slapped his rival before the hordes. He moved in the slowest undulations as Luc gripped Blade's gluteus maximus. With Blade's ass in those monstrous arms, Luc looked like Atlas, holding two worlds in his beef and mechanical hands!

With the sound of "Ooooohhhh!" Luc's tongue darted the air and swiped the pearl of jizz that formed at the wide pisshole. Blade washed his face in it. Man! I'll bet ol' Luc's cheeks were on fire! Boldly seizing the tremendous pipe in his fist, Luc Dane wrapped his burning lips tight around Blade's outsized crown. He groaned as he licked the slimy head, up, down, his wild tongue teasing all around its heavily ridged knob. Soon, Luc Dane commenced to not just suck but chow down on Blade's projecting dick, until his steely jaw grew tired from the thrusts!

Then, I watched it happen. Slowly the mighty Luc turned over and yanked down his unitard! Those big, bullish thighs wavered, like two Roman columns about to topple before the Great Fall. But was he falling from defeat, or falling into lust for Blade's dick? The man lay on the ground of the arena, belly down, grimacing, squirming as four of Blade's fat fingers entered the zone of his heretofore forbidden chute. The groan Luc unleashed racked the ears of all the spectators. It was one small digital lunge for Blade, and one giant finger fuck for all gay mankind.

For a moment, that arena became so quiet you could hear a dollop of come drop.

"Go on. Take it. Take my ass. You won, damn you, Blade! You fuckin' won!" Luc grunted.

Blade mounted him, grabbed a fistful of hair, and pulverized Luc Dane's asshole with his big, hard, 11-inch prick. He jammed so deep he was buried up to the burly

INSIDE THE SLAUGHTERDOME

cockstem in Luc's hole. Blade fucked him, rammed and thrust with hard jolts sure to bust a straight man's cherry.

Seeing their fearsome leader taken down only seemed to inspire the others, not to riot but to join in the horny celebration of victory in the Slaughterdome. Codpieces fell, revealing hard and sturdy pricks that showed no visible signs of defeat. Who were these guys, anyway? Two of Earth's players hoisted Thad Darius over their shoulders. But Thad was one of our alternates! Still, they were picking him up and ripping at his unitard. I couldn't believe it! Earthlings were kissing Thad's moons! Things became even more heated and far more raunchy after that!

Announcer: "Folks, this is madness! I've never seen anything like this! It's a free-for-all! Asses are being wildly fucked! Champagne corks are popping, and oh! the suds are splashing all over naked dicks! Erect dicks. Dicks everywhere! I can't give you a blow-by-blow. It's hard to tell which cocks are getting sucked. Someone zoom in for a closeup! Men are slapping, kissing, licking naked asses! Madness! There's Blade's teammate, Apollo Davis, swinging his big black cock around. Oh, my! Look at those straight guys diving for dick! Blond Butch Branson's taking it in the face, while Corbin Cruz takes care of those big brown nuts! It's absolute pandemonium in the arena! A bucking, sucking, fucking orgy of beef, brawn, and awesome manhood colliding! Hey! Doesn't anyone want the trophy? I—I can't go on! It's too much! Somebody grab my mike!"

"Fuck ass! Fuck ass! Fuck ass! Fuck ass!" the roaring masses chanted.

"Yeah. I think you like this new interplanetary champion cock!" Blade teased.

FULL BODY CONTACT

You could almost feel the ground shaking as Blade's huge throbbing cockhead forged through that narrow opening, pushing through that tight ring of fire! The crowd grabbed the arms of their chairs, gritting their teeth, as if Blade were invading them! One look at his mug and I knew Luc was fighting a maddening pain. A pain I'd grown to endure and love. Luc grunted and buried his humiliated face in the mat. Blade was relentless. He savored his victory, plunging his grotesquely swollen dick deeper, deeper, hotter, and wilder. He wanted Luc Dane to know what a big gay Moon dick buried up straight Earthling asshole felt like. In mid-fuck, he pulled back very slowly, then pushed deep within, ripping that virgin manhole wide open, tearing it apart, like a fiend!

"AHHH! SHIT! BLADE, DON'T—NO MORE! WHOA! DON'T FUCK ME!" he howled.

Announcer: "Citizens. You heard it yourselves. This is embarrassing! He's fucking beggin'!"

"Oh, shit! He's actually getting f-f-fucked!"

"Luc lost to a bunch of gay men from the Moon!"

"Just take it! Damn it! Take it like a man!" assorted voices boomed throughout the arena.

Blade's ramming fuck speed accelerated. That horse-cock began drilling the straight ass into hot queer infamy, plowing, pounding the holy hell out of it. There was lightning in his cock! I was begging to feel envious. There was Blade nailing that ass, hammering it hard and ceaselessly, with a driving mission to come! Pounding. Thrusting. His weighty nuts slapped back and forth with a brutal beating friction. There was no stopping him. Some of us didn't believe Luc Dane, Earth's former slaughterball champ, even wanted Blade to stop.

INSIDE THE SLAUGHTERDOME

What a hot sight Blade was, glistening in metal shin-guards, his ass a hard, thrashing, naked wonder covered in sweat. Groups of men, gay and straight alike, stood in the stands, beating their dicks and writhing their hips in the thunderous celebration.

"Fuck me. No. Stop. No. Don't stop!" Luc begged, both lost and caught up in a thrust. Then Blade picked up the beast, his raging cock still lodged deep in Dane's anus, and walk-fucked him around the floor of that roaring Slaughterdome!

"Ride! Ride that fuckin' bone!" Blade yelled, smacking those boulder-like cheeks.

That was it! Our team dashed toward the arena center, and Earth's team followed. It didn't seem to matter which side you batted on, as long as you got your hands on some-one's bat. Suddenly unitards ripped away and cocks sprang forth like human masts, fighting for attention. Victory and lust was in their blood. As Blade fucked Luc, you'd have thought men fucking men was some glorious epidemic! Men were falling to their knees inhaling, licking, sucking strange, athletic dick. That theater of savagery soon became the arena of the primal fuck! Asses were bent over, cocks were launched, and gay and straight alike were taking it deeply, brutally up the butt. Sweat and muscle, muscle and sweat fell like willing victims in heaps of twisted, humping, bucking ass-sex.

Announcer: "Citizens, what can I say? It's good to be gay in 2069. There sure are some fine slabs of beef on dis-play in this arena! It's enough to make an objective tele-caster bust a nut!"

I dashed up to Blade, and he instantly pushed Luc's well-fucked ass away. We hugged as hard and full as our raging cocks. I grabbed his meat. His huge rod soundly throbbed its quick, wicked pulse in my grasp. His eyes were an ice-green shock to my system. Yes! I, Chan Zeron, was about to get dicked at last!

"Come here, you. I'm gonna fuck the living moonbeams outta that sweet ass!" he joked. Then he wrestled me play-fully down to the floor, bent me over, and gave me what I'd been going crazy waiting and pining for for months. The hot slide of his thick cock burrowed through my chute like a laser saber. But, oh! I loved that heat. Once in deep, he pulled back far, and then slammed me that hot way I need-ed to be slammed! "Yes! Shit! Blade, yes!" AW! Shit! It fuckin' hurt, but I'd waited so long for that fat vascular prick to astound my pucker hole again. Aww! Oh! The thrust of it made me shudder. He went deeper, fucking hard and rough, the way I wanted it. Cock and asshole met in violent clinches and painful withdrawals. But every hard and sweaty thrust felt like victory! Blade pulled out all the way and rammed it in again. Oh! My body rocked. I pounded the floor, grunting as Earth men and Moon men sucked and fucked shamelessly all around us. Muscles were pounding, big pricks were driving, taboos and cherries were being broken that wild night. Strangers resorted to using their "primitive" fists, flogging hot dicks throughout that horny audience. The sex-crazed crowd cheered like savages, the way they did during a rousing game of Slaughterball. But, in the year 2069, we gave it a whole new meaning.

Blade's ramming dick filled me, drilled me with pulver-izing thrusts. Every sinew rippled and lunged. I rocked and shook, so hot, so turned on I could hardly breathe! On hands and knees, I was bravely fucked, unafraid of what our audience thought. But they were so enthralled by the

INSIDE THE SLAUGHTERDOME

clashing of muscle, the lashing of cocks, that most whipped out their Earth pods and flogged along in rhythm with us! Oh! I glanced up, cowering, as Blade ripped up my rectum, to find an arena of nearly 200,000 hard, naked pricks violently saluting us! Instead of grabbing their steely balls and heading home, Earth men decided, they'd much rather play with ours, and bat for OUR team!

Yes. Those Slaughterball Games were brutal. It had been a war. But it was peacetime now, and we were only too glad to welcome the new recruits to our side in the year 2069.

Kill
Randolph Petilos

Game, set, and match point. I knew we had already won and were headed for the finals the moment the ball left my fingertips and described the shallow arc I'd planned for it toward the far end of the net. The quick set is my favorite play and, as usual, our trusty southpaw Jason was there to stuff it into the face of the would-be defender. This would make Jason's 14th kill of the match; you'd think by now the other team—hell, all the teams in the league—would be wise to this ploy. I mean, what clueless losers they must be *not* to see it coming a mile away once Jason steps up to front left.

With an oh-so-satisfying combination thwack-thump, the ball left Jason's palm, rocketed to the surface of the court, and bounced away unhindered to dance among the feet of the bewildered members of the opposing team. The kill was followed by a half-dozen masculine voices sending up a testosterone-drenched "Yeah!" that echoed happily around the gymnasium. And, as usual, Jason high-fived his way through the crowd of sweaty, pumped-up gym rats that made up our team to lift me off the floor and swallow me whole in one of those rough, manly hugs. Turns out, Jason's on-court hugs lifted a few more things in me—and on me—than just my feet off the floor.

"What is it about volleyball, anyway?" I'd muse to myself in more quiet moments. Surely not the opportunity to get the occasional blast from a man's ripe pits when he reaches both arms toward the net for the block, or the momentary slippery wetness of his bare shoulder or arm as you jostle one another for position, or the alluring bump-and-sway of his basket as it surges to eye level and throws a delicious musky odor in your direction as he goes for a kill. Duh, of course it's those things—and more.

After all the high-fiving, the hugs, the affectionate punches on biceps and loud smacks on hard butts, I was surprised to find Jason lingering among our teammates, chatting and "good game"–ing everyone up—not making his usual beeline to courtside for his gym bag then bolting for the door. For the umpteenth time, I took the opportunity to admire him. At 6-foot-1, 190 pounds—just the right ratio of lean to muscle—with closely cropped hair the color of ripened wheat and eyes as blue as an Iowa sky in summer, Jason would be the object of desire in any young red-blooded American queer-jock's wet dream.

One reason I tried so damned hard to excel at the sport was that I'd hoped, eventually, to reap that golden harvest, to win a roll in the hay with this particular hunk-of-a-farmboy in exchange for a few well-set balls, a few winning games. If I'd been at all honest with myself all those weeks, I'd have admitted that that was the *only* reason I worked so hard—simply to gain Jason's notice, his approval, and a chance to turn the bear hug at the end of a point into the more inti-

FULL BODY CONTACT

mate, less hurried variety, after the game, preferably naked and in bed. Aw, hell, forget the bed: fully clothed, on the carpet, in front of my mother. That's how much I lusted after him.

What a different person he'd become over the weeks we'd played together. When I first met Jason on sign-up day for the league, I pegged him for one of two types: 1) shy and hiding his shyness behind a disinterested exterior; or 2) he was one of those hot jocks who knew it and "oh, by the way, fuck you, you can look all you like but don't touch." After we'd played our way through the other teams in the queer recreational league, though, Jason was now relaxed and freer with his expressions of affection for his teammates in general, and his approval of and even admiration for my ability to move the ball. Man, he loved the kill, and it was simply a joy to watch him hang in the air and really let loose on the ball.

What always puzzled me about Jason, though, was the way he never stuck around after games to shoot the shit. He never wanted to go out afterward to the bar that sponsored our team for the customary free rounds of drinks, never wanted to just hang out. Immediately after each game, he'd say his quick goodbyes, snag his gym bag, and disappear. So, of course, being the nosy nelly that I am, I tried to find out what I could about him. I asked the other guys on the team if he had a boyfriend, but no one seemed to know much about him. When I asked our manager, Erik, what the story was with Jason, Erik simply said, "Girrrrl, I wish I knew. That is one hot fucker." *Oh, gee, thanks, Erik*, I thought, *you're just a fount of information. You're our* fucking *manager,* fer crissakes. *Surely you must know something about him.*

KILL

As the season wore on and nobody had a clue what was up with Jason, my curiosity, as usual, got the better of me. Two weeks before the game that put us in the finals, I broke the cardinal rule of gay recreational sports leagues: I asked one of my teammates out for a drink.

"Aw, geez, Rickie," he said, sounding apologetic while giving me a full dose of those spectacularly blue eyes, "I'd like to, buddy, but I gotta go out of town for work early tomorrow and I got some stuff to get done before then. Can I take a raincheck on that?"

"Sure," I said, trying not to seem disappointed but not able to keep a sad smile from creeping onto my face. Of course, what I really wanted to do was rip his gym shorts off and bury my face in his crotch.

"Thanks," he said with a smile. "See you next week. OK?" And with a comradely squeeze of my right deltoid he was gone.

Fuck it, I fumed. *Whatever*. So he doesn't turn on to me. So what? So I'm 5-foot-7, 140 pounds, not overly muscled, brown-colored all over in a nondescript sort of way, and the object of *nobody's* fantasy. He's probably got a hot husband who's got him on a short leash waiting for him at home anyway. Or worse: He's married with kids and a house in the 'burbs and is only playing in the gay league to get his jollies watching all the fags drool all over him. Or unforgivable: He's the worst kind of unrealized self-hating homo, unable to admit that he's attracted to men and living a furtive, miserable, secret lie. *Yeah, right*, my inner voice nagged, *whatever it takes to make yourself feel better, you bitter, lust-besotted, tired old fairy*. Right.

Imagine my surprise then when, after the game that put us in the finals for the trophy, Jason walks up from behind

FULL BODY CONTACT

me, puts his sweat-covered arm around my neck, infusing the air around us with his sweet-sour stench, and says quietly, "So, we're all going to Buckie's for our victory drink now, right?"

I couldn't speak. I just looked at him. In the middle of the raucous celebrating of our teammates all around us, we just stared at each other with silly grins on our faces, the proverbial eye of calm amidst the storm. It's a moment that I'll never forget: Jason's eyes, Jason's hair, Jason's smell, the touch of Jason. For that all-too-brief moment, we were the only two people on the court, in the gym, in the universe.

Then our coach, Erik, shoved us, breaking the moment with a knowing grin: "All right, you two sick homos, that's enough. Good job, Jase. Nice work, Rickie. Get cleaned up and I'll see you two at Buckie's." It wasn't a question.

Before I knew it the rest of the team had whisked Jason off toward the door and were on their way to their respective homes to shower and change before gathering at the bar. What could I do? I grabbed my gym bag and chased after them, tired, achy, and pumped with the sweet feeling of triumph.

Buckie's as a "sports bar" is a misnomer if I ever heard one. From the outside peering in, it may look like any other (straight) sports bar: dart board, pool table, a different game on each of four TVs, banners and jerseys from various teams and sports equipment hanging on the walls—the works. Except for one small difference: Where were all the hot chicks in jean shorts and tube tops? *Right.* Even lesbians shunned this place as not being "serious" enough about sports, despite the decor.

Anyway, I walk in the door and there stands The Incomparable Sam. Sam is always the first to arrive,

KILL

shirtless, of course, it being the height of summer, his gray, well-worn, faded-blue gym shorts riding a little lower on his hips than his tan line, his well-defined legs dropping into a pair of equally well-worn blue-and-white Reeboks. Southern-born and bred, a model of manners and of that famous hospitality, he was simply stunning. From the moment he said hello to me at the league sign-up I fell hopelessly for his cultured plantation accent and his subtle, aristocratic bearing. Needless to say, he had a 6-foot body that anyone would kill for: beautifully defined abs, deep chest, and flawless, creamy-smooth skin where the sun had not warmed it to a delicious honey gold to match his warm brown eyes and short-cropped, dark-brown hair. Buckie, the bar's owner and team sponsor, busied himself with pitchers of beer and munchies in preparation for the celebration while shooting the shit with Sam.

"So," Buckie began, to no one in particular, "we play Stoli next, right?" Since there was no one else in the joint, The Incomparable One and I assumed he was talking to us. Buckie had sparse, mousey-brown hair on his scalp and one of those physiques that was always threatening to get out of control, as though only a strict diet and dutiful trips to the gym kept his belly from doing a middle-age spread. As it was, he was already well on his way to being one of those aging-badly former-circuit-boy burnout-tragedies, if not for his partner Gene's tight rein on the between-meal snacks and the purse strings. Buckie tended to wear loose-fitting clothes these days, like the slimming vertical black-and-white-striped faux-referee shirt and the black chinos he had on today.

"Yes, that's right," Sam replied, in the honey-dripping baritone that matched his golden skin. "Their record is as good as ours, although some might say they had a much easier row to hoe to get to the finals."

"Yeah," agreed Buckie, "their last four matches were against teams with the worst records in the league. We should have no trouble taking them."

"Well," I warned, "we shouldn't get too cocky just yet. Remember what happened to the team from Manscape when they played Stoli last year. Manscape were undefeated and thought they were a lock for the finals and almost didn't get there. Stoli killed them in the first game and made Manscape earn every point before they eventually choked during the third game."

"You know, you're right about that," agreed The Incomparable One. "I remember that match. Overconfidence was almost Manscape's downfall, and that Stoli team's got just about the same lineup as last year, if I recall correctly."

"Yeah, whatever," Buckie cut in. "I still think they're not playing as well as they were this time last year. I'm not worried. My boys'll take 'em easy," he leered at us. The Incomparable One and I beamed with pride.

At that moment, James sashayed in—and I do mean *sashayed*. What always struck me about James was how cute-as-a-button he was, and how he insisted on going by James—not Jim or Jimmy—a formality that was strangely incongruous with his personality.

"Hey, buttheads," he shouted to the entire bar. Believe me, he would have turned every single head in the place—that is, if there were any heads other than the three of ours in the bar just then—even if he weren't wearing a distressed-orange cut-off muscle tank that showed his pecs and tight belly to advantage, and a pair of gray cargo shorts that

KILL

hugged his nicely muscled butt. With deep blue eyes the shade of the Adriatic on a sunny day and hair as dark as any Greek fisherman's, Cute-as-a-Button had the kind of easy, inviting smile that always seemed on the verge of a really raunchy joke—which was usually true. He had a way of putting everyone at ease with his bordering-on-vulgar-but-not-quite-crossing-over-the-line banter and good-natured teasing. At 5-foot-11, with smooth tanned skin and supple muscles rolling beneath the surface, James had a boyish charm that just wouldn't quit.

"Hey yourself, Asswipe," Buckie shouted back, undaunted by James's beauty.

"Where the hell *is* everybody?" James continued shouting, as though he were trying to be heard across a crowded bar. "And where's my goddamn drink? This is supposed be a victory celebration!"

Buckie glared at James and promptly handed him a pitcher and a glass. "All right, all right," Buckie countered in a mock-hurt tone, "quit yer bitching, drink this, and shut the fuck up."

Buckie loved James's rudeness; James loved to goad Buckie on. They were made for each other.

"So," continued James, pouring himself a drink, ignoring Buckie, and crooning in his best Cute-as-a-Button voice, "Rickie, how comes y'all don't set as pretty fer mey as y'all do fer Jase? Yeeoo lahk hayem better'n mey, dontcha?"

Leave it to James to figure out a way to work all three of our last good nerves at once: ignoring Buckie while baiting me in a hick accent that he knew would irk Sam. Buckie just glared. Sam gasped. What else could I do but swoop to defend our collective honor?

"Oh, fuck you, James," I said in my best lecturing tone.

FULL BODY CONTACT

"If I'd placed the ball any more perfectly for you today, you'd have be able to hit it over the net with your cock." Of course, I knew this was just the sort of opening James loved to take advantage of, but I was in a good mood and decided to let him have his fun.

"Oh, yeah?" James said in a faux-threatening tone, reaching for the back of my neck and motioning to make me give him head. "C'mere, you faggot, I'll show you cock...."

Feeling a little frisky myself, and wanting to teach James a little lesson, instead of resisting as I usually do I bent over and let him guide my head to his crotch. When I got there, I immediately locked my teeth onto as much of it as the material of his cargo shorts would allow.

Surprised by my uncharacteristic move, James yelped and jumped back a foot, causing both Buckie and Sam to burst out in huge belly laughs.

"You little prick," James said, trying to recover his composure and grabbing me in a rough bear hug that was more affection than retaliation. He kissed me briefly on the neck before setting me down and laughing along with the rest of us.

Just then the rest of the gang arrived, minus the one person I'd most wanted to see: Jason. What the hell was keeping him, I wondered, and began to worry that he was going to pull another one of his disappearing acts, when Andy came up to me, put one brotherly arm over my shoulders and reached for a glass with the other.

"Hey, Rickie. Good game today," Andy said, with a big smile, one of his more dazzling ones—and, believe me, they were all dazzling, what with his perfect, perfectly white teeth, flawless, silky-smooth skin the color of sweet cream just below the tan line at his belly, where summer sun

KILL

hadn't been able to kiss it to a warm bronze. Andy was Truly Exceptional. "We really clicked today, especially in the first and last games," he enthused as he ran a tanned hand through his normally dark blond hair, now streaked through with summery highlights that played off the golden flecks in his soft, cornflower-colored eyes.

During games, though, I noticed how his usual sunny demeanor would sometimes transform into this "I will brook no excuses" look, a certain firmness of the jaw or a determination about the eyes that spoke of a formidable temper held uncomfortably in check—especially when we were down a few points—or when he was particularly frustrated with the way he or someone else on the team was playing. More than once I caught myself staring at his firm, full, utterly flawless butt, barely contained in the deep-side-slitted Malibu gym shorts he'd wear for games, and the expanse of solid thigh leading from them.

I will never forget that day earlier in the summer when Truly Exceptional and I went to the lakeshore. We were strolling along the water's edge, he in nothing but a midnight-blue racer with Speedo emblazoned in big lemon-yellow letters astride his buns. There were audible gasps from beachgoers reclining on towels or in beach chairs as we made our way up the beach and back, and all conversation around us would abruptly cease until we moved far enough away for the men—and women—to breathe normally again. Truly Exceptional, of course, was embarrassed by it all, but I sure did get a lot of mileage out of that story with the rest of the team.

"Yeah, you had some nice kills today," I replied, aiming for manly but hitting awkward instead. I always get just a little stupid in Andy's presence. It happens all the time when

I'm around guys who are so much more beautiful than I am. It takes me *days* to recover.

"Y'know, Rickie," Andy continued, more seriously, "we couldn't have gotten this far this year without you. I'm not sure how it happened, but ever since you joined the team we've somehow managed to become just that: a team."

"Oh, please..." I attempted to change the course of the conversation, but Andy cut me off.

"No, really, I've talked to the other guys about it. You have a way of sending signals to each of us, a kind of tele-graphic body language that we can anticipate. We know what you're going to do and, in turn, what you want us to do, almost before the ball leaves your hands—all without saying a word. To tell you the truth, it's kind of spooky."

"Oh, geez, Andy," I joked, "I'm about to choke on feel-good...."

"Aw, c'mere, Shithead," Andy cut in, grabbing me about the neck in a headlock, messing my hair, then shoving me away. I took the opportunity to breathe Andy's clean, mas-culine scent, mixed with the pleasant smell of sweat and the clean cotton of his white, torso-hugging T-shirt. "Larry," Andy called across the bar, "Larry, c'mere for a second."

Larry is an M.D.—Oh-So-Cuddly, I like to call him—as well as a terrific defensive player who can dig balls like nobody's business. He doubles as the team physician when necessary. At 5-foot-8, with dark green eyes and a luxurious patch of soft brown curls on his head and on his chest that could stave off any winter chill, Larry was just the sort of queer you'd want to take home to meet the folks. Well-spoken, culture oozing from his pores, he was everyone's big brother and must've had his ear talked off constantly, what with all the guys bringing their problems—both emotional and physical—to lay at his doorstep. He'd quietly listen to your bitching, then he'd give you his take on the situation, and, before you realized it had happened, you were wondering at him, marveling at how thankful you were to have, at last, found the long lost big brother you never knew you had: the one who took an interest in every little thing you did and who was your best friend; whom you could count on to look out for you when you stubbed your toe; who gave you his lunch money when you lost yours, or loaned you cash for rent when you stupidly pissed it away on that DVD player you thought you had to have; who knew you well enough to leave you alone when you wanted to be left alone but would give you advice or help when you needed it the most but were too proud—or just too stupid—to ask.

More than once even I took advantage of Oh-So-Cuddly's nurturing instincts when I had some problem or other with a lover or a family member. Larry was the kind of person who made you feel like you could handle whatever came your way, not with flash or false bravado but by listening quietly without interrupting and encouraging you in subtle ways to let it all out without fear of disapproval or reprisal. I remember once, halfway through the tournament, when I was going through a particularly rough patch simultaneously at work and with my folks, he let me yak for what seemed like hours and was never once anything but sympathetic and supportive. Once you got over how gorgeous he was, the distraction of his olive skin and the furnace that burned in his dark green eyes, a fire that could light up the world, you'd realize what an extraordinary human being he was.

"So, Larry," Andy began, "corroborate my story. The

team's changed since Rickie here's been playing with us, right?"

"Without question," Larry said, authoritatively. "What used to be a bunch of overly muscled hound dogs with self-inflated egos is now a finely-tuned Stradivarius with Rickie's miraculous fingers stroking the strings."

"Aw, Larry," I teased, "keep talking like that and I'll have to suck your dick." Without missing a beat, Larry lifted his black T-shirt over his taut belly and started to unbutton his khakis until I shouted that I was kidding. That got a hearty laugh out of the two of them.

"Seriously," Larry continued, putting a brotherly hand on my shoulder and getting a bit soulful, "I'm not saying we weren't good players, individually, before you arrived, because we were. We just didn't work together the way we do now. It's a cliché, I know, but this is one case where the whole *is* greater than the sum of the parts—all because of you, Rickie. Make no mistake: If we go all the way this year, it'll be because of you."

"See," announced Andy smugly, "I told you."

"Yeah, well," I blushed, "Larry and I'll keep puttin' 'em in the air if the rest of you guys'll keep hittin' 'em down."

An affectionate slap on the butt from Andy and a paternal pat on the back from Larry and the two were off to throw some darts, leaving me alone but bursting with pride. Of course, the minute they left me alone I began to worry about Jason again. *Damn*, I wondered, *where could he be?*

Then, as if on cue, there he was walking through the door. He indulgently acknowledged everyone's shouts, briefly accepted the hugs and pats as the team descended upon him, but pointedly made his way to me through the crowd to wrap me in his arms and lift me off the floor.

KILL

Jason's hair, Jason's eyes, skin of Jason, Jason's touch, smell of Jason. Do I need to say I was in heaven?

When he finally returned me to Earth he continued to hold me close and looked me in the eye, unwilling to break the contact. "Thanks for making me look good again today, Rickie," he almost-whispered through a sexy smile.

I was sure he could feel my woody through my surfer shorts, but at that moment I couldn't care less. "Takes two, Handsome," I replied, matching his tone and smile. "Feels good playing ball with you, Jase." No longer able to keep the innuendo in my voice from seeping out, or the need to get him into bed in check, I asked, "So, what other games do you like to play?"

"Oh, so that's how it is, is it?" he said, coyly, although from his expression I could tell he knew how I felt about him.

Feeling bold, I leaned up to him for a short peck on the lips, which he responded to by quickly grabbing the back of my head firmly with his hand and prolonging the kiss. Jason's mouth, Jason's taste, Jason's smell, feel of Jason. I couldn't think, couldn't breathe, couldn't do anything but melt into his kiss, his body, the feel of his cock swelling to fill the space between us.

When he finally broke the kiss and I collected myself, I said, "Jase, you know, I would like nothing better right now than to take you out of here, throw you onto a bed, rip your clothes off, and fuck you silly."

"What a nice thought, honey," he replied, then looked around us as he continued, "but I think the guys might take offense at our leaving the party early."

When he returned his gaze to me, I smiled, looked around, and said, "Yeah, guess you're right about that. Later, though?" I met his gaze again.

FULL BODY CONTACT

"Later. Definitely. Look, Rickie," he continued, looking down, "I've been meaning to talk to you, to explain my odd behavior over the past few weeks"—but I stopped him by clasping his face in my two hands, forcing him to look me in the eye, and placing a chaste kiss on his lips.

"Don't worry, Jase," I reassured him, "you can explain everything to me later."

"Yes," he smiled, satisfied for now. "A little later." He kissed me again, turned to get a drink from Buckie, and went to mingle with the rest of the team.

"A little later" couldn't come soon enough for me. Feeling elated—and not a little self-conscious—I turned back to the bar to retrieve my beer, and Steve was there beside me, with a knowing smile on his face. "What's up, Steve?" was all I could think to say, then turned to hide the silly grin on my face behind my beer.

"Well, I can see things are progressing with you and Jase," he said, looking and nodding in Jason's direction at the far side of the bar.

I turned to follow his gaze and said, "Yeah, it seems so. Not sure what to make of it, though. I mean, like I told you, he's been awfully secretive and unavailable till now."

The patience of Steve. Weeks ago, I had let Steve in on my crush on Jason and I had been surprised to learn that he already knew, not because he'd heard it from someone else—since I hadn't told anyone—but just through the Patient One's quiet, unerring skills of observation. Steve, our team captain, Steve, of the discerning blue-green eyes, eyes that see everything and assess every person and situation fully and instantaneously.

Tall at 6-foot-3, lithe, sinewy, graceful in motion as at rest, he speaks to you and you get the distinct impression that you and he are the only ones in an otherwise crowded room, the last two people on the planet. You become mesmerized by the unhurried, gentle lilt of his voice, the pleasure he takes in assuming nothing, and explaining everything to you as though you were 7 years old and trying to comprehend trigonometry, a stranger seeking directions, or an initiate who will, at last, share in the well-guarded secrets of the Masons or the Knights Templar.

Then, when he notices that you're watching his mouth move but not hearing a word he's saying, his eyes light up, he smiles knowingly, waits for you to regain your senses, and begins again in that slow, easy manner until you've again fallen under his spell.

Of all the guys on the team, Steve was the only one I'd talked at length with about Jason.

"Yes, it does seem that he's got a lot going on just now," Steve said when I first brought up the subject of Jason's abrupt departures after games, and my frustration with his disinterest. "Well, I don't know anything about his particular circumstances," he said. "All I can do is offer what experience I've had with my previous partners, and now with Joey."

Steve and Joey have been together for six years.

"Joey was the same way when we first met," Steve went on. "There was an unmistakable attraction between the two of us, but Joey had too many balls in the air at the time, and I wasn't in any rush. I could tell that he wanted to get to know me better, but I also knew that it would be a mistake just then to force the issue. To force him to make time for me when he obviously couldn't. Although I can't be sure, of course, my guess is that, if I had pushed him to commit to me back then, we wouldn't still be together today.

Chemical, sexual attraction only goes so far in a relation-ship. Two people need to be secure, solid as individuals, and ready and willing to make time for each other. Otherwise, feelings of neglect, resentment, jealousy, and a host of other relationship-killers could surface."

Steve stopped talking for a moment, smiled, and waited patiently for me to refocus. When the moment passed, I was able to stop watching his sexy mouth for long enough to think about what he'd just said. Hmm, interesting problem, I thought. Timing. A bit like trying to get the timing just right on a jump-serve, where the approach, the toss of the ball, the leap, the extension of the serving hand, and the contact with the ball all need to be precisely in sync or the ball falls short and sails pitifully into the net.

Early in the season, my serves did just that about half the time. Steve had agreed to stay a little later with me after a game that we'd lost, in part because we sided-out a few times too many due to my piss-poor serving. In that utterly patient way, Steve helped me break everything down, from my first step to my feet landing on the court after hitting the ball, to figure out what I was doing wrong. In his own sub-tle way, Steve was, even back then, trying to teach me, simultaneously, how to improve my game while thinking more deeply about my relationship with Jason. He's a sly bastard, and I will always be grateful to him for the coach-ing, with volleyball and life, on and off the court.

"So," Steve said, "what are the two of you doing after this?"

I didn't have to ask whom he meant by *the two of you*. "Dunno, Steve," I replied, looking away. "Jase said he wanted to get together later, but nothing more specific than that."

KILL

"Go slow, honey," he said, before picking his drink up off the bar. "Let it happen when and how it does, naturally, and in good time. And good luck," he said, kissing me on the cheek and moving off to find Joey.

A couple of hours later the party started winding down. During that time I tried to put Jason's and my "get together" out of my mind as best I could. Having James there to make lewd and leading comments helped to distract me a little. I also spent some of the time listening to Andy and Dr. Larry talking about the latest AIDS treatment techniques and meds, and hung out with Sam and some of the other guys from the team who were dishing the team we beat earlier and strategizing about the Stoli team we'd be playing next. Then I got recruited by Erik and Buckie to ask Gene if he would spring for new team jerseys for the finals. Eventually, I joined Steve, Joey, and some of the other guys from the team taking turns at the pool table.

Jason made it a point to talk to each and every player individually, as if trying to make up for the standoffish impression he'd given everyone over the weeks leading up to the finals. I followed him with my eyes, trying to be as unobtrusive as I could, given the lustful anticipation that was building inside me. Every now and then we'd make eye contact and he'd wink at me, causing blood to rush to my face (and other parts of my anatomy). Finally, having made the rounds, Jason came up to me when I was about to sink the eight ball, leaned over, and whispered into my ear: "'A little later' is now, baby. You ready for me?" Without looking at him, I replied: "Just let me put this in the hole and then I'll be ready to fill yours." I tapped the cue ball just hard enough for it to reach the eight and with an unhurried pace, the eight made its slow but inexorable way into the side pocket.

With that I laid my stick on the table but didn't hear the cheering and clapping for my game-winning shot—if, indeed, there was any. All I was aware of was Jason's hand in mine as silently he led me from the table, out the door of the bar, and toward our long-awaited one-on-one volleyball match...only this time Jason would be doing the setting, and I, the kill.

Rugby Filthy
Jay Starre

Daniel came out of the scrum with the rugby ball under his arm and careened down the field. He was tackled into the mud almost immediately, his bare legs coated with the filth. Rain came down in a torrent, but the game went on. The big rugby player wiped the mud from his eyes and plowed through the opposition without a second thought. Daniel was tough. Originally from New Zealand, as a kid he had come to America, where he had taken up the sport of his homeland with a vengeance.

Another player had his eye on the redheaded Daniel. Brandon was tall and muscular, yet not much more than half the size of the burly Kiwi. Brandon was homegrown New York, but loved rugby with equal passion. The two 20-year-olds were on opposing teams and clashed over and over, tumbling to the mud, sliding along the wet grass, crashing through other struggling young men recklessly.

Brandon's lungs were heaving, his shorts and rugby jersey soaked from the incessant rain. It was getting dark as well. He stared around him in the momentary lull of the game and his eyes landed on the figure of the big redheaded Daniel once more. Although he was exhausted, Brandon's dick grew stiff at the sight of the husky rugby player. His thick thighs, his barrel chest, and his broad-nosed good looks had Brandon's balls churning. He wanted to fuck the big jock! As Daniel turned away from him, Brandon got a look at his beefy butt, powerful, big, and meaty. Brandon gritted his teeth and moaned silently. He had to fuck that ass!

The game ground to its inevitable end, Brandon's team delirious in their victory. Brandon spotted Daniel stalking off the field in the near-darkness. He slipped away to follow, hoping against hope something might happen that would throw the two men together. To his joy, Daniel moved off to the darkened stands, possibly to be alone in his misery. Brandon stalked him like a hunter after his prey, glancing over his shoulder into the deepening gloom to make sure no one was following.

He turned back to spot Daniel leaning against a railing, his head down in a dejected stance, his big chest still heaving in and out from the final minutes of the hectic game. The Kiwi's big butt jutted out behind him, sexy as hell, covered with mud and grime from the field. Brandon moved closer, racking his brain for something to say to the man.

"Good game, mate. Sorry you lost." Brandon placed an arm on the losing player's shoulder from behind, trembling slightly at the touch. The guy's back was massive, his shoulder hard as iron. Brandon couldn't help but glance down at the big hard butt now within inches of his own body. God! If he could only get into that!

"You won, and you deserved it. You were better today." The redhead glanced up and stared at Brandon, his green eyes practically invisible in the near-darkness. "But maybe next time you won't be so lucky." He grinned then and turned to press his wet, muddy body directly into Brandon's, his beefy paw coming out to clasp Brandon's where it rested on his shoulder.

They stared at each other, both grinning as they struggled in the falling night. Their bodies were pressed together, as if they were still in the game, and Daniel held Brandon's hand over his own shoulder in a fierce grip that Brandon could not break.

They laughed and tumbled together against the railing behind them, almost falling but then righting themselves. It had started as a friendly tussle, but then they were abruptly in a near-embrace as they shoved back and forth along the edge of the field in the darkness.

"We'll win next time too!" Brandon laughed in Daniel's face, his arms wrapped around the player from the front, his thigh pressed between Daniel's legs and his crotch mashing into Daniel's stomach.

"You might if you play the game with that big hard-on," Daniel hissed into Brandon's face.

Brandon realized with a sinking feeling in the pit of his stomach that he did have a hard dick and it was pressing into Daniel as they shoved back and forth in the rain. He made to move away, embarrassed to be caught out, but Daniel held him tightly, and it was then Brandon realized that there was a growing erection shoving up against his own thigh. Daniel was getting hard too!

It was nearly pitch-dark by then, the field behind them deserted, the few fans who had braved the rain scurrying to drier environs. They were alone. They were in each other's arms and they both had very stiff dicks. What were they to do?

Brandon's arms were already behind Daniel. He had no

qualms about reaching down and copping a quick grope of the big can he had been surveying all during the previous game. He clutched at the hard butt, grabbing two handfuls of muddy shorts and squeezing.

Daniel laughed in Brandon's face and then lunged forward to knock his opponent to the ground, landing on top of him and nearly knocking the wind out of his lungs. "You think you deserve this butt?—well, prove it!" He grunted in Brandon's face as he sprawled on top of the struggling rugby player.

Brandon couldn't laugh back, his body buried under 230 pounds of huge muscle. But he smiled as he heaved upward with all his substantial strength and managed to dislodge the other man while still groping his butt, although by then he had also managed to slide his big hands into the loose rugby shorts and was feeling the furry butt cheeks firsthand.

"Shit!" Daniel grunted, attempting to squirm away from Brandon's probing hands. Those hands had quickly insinuated themselves right up into the crack, feeling for and discovering the slick inner flesh there and grazing across a puckered, snapping hole in between.

The feel of that hefty, silky ass and the slick crack between was incredible. Brandon would not give up now until he had fucked it or Daniel made it clear there would be none of it. At that point, it seemed that Brandon would get what he wanted if he could only pin the hefty rugby player.

They sprawled across the wet field and rolled over and over. Brandon continued to grab and prod at Daniel's big ass cheeks while Daniel laughed in his face and attempted to pin him beneath his larger bulk. The rain kept coming down, and although it was late fall, it had been unseasonably warm before the rain had come and was still warm even with the incessant drizzle that enveloped them.

It could not last. Both men had fought a hard game only a few minutes earlier. They were exhausted. Abruptly they disengaged, both on their hands and knees, huffing for breath, Brandon leaning on top of Daniel.

Brandon was right behind the Kiwi. His hands were on his back and ass. He went for it. With both hands he ripped down the redhead's muddy shorts. The pale ass was exposed, gleaming in the gloom of the rainy night. Brandon dove for it, burying his face in the big buns and shoving them apart at the same instant. His mouth opened, his tongue came out and he was suddenly lapping at a wet, slippery ass crack. Then he was up into that crack and tickling a palpitating, snug butt hole.

Daniel was on all fours, his head hanging down. He had enjoyed the wrestling match; the other rugby player was certainly a hot guy and he had not failed to notice him during the previous game. That he had come on to him sexually had been a fantastic bit of luck—Daniel had just not wanted to seem too easy. Let the tall fucker work for it. But now that Brandon's handsome face was buried up Daniel's ass, the Kiwi shut his eyes and inhaled sharply with a big snort as he felt that tongue moving up and down the sensitive area.

Brandon had shoved the muddy shorts out of the way and let the rain wash clean Daniel's butt only for a brief moment before getting his face down there and eating butt. It was fantastic. Raunchy, sweaty ass in his face, big beefy buns with a coating of silky red hair over the hard musculature—it couldn't have been better. He jammed his cheeks between the rugby player's ass cheeks and tongued wildly, tickling and jabbing at the puckered butt hole he found there. He teased it mercilessly, vindicated by the snorts and grunts he heard coming from the general direction of Daniel's head. Brandon had both hands on that butt, spreading it wide as he chowed down on male ass, and was unprepared when Daniel suddenly reared backwards and upended him.

The tantalizing tickling of his butt hole was almost too much. Daniel's cock reared up stiff and drooling where it was trapped in his tight jockstrap. The hands spreading his ass were insistent and powerful. He managed to catch his breath and then decided he wanted more. He rose up and shoved Brandon backward with his face still buried in Daniel's ass. In one swift move, Daniel was suddenly sitting on Brandon's face, his beefy asscheeks burying the other rugby player in stinking ass flesh. Almost simultaneously, he ripped down Brandon's shorts and jock, revealing the big boner that leaped out into the night air. He swooped down and enveloped it in wet, sucking mouth.

Brandon reared up, the mouth on his dick feeling incredible. He had not expected that. And the ass over his face was just as awesome. He spread the cheeks wider and jammed his tongue right up the now-gaping slot. He tongued hole while his cock was lavishly deep-throated.

The rain came down harder, the two men writhing in the mud but getting washed clean at the same time. One had his tongue up the other's ass, the other had his tongue wrapped around a big juicy dick. They both slurped and lapped enthusiastically in the darkness.

Brandon wanted to fuck. From the way Daniel was grinding his hips into his face, his asshole obligingly opening up for Brandon's tongue, he believed the Kiwi was ready for it. He was certainly sucking avidly on Brandon's dick! Brandon went for it. With the remaining strength he possessed, he upended the bigger player, throwing him forward onto his hands and knees. He didn't wait for his reaction before leaping forward to shove his hips up into Daniel's spread butt. Brandon's hard, spit-slicked dick ended up where his tongue had just been, poking at the moistened entrance to Daniel's jock butt oven.

"I'm gonna fuck your big beefy ass, and you're gonna love it!" Brandon shouted into Daniel's ear above the sound of the falling rain.

Both of their shorts were down around their knees, and Brandon reached down to rip his own off, then Daniel's as well. The other player offered no resistance, his head down again and his big biceps bulging as he held himself up on all fours. He seemed to have accepted his defeat, and when Brandon shoved his dick back between his parted butt cheeks, Daniel shoved backward to meet the thrust. In one sudden stab, Brandon's dick sunk into Daniel's trembling butt hole.

"Fuck me, you little shit!" Daniel growled back at Brandon. Then he proceeded to buck and rear backward, driving his own asshole over the hard spear impaling him from behind. Before Brandon could react, his dick was buried in pulsing, hot male butt hole. He shouted out in glee, grasping Daniel's huge shoulders and shutting his eyes as he obeyed the Kiwi's command.

The two men squirmed and writhed in the mud on all fours as Brandon drilled Daniel's butt with his hard dick. He rammed it in and pulled it all the way out, then rammed it back in. Daniel accepted it willingly, throwing his thighs wide and locking his elbows as he took the harsh ride without a whimper. His grunts were clearly audible though, and Brandon had the weird sensation that he was fucking a pig for a moment, a big muscular hairy pig that snorted and bucked and took his dick to the hilt.

Their knees were coated in filth, their bodies drenched by the falling rain. Their crotches were on fire with the furious fucking. They fucked like dogs in the dirt. Brandon slammed into Daniel without mercy, his dick stretching open the previously tight sphincter until it was a gaping, sloppy glove that gave it all up to the tall American. Both men were in an ecstasy of sexual delight, grunting, groaning, and gritting their teeth as their dicks grew stiffer and more sensitive with the fury of their fucking.

Daniel felt every inch of Brandon's hard meat as it slid relentlessly in and out of his battered butt hole. It ached as it slammed against his prostate, it tickled as it massaged his sensitive buttlips. It never ceased its pounding rhythm, causing his dick to twitch and throb up against his belly. He could hardly believe he was on all fours in the mud, naked from the waist down, getting a big dick shoved up his willing ass in the dark and rain. The humiliation of it was a total turn-on, the raunchy animal-like way Brandon fucked him from behind like a dog was sexy as hell. And the incessant squirming of that fat snake up his ass was absolutely awesome. It all went to his head and he realized his balls were roiling with a load, and his dick was ready to blow.

"I'm gonna come, fucker!" Daniel shouted.

"You're gonna come with my big dick up your ass?" Brandon growled back in Daniel's ear, nipping at it.

That did it for Daniel. His asshole clamped down over the snaking dick, his balls churned, and his boner exploded. Jizz flew out of his untouched dick. He rolled his eyes and howled as he shuddered from head to toe in the throes of his orgasm.

RUGBY FILTHY

Behind him Brandon was equally agitated. The brutal fuck in the filth was just as exciting for him as for Daniel. The giant rugby player on all fours with his ass wide open, taking Brandon's hard bone to the hilt and loving it, was an unbelievable experience. And his dick was red-hot with the friction of his rapid fucking. When Daniel's asshole began to spasm and clamp down over it as he came, it proved too much for Brandon. He blew his own wad.

"I'm shooting up your beefy butt! I'm filling your stinking hole with my come!"

The two men fell to the muddy grass in a near-faint as both of their bodies quivered with post-orgasmic shivers. Daniel had his belly and face in the mud, Brandon had his dick still planted up Daniel's ass, draining into the Kiwi's throbbing rectum. It was awesome.

"Get off me, you big fucker!" Daniel finally growled, rolling over and dislodging Brandon. They faced each other, both spent from the game and the pounding fuck.

"I'm Brandon."

"I'm Daniel. What now?"

They eyed each other, both muddy and exhausted.

"You wanna fuck me?" Brandon finally laughed, reaching out to clutch at Daniel's stiffening dick.

"You better believe it, boy!"

It was another good 30 minutes before they finally found their way to the deserted dressing rooms. They were on their own again. This time they fucked clean, soap and water and a tiled shower stall with bright lights their trysting spot.

But they still fucked like dogs.

You can wash the filth off a rugby player's body, but apparently not out of his mind.

FULL BODY CONTACT

High Sticking
Chip Capelli

Ice hockey and men: both have been in my blood for as long as I can remember. At 13, when realized I was gay, I saw my childhood heroes in a new light. They were no longer untouchable idols, but men whose bodies I wanted to devour. They had the hottest, most graceful, powerful, and muscular bodies I could ever wish for.

As a boy, I mowed lawns, delivered newspapers, and did whatever else I could to earn enough money to buy season tickets for the Philadelphia Flyers, our local NHL franchise. Everyone thought I was industrious, working hard to enjoy my favorite sport. But I was feeding my lust, fueling my adolescent fantasies.

The skating, slamming, fighting, sweating, and nonstop movement all provoked dreams that led to many hours of jerking off. Some of the hockey cards in my collection became glued to one another.

I played intramural ice hockey all through college, drawn by the strength, smell, and look of my teammates and opponents. The coolness of the ice offset the heat of the players and made me one giant skating hormone.

But my preoccupation with turning locker room fantasies into reality kept me from being a better player. I was always the guy willing to help out an injured teammate, giving massages, rubbing in ointment, wrapping ankles, or helping with at-home physical therapy. Most of the time, the male bonding led to strong friendships and nothing more. But sometimes I found a teammate who was exploring his own sexuality, or just plain horny. Usually, it started (and often ended) with a tentative hand job. But either way I was happy to help out a teammate.

After college, I left competitive hockey and spent my time like everyone else: working too hard, falling in and out (mostly out) of love, and living life. Deep down, hockey remained a source of passion. I kept my season tickets and, though I couldn't quote the NHL stats like I used to, I kept up with the Flyers and always knew which players had the best bodies.

At 33, I had made a name for myself as writer. As such, I enjoyed a certain amount of recognition and was often invited to black-tie functions. These were usually good opportunities to remind people about my last book, my upcoming book, and so forth. Unlike most of my colleagues, I enjoyed these formal affairs. For me, the only thing as hot as a man in a hockey uniform is a man in a tuxedo. The white shirt, bow tie, cummerbund, the air of being uncomfortable. It adds up to one very sexy package.

At one such function, I ran into Billy DeYoung, editor of *CityLife,* the local bible of what was hot.

"Rickster, loved the new book," he said, before even saying hello. "Who would've picked the old maid librarian as the killer?"

"Still waters and all," I said.

"If you ever want to tackle journalism, call me. You could be the next Dominick Dunne."

"Fiction is all I can handle right now."

"The offer stands," Billy said, walking away.

"Great tux," I yelled after him.

"Slut!"

My reputation preceded me.

The next week, I read an interview with Donald Spellini, the Flyers' star and arguably the best goaltender in the NHL. With 2.04 goals against average, he was so hot that his crease hissed steam. I was embarrassed at getting all tingly over him. I felt like a lovesick schoolgirl mooning over Brad Pitt. But despite my lust, I was able to see that the interview was nothing but drivel. It was hardly enough to divert my attention from the great chest shot of Spellini that accompanied the story.

I decided to call Billy DeYoung.

"Bill, I just read an interview with Spellini. He sounded like a dolt. I know his background. He's smart. These schmucks who write the sports page are way off the mark."

"Plus he's not too hard to look at."

I ignored his remark.

"I can get him to talk. *CityLife* will get a great story. Spellini will get good press and maybe even break the dumb jock rep he's gotten."

Billy was silent.

"If he's as smart as I think he is, he won't forget my help or *CityLife*'s," I amazed myself at my persuasive powers when there was a sexy man at stake.

"If I can set something up, it's yours."

"If? Billy, you've been begging me for years to write for you."

HIGH STICKING

"I know what you're thinking. Spellini's the only starter on the team who doesn't have a rep as a ladies' man. What happens if you make a play for him and he puts your lights out?"

"You know me better than that."

"Give me a few hours," a defeated Billy said.

Later that afternoon, Billy called to tell me that the interview with Spellini was scheduled for five days later. My work was cut out for me.

The next few days were spent making calls and gathering background on Spellini. Since he had spent 12 of his 14 professional years in Philly, I knew his stats like any good hockey geek. Everybody from the front office staff to the Zamboni machine drivers mentioned what a great guy he was.

On the morning of the interview, I took a hot shower, taking time to beat off to reduce any high testosterone levels that might lead me to act against my better judgment.

I arrived early to watch the team finish practice. Don's solid form gracefully sped across the ice. He slowed at the net and ripped off his mask with a primal passion. His face glistened with sweat, giving him a sexy glow. As Don's teammates left the ice, some slowed to exchange high fives before disappearing into the locker room.

As Spellini showered, I reviewed my notes, but my thoughts kept coming back to how perfect he looked, even under the heavy hockey equipment. Wondering about the man lurking behind that mask, I was startled when the press agent snuck up on me.

"Perretti," Phil Miller barked.

"Yeah, what's up?"

"Spellini's ankle's acting up. He's down in the whirlpool

FULL BODY CONTACT

room. If you don't mind, you can start down there."

Mind? Was he nuts? Me, in the same room with the hottest hockey star in North America while he soaks in a hot tub?

I feigned annoyance. "Sure, whatever."

I followed Phil through the locker room and casually checked out the players. Judging from what I saw swinging, there's a definite correlation between cock size and hockey skill. The delightful melange of sweat, colognes, steaming showers, and medicinal rubs together with the look of strong muscles, wet hair, and scarred body parts slick from sweat or showers brought me back to my glory days of college hockey. We passed through the rear of the locker room, where a player was being rubbed down by a massive blond who clearly enjoyed his work. The player's guttural groans stirred my rising crotch. When we arrived in the back room, Don was soaking in one of three large whirlpool baths.

"Don Spellini, meet Rick Perretti," Phil said.

Don shot me a broad smile and extended a muscular arm to shake hands. "Good to meet you, Rick. I would get up, but..."

He motioned downward, implying that I might somehow be offended by his nudity.

"No problem." I tried to sound relaxed as I took a seat on a rickety folding chair, crossing my legs to hide my crotch.

My eyes were drawn to Don's chest. It was covered with thick black hair from one broad shoulder to the other. Even through the fur, I could see how solid his shoulder and pectoral muscles were. In addition to being in great shape, Don oozed sex appeal as well, a combo rare in professional athletes who regularly get their noses broken and teeth knocked out. His face was ruggedly handsome, with a wide smile offset by deep dimples in his cheeks. His deep brown eyes were surrounded by laugh lines. Dark stubble shadowed his jawline, which was tipped by a goatee. His black hair was slightly receding, cut short to give a clear view of his perfectly shaped ears, which were red from rising steam. The entire picture gave Don the dangerous yet seductive appeal of a schoolyard bully.

"I'll leave you to it," Phil said as he turned to Don. "Unless you need me to stay."

"No, Phil. We'll be fine." Don rolled his eyes and smiled at me.

"I'm out of here then," Phil said, leaving the room.

Don winked at me. "He's a nice guy, but a bit of a mother hen."

Don's "regular guy" demeanor was refreshing. I had worried that he might turn out to be a media-hyped personality, thereby shattering my fantasy.

"I saw you at practice. What did you think?" Don asked.

"The best team on ice."

"We try." Don's smile was warm enough to melt polar ice caps.

Awkward silence followed.

"Sucks about your ankle," I said, noticing that Don was staring right into my eyes.

"Yeah, it's an old injury acting up. On ice I'm great, it's wearing those fuck-me pumps in the off-season that are a bitch." Don flashed his great smile again.

I returned his gaze with a tentative smile, thinking that Don's appearance, his performance on the ice, and his amiable personality provided a definite study in contrasts.

FULL BODY CONTACT

"You've got a great mouth," Don said quietly. "Those teeth are all yours, aren't they?"

"What can I say? Writers don't get slammed in the face nearly as often as hockey stars." I almost said "studs."

Another silence followed.

"What does *CityLife* want to know about Don Spellini? I'm an open book," he spread his arms, showing off his magnificent upper body. The breathtaking view of Don's outstretched arms, exposing his thickly furred armpits, made my mouth dry. *I could spend a week chewing on them,* I thought as I looked at my notes.

I'd been an armpit fan since my first taste in a college dorm room, when I bit into one to stifle my cries of passion. The taste, smell, and feel of the thick hair has always brought me back to the heart-racing excitement of forbidden passion I felt as an inexperienced kid.

"Tell me something about Donald Patrick Spellini that no one knows."

Don rubbed his chin, stroking his goatee. I wondered if his long fingers were an accurate indication of what was floating between his legs. "What makes you think I'm hiding anything? I think I'm a what-you-see-is-what-you-get kind of guy," he smiled.

"There must be something that I can't read on the back of your hockey card."

"True, everybody has secrets. Even you."

"Me?"

"You did research on me, I researched you. I found out a lot about you."

"Find anything good?" I played right along.

"You're damn good at what you do. Plus, I've read all of your books. The new one was great. The librarian as

HIGH STICKING

the killer? Fucking genius, man," Don laughed.

"The pressure's on to write a Pulitzer Prize–winner."

"Not at all," Don laughed as he put his hands into the water. I musingly wondered if he was touching his dick.

"I'll ask what everyone wants to know. Is there a special lady in your life?"

Don almost sneered. "That's not for me."

What the hell did that mean? How should I react?

"Must make for a lonely off-season," I observed.

"I do OK. Don't worry about old Donny."

"Let's talk hockey," I said. "You made 11 saves last night. Is it safe to say that nothing much gets past you?"

"Nothing gets in unless I want it in. When me and my stick are in charge, watch out." Don adjusted himself in the tub.

"What a stick it is."

"Only as good as the man in control," Don countered.

"Then, what control."

Don smiled and the interview went on—40 minutes of questions and answers, mostly about the team's chances in the playoffs and Don's future in Philadelphia. Throughout the interview, my dick was in a state of arousal, but I worked hard to remain professional, for Billy's sake if for no other reason.

Suddenly, Don smiled, raised his left arm, and wiped his brow, giving me another great pit shot to torture the bulge between my legs. He looked at his hands and hoisted himself from the tub. "Christ, I'm turning into a fucking prune in here."

The sight of Don rising from the tub made me weak. His matted chest hair continued down his rippled stomach, spreading out into the most magnificent crotch I had ever seen. His thick, long cock was in a floppy, semierect state, with his ample balls nestled behind it. His muscled thighs led down to solid calves covered with the same dark hair that dressed the rest of his body. He stepped away from the tub and reached for a towel. The rear view was spectacular. His well-defined back led down to two delectable half moons. Michelangelo never chiseled a more perfect ass.

"Now I can relax." Don unfolded a chair and gave his toned body a quick drying before sitting down and resting the towel over his left thigh.

"What...what about your ankle?" I tried to hide my excitement at seeing my dream man in the flesh.

"It's fine," Don said as he rotated his head. "There's a bitch of a kink in my shoulder, though."

"Should I get the trainer?" I asked through a lump in my throat.

"You take a shot at it. I bet you've got good hands."

"I don't know how good I am," I said, approaching him from behind. "But, anything for the team."

"You'll do great," Don said, removing the damp towel from his thigh and tossing it on the floor.

"Here goes." I rubbed my palms against the moist flesh of his shoulders. His muscles were firm but tense, giving very little as I dug in deeper as if to channel my sexual energy away from my dick.

"To the right."

"Like this?" I said, trying to follow his direction.

"Up a little."

I repositioned my hands again.

"No, like this," Don's strong grip guided one hand over each shoulder, grinding my fingers into his shoulder blades.

"Got it?" Don turned his head and smiled, still holding my hands.

HIGH STICKING

"Got it." I felt faint from my blood pumping into my cock rather than to my brain.

I massaged his shoulders for several minutes as Don rolled his head from side to side. I glanced downward and noted that his dick was bigger than it had been earlier. I decided to risk it all and gently pulled some hairs on his upper chest.

"Magic touch, man," Don moaned, "that's what you've got."

"All for the story," I said as I continued kneading my palms into his firm flesh.

"You've got great hands. I bet you're good at handling a stick too."

"Depends on the goal," I said.

"What's your goal?" Don asked, rotating his head.

"A great interview that makes us both look good."

"Looking good, feeling good, helping out a friend. That's what it's all about."

I kneaded his shoulders in a slower, more sensual manner. I pressed my cock ever-so-gently against his back as his moans became more frequent and audible.

The sound of a locker slamming shut from the adjoining room suddenly jolted me back into reality. Don abruptly stood, grabbed his towel from the floor, wrapped it around his waist, and walked toward the now-empty locker room.

"I've got to get home," Don said with his back to me.

"What about the interview?" I asked as I followed behind.

Don silently dropped the towel and quickly dressed in a pair of jeans, a sweatshirt, and boots.

"Follow me in your car," Don said. He didn't look at me as he tied the laces of his boots. "We can pick up at my place."

FULL BODY CONTACT

"Sure," I said.

"What are you driving?" Don asked in the parking lot.

"The Bronco," I said, pointing to a parking space a few yards ahead.

"I'm right here," he said as we approached a black Lexus. "Follow me."

As I followed Don through the city to the pricey Main Line, my heart raced in anticipation of what lay ahead.

Twenty minutes later, I pulled into the driveway of a small estate. Don parked and walked over to open my door.

"What a gentleman," I said, immediately regretting it.

Don just smiled.

"Very impressive," I said, taking in the medieval look of the property.

"It used to be a monastery," he laughed.

We entered through the kitchen, and I was amazed by stained-glass windows that wrapped around the room.

"I heard about this place when I was researching the article. It's something," I said. "Can we set up a photo shoot?"

"Sure. I love it here. It's a good place to escape from reality. It almost brings me to another time," Don said.

There we stood, in the middle of his kitchen, experiencing the same awkward silence we encountered earlier. Finally, Don opened the refrigerator.

"Beer, soda, juice?" he asked.

"Whatever you're having."

Don took out a bottle of cranberry juice and poured two glasses.

"To our urinary tract health," he said, handing me a glass.

I raised my glass, gulped the tart liquid, and placed the glass down on the counter.

HIGH STICKING

"Want a tour?"

"Sure."

The large living room was what I expected of Don now that I had gotten to know him a little better. The Old World stone walls contrasted against the modern art and mirrors. Leather furniture was tastefully arranged throughout the room. Thick, ornamental braided rugs covered the hardwood floors. In one corner there was a large glass case with various certificates, medals, and trophies attesting to Don's successful hockey career. Another corner housed a large-screen television and stereo system in an oak entertainment center. If someone had described the room to me, I would have expected it to be gaudy. Seeing it in person illustrated how one's separate tastes can come together to make a powerful statement.

"This is where I live," Don spread his arms to show off the room as if he were Vanna White.

"It looks like you get a lot of use out of it."

"I usually crash on this couch, it's almost as wide as a double bed and more comfortable."

"A photo spread in here would be great." I was trying to keep my mind on the interview.

"What kind of pictures do you see?"

"You, lying on the sofa, a pair of gym shorts, no shoes, a Flyers tank top, smiling with the remote in your hand."

"Sounds like a night at home," Don smiled.

"Ah, the solitary life of a hockey superstar."

"It's not too bad. But I do get lonely once in a while." Don walked toward me.

"Good-looking guy like yourself? I'd think they'd be waiting in line."

"Hardly," he laughed.

FULL BODY CONTACT

"Their loss," I said as he got closer, so close that I could feel his breath on my face.

We were gazing into each other's dark eyes. I could feel myself breaking out into a nervous sweat.

He moved in close to me and pressed his body against mine.

"Do you think I came here just to get some goalie cock?" I felt his crotch against mine.

"Didn't you?" Don squeezed my ass even harder.

"I think you brought me here to get into my ass."

"Pretty high opinion of yourself, Perretti. I like that."

"I can feel your dick begging right through your pants."

As Don released his grip, I reached for his crotch. "Pretty solid stick." It grew harder by the second. I unzipped him, reached in, and grabbed his cock. It was hard as steel, hot to the touch, and very thick.

I grabbed a handful of Don's sweatshirt and pulled it over his head, getting a terrific view of his armpits in the bargain. I unbuttoned his pants and shoved them down to his knees. We took a minute to liberate ourselves of whatever clothing we had on. Once situated, I faced Don and took a nipple in my mouth. At 5-foot-10, I was six inches shorter than Don. He used his height advantage to rub my shoulders and back while I chewed on his nipples and chest.

Don embraced me in a solid body lock with his arms, chest, and shoulders, his strength encompassing me with lust and hunger. Spreading his legs and squatting as he gently yet firmly maintained his awesome hold, he lay me down on the long leather sofa.

After rubbing his dick into mine, Don stood up and surveyed the scene. I flipped over, sticking my ass up ever so slightly, anticipating what Don wanted. He immediately

HIGH STICKING

and mercilessly plunged his middle finger into my willing hole. Even dry, it felt good. He quickly pulled it out and replaced it with two fingers. As he stretched me wide open, he kneeled between my legs. Each time he pulled out, he replaced whatever was in me with something else. A thumb, two fingers, the middle finger from each hand. He covered his fingers with saliva to provide some lubrication, making each plunge even hotter. I looked across the room and found an ornamental wall mirror where I could see our reflection. Though the image was somewhat distorted, I could still see our reflection on the sofa. Watching my fantasy man, this hockey superstar, perform a digital assault on me drove me wild. Don's talented hands were not limited to his handling of a hockey stick.

"Like that?" Don asked.

I responded with a loud moan.

"You ain't seen nothing yet!" Don promised as he took his hand out of me.

He disappeared through a doorway that I assumed led to a bathroom and returned with a tube of lubricant and a few condoms. He knelt between my open legs, ripped open the package, unrolled a condom onto his tool, slathering it with lubricant. I could feel his cock's bulbous head ease into me. Once he'd gained entry, Don went for broke and drove his cock home.

"Man, you are hot!" Don screamed. The reflection of his hairy, sweaty, muscular upper body contorting in pleasure in the mirror drove me wild. I tightened my hole in response.

"Keep it tight, make me work for it." Don was getting into it. The faint odor of chlorine from the whirlpool added to the mix of sweat and leather, giving the perfect aroma for hot sex.

Don continued his rhythmic, powerful fuck as I was getting more lost in the reflection. His hands grabbed onto my waist and pulled me to my knees, allowing him to fuck me with even more vigor. He rubbed my ass as I forced myself back onto his heavy root. The friction from our hairy thighs rubbing together felt great. My cries of delight were so loud that I could barely hear the creaking sounds of the sofa springs. The blood-boiling concoction of erotic pain and pleasure brought me to new heights. Suddenly, Don broke me from my trance with a hard slap to my ass.

"I'm shooting, man," he screamed as he shoved his cock into me and held it in position. He resumed thrusting, more forcefully but slower, as if he was trying to get every second of pleasure before he popped. Swollen balls slapped against mine as he blew a wad of jism so powerfully I swore I could feel the latex barrier expand within me. I watched Don's reflection as he locked his hands behind his head and banged me for all he was worth, letting every drop of juice flow into the straining rubber. I spied his hot pits in the mirror once again and felt a desperate urge to coat the sweaty, musky hair with my spit. I shot my load without even touching my dick, spewing out heat I hadn't felt in a long time.

He pulled out of me, ripped off the condom, tossed it aside, and flipped me over, careful to keep me from lying in my own come. I felt empty without his magnificent hose inside of me. His cock was a beauty: long, red and slick from the load that had coated the inside of the rubber. His balls were hanging low.

I got up and stood next to Don, ready for that awkward post-fuck moment. "I guess I ought to clean myself up and head out."

HIGH STICKING

"You're leaving?"

"Do you want me to stay?"

"I do," he said as he put a hand on my back.

We embraced and he pushed me back onto the sofa with the same gentle force he had used earlier.

"Did you think I would let you go after that?" he asked as he smiled into my eyes.

He drew his sweaty face closer to mine and invaded my throat with his long hot tongue. He hadn't kissed me up to then; I'd assumed that Don was an "as long as we don't kiss, I'm not a fag" guy. But, like his cock, his tongue had a will of its own. He scorched my lips with passionate kisses. After a timeless moment, he broke away and covered my neck and chest with small kisses as he ran his hands over my shoulders, neck, and head. I lay back and happily found my nose right in the middle of his armpit. I hungrily feasted on the thick, wet hair, biting the underlying flesh, to Don's delight.

As he brought his flushed face to mine, his sweat dripped onto me. This time, the silence spoke volumes. He nuzzled my neck, rolling partway off of me and tossing aside the back cushions, proving that the couch was indeed nearly as wide as a full-size bed.

The next thing I knew I was waking up under a thick wool blanket with Don at my side in the same position. I briefly wondered how the blanket got there, but given that it was January and I was naked in a stone-walled house with no visible insulation, I was just happy it had appeared. Don seemed to be in a deep sleep and I thought it rude to just leave, so I drifted back to sleep.

The next time I woke up, I was alone, wrapped in the same blanket. I was a bit disoriented, not sure of where I was or how I had gotten there. I stood up, stretched, and looked around for my clothes, figuring it was as good a time as any to get dressed. My clothes were nowhere to be found. I headed for the only other room in the house that I knew of—the kitchen.

"Hey, sleepyhead," Don said.

I rubbed my eyes to gain focus and saw Don standing at the sink. He was dressed: sweatsocks, navy sweatpants, and a grey sweatshirt with the sleeves cut out, giving me another great pit shot.

"Didn't know what you'd want to eat, but I figured with a nice *paisan* like you, spaghetti is always a safe bet, so voilà."

Don pointed at the intimate setting in the dining alcove. Red-and-white-checkered tablecloth, bread basket, wine glasses. All the makings of a romantic dinner for two. "I folded your clothes. They're in the laundry room. But I pulled out some sweats and a shirt for you too. They're much more comfortable and much sexier. Not that you don't look great the way you are now."

I looked down at myself, naked except for the wool blanket I had haphazardly wrapped around my body.

"I could give you a robe," he offered.

I didn't answer, I just stared.

"Are you OK?"

"Yeah, I'm fine," I said, not quite sure that I was.

"You're surprised. I guess I am too."

"I didn't expect this," I said.

Don disappeared for a second and returned with the promised casualwear. I quickly dressed.

"Sit," Don said.

I climbed on a stool under the island in the center of the kitchen as Don handed me more cranberry juice.

"When I said I did my homework on you, I meant it.

You know, Billy DeYoung is your biggest fan."

"Billy?"

"He thought we'd hit it off. He told me that I should get to know you, interview or not."

"Billy knows you're gay?"

"I came out to him years ago. It helps to have a friend in the press that I can trust." Don put spaghetti into the boiling water. "I know I should have just asked you out, but you were so damned irresistible sitting in that chair, I couldn't hold back."

I was having trouble processing what was going on around me.

"Billy set me up?"

"He thought we'd be simpatico. He said when you called him about the interview, it hit him like a ton of bricks."

"I really enjoyed being with you."

Don came over to the stool and stood between my legs. "I can't predict the future, but I know that I like what I see. You're fun, sexy, smart, independent. Hell, I wanted to fuck you ever since I saw your picture on the back of your book a few years back."

I was flattered. "I've wanted you since I got your rookie card 14 years ago."

"Looks like we've got a lot of time to make up for." Don rubbed his rough chin into my neck.

"No promises. Except to be honest with each other." It was hard being sensible with him so close.

Don looked me squarely in the eye. "Agreed."

He smiled, and I knew that no matter what happened, I would be a better person because our paths had crossed.

FULL BODY CONTACT

Starting in the Start Position
Joel Arthur Nichols

We walked back from the party holding hands. It was my first time holding hands with a boyfriend in public, letting everyone around see that two guys were taking each other home. We went up to my room and over to the bed without turning on any lights. My bed lay under the tall windows, and the bright light from the dorm courtyard was enough to let us make it across the room. I kissed him. He kissed me back, and I pulled him on top of me. He was the first one I kissed, tongue to tongue, and I think I was his first too. I couldn't believe how different his mouth was from a girl's; knowing that a man was behind the lips and teeth, feeling the stubble starting to sprout around his mouth, and having my back cupped by his hands exhilarated me. I would have liked to push him down and unbutton his shirt. I would have fucked him that night, on my green comforter, beneath my college sophomore decorations, but he had to get up early the next morning. I walked him back to the door and pushed him up against it, again pushing my tongue into his mouth and feeling his dick on my hip. "I'll see you tomorrow night," he said, and walked out the door. I watched him through the peephole until the end of the hall.

The first time I went to his room, he gave me two glasses of red wine in quick succession and I was almost too drunk to leave and meet friends at a party across the street. He had to work.

The next night, I wasn't going to leave after a few kisses so he could get back to the web design that took up all his free time. I went into his room and sat down on the weight bench. It was white and had a black cushion with books piled on the end. A white towel hung over the barbell, and I saw his workout clothes on the pile of dirty laundry. Gray tank top and blue mesh shorts, like basketball shorts but not as long. I thought of him lying there on his back, chest and arms straining to take the weight from the rests above his head, lower it, and then put it back up—his pit hair sweaty and his thigh muscles showing their cleft as he did it. I imagined the deep breaths and groans as he lifted.

I asked him about his life before he transferred to our school. Two years at a conservative little college I'd never heard of, frat-centered and sports-run. He was closeted to everyone. Wrestled. "You wrestled?" I thought of my freshman-year roommate and his best friend. One a hockey player and the other a wrestler. One morning, a few weeks into our first semester, I had looked through the peephole in the doors separating his room from mine and seen him change from a towel to clothes after a shower. As he dropped the towel to dry off his balls and put on an ugly pair of straight-boy plaid boxers, he had turned so I could only see the curve of his ass and hip. I'd wondered if he suspected I was looking, and so had turned away from the

FULL BODY CONTACT

peephole. I was repulsed and attracted to his hockey gear, a stinking pile of plastic and nylon heaped in a corner of the room or on the balcony we shared. I wanted to see his jockstrap.

"Yeah, in high school too." High school wrestlers were even hotter than college wrestlers. I remembered getting changed for gym class near the end of the day when the wrestlers were getting ready to travel to a meet. Wrestlers always walked around the locker room naked while the rest of us struggled to stay covered at all times. They were all older boys. I was fascinated by their hair—on chests and legs. Some had that discernable treasure trail leading to their dicks. My eyes were always going to their treasure trails, wanting to look at their dicks. I wanted to be able to have a clear picture in my head forever, so I could go home and jack off. Now I was kissing a former wrestler. "Wow. You actually used to wrestle at school. Didn't you get turned on?"

"Not really. It was the weigh-ins that were tough. We all had to stand there in our underwear while every guy weighed in. When it was our turn, we dropped our underwear and stepped on. Everyone looked."

"Hot. How'd you not get turned on?" I pictured him a few years younger, surrounded by the jocks from my memory. They were in the team room from my high school, standing variously in white briefs or jockstraps. The first time I saw a jockstrap in that team room, my dick was so hard I almost had to run out of the room or explode. I thought I'd never see anything that would get me that excited again.

"I had to concentrate so hard...focus attention away from all the guys standing there almost naked." I wanted to ask him to describe every guy in that locker room, every stomach and the hair on it, every ass and back, every pair of balls hanging under every dick. I wanted his attention focused on those guys.

I wanted all his attention focused on me.

"Will you show me a move?" He laughed a little. I don't think he'd expected me to be so forward in getting him on the floor. After nights of getting scared off and blaming work, I think he knew that we were going to finally hook up.

"Really?" He seemed like he couldn't believe I was serious, but he knew I was.

"Yeah. What should I do?" I looked at the weight bench again and my imagined picture of him straining on his back floored me.

"Um, I'll show you the start position. Get on your knees." I got down and he knelt behind me. I couldn't see him, and I really wanted to lean back to feel if his dick was getting hard. "Now bend over and put your hands on the floor." I did it and he bent over me. I pushed my ass back against his hips and felt his dick. He felt me feel it and breathed in quickly. "This is it...how we'd start." I reached back and put my fingers around his calf. I squeezed a little and started to massage it. He kissed my neck and started rubbing my shoulders. I went all the way down to the floor and he put one leg on either side of me, rubbing my back and shoulders. After a few minutes, I rolled over and kissed him. Pulling his head down so I could get his lips to touch mine, I felt a little sweat on the back of his neck. I thought of him on the bench again and my dick strained forward, pressuring me to open my zipper and touch it. He felt it and kissed me harder.

"Let's get on the bed," I said, and pulled myself up. He switched off the light and turned on a mix tape. Courtney

FULL BODY CONTACT

Love sang while I unbuttoned his pants and pulled them down. Sitting on the edge of the bed with his crotch at eye level, I saw the blue and yellow waistband of his briefs. I could have grabbed my cock and finished right there, knowing that he had on white briefs. I left his pants around his ankles and ran my hands back up his legs, over the knees and hips, and then brought them together at his briefs. I could see a lump of balls and dick, but couldn't make out anything definite. I pressed my thumbs against his lower stomach, right above his dick, smoothed my palms over his stomach and chest—his stomach was firmer than I had imagined—and then I felt his ribs. I moved my fingers across his chest to the thick patch of hair right below his collarbone. I touched his nipples, which surprised him. Putting my cheek against the now-bigger shape in his briefs, I noticed a little hole where the cotton had given out. I pinched his nipples. He had his hands all over my head and neck, and I pulled him down onto the bed.

Soon my pants and underwear were off and I was left in a white undershirt, kneeling on the bed with the head of his dick in my mouth. It curved toward his stomach and wouldn't bend straight. I had to put one ear below his ribs and take it sideways into my mouth. I wanted to take it all the way in, but my throat resisted. He grabbed my hips and held my legs from the back of my thigh. With lotion that seemed to appear from nowhere, he started to jack me off and suck the head of my cock. The weight bench was to my right. I saw the white frame and black cushion and the towel. He groaned the way I had imagined him doing when I stuck the tip of my finger, wet with spit and lotion, into his ass. "Yeah," he said as I started fingering him, and I came all over his chest and in his hand. I took his dick in my mouth and put more of my finger in his ass. I shifted to be below him as he jacked off and I continued to fuck him with my finger—now two fingers. I could see the blue mesh shorts in the laundry pile and the white briefs on the floor. He started to come and I thought of all the wrestlers I hadn't seen since high school and would never see again. We lay on his bed, out of breath from coming, chests heaving—mine in a white T-shirt, his in a uniform I'd imagined there, over the layer of sweat.

Kleet
Mark Wildyr

I pushed through the door of Biggs Gym for the first time in over a year. A police exercise hangout and boxing club, the place was no Stilman's New York or Johnny Tucco's Vegas, but neither was it an automated Gold's—although there were a few new body-shaping machines in the back. Nonetheless, it looked the same and smelled the same and Jimmie Biggs still propped up a corner post of the boxing ring. He probably hadn't moved since the last time I was here. The grizzled old retired cop pried himself off the ropes long enough for a grimace that passed for a smile and a hard handshake.

"Hal! Long time, no see. Heard you got shot. You OK?"

The blunt, gruff greeting brought a genuine smile. "Caught one in the side, Jimmie. Nothing you haven't gone through once or twice."

"Yeah. Comes with the territory. But you're OK now, right?" The old cop barely waited for my nod before turning back to the ring. "Got something you gotta see. Look at this kid!"

He didn't need to be more specific. A tall, dark young man sparring with his partner was the "kid." The boy dominated the ring, pushing his heavier opponent around virtually at will. As I watched, he loosed a furious series of jabs and rattled the other boxer with a right cross to the jaw. Jimmie immediately called a halt to the session.

"Come here, Kleet," the manager called, after making certain the other boxer was OK. "Meet Detective Lieutenant Hal Marcus outta downtown. Hal, this here's Kleet Drum, cycle cop outta the Far North Precinct. Kleet, Hal usta be my best boy, 'fore he got hisself promoted to lieutenant and claimed he was too busy for the important stuff." Jimmie pried the kid's mouthpiece out.

"Lieutenant," the boy acknowledged, touching his gloved hand to the fist I offered. "Nice to meet you. I heard of you. They say you're pretty good."

"Was," I acknowledged. "Time and circumstance caught up with me."

"Don't let 'im bullshit you," Jimmie cut in. "Youngest lieutenant on the force. What are you, 28...29? That ain't old. So what if you got shot up a year ago and ain't put in your time? Bet you're still damned good."

"Be glad to go a round," the boy offered, holding out his hands for the trainer to take off the gloves. He ripped off the headgear Jimmie insists his boys use in practice, and I almost gasped. The kid was as handsome as sin. No wonder he was so dark, he was an Indian, but not one from around here. At about 160 his body was compact, despite his 5-foot-10 frame. The chest was probably 45 inches...hell, Charles Atlas's was only 47. Heavy pecs, defined lats, flat belly, good thighs and legs. The kid's biceps and triceps rolled with controlled power every time he moved. There wasn't a hair on his smooth, dusky body that I could see, although an ebony mop plastered down by the sweat of his efforts covered his head. The broad forehead was smooth and unmarked except by finely curved brows. Sensitive black eyes danced restlessly. Black eyes are hard to read, and his were doubly so for some reason. The nose was straight and a little fleshy, as were the lips framing the wide mouth. A firm jaw, slightly rounded; skin that looked Hispanic with a rosy overtone.

In the nanosecond it took to size him up, I flashed on my ex-partner when we were his age, probably not much over 21, and for the first time in five years I suffered a hunger not experienced since Bryan resigned from the force and moved away.

"Let me get back in condition," I said, slapping my lean belly, "and I'll take you on."

"Fair enough. Let me know when you're ready. I'm here most nights." The boy turned away, giving me a good look at his wide, tapering back.

"Gonna enter the departmental bouts." Jimmie's voice interrupted my inspection. "Take the belt most likely. He's good, Hal. And that's why I'm glad to see you."

I looked at him suspiciously. "Why's that?"

Jimmie placed a hand on my arm and motioned me to the side of the room, although there was no one within hearing since Kleet had left the ring for the light bag. "I...uh, I got a problem, Hal. I...uh, I gotta go in the hospital. Put off taking care of a damned hernia and the doc won't let me stall no more. Got me scheduled for the 15th of next month. Kleet's first fight's that night. Need you to stand in for me. Maybe for the next bout too."

"Me? Hell, get somebody who's been around, watched him, knows his moves."

KLEET

"Ain't nobody I'd trust like you. Kleet don't know about it yet, so don't say nothing, but I sure need you to back me up on this."

"Give me a week," I sighed, mentally rearranging my schedule. "Let me see how I come along."

"Good enough," Jimmie smiled, knowing he'd suckered me into it. "Do your stretches and hit the rope. Then take the heavy bag." He gave orders like I was a kid who'd just signed on.

I was on the bag, beginning to get back into my rhythm when someone steadied it from the other side. Although I couldn't see clearly through all the sweat in my eyes, I knew it was Kleet Drum. He leaned into the bag while I punished it with everything I had for five minutes. Then I stepped back.

He came around the bruised bag and gave me a grin. "You've done this before," he said. "You a southpaw?"

"No, why?"

"Hitting it harder with the left."

"Got shot in the right side. Guess I'm holding back. Thanks for pointing it out." I went at it for another 10 minutes. He stayed and watched, until I gasped and gave it up.

"Not bad for the first workout in...what?" he asked.

"A year."

"Not bad at all." He gave me a crooked smile that lit up the room and turned his back on me. "Gonna hit the showers."

"Me too," I panted, "if I don't collapse first."

I consider the shower room one giant, fucking trap. I grew up in shower rooms, first in public schools, then in college and on the job. They never made me uncomfortable, until Bryan Shalter that is. Like most street partners, we became friends in the cruiser and buddies at bars and ball games. Neither of us was married, so we bummed around;

FULL BODY CONTACT

joined at the hip, some of the guys used to claim. They didn't know how true it was. Our second year together, he broke up with the girl he planned to marry, got drunk, and came over to my place, where we ended up in bed. The next morning we swore it would never happen again, but when we showered in the locker room after work, our eyes betrayed us. I followed him home and butt-fucked him with both of us stone sober.

We never moved in together, but we spent most nights with each other. If social activities dictated dates, we'd meet after taking them home. Fucking the girls merely seemed to whet our appetite for what we shared. We loved each other without words for two years. A week after I verbally declared my devotion, he turned in his badge and moved to the West Coast. He tried to tell me why, but never quite got the words right. It didn't matter; I understood. We were getting in too deep. He knew we'd eventually come out of the closet if we remained together and wasn't certain he could handle it. Beautiful, blond Bryan. I wondered how he was doing.

Ever since, I've been leery about shower rooms. Couldn't avoid them, just been a little defensive. Justifiably so, if my reactions now were any measure. Kleet, in the shower opposite me, was of more than passing interest. I completed my inventory: lean, powerful thighs; a patch of curly black hair clustered around his long, thick, uncircumcised cock. I'm no expert on men's cocks, since my experience was limited to Bryan's and my own, but this one looked as if it would be a monster when roused. As he washed himself, it almost got out of hand, thickening and stiffening a little. Self-consciously, he turned into the spray, and I studied his tight buns until I felt the need to turn away myself.

I started my regimen in earnest after that, greeting the

KLEET

road at 5 o'clock every morning for a run. When I worked up to five miles, I found out where Kleet Drum ran and joined him occasionally.

The first time I climbed into the ring with him I worked the pads, holding up the big mitts for him to jab. The most important thing I learned, beside the fact that he could punch like a pile driver, was that he had developed a pattern...four left hooks before he crossed with the right. He heard my warning, but didn't really heed it until we sparred a couple of nights later. I counted four jabs, slipped the right I knew was coming and landed a hard right to the ribs. He recovered nicely, but he'd gotten the message loud and clear.

Our force isn't big on departmental strata, and the camaraderie of the gym was pretty democratic, so it was natural that we developed a friendship. This meant accepting his cycle buddy, as well. Andy Lawson was a blond kid Kleet's own age whose fair Midwestern good looks made me think of Bryan. Most of the time Andy worked out on the machines at the back, but occasionally he joined us at ringside to watch his partner work out. I soon realized the blond adored the Indian, probably more than was socially acceptable. He covered it well except when he watched from ringside; then it was apparent for anybody who wanted to see.

The night Jimmie told Kleet about the hospital and formally turned the kid's training over to me, we ended up in a neighborhood bar without Andy, who was on a date. Kleet permitted himself two beers three nights a week while in training. Tonight was one of them.

"Well," he ventured after the first long sip. "If Jimmie's gotta hand me off to somebody, glad it's you."

"I've gotta warn you, I'm gonna change a couple of

FULL BODY CONTACT

things. You're too aggressive. You don't pay enough attention to defense. Nobody ever hurt a good defensive fighter, and they've won lots of fights."

"Yeah, I know," the kid acknowledged. "I trust you, Hal. You say it, and I'll do it."

After a few minutes of ring talk, we turned to the job. He liked being a cycle cop and thought Andy was a good, reliable partner. I learned he came out of poverty on a northern reservation, which he escaped by joining the army, apparently right ahead of the local sheriff. In turn, I told of the arrest of a burglary suspect with no history of violence that went wrong, resulting in a hole in my side. I didn't realize that my leg was leaning against his beneath the table until he shifted.

"Sorry," I mumbled, moving my leg and glancing up into his black, unreadable eyes. He shrugged and changed position again. The calf of his leg rested against my shin for a long moment. So help me, I got an erection.

He drained his glass and shoved it aside. "Think I'll pass on my second one," he said casually. "You ready to go?"

Suddenly uninterested in the taste of alcohol, I rose, turning awkwardly so he wouldn't see my condition, not certain I was successful. We walked the block to the gym. My car was the only one in the lot.

"Where are your wheels?" I asked.

"Walked over," he said. "It's only a couple of miles. Needed the exercise."

"I'll take you home," I volunteered.

Kleet crawled into the passenger's side. "Nice car," he noted approvingly. "A detective lieutenant's pay must be better than a cycle cop's."

"Supports a bigger car loan," I acknowledged.

KLEET

Once we were out of the parking lot, he turned in the seat to face me. "Probably should have jogged. I'm sorta restless."

Somehow we ended up at my place trying out a sweet nonalcoholic wine I'd bought earlier. The kid was wired, and I wasn't in much better shape myself. I kept thinking of his warm leg against mine at the bar, the sight of him naked in the shower, the look in his black eyes. My erection returned. Abruptly, Kleet put down his glass of fake wine and stood up from the table in my kitchen. Grabbing my arm, he hauled me to my feet.

He took a stance, and I slipped into my own. He threw a few light jabs that I blocked. Even his light jabs stung, so I walked into him, going into a clinch. Surprisingly, he permitted it, snuggling close and giving me some pseudo-jabs to the sides. Then he dropped his hands to his sides, head on my shoulder, body against mine. If he didn't know before, he knew now. My bone stabbed his groin. Neither of us moved. Finally, I pulled away and cleared my throat roughly.

"Need another shower. I'll leave the door open in case you wanna use the can or something." Those black, black eyes studied me as I spoke.

After I was in the shower, he entered the bathroom. In moments, it sounded like a horse was pissing in a bucket; my cock reared up against my belly. Through the frosted glass of the shower enclosure I saw him turn and stare at my blurred image. My cock got harder. Then he walked out. Disappointment clutched at my guts.

I dried off as quickly as I could and went back out into the living room. He wasn't there. Nor was he in the kitchen. He wasn't anywhere. He had left. Concern puddled with disappointment in my belly. Damn! What had I done?

Deciding the long walk would be good for what ailed him, I took a slug of whiskey and tossed and turned in bed for an hour before finally going to sleep.

The next morning, I made a point of driving over and joining Kleet for his run. He threw me a bright hello while we did our stretching exercises, with no sign of distress over the night before. Taking my cue from him, I avoided the subject.

Andy stuck close to us the rest of the week, which was probably a good thing. The blond kid was learning a lot about boxing, and I even put him in the ring once as a sparing partner when all I wanted was to point out a couple of things to Kleet.

Friday night, Kleet surprised me by announcing he had a date after the workout. Apparently he threw Andy a curve as well. The kid gulped a couple of times and watched his partner out the door after their shower. Then the boy turned and looked at me as if to say...do something! I did; I took Andy to the bar for a drink and watched him down a pitcher and a half. When it was time to leave, I wouldn't let him drive.

"Live clear...clear on other side town," he slurred when I offered a ride home. "Take bus," he announced solemnly and started for a nearby bench. Buses had quit running hours ago.

"Afraid not, Andy. Buses have gone beddy-bye. Come on, I've got a couch you can use. You on duty tomorrow?"

He shook his head loosely. "Nope."

I gave the kid some bed linen and a pillow and went to change into my robe. When I checked on him, Andy, clad only in his jockeys, was on his knees beside the couch

KLEET

fighting with a sheet. It was almost like seeing Bryan in the house again. I swallowed some painful memories and went to give him a hand. He suddenly turned his head. Whether by design or accident, his nose was in my crotch. We both froze for a second, and then his arms went around my hips, pulling me into him. He moaned as he opened my robe. I was naked beneath it.

The boy sucked the end of my flaccid cock into his mouth. One hand clasped my balls; the other steadied my growing erection as he took all six and a half inches. I braced my arms against his shoulders as he worked on me. It had been a long time, and I got there in a hurry.

"Andy!" I warned, but he kept sucking and stroking. I shot. "Oh, man!" I groaned, thrusting at him as my load pumped through me. He took all the come I could deliver. After I worked through my orgasm, he remained on his knees, my flagging prick in his mouth. I don't think he knew how to end things.

"Oh, shit, I'm drunk!" he managed to mumble around my glans without biting me. Then he reared back and looked up the length of my torso. "Am I in trouble, lieutenant?"

"I don't see any lieutenant here. Just me, Hal. The lieutenant's probably at the station."

The kid breathed a big sigh of relief. "Sorry, man. Don't know what got into me. But...but...well, you're a hunky son of a bitch."

I pulled him to his feet. "So are you, Andy. So are you." He accepted my kiss hungrily. I stripped away his shorts and led him into the bedroom, where he flopped facedown on the bed. I stretched out beside him. His shoulders were firm and freckled. I ran a hand down his spine and over the smooth buttocks. After five minutes, I was ready again. He parted his legs as I moved atop him. He took me effortlessly and, enjoying the freedom of this larger orifice, I fucked him energetically. For a few seconds it was Bryan beneath me again. As I indulged my fantasy, I'm sure he had his own. No doubt in his own mind, it was Kleet's big cock fucking his ass.

Andy was quiet after I cleaned us with warm water and a washcloth. He was probably a cuddler, but was a little on edge after getting it on with a lieutenant. He couldn't contain himself forever. "You do this with Kleet?"

I tousled his mop of straw. "No," I answered without thinking. "But don't ask me that again. Would you like me to discuss what we did with him?" The brief silence before he answered no was revealing. "You love him, don't you?"

The head beneath my hand nodded once. "How did you know?"

"By looking at you."

"It shows?" he squeaked alarmingly.

"Sometimes. Sometimes it's right there on your face."

"You think he knows?"

"No, I don't believe his mind works that way. He probably understands on some level that you love him, but he'd think in terms of 'best buddy' or 'brother,' not the way you feel it."

"Doesn't matter," Andy said bitterly. "If...if he was going to do it with a guy, it'd be somebody like you. Somebody he looks up to and admires."

I didn't know what to say, so I said nothing. Soon his breathing told me that he was asleep. I followed him to dreamland soon thereafter. He woke me at dawn, sucking my cock so thoroughly that I abandoned the idea of joining

KLEET

Kleet for the morning run and fought hard to make five miles by myself.

For the remaining time until the fight, I made Kleet concentrate on defense and conditioning. We ran together five days a week. We worked the medicine ball until I thought my belly would crack open like an egg. I put on the gloves and tried to put him down, forbidding him to do anything but defend himself. The night before the bout, I turned him loose and had bruises to show for it.

Kleet's opponent for the first match was a big sergeant from the southwest precinct by the name of Butch Class. He was older by five years, but also a lot more experienced. I'd already given Kleet his instructions, so for the most part I left him alone to do his mental preparation after he climbed into the ring. During the preliminaries, Butch put the stare on him, but the kid refused to be intimidated. The bell rang, Kleet exploded from his corner...and led with an uppercut! It connected and Class went down.

Andy, who was acting as cutman, and I both went nuts! Nobody *ever* leads with an uppercut; even the rankest amateur knows that. But he had, and it worked. After a standing eight count, the bout resumed. Class was slightly confused. He'd heard that Kleet Drum was a savvy fighter, but he'd opened with a boneheaded move like that...even if it had decked him. To make matters worse, Kleet was a peek-a-boo fighter and could let go with either hand. Class spent the rest of the round waiting for my boy to lead again with his right, but it never happened.

The second round was totally different. Butch Class was pissed and went on the offensive. Kleet closed up and did a magnificent job of slipping and blocking...and even ducking. Butch never managed to land a clean blow in the entire three minutes between bells.

The third round was all Kleet's. He defended, but toward the last he turned aggressive, blocking the ring, jabbing with that piston-like left, and then crossing to land a solid punch on the jaw. Immediately, he followed up with a flurry of body blows. Class never went down again, but he was beaten. The decision was unanimous. All three rounds went to Kleet.

It took some time to get back to the dressing room because all the fans wanted a minute with the winner. When we finally arrived, Kleet put Andy on the door and told him to keep everyone out, saying he wanted a critique.

As soon as the door closed behind him, he locked it and went wild, dancing around the room and hugging me in glee. He stripped off his trunks, got out of his cup, and threw them in the corner.

"We did it!" he almost shouted. "Man, we did it!"

"You did it, Kleet. You were great...except for the uppercut. What the hell got into you?"

"He was too confident. I had to make him more cautious. His chin was right there, so I did it! And it worked."

"Yeah, it worked. And I don't ever wanna see you do it again, you hear?"

"Yeah," he agreed, standing there in his magnificent nakedness.

I couldn't help myself. My eyes raked his fine body. He seemed half-aroused. Suddenly, he grabbed my shoulders, whirled me around, and bent me over the massage table. My trousers hit the floor, and he was on me. The entry was painful despite the fact that his cock was coated with his sweat. It felt as if he were splitting me in two. I cried aloud. His hands, still taped, brushed my shoulders roughly, mov-

KLEET

ing down my back and pulling my buns apart, giving him better access. His cock bit deeper. I groaned again.

Then it was all right. He was buried to the hilt. He withdrew and lunged again. The excitement of the entry behind him, he settled into a rhythm, ignoring sounds at the locked door as people tried to get past Andy. He fucked me then. He fucked me with a passion, energy, and intensity I'd never experienced. The few times Bryan had mounted me, he'd almost been apologetic. Not Kleet! He fucked as if he had a right to my ass. He claimed me so totally that I was torn between needing to experience his climax and never wanting it to end. But the end came. He came. He came with an explosion of hard, urgent thrusts and long, hot spurts of semen deep inside my bowels.

Then he pulled me back against his body, and with his cock still inside me, beat my penis until come poured out onto the table. As my internal muscles contracted, I felt him harden again. He pressed me flat against the table and fucked me unmercifully, beautifully. He fucked me like a man fucks his woman. Like a lover pleasures his *amorata*. Like a bull takes a cow. Like a stallion!

While he showered, I cleaned things and staggered over to open the door. The wounded look in Andy's eyes told me he knew what had happened. There was a crowd of people, mostly cops, behind him, pressing to congratulate their hero of the moment. Kleet came out of the shower naked and unconcerned, shaking hands with each well-wisher before bothering to cover himself with a towel.

All during the next week, I expected Kleet to make some move after our training sessions, but it was as if he had forgotten anything had happened. Andy stayed away from the gym for a few days, and then showed up on my doorstep late one night. "Do me like he did you," he begged. I did my best for him.

Jimmie Biggs came back, insisting he wasn't strong enough to take over Kleet's training, but he did some nosing around and came up with the fact that the kid's next opponent out of the North Valley Precinct was a southpaw. That was bad news. Everyone hates a southpaw...even another southpaw.

We found a left-handed sparring partner, and even though he wasn't that good a boxer, Kleet had trouble with him. The second night, I heard Kleet swear through his mouthpiece as he switched to a left-handed stance. They both had trouble after that, but at least Kleet was landing some punches.

I quickly glanced around the club and failed to spot any strange faces. Not willing to trust to luck, I stepped into the ring and put a stop to the session, loudly berating Kleet about switching stances. He started to give me lip, but suddenly caught himself and accepted my abuse.

Later in the shower room, he saw that no one else was around and turned on me. "You thinking what I think you're thinking?"

"Absolutely. We're going to work later so I can close the gym. I don't want anybody to see what we're doing. Think John will go along?" I asked, meaning the southpaw sparring partner.

"You bet. Only got another week before the fight, but that's plenty of time."

When Kleet Drum climbed into the ring with Robert Hoya and took up a southpaw stance, the valley cop's strategy was destroyed. Remember, nobody likes a southpaw...even another southpaw. Kleet took the round from his strong, beefy opponent. When he came out for the second round in his regular stance, it took his foe a precious minute to reshape his thinking. By that time, Kleet had landed two hard blows to the body and a clean one to the head. The other fighter was into clinches by then, and the referee didn't like that. At the beginning of the third round, Kleet started falling into his old pattern of four jabs and a hook. When it happened for the fourth time, I could see that the other boxer had caught on. Hell, it was so obvious even Andy saw it.

"You gotta do something!" the boy exclaimed. "Kleet's gonna get clobbered!"

"He knows what he's doing," I said hopefully.

He did. He loosed two vicious jabs and followed with a hook, catching the man totally off guard. Hoya had figured that after two more jabs, he'd slip the hook and catch Kleet off balance. Instead, he landed on his ass and took an eight count. From there on, he fought flat-footed. His legs were gone. Less than 30 seconds later, a straight right hand put him down for the count.

Andy took up his post before the door without even being told. As soon as the door was locked, Kleet stood still long enough for me to remove his gloves and bindings before stripping us naked and pushing me flat on my back atop the massage table. Standing at the edge, he put my legs on his shoulders and pulled my hips forward, entering me without once taking his eyes from mine.

It was a rush watching him as he fucked me. His confidence was amazing. His technique was more evident this time. He started slowly, built to a tempo that about brought him over the edge, and then stopped to lean forward and kiss me deeply. Then he began again, this time holding my own swollen cock in his hand as he beat himself against me. He fucked without stopping until his eyes rolled up in his head and he shuddered through a tremendous orgasm. Once he recovered, he stroked me to climax, enjoying once again the massage my internal muscles gave his huge cock when I came. And then, as before, he proceeded to fuck me again.

When we were both exhausted, he stood with his cock still half inside me and leveled the stare boxers use to intimidate others. "You may be a lieutenant, and me just a lowly patrolman, but your ass is mine from now on, you understand?"

"Any time you want it," I sighed, beginning to regain my breath. "But what about Andy? He's hung up on you, you know."

"Yeah, I know. And I know you've been fucking him too. Well, we'll just have to figure out what to do about Andy, won't we? But I'm the only guy who fucks you...right?"

"Right, Kleet. Absolutely right!"

A Shadow's Dream

Ernie Conrick

Throughout all of Hellas the poets sing victory odes about the beautiful wrestler Alcimedon of Aegina, and of his Athenian trainer Melesius, who is said to be as swift as dolphins in the sea. At the Pythian games at Delphi Alcimedon brought Melesius his 30th crown by sending four boys back home to the shameful silence of their families, to walk the alleyways and lick their losers' wounds.

The poets sing songs of athletes, and it matters not to most if these songs be true, but only that they satisfy the ear. Alcimedon's name will echo through time for as long as people have ears to hear, but these songs don't tell the whole story. I know, for I was one of those boys he sent home to silence and shame, though in truth his crown of bay leaves should be mine. I lost it to Alcimedon for reasons that had nothing to do with strength or courage. Rather, I lost a contest of a different sort.

My name is Strophius of Thebes, son of Theoxenus. It is a name, I have no doubt, that you have never heard. Neither Pindar nor Bacchylides or any of the singers who have traveled from game to game through all the successive Olympiads sing odes of me. Poets, like whores, want money for their attentions, and I have none to offer them. So I will tell the story in my own way and, if the hearer can endure my rough speech, he will find that what I have to say makes up in truth what it lacks in meter.

From birth my face was crooked, with a nose going in one direction and teeth in another, so that I have always looked as homely as the men who waste their days in the marketplace of Athens talking nonsense from dawn to dusk, debating the existence of phantoms. As I grew, my hair became thin and my skin discolored in uneven areas around my eyes and mouth, so that I appeared as one afflicted by illness.

Despite my appearance, however, I was vital and strong and I grew tall and vigorous, such that the children who tormented me for the shape of my face paid dearly for it by the shape of my arms. My teachers at the gymnasium saw something of value in this and turned me over to the tutelage of Tithonus the Champion at his private palaestra. By the age of 12 I could not be defeated by any wrestler under the age of 15, and by the time I completed my 15th year even Tithonus himself had difficulty throwing me.

At the local festivals I was beaten only twice in two years, and both times it was while I suffered from injuries. At all other times, too many times to count, it was I who threw my opponent. My strength was such that I had only to firmly grasp the other boy's hand in mine to know that I would be victorious. From that simple grip my arms would bring him to my torso, where the sinews of my chest and neck would grind him like grain against the miller's stone. My forearms grasped and twisted, rent and crushed the arms of them all until I would squeeze the very courage out of their bodies like the washerwoman wrings water from a cloth.

Each victory was sweet, but also bitter, for I knew that many of my vanquished opponents enjoyed the attentions of lovers, while I, despite my strength, went utterly unnoticed. At the symposium, I could see them reclining on couches in the arms of attentive men. I could see their lovers plying them with choice wines and expensive fruits, teasing them with figs, and rubbing their shoulders with fragrant oils, while I sat apart and alone chewing only on my own spite. So each boy that entered the wrestler's ring with me was the target not only of my strength, but also of my jealousy and hatred. More than one of them turned and fled before our skin had met.

Tithonus the Champion was sure that I would bring him crowns from all of the games, and that I would go to Olympia and increase his glory in the eyes of all of Hellas. And so, when I had reached the age of 18, he took me on the long trip to Delphi, there to display my strength and skill before the entire world at the Pythian games given for the pleasure of divine Apollo.

It was there, at the temple Apollo Nymphegetes, on the eighth day of the month of Gamelion, during the performance of the divine sacrifices, that I first saw Alcimedon, as if in a vision. His eyes were as dark as a starless night and his hair was as fair and fine as the threads of a spider's web. His face held an unearthly beauty, and each limb was in perfect proportion. His demeanor was modest and his eyes cast always to the earth. From the sandals on his feet to the slender fingers on his long hand he was incomparable to any boy or man in all the world from its creation to this day.

When I saw him and beheld his face wavering in the

smoke of the sacrifice, my heart, which had always been hard and seamless like a gem, jumped in my breast. I remember nothing of the sacrifice but his face, and if asked I could give no account of the pronouncements of the oracle.

With him was Melesius of Athens, the famed trainer who was said to be as swift as dolphins in the sea. Certainly this was true at one time, but at the Pythian games he looked as massive as a cow carrying a pair of calves in her belly. His limbs had grown heavy and his hair had fallen out such that his head reflected the light of the sun like a polished shield. His girth pushed the cloth of his garment outward so that the shape of his chiton was like a shepherd's tent and his nose was red from drinking.

At the banquet that night I watched young Alcimedon recline in the thick arms of Melesuis, who, on the thin premise of instruction, grasped the boy's arms and legs and held him tightly to his broad chest. Each time his charge's cup was empty Melesius would have it filled immediately with the choicest vintage. Whatever Alcimedon wanted, Melesius would have it brought, from roast duck to special breads and cakes to honey candy. In the same way that a trainer feeds his prize falcon, Melesius fed Alcimedon from his own hands, holding each fig or cake before his beautiful face with his thick fingers and whispering into his delicate ear until Alcimedon's face blushed and his scarlet lips parted and he swallowed what was given to him.

The great banquet continued late into the night. No expense was spared for the entertainment of the athletes. Female slaves and singers filled the hall with the sound of the lyre and the harp and the flute. A chorus of boys sang odes to Apollo and to the inhabitants of Delphi and to the gods and heroes. Bacchylides himself was there, although

A SHADOW'S DREAM

he did not sing, and each of the contestants tried to speak to the poet, the one who alone could make them immortal.

It was the richest feast I had ever attended, but it gave me no pleasure. My heart was dark with jealousy and desire for Alcimedon, such that I could not eat and the music seemed barely to touch my ear. It was not until a servant girl sang love verses to the sound of the harp that I awoke and listened and was carried away by a verse from the poetess of Lesbos: "Then love shook my heart like the wind that falls on oaks in the mountains."

Tithonus, thinking that my lack of appetite and my melancholy demeanor came from the desire to vanquish my rivals at the games, commended me on my seriousness and boasted of me to others. "This boy," he said, "thinks of nothing but winning the crown."

Hypnos, god of sleep, did not come to me that night. When I closed my eyes a vision of Alcimedon's face appeared before me, smooth, beardless, angelic. Then came Melesius's corpulent shapeless visage and I would awaken. At last, I raised myself from my bed and sat on the steps of the court-yard, leaning against a column. Above me Orion the hunter was high in the sky, fearlessly hunting his quarry.

I looked at the myriad of stars in the cosmos and consid-ered that all our fates are written in their movements and in their turning. Scanning the heavens, I considered each star and wondered which one in particular had caused me to be born wholly without beauty and to be struck by a love so hopeless as mine for Alcimedon. Each star twinkled back at me inno-cently, as if to deny its responsibility for my misfortune, and so I cursed them all. If only my misfortune could be clothed in the skin of a man and brought to the stadium, I thought, I could then change my fortunes by my own strength.

FULL BODY CONTACT

At that moment I heard the shuffle of sandals and I looked to see who, like myself, could not find sleep. Across the courtyard in the darkness between the colonnades I saw Alcimedon himself, returning from Melesius's quarters. His chiton was crooked and the beauty of his legs was revealed in the starlight. Full of wine, he could not walk in a straight line, and he embraced each column as he went, as a whore loves each of her customers in turn.

His arms around a column, he turned to me suddenly, noticing me for the first time. He did not speak, and in the dimness of the courtyard and with the blurring of his vision I do not think that he knew my identity. As for myself, I thought it fortunate that there was no moon on that night, for my ugliness was hidden from him. He called out his greeting to me in an unsteady voice. I answered him roughly. Then on he went to the next column and then the next, until he was lost in the shadows.

✪ ✪ ✪

The next day, while the chariot races, the stadiodromos, and the pentathlon were held in the stadium, the boxers and the wrestlers trained at the palaestra. The cheers and jeers of the crowd could be heard by all of us, and the knowledge that tomorrow we would be the objects of either praise or derision sobered us all.

Tithonus introduced me to some of the older wrestlers who, he said, would soon be my rivals when I turned 20 and had to compete with men instead of boys. I wrestled with Ephermostus of Opus and Theaeus of Argos, but I was tired from the previous night and could not concentrate. Theaeus threw me twice and Ephermostus once. In neither

A SHADOW'S DREAM

case did I show great courage or skill, and I could see that Tithonus was unhappy with my performance.

Diagorus of Rhodes, an old friend of Tithonus and a champion once at the Olympian games, believed it was nervousness that hindered me and tried to take my mind off the next day's competition by instructing me in boxing. I had no skill at this game. My arms, trained for grasping and lifting, swung slowly when thrown behind a fist, and my thick neck and torso lacked the dexterity to dodge his blows.

Far from hurting me, however, the fists of Diagorus cleared my head, and my melancholy, so pronounced since the day before, seemed to shake free from my heart. Soon enough I was playing at the pancratium with both boys and men, all of us talking of the morrow and our chances of taking home the crown. I knocked one man to the ground by sweeping his leg from under him in a way that nobody had seen before—the move being one that Tithonus, and few others, used.

As I oiled my body, Tithonus approached me with Melesius and Alcimedon. Seeing Alcimedon, naked and oiled for the palaestra, all my melancholy from the previous day returned, and I could not lift my eyes to look at him. When I did, I could see that not only were his face and his limbs beautiful, but that his torso and chest were of excellent proportion, graceful and dazzling, his entire body brown and slick with oil—perfection embodied.

Melesius suggested that Alcimedon and I wrestle together in preparation for the competition. Tithonus agreed, oblivious to my averted gaze and my shaking hands.

How can a man strive with that which he loves? Watching Alcimedon's graceful form in the ring of the palaestra, my heart was torn asunder. Each movement of

FULL BODY CONTACT

his limbs was poetry, as his feet shuffled in the dust and his unmarked skin glistened in the sun.

He was quick and graceful in his movements but lacked any great strength. Several times his oiled limbs slipped through my fingers, which, when grabbing hold of his beautiful form, seemed to have lost all of their power. Finally, catching hold of his arm, I pulled him close into my chest and enveloped him with my tree-like arms. Like a sparrow caught in the talons of a hawk, his graceful form struggled in my grasp, his chest against mine, his legs wrapped around mine as a vine wraps around the trunk of an oak tree.

Pressing him close, I could feel his hairless brown skin against mine and smell the oil in his hair. It would have been no great feat to throw him, but instead I let him slip from my hands. Twice more I pulled him to me, crushed his form in my grip so that the very breath in him was wrung from his frame. Each time I wanted only to grasp him, to mangle his beautiful body like grapes in the vintner's press, until his essence flowed from his frame like wine.

Only when Tithonus cursed my gentleness and threatened me with a beating for my courtesy, which he perceived as girlishness, did I end the match, laying Alcimedon's body down in the dust of the palaestra as a mother puts her infant into the cradle.

That night, as I slept, the god Morpheus, son of Hypnos, sent me a dream. In this dream I wrestled with Alcimedon again, in the palaestra. In my dream the building was deserted except for the two of us. As before, I brought his body close to mine and held it as he struggled. Gently I turned him and threw him to the dust, grasping his middle. This time, however, I did not let him go but, holding him tightly to myself, I took him as men take boys in Hellas. We were covered in dust and oil, and in my dream Alcimedon stopped struggling and gave himself to me, his dark eyes flashing over his oiled brown shoulder, his voice crying my name quietly in a soft voice over and over again.

In my dream I felt such pleasure as surely is reserved for gods. Lost in my passion I called out his name, "O Alcimedon," I said, "most beautiful of boys, Alcimedon!"

At that moment, however, he answered me in a different voice. "But you have made a mistake, my friend," he said, "I am not Alcimedon but Antaeus, the son of Poseidon, the giant of Libya, collector of skulls, who takes my strength from the dust of the Earth."

I laughed at him, and thought that he must be jesting, but suddenly I could feel his girth and his strength increase beneath me, and he shook me loose and rose to his feet. Again we came together, but he was stronger now and I had great difficulty in moving him. I picked him up off of the ground to throw him, but he had grown heavy and large and he slipped from my grasp. When he touched the ground he became yet stronger and now it was I who was trying to avoid his grasp.

In my dream Alcimedon grew large before my eyes, so that he was truly Antaeus, the giant of Libya, and he towered over me, picking me up in his massive arms and shaking me violently. "Antaeus!" I cried, trying desperately to fend him off.

At that moment I opened my eyes and it was not Antaeus the giant, but Tithonus who was shaking me awake. Outside the sun was rising and the day of the games had arrived. "Antaeus?" Tithonus laughed at me. "Are you Hercules himself to strive with Antaeus?" I said nothing, and did not speak of my dream to him.

FULL BODY CONTACT

Tithonus had told me that the crowds of spectators are fickle, and that both their affection and their derision are short-lived. He therefore urged me to ignore all people but my opponent when in the stadium. I had always followed his advice, but in the stadium of Delphi on that day I could hear all of the comments made on my entry. "How thick his limbs are!" one man would say. "And how ugly his face!" came his companion's inevitable response. When Alcimedon entered, however, the crowd could not contain their interest, greeting him with cheers and whistles. "Ganymede has returned from Olympia!" cried one man, carried away with his beauty.

My first contest caused me no difficulty. My opponent, a youth from Corinth, was strong but unsteady on his feet and unskilled in his movement. I wasted no time, but threw him two times to the dust, separating his arm from his shoulder with my viciousness. The crowd reacted with calls of derision as the pride of Corinth was carried from the stadium, attended by his trainer and his brothers.

When the crowd saw Alcimedon's graceful oiled form wrestle, on the other hand, they were instantly charmed. Although smaller than his opponent, Pytheas of Cyrene, he avoided his clumsy grasp with quick steps and dexterous hands. Time and time again his opponent would try to draw his body to his own, only to end with an armful of empty air. Eventually Pytheas grew tired. His chest heaved and his head began to lower. Now Alcimedon, seeing his opportunity, dragged him from side to side until his feet tripped over themselves. Then Alcimedon, like a wolf on the back of a stumbling goat, forced him to his hands and knees. A

A SHADOW'S DREAM

cheer such as I have never heard rose from the masses of spectators.

My next opponent, Xenacres of Attica, was almost as ugly as myself. Looking at his face—his oversize nose, his small eyes, his missing teeth, his head shaped like a melon—I was reminded of how others must feel when looking at my own face. And so, as if trying to destroy my own ugliness, I vanquished Xenacres, running his misshapen head into the dusty ground with such force that he too was carried from the stadium by his family, never to wrestle again. In the crowd there was such an uproar against me that I feared for my life. Men tossed apples, eggs, and rocks at me until Tithonus stood over me and shielded me with his cloak.

Later, Doryclus of Sicily won the second throw against Alcimedon with a skillful headlock. Tied at one throw each, Doryclus menaced the beautiful Aeginan with his strength and endurance, time and time again tying up Alcimedon's graceful limbs in his python-like arms. Alcimedon tired and could not stand without leaning on Doryclus, his mouth opened and his eyes watered and his knees bent. Gathering all his strength, the boy I loved pushed the Sicilian away. Nonplussed, Doryclus tried to close with him again, chasing him around the ring, stalking his quarry such that it had nowhere to go.

At that moment I saw, as all people present did, a sudden cloud of dust rise from Alcimedon's foot and cover the eyes of Doryclus. Blinded, the boy clawed at his eyes and shook his head. Then Alcimedon, seeing his chance, jumped on his opponent, who could not see him, and threw him to the ground.

Though Doryclus and his trainer protested, and though I am convinced there was not a person in the stadium at

Delphi who did not see Alcimedon's treachery, nothing was done. Melesius protested that the dust was a simple consequence of Alcimedon's stumbling feet, and with shrewd arguments and subtle wording he eventually prevailed upon the judges. The crowd, for its part, did not desert Alcimedon for a moment, but chanted his name in a tremendous roar. The judges, afraid to anger the crowd, deferred to Melesius, and Alcimedon raised his hands to the laudatory yells of the spectators.

As I watched, I was heartbroken to learn that his beautiful form was wholly without virtue. As he stood there with his arm raised into the air by Melasius, I was filled with anger. In my final match of the day I sent Hieron of Syracuse home to lick his loser's wounds, defeating him in two straight throws. This I did as Melesius and Alcimedon looked on, and when I raised my hands in victory I scowled at both of them. And when the crowd pelted me with apples and rocks, I reveled in their hatred. *Here are the people of Hellas,* I thought to myself bitterly. *They make a hero out of a scoundrel and praise deception over honesty.* I looked into their faces, which were drunk with wine and with lust, and I could see that the farther away they were from myself, from the stadium floor, the braver they appeared and the louder they shouted. They who love beauty over virtue, they who despise me for my ugliness but love Alcimedon despite his treachery. I hated them all.

When Alcimedon won his final match of the day I was elated, for I knew that we would meet the next day and fight for the crown. For the remainder of the day my mind was full of dark fantasies. I imagined how I would twist his arms and snap his bones, how I would pick him up over my shoulders and break his back. All of the spectators would see their

A SHADOW'S DREAM

hero maimed in front of their eyes. I myself would do it. I would punish them for loving him and punish him for being a scoundrel and the gods for creating us both as we were.

So dark was my mood that in the evenings I did not hear the sound of the flute and the lyre. My hatred for all of Hellas ate at me from the inside like a worm at the core of an apple. I sat by Tithonus's side, not speaking or smiling. Near us in the odeion Melesius and Alcimedon sat side by side, Melesius whispering in Alcimedon's ear with great seriousness. I dared not look on his face.

The songs went on and on, and I did not listen to any of them. The myths of Hellas seemed intended for somebody else. They were full of beautiful nymphs and handsome gods, courageous heroes and wise kings. What had I to do with any of them?

And then, almost as if in answer to my own question, a slave girl sang of Aphrodite and Hephaestus, the son of Zeus cast out from Olympia for his own ugliness. Aphrodite loved him anyway, sang the slave girl, because of his skill as a craftsman and his good heart. As the music played, my heart, so dark just a moment before, stirred.

At that moment, unable to help myself, I glanced in the direction of Alcimedon. His eyes, large and dark and shining in the dimness of the odeion, were fixed on me, and he returned my gaze for a long moment. Far from the stare of an adversary preparing for battle, his expression was one of gentleness, docility, and remorse.

In my breast my heart leapt, and I imagined that perhaps, as the beautiful Aphrodite was drawn to the ugly Hephaestus, Alcimedon was drawn to me. Now each note of the music and each stanza of the odes echoed in my heart, and my fantasies of violence turned to fantasies of love.

FULL BODY CONTACT

In my bed I could not sleep, but lay awake, drunk with desire. While I should have been imagining the next day's bout and the glory of winning a crown for Tithonus and the city of Thebes, I thought only of Alicmedon's eyes, his soft expression, the small bruise on his lip, his hair as fine and fair as a spider's web.

I arose and went to the courtyard, hoping that perhaps I again would see him there, as I had the first night. As on the first night, the stars were bright in the sky above me, but just as impenetrable. Somewhere in the heavens, I told myself, was written my fate, what crowns I would wear, what banquets attend, what victory odes my name would appear in. Also written there in the heavens before me—in the steely blue light of distant stars—was the outcome of my love for Alcimedon. So I stared with intense concentration on the constellations and, in my fatigue and my excitement, I imagined that the stars in Cassiopeia blazed in the darkness as I looked at them, and took this for an omen.

A short time later, as I had hoped, I saw Alcimedon walking along the colonnade, returning from Melesius's quarters. In the starlight his chiton glowed a bluish-white against his dark limbs. I wanted to approach him and speak what was in my heart, but suddenly, as I watched his form pass between each column, appearing and disappearing with each passing second, my courage, which in the gymnasium was unflagging, deserted me completely.

He did not seem to see me, and was about to pass out of my sight when suddenly he turned his head in my direction. In the starlight I could see his white teeth bared as he recognized me and smiled. Immediately, almost without a thought, he turned and walked toward me, calling his greeting as he crossed the courtyard. And so he who I had

A SHADOW'S DREAM

thought a coward showed more courage than myself in this matter. While I sat unable to move, my back against the column as if I were a statue in a fountain, Alcimedon, showing no fear, approached me and I was ashamed.

"I was hoping I would see you," he said. He then praised my skills and my strength, saying, "Without doubt, on the morrow, the crown is yours."

He speech was as fair as his form and as he spoke my heart was wholly opened to him.

"The crown means little to me," I said, "except that it gives me reason to hold you close to my breast." At that, even in the dimness of starlight, I could see that his face reddened, and he smiled silently back at me. Then, standing close to him, his back against a column, I told him of my love for him, how I could not sleep because his face was always before my eyes, how I felt that I would rather depart for far off Hades than be parted from him, how there was no crown in all of Hellas that compared to a moment with him in my arms.

Against the column I caressed him, pressing my body against his, kissing his neck and his face and unfastening his chiton so that it fell to his feet and he was naked before me. And he returned my kisses and flung his arms around my neck and drew me to him, yielding himself to me in the courtyard, naked and shameless in the starlight.

Suddenly he tried to pull away. He protested that we should sleep in preparation for the morrow. He tried to dress himself, but I placed my foot on his chiton and would not move it. Now, naked on his knees, he tugged at the garment and pleaded with me to let him go, but I would not.

"Does the lion release the gazelle once it has tasted its blood?" I jested. He looked up at me, his dark eyes wide and

FULL BODY CONTACT

docile, and placed his hands on my thighs. He said that if I would give him his garment, he would take me to a place where we could spend the remainder of the night undisturbed.

I yielded and he dressed quickly. Slipping out of the palaestra, we crossed the agora together. All of Delphi slept, the windows of all the buildings were dark and the fires at the temples extinguished. In the starlight the buildings were pale and seemed almost to turn a delicate shade of blue. I followed Alcimedon's white chiton through the streets, pausing in front of the fountain of Poseidon to embrace him again. Later, a strong wind swept over the hills, pressing Alcimedon's chiton to his body. I imagined that Zephyrus, the god of the west wind, had seen him and, unable to control himself, was tearing at his garment.

At a traveler's inn on the slope of the valley on the road leading to Athens, Alcimedon made arrangements for a room. As soon as the door closed behind us I was upon him, greedily gathering his body to myself and kissing his upturned lips. Inspired by Zephyrus, I did not unfasten his chiton, but ripped it from his body, rending the seams with a single tear. He did not protest, but entwined my legs with his and pressed his the maddening suppleness of his body to mine.

Soon we were a tangle of arms and legs, knotted together on the bed. In the dark I held his body between my hands and I caressed him and covered him in kisses. My lips lingered on his lips, my hands rubbed the fullness of his chest. When I took him as men take boys in Hellas, he uttered a cry, for my manhood is as thick as my arms.

"Stop!" he pleaded. His cries were like music to me: I was happy to know that Melesius's girth did not extend beyond his stomach, and that none had loved Alcimedon as

A SHADOW'S DREAM

I had. Soon his cries of pain turned to cries of pleasure and he no longer told me to stop.

Before dawn I loved Alcimedon no less than four times while he lay on his stomach in the dark. In the starlight he was only a dark, fragrant shape, his skin was of an impossible smoothness, and his hands were as small as a girl's.

Between raptures I lay on his back kissing his hair and we talked of many things, of his childhood in Aegea and the customs of that place, and of his late father, Iphion, who had passed away in his sleep only two seasons previous.

"With his passing," he said to me, "all of life seemed without purpose. To what avail do we struggle? What crown can be won that will save us from Hades?"

"Man is but a shadow's dream," I answered. "Or so says Pindar the poet."

Alcimedon lay his head on his arm and sighed, "What else says the poet?"

"'Men's happiness is early-ripened fruit that falls to earth from the shakings of adversity.'"

"So is this our salvation then?" he asked as if disappointed. "To enjoy what advantage we can till we are laid low by fate?"

"Perhaps," I answered, "that we find a type of immortal life in the victory odes of poets who preserve our names throughout the ages."

"And what of those for whom no ode is written?"

"They pass from the earth without a whisper."

"A shadow's dream?"

"So I suspect."

He shuddered beneath me and closed his eyes. "Love me again, Strophius, that I may forget this talk."

When Helios climbed the slopes of Mount Parnassos and

FULL BODY CONTACT

vaulted into the heavens, and the skies of Hellas reddened with the arrival of Eos, the goddess of the dawn, Alcimedon and I sat upon the edges of our bed, our eyes red and swelled with sleeplessness.

Settling into my arms, his dark eyes on mine, he said, "I cannot strive with you today."

"Nor I with you."

"And yet all the stadium will soon fill with those who wish to see us darken each other with blood."

"I care not about those in the stadium."

"But what of glory and victory odes?" he smiled shyly at me.

"The only glory I desire is your presence, and I would rather the poets write love verses of us both than victory odes for one."

With that we decided to run away and leave Greece altogether. At the coast we planned to find a ship and sail for Crete. We even imagined, after a time, to reach Egypt. I told Alcimedon what I had heard, that in Egypt there are no mountains, so the kings of Egypt built their own mountains out of stones.

"Can you climb them?" he asked incredulously.

"I know not why," I answered. "Surely we shall climb them."

Alcimedon was silent for a moment.

"I know of a place not far from here," he said, "on the road to the coast, a secluded glen where we can meet." He told me its location and how to find it. "Go to the market," he instructed. "Buy provisions for our trip, then meet me there in the third hour. I will collect what I can of my inheritance from my brother and meet you there."

Then, with fair words, we parted, I for the marketplace and he for his brother. My heart was light, and I had not a

A SHADOW'S DREAM

care for Tithonus and the crown, for I had traded it all for something far better, the love of Alcimedon. It was early in the marketplace and the merchants were just erecting their tents for the day. I filled my traveling bag with dates and raisins, figs and olives. I added to it a skin of what wine I could afford and several woolen garments to protect us from the cold winds of the Aegean.

With a heavy bag and a light heart I set out from Delphi, avoiding others as much as possible. I reached the place described by my lover, a shady copse hidden from the road. There I set my provisions down and waited. I imagined the stadium filling with spectators, their bloated faces and loud voices, and I imagined Tithonus and Melesius walking nervously through the crowd, looking for us in vain. Slowly it would dawn on all of them that those who were to spill their blood and break their own bones for their entertainment and enrichment were gone forever. I was sure that neither they nor the poets would ever forget these games.

As I sat there lost in my own pleasant thoughts, three men suddenly set upon me. They grabbed my arms and forced me to the ground. I resisted with all my strength, but they were heavy men and I could not escape. Once atop me they bent my arms behind my back until one of my clavicles snapped in two. Then one of them set upon my ankle, twisting my foot so that there too I heard the crack of bones. After they had done thus to me they departed, as quickly as they had come. I cursed after them and rolled upon the ground in agony. I do not know how long I lay there on the ground. After a time had passed and Alcimedon had not arrived, I decided that something must have delayed him and that I would walk back to Delphi to find him.

My ankle was so swollen that every time I took a step,

pain paralyzed my body. At last a farmer in a wagon stopped and, accepting a coin as payment, transported me to the marketplace of Delphi. It was now midday, and the market was full of people. Thanking the farmer, I searched the faces in the crowd for Alcimedon, but he was nowhere to be found.

Suddenly a group of men approached me. "Look," cried one of the men, "it is Strophius the athlete!" Before I could escape, these men surrounded me. "Where are you going, Strophius?" they asked. "Alcimedon of Aegina waits for you in the stadium!" I did not say anything in answer but simply stood silently and considered what they had said. "He is running from his opponent!" cried one of the men. "He is trying to leave Delphi because he is afraid!" Now they began shoving me and dragging me toward the stadium. I tried to tell them that I had been beaten and could not wrestle, but they called me a coward and pushed me more. Soon other men had joined the crowd. "Look!" they cried to anyone who would listen, "it is Strophius of Thebes, the son of Theoxenus, the student of Tithonus! He is trying to run away from his opponent!" They laughed at me and spat in my face. "Let us bring him to the stadium and see if he is as strong as he thinks he is!"

A large crowd gathered, and I was carried and shoved into the stadium, my right foot and left arm useless. Twice I fell to the ground in agony as my ankle twisted, but they picked me up again. When I entered the stadium at the head of this mob, the spectators rose and shouted and laughed. "There he is!" they cried. "The boy who was so brave yesterday!" They mocked me and threw eggs and rocks at me.

They brought me to Tithonus who asked me where I had been. "I found your bed empty this morning!" he declared in anger. I explained that I had been attacked in the woods

A SHADOW'S DREAM

and that I could not wrestle. He cursed me over and over again. "Are you a coward?" he asked. "Have I brought a coward to Delphi?" Then to the cheers of the crowd he struck me and declared, "You will come and do what I brought you here to do."

With those words Tithonus himself ripped my chiton from my body and dragged me to the ring to the wild cries of the spectators. There waiting for me was Alcimedon, who only that morning I had held in my arms and pledged my life to, oiled and naked, standing by Melesius's side, the width of his body only exceeded by the width of his smile.

"Ah," he said, "they have found you at last. Alcimedon has been waiting here for some time."

I looked at Alcimedon but I saw nothing in his expression, and his eyes were like polished black stones. I cursed him vehemently and called him a dog and a whore.

"Save your anger for the match, boy," replied Melesius. Alcimedon said nothing.

As I looked at Alcimedon with his gaze averted, my heart rent in two and tears welled up in my eyes. But before the first tear had fallen to the dust, the signal was given and the match began.

As Alcimedon circled me, I stood rooted to the spot, my right ankle now so swollen that I could not stand on it. My left arm hung limply by my side; I could not raise it. Before me Alcimedon darted to the left and to the right, feinting and dodging. He need not have moved so much.

As he circled closer, I considered that even now, after his treachery and his deception, still his physical beauty was unparalleled. To know that only hours before I had possessed him and had made him cry out in passion, and that I had now lost him, was enough to render me insensible.

FULL BODY CONTACT

He made short work of me for the first throw. Moving laterally, I was unable to follow him and, with a torturous pain, my ankle twisted upon itself and I fell to the ground and rolled in the dirt in agony. The crowd roared, and Melesius jumped in the air. For some reason I stood up. It was not courage or shame, it was simply that I no longer cared. Let Alcimedon kill me, I thought, let the crowd rip me to pieces, such is my fate. Were there not worse fates than dying for love? I considered. Hadn't better men died for worse reasons?

I stood resigned to my end. Alcimedon, however, just when victory was his, grew foolish. Flush with confidence, he approached with his head too low. Instinctively, I reached my right arm around his neck, and, pivoting on my one good leg and gathering what strength I had left, I forced him with one mighty heave to the dust. The crowd was quieter then.

As I watched him pick himself off the ground and brush the dust from his stomach, a thought occurred to me. What if Alcimedon, my lover, this most beautiful of boys, had really intended on leaving Delphi with me? What if, perhaps, Melesius had caught him as he went in search of his brother? What if, threatened by Melesius and the crowd, he had simply returned to the stadium out of cowardice? In that case, I considered, there was no reason to hate him. Weakness is simply a loss of courage, not wickedness itself.

As I thought this, Alcimedon came once more into my arms, grappling with my broken shoulder. As the pain shot through my body I looked at his eyes, searching them for some sign of love. If he were only a victim of circumstances, I thought, then I could forgive him his weakness and love him again.

A SHADOW'S DREAM

His eyes looked back at me, however, with an expression that was cold and viscous, the eyes of a python. As he stared at me, his muscles straining against mine, his thin, beautiful lips curled into a cruel snarl.

"To Hades with you now, you ugly dog," he sneered, and with these words he swept my feet from under me with his thin legs, snapping the bones of my ankle asunder.

I would gladly have accepted death at that moment, rolling in the dust, pelted with rocks and eggs, the object of a thousand jeers and catcalls. But even in this matter fate was unkind. My eyes did not shut, and my breath did not desert me. Worse, through a veil of tears I saw Alcimedon's arms raised in victory, a crown of bay leaves on his brow. I heard the roar of admiration from the crowd. I survived to hear the victory odes sung in the Odeion of brave Alcimedon of Aegina, the gods be damned.

From that day forth, I grew old and lame, a bitter man by the age of 20. The stars hid a grim fate for my life, and there is no court in which to plead my case. Sometimes at night, however, I still watch the stars and wonder if they hold yet greater secrets. I feel that the world cannot continue long as it stands, but that someday, somewhere far away—in the swirling sands of distant Egypt perhaps—a new secret will be discovered, such that man will not strive for the empty words of poets, but for immortality of a different kind.

FULL BODY CONTACT

Backstage With the Bulldogs

Aaron Travis

The lights go down in Ringside Coliseum. The fans go wild. The announcer barks into his microphone: "And now, ladies and gentlemen, the match you've been waiting for, the main event of the evening: The Lightning Kid versus Leo 'Hit Man' Logan!"

The Lightning Kid is already in the ring, soaking up the crowd's adoration. Tonight he wrestles solo, but he's usually part of a team, one half of the Baltimore Bulldogs. His partner, Lanny Boy Jones, stands outside the ring, playing manager tonight. Both Bulldogs look fantastic. They've been training like devils, pumping steroids and iron, hardening their short, stocky physiques to join the upper rung of wrestling superstardom. Even the TV announcer can't contain his enthusiasm: "Get a look at the superb physiques on these fine young athletes!"

Despite the fact that they could almost pass for twins, the Bulldogs have never been billed as brothers. The only logical alternative, from the way they casually touch each other on the rump and embrace before and after every match, is that they're lovers. Lanny Boy is obviously the top; he's a little chunkier and smoother, with huge slabs of pecs, massively muscled shoulders, a big boulder ass and just a trace of a gut. Something in his swagger tells you he's got an enormous clubcock between his legs, something the Kid loves going down on after a hard match in the ring.

The Kid's the bottom, with his etched-in-steel physique and hard round ass. He suffers more beautifully in the ring than anybody else. And he gets plenty of chances to suffer when they pit him against Leo "Hit Man" Logan. As the crowd boos, Logan swaggers in wearing a black tank top that clings to his pumped-up pecs, sporting his trademark mirror shades and a smart-aleck smirk.

The bell sounds. Logan proceeds to put the Kid through his paces. Slamming him against the boards. Throwing him clear out of the ring. Following him out and yanking him to his knees by a fistful of hair. Calmly dragging him back into the ring for some more punishment of that godlike young body.

Logan wraps the Kid's outstretched arms in the ropes, then steps back and gives his bound half-naked body a leering once-over. He makes a fist and starts pummeling the Kid's iron-banded stomach, slaps his face and knees him in the groin. They've done this routine before—in private, with both of them naked and the Kid begging through busted lips for the privilege of kissing Logan's donkey dick.

The crowd starts screaming: It's Lanny Boy, bounding over the ropes to come to the rescue, breaking every rule. He does a quick takedown on Logan, then rushes over to check on the Kid. The Kid lies there, glistening with sweat, breathing hard, his face screwed up with pain. Lanny Boy helps him up and out of the ring, but the Kid can't stay on his feet. Lanny Boy cradles him in his big arms and carries him up the aisle, one hand under his shoulders, the other firmly holding his rump. The audience goes wild—hands reach out to grope a fleeting touch, flashbulbs spark. The Bulldogs disappear backstage.

Alone in the dressing room, Lanny Boy starts getting hot and smoochy, kissing the Kid's bruises, stroking his hard buns. "Pull down your tights," he says, his voice deep and breathy. The Kid hangs his head. He strips for Lanny Boy, and underneath his tights he's wearing nothing but some Frederick's of Hollywood black satin panties, stretched so tight across his hard bubble butt they're about to split.

Lanny Boy likes the idea of the Kid wearing those panties under his tights when he's in the ring, getting the shit beat out of him by the Hit Man. "Good boy," he whispers. "Now take off your panties."

Sure enough, there's a puddle of come staining the front panel. The Kid couldn't help it; it happened when Logan had him bound up in the ropes, slapping him around. That wasn't agony on the Kid's face; it was pure, helpless lust.

"Guess the Hit Man worked you over pretty hard," says Lanny Boy.

"Yeah," the Kid answers, hanging his head.

"And I had to come in and rescue you," smirks Lanny Boy. "Just like always. Shit, maybe you ought to at least say thank you."

"Thank you, sir," whispers the Kid, staring downward.

"Maybe you ought to show me instead of just saying it." Lanny Boy pulls down his tights. His massive dick flops out.

"Yes, please, let me," gasps the Kid, dropping to his hands and knees and crawling toward Lanny. The Kid's own cock presses rock-hard up against his belly. It's a little dick, despite all those big polished muscles, not more than

BACKSTAGE

four inches—just a weenie compared to the plump forearm of meat hanging between Lanny Boy's muscle-bound thighs.

The Kid takes the whole thing in a single swallow and starts fucking his face on it while Lanny Boy settles into an easy chair for a long blow job. There's a knock at the door. The Kid jerks, but Lanny Boy holds him in place and yells, "Come in."

It's Leo Logan, all sweaty and pumped up after the match. He's wearing a skintight tank top, faded jeans, and mirror shades, and he's got a twisted grin on his face. "Already at it," he sneers.

"Go ahead," sighs Lanny Boy, "the Kid really knows how to deepthroat a guy—take a piece. You earned it."

"Sure." But first Logan grabs his belt buckle. The long leather strap slithers through the loops and cracks in the air as he pulls it free. Logan stands behind the Kid, staring down at his hard pale ass and the way it juts up round and plump above the silky small of his back. He swings the belt and lays a stripe across the Kid's rump.

The Kid squeals and chokes around Lanny's meat. "Shit, that felt great," sighs Lanny. "Do it again."

"Hell, they don't call me Hit Man for nothing," Logan smirks, drawing back his arm and laying on another blow. He proceeds to crisscross the Kid's ass with welts. Every blow makes the Kid squeal around Lanny's cock. The vibrations drive Lanny wild.

Finally Logan's had enough; he wants his dick up the Kid's ass. He makes the Kid stand up for it, bent double so he can still suck Lanny's cock while Logan slides his greasy pole deep inside the Kid's guts.

They doubledick him until the Kid can hardly stand. Logan really pounded him out in the ring, and he's exhausted. But Lanny and Logan are fired up and ready to go on for hours. They change places and doubledick him again, then settle back for a breather while they make the Kid mince around the room with his little cock pushed out of sight between his legs, taking cracks at his ass with the belt. The Kid's so shaky, he can hardly stand. He's covered with sweat and breathing hard.

There's a rattle at the door, and in comes Larry McMasters, with his slicked-back hair and hand-tailored polyester suit. McMasters is the Bossman, head honcho, lord and master of the wrestling circuit. He locks the door behind him. "Having a party, boys?" Logan and Lanny Boy laugh and nod.

McMasters stares at the Kid, who's standing stock-still, quivering and blushing deep-red from head to toe. He looks at the Kid's crotch, where there's nothing but naked flesh and a frazzled tuft of pubic hair, the smooth sweaty muscles of his hard belly and thighs curving into a deep pocket of flesh that begs to be fucked but can't.

"Well, well," McMasters booms, "my favorite piece of Baltimore ass." He walks over to the Kid and runs his hands all over his hairless, muscular flesh, pushing his middle finger between the Kid's legs, filling his hands with big hard pecs and pinching the Kid's nipples. Finally he pushes the Kid to his knees. McMasters pulls his cock out of his pants.

The Bossman is number one in the dick department—his foot-long tube of meat is one of the ways he keeps his boys in line. It's as thick as a man's forearm, plump as a family-size sausage. He rudely shoves it into the Kid's mouth, but the Kid can only take about a third of it without splitting his lips and choking to death. The Kid wraps his hands around the rest of it—his fingers and thumbs hardly meet—

BACKSTAGE

knowing that's the way the Bossman likes it. McMasters fucks face for a while, but it's not easy for him to get a good blow job; Tommy Dakota's the only one with a mouth and throat that can really satisfy him. He pulls the Kid back to his feet.

"Hold him," he says. Lanny and Logan each take one of the Kid's arms. The Kid loves taking the Bossman's cock; eventually. But every time, for the first five minutes or so, he fights like a hellcat to get off it. McMasters walks around behind him and lubes up his dick—he's still wearing his suit, just his cock and balls hang free—and abruptly pushes the whole thing inside the Kid....

...who lets out a howl that even the screaming fans out in the auditorium can hear. Then he starts blubbering and whimpering, begging the Bossman to take it out. McMasters ignores him and starts pumping away, holding the Kid by the hips. He's a hard fucker. The Kid keeps begging nonstop, pleading with McMasters to please take it out. It's all he can think of, getting away from that monster up his ass. McMasters even teases him a few times, pulling all the way out but before the Kid can catch his breath, he shoves it back in and fucks harder than before.

Finally, after five or 10 minutes of sheer torture, something breaks inside the Kid. He never stops begging, but now he's begging the Bossman to fuck him harder and never stop. He goes crazy for the cock up his ass, rotating his hips and fucking back against it. McMasters pulls it out with a laugh; the Kid gyrates his greasy ass in lewd circles, searching for the Bossman's cock until the blunt tip pokes his swollen hole. The Kid opens wide and squats back on it, sucking the whole thing inside.

But not for long. McMasters laughs and pulls out of the

Kid's ass with a loud liquid plop. He reaches for the Kid's Frederick's of Hollywood panties and wipes off his drooling, rock-hard dick. "Sorry, Kid, but I can't give you my load. Gotta keep it hot and ready for my date tonight with Tommy Dakota!" He stuffs his cock inside his pants, gives the Kid a hard swat on the ass and heads for the door. "You boys put on a great show in the ring tonight," he calls over his shoulder. "Have a good workout."

The Kid's a sobbing, quivering, sweat-drenched mass of muscle on the floor. His face is pressed against the carpet. His ass sticks straight up, making circles in the air. He reaches back with both hands and spreads it wide open. He drools on the carpet and whines: "C'mon guys, fuck me. Fuck me! Fuck my ass, please!"

Meanwhile, Lanny Boy and Logan rummage through the Kid's footlocker. Lanny pulls out a pair of handcuffs, a leather paddle, a braided whip. Logan smirks and pulls out a wicked-looking pair of tit-clamps, an official Baltimore Bulldogs dog collar, and his favorite sex toy, a bona fide Larry McMasters-size dildo.

CONTRIBUTORS

Clark Anthony has northern roots but lives and goes to college in the southern half of the U.S. With tastes and predilections ranging from mild to wild, he never has a problem figuring out what to do on weekend nights. He's no wrestler (at least not for the NCAA) and no gymnast (although he's renowned for his flexibility), but his basketball skills are unmatched. This is his first porn story, so feel free to let him know what you think at clarkanthony100@hotmail.com.

Chip Capelli, 36 and single, makes his home in the City of Brotherly Love. His hobbies include reading, mah-jongg, spending time with his family, and of course, hockey. Previous works of fiction have appeared in *Hot Shots, FirstHand,* and *Cobblestones*, the literary journal of the Haworth Society. While writing remains his passion, Chip spends his days as Director of Finance at MANNA, a nonprofit agency that provides meals and nutritional counseling to people living with HIV. Currently, he is finishing his first novel, a murder mystery tentatively titled *Murder at the Apothecary*. E-mail him at CapelliChip@aol.com.

Dale Chase has been writing erotica for several years. His work has appeared in *Men, Freshmen, In Touch,* and *Indulge* magazines and in several anthologies, including the *Friction* series, *Twink,* and *Bearotica*. He lives near San Francisco.

M. Christian is the author of *Guilty Pleasures: True Stories of Erotic Indulgences, Midsummer Night's*

Dreams: One Story, Many Tales, and *Eros Ex Machina: Eroticising the Mechanical.* His short fiction has appeared in over 100 anthologies and periodicals. His short-story collection, *Dirty Words,* is forthcoming from Alyson. He lives in San Francisco.

Ernie Conrick is a freelance writer living in NYC, an adjunct professor of religion at Sacred Heart University and Iona College, and the former senior editor of *Tricycle: The Buddhist Review.* His work has appeared in *Best American Erotica 2000* and *2002* and on Salon.com. His novel *Safe in Heaven Dead* was a finalist in the Heekin Group Foundation Awards in 1995. A wrestler in high school, Ernie went 1–7 during his only year on the varsity team.

Kieron Devlin has written for *The Village Voice, Prose-In-Fiction* magazine, Smackdabmedia.com, and *Tattoo Highway.* His short fiction has appeared in *Erotic Travel Tales,* published by Cleis Press. He won the Hayward Fault Competition at Doorknobs and Bodypaint, www.iceflow.com. He helps to edit fiction for *LIT* magazine at the New School. He is working on a novel and a short story collection.

Hank Edwards has just recently begun publishing fiction and has had stories published in several magazines including *Honcho, Bear,* and *FQ.* He is the author of two upcoming comic/erotic novels, *Fluffers, Inc.,* due in fall 2002, and *Carnal Cruise: Fluffers, Inc. 2,* due in 2003 from Alyson Publications. Hank lives in a northern suburb of Detroit, Mich., and works as a software trainer for a multinational company. He shares his home with Fred, his partner of six years, and an orange tabby cat named Tom.

Darrell Grizzle is a large but friendly bear who lives in Atlanta, Ga., with his partner and way too many books. Darrell's writings on gay spirituality have been published in such magazines as *RFD* and *White Crane*.

Alex Hamilton lives and writes in Northern California. After studying classics at Amherst College and U.C. Berkeley, he left academia to devote more time to creative writing. He welcomes comments on his fiction by E-mail: hamilton@calcentral.com.

Greg Herren is the author of *Murder in the Rue Dauphine* and the forthcoming *Bourbon Street Blues*. His fiction has appeared in *Men, Harrington Gay Men's Fiction Quarterly, Rebel Yell 2, Men for All Seasons, Friction 4, Friction 5,* and *Best Gay Male Erotica 2002*. An avid wrestler, he lives in the city of New Orleans with his partner of seven years, Paul, and can be reached at gregh121@aol.com.

"What Are You Going to Do?" is Brian Lieske's first published piece of fiction. He grew up in Maryland and earned a Master of Fine Arts in Creative Drama and Youth Theater from the University of Texas at Austin. He moved to San Francisco in 1991, where he lives happily with his life partner, Michael. By day, he is the registrar of a small graduate school of psychology.

David May was a nice boy from a good family who fell in with the wrong crowd. He is the author of the SM-oriented *Madrugada: A Cycle of Erotic Fictions*. His work, both fiction and nonfiction, has appeared in numerous magazines and journals, as well as in the anthologies *Rough Stuff 2; Afterwords: Real Sex from Gay Men's Diaries;*

Kosher Meat; Bar Stories; Midsummer Night's Dreams: One Story, Many Tales; Cherished Blood; Flesh and the Word 3; Meltdown!; Queer View Mirror; and *Rogues of San Francisco.* He lives in San Francisco.

Adam McCabe is the pseudonym of a well-known author and black belt in tae kwon do. His work, including the story "The Maltese Dildo," which appeared in the Best American Erotica 2000 collection, has appeared in a number of magazines and anthologies.

Joel Arthur Nichols grew up in Brandon, Vt., and studied German at Wesleyan University in Connecticut, where he translated Peter Altenberg's 1896 *Ashantee* as an honors thesis project. He has been writing since he attended the New England Young Writers' Conference in high school. His work has appeared in Vermont's only queer publication, *Out in the Mountains,* in the Wesleyan magazine *Hermes,* and in *The Reporter of the National Lesbian and Gay Journalists Association Convention.* "Starting in the Start Position," written in a humid Burlington summer, is his first piece of erotica.

Born and raised in Hawaii and educated at Harvard University and the University of Chicago, **Randy Petilos** is a university press acquisitions editor by day and an early music performer and enthusiast by night. He lives, works, sings, and shoots pool in Chicago.

James Ridout is a graduate of the University of Maryland with a Master of Science in Human Resource Management. He is a resident of Washington, D.C. Ridout has been with

The Washington Post for 15 years. His first book, *Plantation Secrets,* was published in 2000. He is currently working on his second novel.

New York-based writer, critic, and poet-playwright **L.M. Ross** has published work in various media. His erotica has graced the steamy pages of many popular magazines and anthologies. His eagerly awaited novel, *The Long Blue Moan,* is forthcoming from Alyson.

Lukas Scott's first novel, *Hot on the Trail,* put the "wild" back into the Wild West. Recently published short stories include "Moon," in *Buttmen*; "scar," in *Ophelia's Muse*; and "There's More To Love (Than Boy Fucks Girl)" at *MindCaviar.* He has been a university lecturer, queer activist, theater director, bookseller, television and film extra, counselor, and safer-sex worker. To find out how he likes to be tackled, visit www.LukasScott.com.

Simon Sheppard is the author of *Hotter Than Hell and Other Stories,* and the coeditor, with M. Christian, of *Rough Stuff: Tales of Gay Men, Sex, and Power,* and *Rough Stuff 2.* His work appears in over 70 anthologies, including *The Best American Erotica 2002, Best Gay Erotica 2002, The Burning Pen,* and *The Best of Friction.* He's currently semihard at work on a nonfiction book, *Kinkorama.* Visit him at www.simonsheppard.com.

Mel Smith's stories have appeared in *In Touch* and *Indulge* magazines, online at *Velvet Mafia,* and will be appearing in the forthcoming anthologies *Best Gay Erotica, Friction: Best Gay Erotica Vol. 5,* and *Best of*

Friction. Mel has wanted to be a writer since the fifth grade but got sidetracked by a stint as a firefighter and 13 years in law enforcement, where the men were plentiful and easy. She left law enforcement for single motherhood, which is tons more fulfilling, but she does miss the men.

Jay Starre writes from his desk in Vancouver, B.C. He pounds out porn stories by the hundreds, having written for such magazines as *Honcho, Torso, International Leathermen,* and *Bear.* His stories have also appeared in numerous anthologies, including *Freshman Club, Rentboys, Skinflicks 2, Hard Drive,* the *Friction* series, *Twink, Buttmen,* and *Hard Wired 3.*

Troy Storm has had more than 200 erotic short stories published in various gay, straight, and bi publications. He has contributed to the *Men for All Seasons* anthology and has stories scheduled for the *Buttmen* series. His collection of gay erotic short stories, *Gym Shorts,* is published by Companion Press (check www.companion-press.com). Although generally a peaceable, semi-nonathletic type, Troy considers himself definitely a full body contact kind of guy.

Aaron Travis is the pseudonym of Steven Saylor, who spent the Reagan years editing incredibly raunchy gay magazines like *Drummer* and making a living (sort of) by writing gay erotica. Nowadays he writes historical fiction and mystery novels (including *A Mist of Prophecies* and *A Twist at the End*). After 20 years of going back and forth, he still can't decide between the San Francisco Bay Area and Austin, Tex., but he can always be found at www.stevensaylor.com.

Born and raised an Okie, **Mark Wildyr** graduated from Texas Christian University with a degree in government and history. Following service in the U.S. military, he worked in banking, finance, and administration. He has authored several novels, most with contemporary settings in his adopted state of New Mexico. Multicultural interactions are of particular interest to him. More recently, he has turned his attention to writing short stories exploring personal development and sexual discovery. He is married with two adult children and resides in Albuquerque.

Duane Williams lives in Hamilton, Ontario. His fiction has appeared in *Queer View Mirror, Contra/Diction, Velvet Mafia, Buttmen,* and *Harrington Gay Men's Literary Quarterly.* He is currently at work on a first collection of short stories.